BENEDIC

Benedict Kiely has come to be reg
admired literary writers. Born near ᴅ⸗⸗⸗⸗⸗, ⸗ ⸗⸗⸗⸗⸗ ⸗
1919, his long and successful career spans the writing of novels,
short stories and memoirs. He is well known as a raconteur and
broadcaster on TV and radio. In 1996, he was presented with the
golden torc of a Saoi of the Aosdana by President Robinson.

His novels include *The Captain with the Whiskers*, *Honey Seems
Bitter*, *The Cards of the Gambler* and *Dogs Enjoy the Morning* (also
available from Wolfhound Press), among many other works.

REVIEWS

'Benedict Kiely is the Irish Balzac.' Heinrich Böll

'One of Ireland's most significant writers .... There is truly no more
numinous writer than the Tyrone seanachie.' Sean McMahon

There Was an Ancient House

In the ancient house of the title live thirty novices of a religious order. This
is the story of their attempts to conform to the pattern laid down by rule.

'The human struggles, even the careful humour of scholars within these quiet
walls, are beautifully conveyed, but the power of the book lies in its richly
poetic quality and vivid evocation of scene and atmosphere.' *The Scotsman*

'The picture of everyday religious life is bright and true, obviously first
hand.' Maurice Richardson, *New Statesman and Nation*

The Cards of the Gambler

'An astonishing book ... What is uniquely Kiely's, his thumbprint, is his easy
mastery of the lyrical, and the feeling of felt life, felt experience, just beneath
the surface of his prose.' Thomas Flanagan, author of *The Year of the French*

Also by Benedict Kiely

Dogs Enjoy the Morning

'There is a gusto and a joy of life in Benedict Kiely's novel, first published in 1968, that is missing from most Irish fiction since. He creates a village of Cosmona, around whose hospital with its long-stay patients most of the action turns, on his dreamy girls, boozy men, flighty floozies and pliable priests. A very welcome return for a very funny book from the new Saoi.' *Sunday Tribune*

Drink to the Bird

'Mr Kiely is one of the last of the literary gents...His learning is extensive and he is excited by popular as by high culture. If in one chapter he is recalling the effect of Irish rebel incursions on the writing of Spenser's *Faerie Queen*, in another he salutes the Everton centre forward Dixie Dean as the only footballer ever to establish a hairstyle: the sleeked-back, middle-of-the-skull parting...A charming and civilised book.' *Sunday Times*

Nothing Happens in Carmincross

'I have been waiting for a novel as full of rage about contemporary Ireland as this one. And this is the book I have been waiting for.' Frank Delaney, *BBC*

A Letter to Peachtree

'There are so many Irish people who write short stories, and so few who are real storytellers. Ben Kiely is one, and he should be preserved in aspic or crowned high king or just bought in huge numbers.' *Sunday Independent*

'Benedict Kiely is one of the supreme masters of the short story in our time.' Augustine Martin, *Irish Times*

'Stylish, gabby, using language like a fallen angel, he mixes his feeling with a true storyteller's verse that looks like superb skill but is in fact something better. Call it instinct.' *Guardian*

Proxopera

'Compare him with whom you will, the gentle Gogol, the percipient Gorky, Benedict Kiely defies comparison.' Dominic Behan

To
MAUREEN
And with a debt of gratitude to
SEAN WHITE

there was an ancient house

BENEDICT KIELY

WOLFHOUND PRESS

This edition published 1997
WOLFHOUND PRESS
68 Mountjoy Square
Dublin 1

© 1955, 1997 Benedict Kiely

First Edition Methuen and Co. Ltd., London 1955

Wolfhound Press receives financial assistance from The Arts Council/An Chomhairle Ealaíon, Dublin, Ireland.

This book is fiction. All characters, incidents and names have no connection with any person living or dead. Any apparent resemblance is purely coincidental.

A catalogue record for this book is available from the British Library.

ISBN 0-86327-576-1

Typesetting: Wolfhound Press
Cover design: Slick Fish, Dublin
Cover illustration: Includes the painting 'Rossenarra' by Edward McGuire.
© Eamonn McEnery
Printed and bound by The Guernsey Press Co. Ltd, Guernsey, Channel Islands

Contents

There was an auncient house not far away,
Renowned throughout the world for sacred lore,
And pure unspotted life ....

The Faerie Queene

ONE: ANIMA

I

It was a white world. He opened his eyes slowly, wondering. He said to himself: How and When? Why? He repeated several times: Where? Pure white curtains on railings around his cubicle trembled in the flow of air from the open window. He touched the white coverlet with his right hand and thought that his hand was suddenly white, fragile. Sunlight came with the air through the window and brightened the white wall. Beyond the curtains somebody scraped a foot on the wooden floor, and coughed. Outside in the sunshine and free air a great-tit was squeaking like an unoiled bicycle pump. He thought again: Where? and, now that he was properly awake, laughed at his own attempt to deceive himself, for he knew when and where and how, but he wasn't too sure of why.

All the whiteness made him afraid. Was it white or black was the absence of colour? Outside, the great-tit was squeaking and that meant colour of plumage, of leaves and branches, of grass, flowers, brown earth. Colour began outside his white-curtained cubicle. He closed his eyes again, looked beyond the squeaking, plumaged bird and the woods and fields all round the house; and in the patchwork-coloured world he had yesterday abandoned he went searching for why. Back over it step by step, he thought, for I have time and on my first novitiate, neophytical morning I can lie late. Was it wrong to look back and not instead to look forward into whiteness and whiteness as radiant as flame? Yet, this was a neutral moment. His old life, the world, was behind him. Until he put his bare feet on the floor beside the bed he had not commenced living the new life. So he shut his eyes and looked back and saw a town, a school, his first Communion morning, several girls, a clerestory window, angels carved in wood, a lifted golden monstrance, a visit to wise priests in a tall still house behind a church in the middle of a city.

On his first Communion morning he had worn a jersey as white as the cubicle curtains and been chill with worry in case the host might touch his teeth. Afterwards, kneeling beside his mother he had prayed that he might be a priest. Dear Jesus who hath this morning come into my soul for the first time, help me, when I grow up, to be a priest. Three Hail Marys that I may be able to be a priest. Then home to porridge, rasher and eggs, tea, lemonade, money to spend and down the sunny town to a photographer in a room above a sweetie shop, and sixpence and a smile from the photographer, and sweets in the shop on the way out from a smiling shopgirl who patted him on the head, to his great pride and delight, because seeing her dressed up and walking the way between her home and her shop he had always thought her the stateliest lady in the town.

The town, too, was the centre of the world. It wasn't always sunny as it had been on that morning. There was a grey afternoon, cold like a dead fish wrapped in scabby grass and coiled in a basket. Fish; he thought of fish because the pavilion, a green tin hut, in the school football field, had always smelled of fish: air from a dripping closet with its bowl stained yellow and green, the floor damp always from damp feet slapping fishily out from the showers, the stale smell of sweat, the smell of clay scraped from football boots. The voices were boisterous, some shrill, some double-noted because they were breaking, some hoarse with a gravelly cat-hairiness of approaching manhood.

'You missed the goal, MacKenna, you missed the goal.'

'He didn't miss it, he was fouled off the feckin' ball by Snifter Hannigan.'

'Brother Higgins is as blind as a bag, him for a referee, he couldn't see a poultry yard, let alone a foul.'

'Shut your eedjity gob, if Higgins the stiggins hears you at that, you'll have a sore ass for a week.'

'He can't hear me, he's off to high tea in the attic with Matilda Blythe.'

'Her name isn't Matilda.'

'Higgins'll give her a sore ass no matter what her name is.'

'None of that talk, Snifter Hannigan. MacKenna's listening to you.'

'Who's MacKenna?'

'MacKenna's going to be a priest.'

'Did you hear what Geordie the Duke of Saxe-Coburg heard Higgins saying to Matilda up the railway bank by the Crevenagh Road?'

'No! Tell us, go on, tell us, Snifter Hannigan.'

'MacKenna wouldn't let me.'

'MacKenna won't listen, he's going to be a priest. Go on, Hannigan, spill the beans, spill the beans.'

Even now he wasn't certain whether to be glad or sorry that they turned their backs on him while the beans were spilled, turned their faces together like chickens dabbling at the one pile of food, left him out of the circle while they whispered and laughed at their steaming fantasy about the good brother and the elderly hirsute lady in whose house he so frequently had tea. Probably in their raw young minds their exclusion of him was a recognition of difference, a tribute to separateness, sacrosanctity. He had always wanted to be separate and different, to feel as he now felt: white, curtained-off, sacrosanct, protected. They didn't like him the less because he was slow to learn about the secrets they whispered in the grinning, fish-smelling circle. He learned in the end, anyway, from some of their talk overheard; and at other times and in other ways when the town wasn't grey or white and sunny, but black and spotted with points of light, the dark back of a prowling night animal with odd glittering scales.

Bridges seemed to have something to do with first knowledge. Pontifex, Chesterton said, was the builder of bridges, but Chesterton meant the Pope, and the Pope wouldn't have had hand, act or part, in the sort of bridges he was thinking of. Not a tree and an apple and who should eat it, but a bridge and who built it and who shall cross it. There was a bridge over a burn two miles from the town, spanning the burn just above a brawling waterfall widening out into a deep sally-shaded pool. The noise of the fall, of the wind in the sallies, mingled with his laughter, and Frankie's laughter, and the laughter of the two schoolgirls. One girl was dark-haired and sallow-skinned. One was a redhead with teeth slightly protruding. They glistened in the night and hurt his lips when he kissed her. Degged with dew, dappled with dew are the groins of the brae that the brook treads through – a member of a religious order had written that, and the image could still, in spite of whiteness, trouble him with memories of the brawling burn, bending sallies, red-and-white laughter, the feel of her thighs, groins of the brae and the treading brook, young and innocent under school-uniform serge. Frankie and he ran all the way home that night to be on time for the family rosary in their respective homes: Thou, O Lord, wilt open my lips, but when he opened his lips he could, while his people prayed around him, still taste young kisses, feel the touch of glistening teeth.

Frankie was a good friend. Frankie was alone now in the town, his best friend gone, to Frankie's undoubted bewilderement, to live in a world as white as the Arctic circle, as cold too, no more kisses, no more French, by brawling burns and bridges; the railway bridge where the brown-haired girl had nearly but not quite made him do something he only half understood, only half-wanted to do. She was a daring hungry knowledgeable girl. Frankie had just saved him from her educative efforts by sliding down the summery velvety railway embankment to shout: 'Jim MacKenna, Jim MacKenna, Brother Higgins is walking up the line.' The brown-haired girl, he couldn't see why, would never meet him again. Afterwards when Frankie knew finally that his friend was going away to be a priest he said that, according to his grandmother, the boy who had a true vocation could never lose his purity all the way. His guardian angel was there to see to that, a high white angel pushing Frankie slithering down the bank or urging Brother Higgins' thick-soled boots from one creosoted sleeper to another in order to cool and quench the warmth of the brown girl.

No matter what colour, at any time, the town was, the golden monstrance stood above it all like a torch. It was gilded like the sun. It was terrible as any army in battle array. In the oaken loft the choir sang:

Qui vitam sine termino
Nobis donet in patria

Singing with them and looking at the white centre of the monstrance, he saw *vitam sine termino* here in his own *patria*. Bells divided the calm day. The air was cool with prayer and clean like altar linen. Tall priests came and went, preached to the people, raised clean hands in God's forgiveness, held aloft the world in the white Host, or in the quiet night read and wrote learnedly. That was the how and the when of it. At that moment the town, the scabrous young men, the girls, the burns, bridges and railway banks, dissolved like inferior metal in the monstrance's golden flame. It went before him, the pillar of fire, to that house behind a busy city church, to calm searching questions from three of the wisest men the Order had.

What first put it into your head that God had called you to the religious life?

His answer had been honest, but he couldn't all the same talk about the white first Communion morning, the white jersey, his mother's prayers, the vision of the monstrance like the burning bush. Their calm unsettled him and yet at the same time put him at his ease. His faltering answers must have satisfied them. Otherwise he wouldn't be here. Quick jabbings of gooseflesh had assailed him as he sat with them and had a flashing memory of Frankie's farewell words. When you're at your prayers there, pray for me and Delia rolling in Killyclogher wood. Those learned fathers had humour, but they'd hardly laugh at that. Their sense of humour worked in other ways.

Why us now, instead of the Jesuits or Dominicans? Gentle smiles smoothed that question and fingertips were firmly pressed together and meditated upon. But that admission into the circle of their family jokes did everything that was needed to ease his doubt, to hint to him that he belonged, at least that he had been accepted as one who could be put to the tests that only the fit and few survived.

His mother fretted over the list of necessary clothes which came two weeks later with a letter from the Father Provincial. All that linen, and that black ominously-impressive Chesterfield suit. Relatives came with gifts and good wishes. He felt uneasily like the sacrificial calf on its way towards the knives and the smoking altar. On the top of a brown mountain in the course of a Sunday's walk his elder brother and himself talked seriously about the world's need for good priests, never more than today with everything the way it was, for good priests who understood the people. Brown mountain, black Chesterfield coat, soft green midland country, the train going through pine woods, the railway station in a sleepy old town that exiled Huguenots had built, the proud grey heavy ancient houses, the V-8 from the monastery following a narrow road deeper and deeper into pine woods, the greeting on the broad front steps, Doric columns and two stone lions, the polished floors of the main hall and the chapel, faces and faces and dark gowns, and supper in silence in a refectory that had once been an Earl's ballroom, and the litany of saints in the chapel, and awakening in a white world to drowsy retrospection.

The great tit was still squeaking from the woods below the house. A bell rang. Outside his curtain a voice said: 'Brother MacKenna, benedicamus domino'. He answered drowsily, wondering, half-amused at himself: 'Deo gratias.' His feet were on the bare wooden floor and a new life was beginning.

II

His angel, wearing a long black gown, stood waiting for him as soon as he had dressed and pulled back the curtains of his cubicle. This was one case where a dark angel was a good angel. Last night the tall dark-chinned bespectacled novice had explained to him the angelus-anima relationship, the neophytical soul and the guarding angel putting it wise, showing it the ropes for a week's probation that preceded the noviceship proper. 'We live by tradition, you see. It's a system we borrowed from the Jesuits. They're the great men for running novitiates.'

'They're very learned.'

'There's more to them than learning. Our Father Master, that's Master of novices, is strong on that point. Our father founder was a great admirer of Saint Ignatius of Loyola. What the Jesuits aim at first is a sound basis of devotion and commonsense. The learning can come after.'

Outside on its branch the great-tit still squeaked. Morning sunlight emphasised the frayed shabbiness of the guardian angel's gown. He leaned forward and whispered, while deep in the belly of the house the echoes of the bell jammered into silence. Angels could whisper to the souls they attended, for Angeli and Animae were not bound by the great silences that for most of the day kept all the other novices in a religious peace. 'We'll go down now directly to the chapel for morning oblation.' His breath smelled markedly of some strongly carbolic tooth-cleansing concoction.

The house was astir: Animae rising from beds, Angeli and other novices, priests and lay-brothers straightening up from meditative prie-dieux, turning towards chapel and morning oblation. Last night he had been told: 'For the week of your probation you don't talk to anybody except to the new novices like yourself, and to myself.'

He hadn't been able to think of any comment. The rule of silence had been no part of the life without end, vita sine termino, he had looked forward to. 'You'll get used to the silence very easily. As Father Master will show you, it's a necessary condition for true advance in the spiritual life. Especially for novices. We're beginners and we have to make extra efforts.'

Remembering those words as he went down the first stairway, he wasn't at all sure that his angelus hadn't been talking through his hat. Did the saints relax, ease off, rest on their oars, freewheel into heaven as the reward for earlier upward efforts?

The long dusky corridor on the first floor was crowded with gowned novices moving towards the chapel, their elastic-sided house shoes pattering on polished brown lino, with ungowned probationers clattering along, looking and feeling awkward, in all sorts of boots and shoes, mere beginners in the spiritual life. Before a statue of the Sacred Heart inset to the wall a red lamp burned. Beyond the head of the main stairway a blue lamp burned before a similarly inset statue of Mary, the Mother of God; and an extra fervent novice dropped for a moment like a sable roosting bird to the prie-dieu before that statue, whispered for a moment, his thin earnest face pale in blue light, then arose refreshed and followed his fellows. Doors opened and closed, gashing the corridor with morning light, as novices and probationers came forth from white rooms. In one room a slow-moving probationer, still dazed with the shock of waking up in a new world, was pulling across his cubicle curtains, and iron rings grated on iron curtain poles. A distant window showed the ridged outline of an oak wood, leaves still green though the great beech trees he had seen yesterday were sky-high flames like eastern visions of God. In the oak wood now there was sunlight on old branches, birds calling and rusting in undergrowth. But in the vestry hall outside the chapel the oaks and beeches, birds and the revolving world were cut off as if they never had been. This was the beating heart of the house of God.

Consummatus in brevi, said the plaque at the chapel door, explevit tempora multa. The Book of Wisdom spoke to him from a brass plate like a plate picking out the house of a dentist, a doctor or a veterinary surgeon. From a schoolboy acquaintance with the Latin of the liturgy he could stagger at the Wisdom words that followed, could translate them, and he knew that they applied to those who died young in high holiness: Kostka the Jesuit Polish boy; Aloysius Gonzaga, a prim stiff youth; Rose of Lima, or Maria Goretti defending to death her rose of purity against a foaming lustful cousin. Had a novice once died in this house and his soul spiralled upwards, morning mist from spring meadow, to the choirs of heaven? Placita enim erat deo anima ilius, and his name was remembered out there on the brass plaque. Pray for him, or ask him to pray for us, for he died young and in a holy gown. Being made perfect in a short space he fulfilled a long time, for his soul pleased God. His living brothers knelt down before God's altar. The narrow kneeling boards were mollified with green baize. Professed fathers and brothers knelt at the back of the chapel. Probationers and novices knelt in the front rows, close to the altar, separated from the sanctuary by no marble railings nor closed golden gate. The roof circled above them, God's tabernacle, as once in ungodly days it had circled over worldly grandeur, here in the great drawing-room the fine talk of eighteenth-century ladies and gentlemen, music and dancing next door where the refectory now was.

'When we kneel in the chapel,' the good black angel had advised, 'we don't slouch with our elbows on the bench. Novices only rest

their hands on the bench in front of them. It's just a custom. A little
act of mortification.'

So he knitted his fingers together and knelt straightly, his back as
stiff as a ramrod. Still remembering Wisdom, he thought: the just
man if he be prevented with death shall be in rest. No rest, they said,
for the wicked, but here was no rest for the elbows of the just. A
frivolity native to him could have twisted his face in smiles, set his
shoulders shaking, if he hadn't been impressed into awed solemnity
by the nearness of the altar decked for Mass, by the dark figures
around him silently offering the day to God. They seemed tense with
devotion as if netted by strong cords and bound fast to the life living
behind the tabernacle's golden door. He felt his rawness, the rawness
of the other probationers, of the undisciplined undevoted world. The
smells of carbolised tooth-cleansing mixture, of the polish that kept
the chapel floor shining, of incense still in the air from last evening's
benediction, of burning candles, all mingled to make, he fancied, the
odour of sanctity. Without a gown, wearing a suit once worn in the
world, he felt as naked as a dug-up root.

In the refectory after Mass, Communion, and a fifteen minutes'
thanksgiving, he had his chance of looking at the other faces.

Last night everything had been so confused that all faces looked
alike; and on the train from the city he had been shy of saying a word
to the fresh-faced fair-haired fellow who'd shared his compartment.
You couldn't say to a complete stranger: 'Look, I know by the scenes
I saw at the station, your mother's proud tears, etcetera, that you're
off to be a novice in a religious order. So'm I. So let's get together.'
It wasn't like going to boarding school or like going to join the Army.
There was something one had to be shy about. There was a secret as
soft as a dove but still strong enough to enable a fellow to turn the
back on father and mother, home and kindred, and to follow Christ as
the twelve fishermen followed him, or to follow the high monstrance
flame as the people of Moses followed the pillar of fire. In the chapel
at Mass he'd seen only the altar and the backs of heads, some dark,
some fair, some thin pale necks, some thick sun-tanned hairy necks.
The gowned novices kept their eyes reflectively cast down towards
the tablecloth. He knew what that was: custody of the eyes so that the

soul might not be distracted by outward things. Custos oculorum, said his Angelus, and made some Latin joke about oculis dimissis, omnia videns, eyes cast down, seeing all things, like the nuns in the convent in the town at home who never passed the gate of their grounds and never peeped round the white edges of their bonnets, but who still knew all the gossip for ten miles around, knew who married or died, got engaged or born or bankrupt or arrested. The reflective novices, the few fathers at the T-top of the long table, were not just studying the tablecloth and waiting for their porridge. Their souls were away on wings and their eyes saw not the world. Probationers had livelier eyes, more supple necks. Looking up through the steam of his porridge, he caught one pair of those eyes, dry blue eyes, silently laughing at him out of a bronzed thin face. The laugher was a tall fellow with brick red hair and rimless spectacles. He was older than the average run of probationers, a late vocation: and the creases around mouth and eyes marked him, perhaps, as a man made pleasantly cynical by living, but still believing enough in the world to turn his back on it, to work and pray for the world's good, for the good of his own soul. That was what Brother MacKenna thought. Behind the redheaded probationer was the refectory's wide bay-window showing descending lawn, freshly dug flower-beds, then autumn woods reflecting and transforming the sunlight. On one side of the red-headed man sat a handsome dark-haired novice, eyes on his plate, long fingers delicately holding his porridge spoon, cheeks pink-and-white and fresh as a girl's. On the other side a snub-nosed novice peered comically at his food through thick opaque lenses. Lay-brother novices, gowned in white aprons, served at table. Everybody did for God's glory his appointed task, the hands the work of the hands, the feet that of the feet, the belly the work of the belly; and only in God's charity could such subordination smoothly exist. The food was good. Last night his Angelus had jested, but not quaffed and sworn like the drunken private of the Buffs, about the two Nelson Pillar apple-wives walking past the Jesuit house in Gardiner Street, sniffing appreciatively, like the ragged children in the Bisto advertisement, the odour of cooking from the Georgian area, saying one to the other: a grand atin' ordher, glory be to God.

'St Ignatius, you see, was a humane wise man.' The Angel wasn't completely free from stilted phrases or from a certain pride in the fact that he had information to give. 'Saint Ignatius knew that a healthy body fitted a religious for the hard life of an active order. Our father founder followed his idea. We're preachers and teachers, not complete monastic ascetics. We're sort of junior league Jesuits.'

He relished his good breakfast, building himself up to preaching-teaching trim. He glanced now and again as deeply as he could into the beautiful mellowing woods. He knew, for he had a good memory for timetables, what the routine would be after breakfast. Up the stairs to his room. Each room was called a camerata. Make his bed in silence. He was used to making his own bed. But it would be odd to make it in white silence, two black-gowned figures also bending bed-making in the same room, his Angelus and another novice, long-nosed, sallow-faced, to whom even during recreation he would not yet be allowed to speak. At home he had slept in a blue room whose ceiling sloped down with the low sloping roof, whose window looked out over the town to brown lonely Ulster hills.

With his bed made he'd have a few moments to inspect his table, which his Angelus had stocked with the books a novice needed: a rule book, a missal, a book that gave points for meditation, one of the three volumes of the spiritual treatises of the Spanish Jesuit, the Venerable Father Rodriguez, a card with a prayer printed on it and lying on the card a metal crucifix, the life-story of some one of the saints of God, a notebook – because the novice master was a strong man for advising his neophytes to get some of their thoughts about the spiritual life methodically down on paper. That table, a chair, a wooden kneeler softened by a red rubber pad, a washstand, a bed, white curtains running on iron rails, a high window over midland autumn woods, made up the one corner of the world in which he would now find complete privacy. Curtained-off as he was by fields and deep trees and the walls of a religious house from the rush of life, he was yet more than ever a part of a body, a cog, his Angelus might say, in the machine of community life.

Bed made, table inspected, teeth scrubbed and slops emptied in the washroom, he would join the other cogs in indoor works, sweeping, polishing, scrubbing, learning humility in humble tasks, for an hour, until the old house where lords had once lived shone like the deck of a destroyer. Then to the chapel, one body with many members, vine with thirty branches, to beseech for five minutes the Holy Ghost. After that the novice master in the conference room would speak to the new arrivals.

He sipped the last of his coffee, placed knife and fork tidily parallel on his plate. As well as learning and piety, a good religious who had to face the world needed good table manners. The town was far away now, the fishy football pavilion, the bridges. He was cold now with eagerness to know this place, the paths down through the blazing woods, the lake he had heard lay behind those woods; to know the people now holily silent around him, to hear them talk, to learn the thing that brought them, himself included, from all over Ireland and held them there together in a secret sheltered place among midland trees.

III

In the conference room the master of novices spoke to the eighteen newcomers. The delicate Adam ceiling of spacious sinful days had been carefully preserved. When the Order had bought the house and taken it over, invading grass had already burst up, a sickly unhealthy yellow, through the oaken boards that floored the semicircular entrance hall. That unholy growth out of foundational darkness had symbolised decay, days gone in drink and dice, in dissipation. Now the boards shone like bronze because holy hands had zealously waxed them, pushed and pulled over them polishing cloths weighted with monstrous squeegees made from heavy logs fitted with iron handles. Decay had stained and peeled walls and ceilings, but, with fervour and taste, the people of God had come to restore; with respect for what of good the worldly past had contained. Except that the long high orange tables in the conference room screamed out like charging vandals against the Dresden demure grace of eighteenth-century walls and ceilings.

The new nervous eighteen stood between their chairs and the tables waiting for the advent of the man who was to guide them towards God, their ghostly father, eighteen souls waiting like Gerontius. The thin brick-red-headed man stood at Brother MacKenna's left hand. The flaring orange paint on the tables had blistered badly. Three tall windows revealed another aspect of sloping lawns, bleeding newly-dug flowerbeds, walks lined with stiff clipped yew trees, white goal-posts on playing fields, and, cornering around the woods, the glint of a lake. A cloud of starlings whipped like a black cloth past the windows, vanished, all as one, seeking red pulpy berries in a yew tree's breast, just as the ghostly father came, shoes creaking, across main hall, along a short shadowy corridor lined with bookcases, up the passage between the blistering tables to a tiny rostrum. At school or college pencils or penknives would have pierced those blisters and peeled away the punctured paint. But here the holy rules protected them.

Behind that bulwark they shone, they smiled, orange little mountains, smooth mounds of sand. The world outside, quiet as a picture, lay waiting to be discovered. On eighteen tongues words waited eagerly for the release that the day's first recreation would give. The room was loud with expectation.

Send forth thy spirit, prayed the master of novices, and they shall be created; and thou shalt renew the face of the earth.

Come, O Holy Spirit, fill the hearts of thy faithful, and kindle in them the fire of thy love.

Noisily they rose from their knees. Chairs scraped on polished wood. They hadn't acquired the deftness that novices with twelve months' experience had in kneeling, rising, folding gowns around knees, sitting down.

'Dear brothers, it is a pleasant sight to see eighteen radiantly healthy faces here before me this morning.' Eighteen healthy faces smiled eighteen uncertain smiles. The smile on the priest's pale face was quiet and assured as the gentle touch of wind on calm autumn waters. His grey hair was closely clipped, accentuating the length and the regularity of the oval shape of his head. Rimless spectacles sat firmly on a Roman nose. A mole marked his right cheek.

'Healthy faces in the morning mean that we've all slept well, healthy consciences, and that we were all tired after our journey and that we didn't find the surroundings too strange. The life we live here, dear brothers, is very different from the lives we've been used to in the world, but it's easier on the nerves, I think you'll find. And it's a happy life, a very happy life. Father Willy Doyle, the Jesuit who died almost a martyr's death when he was a chaplain in the first world war, was fond of saying that if people in the world only knew the happiness of the religious life they'd break down the doors to get in. That was why I kept the front door so carefully open when all you healthy young men were arriving ....'

His smile was answered by eighteen smiles. He had a pleasantly soothing comforting fatherly voice, a consolation and recompense for eighteen worlds abandoned.

'We've all done something for our divine Lord in leaving our homes and our people as we've just done ....' This grey quiet experienced man was before God a probationer talking to other probationers. 'The renunciation is severe for a time, but no one could expect it to be otherwise. We've been accustomed to so many little things in the world that we now train ourselves to do without. But our Lord is a generous master. His own words tell us how His yoke is sweet and His burden light. We can rest assured that everything we do for Him will be made up a hundredfold, pressed down and flowing over, to us and to ours. Give willingly and God will return generously. The Lord loves a cheerful giver. Bis dat qui cito dat. I'm sure Brother Barragry, if he hasn't forgotten in the hurly-burly of journalism the Latin I taught him once upon a time, will be well able to translate.'

Brother Barragry, a hard friendly voice, said: 'I think I could just manage that, Father.' The nineteen-fold smile shone alive again. Or was it one smile reflected in eighteen mirrors? Brother Barragry was the late vocation, the brick-red lean man; and, remembering Father MacGrath from his schooldays spent in a college run by the Order, he knew that the simple Latin phrase was not a test for his translating powers, but a rope thrown spinning out to bind eighteen men to their leader. Hadn't a pun about Peter the rock once bound twelve men to a Master and founded a church?

'You may find things strange here for a while and probably a great deal different from what you expected. We don't study much here in the novitiate, just a little Latin to keep our Latin from rusting and because the language of the Church is so important to us. Later on you'll have all the study you could possibly desire, perhaps more than most of us would desire.'

His smile was reflected only in some of the eighteen mirrors. Were the minds behind the unreflecting mirrors just a little awed by thinking forward over years of study and training, of Latin disputation, onwards to ordination and the preaching, teaching, hearing confessions, visiting the sick, offering sacrifice, that would follow?

'For two years here we'll concentrate on learning how to pray, a quiet life, building up soul and body for the work to come, down here among these woods that God has made so beautiful. We have to put first things first, for our main purpose is not to be scholars but saints. Scholarship stands up better on a good sensible foundation of sanctity. That wise holy man Thomas à Kempis knew what he was talking about when he said: "I would rather feel compunction than know how to define it. If thou didst know the whole Bible outwardly, and the sayings of all the philosophers, what would it all profit thee without charity and the grace of God." ... Now I'm beginning to preach.' The calm autumnal breeze of a smile on autumn water smoothed away any sterness that eighteen nervous beginners might have imagined into his words. Seventeen mirrors shone. Brother Barragry was studying seriously the red-haired backs of his bony big-knuckled hands. Brother MacKenna thought how many miles away all this is from the pulpit sermons in the parish church at home: from the parish priest himself reading out the list of contributions to Peter's pence or the harvest dues; from the white-robed Dominican missionary proclaiming to the town's most respectable grocers – how often, brethren, has the light of a passing car picked you out in your sin on the side of a lonely road – while the town's prurient adolescents wriggled with glee at such entertainment where it was least to be expected; from the stern thundering Redemptorist shaking a crucifix above his head and demanding of spent dowagers and dry spinsters – shall I curse the company keepers? Here the air was different. The contaminating world was at bay, held restless and foaming beyond the woods. There was a sense of age, of holy quiet around dark yews, white goal posts, woods as deep as the ocean, the still lake. Nothing moved but the sky and the starlings.

'Dear brothers, I'm not here to alarm you, nor even to brace you up with a pep-talk like an American general exhorting his troops.' The slang words were gently, neatly nipped off, crisp celery snapping, by lips more accustomed to the words of God, to the breviary's sonorous Latin, the words of the Mass, but yet ready to use the words of the world for the good of the world. 'I'm just here to welcome you. Your respective Angeli in the course of your probation will initiate you into the ways of the house. The door of my room, too, is always open at any reasonable hour, shall we say after supper every night. And Father Socius will be in his room at the same time. Don't be shy about coming to talk to us. We're both quite harmless.'

He stood up slowly, smiling, eyes opaque behind spectacles, his right hand holding a book, a thin scholarly wise man who had, every novice knew, come from a wealthy family and in his youth in the world had driven at Brooklands. He had known the world. He had turned his back on all that: money, speed, the trapeze swing up and down on the curves of the banked track, the cheers, the laurels, the corruptible crown. He had also been a well-known amateur footballer. The probationers rattled awkwardly to their feet.

'Dear brothers, we'll all get along together here, with God's help, like one happy family. We have, I think, a charity that you don't always find in the world. And among thirty or forty young men you'll hear a great deal of interesting talk – at the times when talk is the principle.'

That was worth a nervous eighteen-barrelled laugh.

'Some have their main interest in birds, some in fish or stars or trees, or flowers or boats or football or books. Contribute each of you what you can and learn too by listening to others. We have to face the world you know, to be all things to all men, omnibus omnia as the apostle says, and such knowledge never goes astray. It's the good God's creation too and the more we know about it the more we love the Creator. Just look at those trees.'

Eighteen heads swivelled. Oh, sloping autumn grass; oh, yews and whipping starlings, oaks and beeches and the distant glitter of sword-like water. They looked until their Father Master's creaky shoes had gone up the dark book-lined corridor. Then Brother Barragry, being the eldest, led them to the main hall where black Angeli stood on polished wood silently waiting. Below in darkness rank unhealthy grass, emblem of decay, died defeated. They went back to their cameratas. Before lunch, a half-hour for spiritual reading, a half-hour free time, fifteen minutes for their first examen of conscience according to the method described by Saint Ignatius of Loyola. Opening his yellow-backed Life of Saint Gemma Galgani, Brother Barragry read at random: 'Notwithstanding so many obstacles – in the midst of so many torments and such fierce battles – Gemma found time to treat with God familiarly. O where art Thou, Jesus, she used to be heard saying after her battles with the infernal enemy.' Distracted from the writing of Father Germanus, spiritual director of the holy maid of Lucca, Brother Barragry, remembering Spenser, thought: there was an ancient house not far away, renowned throughout the world for sacred lore and pure unspotted life. Kneeling down to examine his ex-journalist's conscience, he followed his distraction further: so well, they say, it governed was and guided evermore, through wisdom of a matron grave and hore. Walking down the stairs to lunch he meditated on the hore matron whose only joy was to relieve the needs of wretched souls, and help the helpless poor. His Angelus walked before him: a dumpy curly-headed novice with upturned nose, thick opaque spectacles, a gown too long for him, menacing his steps as he descended. No Seraphim he; at least not in appearance. Brother Barragry liked the look of the thin dark-haired probationer whose name he knew as MacKenna and who had written a poem, not bad for a young fellow, in a Dublin magazine for which Brother Barragry had once been assistant editor. Fancy meeting you here. If we could only talk.

Appreciated your poem about ... what was it about? Helped to publish it, in fact. It is, or was, a small world. With his first bite of brown bread Brother Barragry remembered that the matron grave and hore had spent her nights in bidding of her beeds and all her days in good and godly deeds. In twenty minutes now he could talk.

IV

They finished the fifth decade of the rosary where the avenue under golden beeches topped a low ridge. Below, they could see where one of the gates of my lord's estate had formerly allowed horses and carriages out to the village's one street, and along that street towards the world. The beeches stood up radiantly above a silent unwaving dark-green sea of young conifers, planted in regular lines, spaced out with rides where forestry men could go. Brother Flynn, the Angelus, slipped his rosary beads back into the pocket of his jacket. Outside the house, and with no dark gown to flop and flap about his outsize determinedly-striding feet, he looked curiously naked. 'Every walk we go on,' he said, 'we always say the rosary at the outset.'

Brother MacKenna sniffed the peace of the pine woods.

''Tis ever sweet,' he quoted, 'among the pines to lie.' 'In a month with an R in it,' Brother Hanlon jested, 'novices should not sit down on the grass – nor on the pine needles.'

To Brother Hanlon, allowed on his walk, as a special feast-day concession, to join the company of Angelus and Anima, Brother Flynn explained:

'Brother MacKenna writes poetry.'

'We need good writers in the Order.'

'The men in the English Province seem to be much more active with the pen.'

'But then their two best writers went to them from Ireland.'

'Brother Barragry was getting to be well known in the journalistic world.'

'But he was a journalist pure and simple.'

'Still, he'll have a gift of presentation. It caused a big shock to everybody when he decided to enter.' Gravelled ground where the estate gate had once been, crunched under their feet. A head peered out of the door of the village pub, a hand adjusted the peak of a cap, the head vanished again. Around the parish priest's house a beech hedge, solid and clipped like battlements, resplendently held its leaves and would hold them, Brother Hanlon said, all winter long. It was, he said, the best beech hedge in Ireland.

'Brother Hanlon is our authority on hedges and trees. Just as Brother Guinan is on birds. Brother Guinan, the dark funny little man with the glasses and the turned-up nose. You probably saw him in the chapel.'

Brother Hanlon saluted two barefooted children mournfully crust-chewing at the school gate. 'Brother MacKenna was keeping custody of his eyes in the chapel as his Angelus told him.' They laughed. In a world of silence and prayer Brother MacKenna was discovering it was possible to laugh unrestrainedly at tiny jokes. Rooks flapped like black rags above trees near a threshing yard. Brother Hanlon looked at them, gently as he had looked at the chewing children: black rooks and barefoot children, all God's creatures. 'Are you interested in birds, Brother MacKenna?'

'Big ones, cooked,' Brother Flynn said. The big black-chinned angel had his sense of humour, coming out now and again through the strained, slightly stilted talk imposed on young tongues both by rigid religious rule and by seclusion in the woods from varied topics of the world. They laughed again. 'Ours,' gently smiled Brother Hanlon, 'should not make food a matter of conversation.'

'Except in a general way.'

Brother MacKenna walked wonderingly in a strange land. Hints and lessons from eight days of probation jostled each other in his brain: ours when walking shall not show undue haste, nor swing the arms immoderately, nor look unnecessarily about them, but downcast eyes should indicate the inner repose of the soul; the bread eaten in the refectory shall be plain and of two varieties, brown and white; excessive corporal mortifications shall not be undertaken without the special permission of the ghostly father, but all shall in this matter follow the injunctions laid down, each following those that apply to his own particular status in our Order.

The injunctions laid down.

Two days previously on a narrow pot-holed road that ran between marshy entangled woods away on the far side of the lake, Angelus Flynn had shyly produced from his pocket the two weapons allowed or enjoyed for the mortification of the novices' flesh. Brother MacKenna had had uneasy memories of the first time a school-friend, on the way home from the fishy pavilion, had produced a crumpled coloured postcard. But this was all different. The objects produced were different and the silent dank surrounding woods, and the spirit in which such objects were made and used; a small five-tailed whip of hard white cord, a chain of fine wire with points turned inward so that it resembled a fragile elongated harrow. 'Not as bad as it sounds,' the Angelus soothingly said, that hint of humour holily suppressed in his deep voice. 'We're not desert fathers. If you're right-handed you hit your right shoulder-blade. If you're ciotóg your left shoulder-blade. Twice a week at bedtime like medicine. In the cameratas with curtains drawn, naturally, to comply with the rules of modesty. The head novice in the camerate recites the *De Profundis.'*

The first impulse was to laugh, then to feel tingles of a mild shame. 'That's appropriate,' he said. 'The *De Profundis.'*

'One novice used to translate the domine, domine quis sustinebit as Lord, Lord, who can stick it. He left afterwards.' Their laughter disturbed the deep silence of the woods. A waterhen, startled, fluttered for cover by a pond's still edge. 'It's not just mortification for its own sake,' the angel said lamely, recovering his status as guide, consellor and friend. 'It's just a token to remind us of the sufferings of our Lord and His saints.'

'Dear Angel, say,' said Brother MacKenna, 'Why have I now no fear at meeting Him? Along my earthly life, the thought of death and judgement was to me most terrible. I had it aye before me, and I saw, the Judge severe e'en in the Crucifix.'

'Don't let the shock unsettle you.'

'That's what the soul says to the angel in the *Dream of Gerontius.'*

'The Magnov loves Newman. Last night he was showing me Father Rickaby's index to Newman's works.'

He knew now that Magnov was magister novitiarum, master of novices; that Peesock was Pater Socius, companion to the Magnov. Even novices thought of nicknames.

A labouring man, spade on shoulder, stepped slowly over a trailing barbed wire fence. Quickly the angel concealed the instruments of mortification. Down a long wet slope, glistening with puddles they looked at the unmortified world: a low huddled town where the Huguenot houses were, the white bellying cooling-tower of a new factory emitting periodic steam-puffs as if the earth belched.

Novices wore the chain, points to the flesh between wrist and elbow, every Friday forenoon. 'No cart-chains for us. We're not Matt Talbots.'

The injunctions laid down: the prayers to be said, morning oblation, morning meditation, examen of conscience, evening meditation, litany of the saints, then the great silence; the books to be read: Father Rodriguez, Father Faber, Père Raoul Plus, Father Gallwey, Abbot Marmion, Abbot Vonier, Abbé Fouard, lives of the saints that made Stanislaus Kostka, Paul of the Cross, Thérèse, The Little Flower, Francis of Assisi, Ignatius of Loyola, familiar friends and models – all these were the practices of a little world turning in on itself, hiding in the woods to find God. Now on a feast-day walk outside the curtain of woods and the barrier of demesne wall, the house and its way followed them, cut them off from the people they met on the roads, externs, as effectively as if they had been invisible. A red-coated girl cycled before them up the long slope from the village. Her presence meant as little as the straw on the roadside, blown twisting from the threshing yard. Invisible beside the three striding brothers in Christ walked the holy father founder, missionary and martyr, admirer of Saint Ignatius. His long bearded face brooded over the damp flat countryside and made it his own, the heart of his empire where his soldiers learned their drill. The countryside, too, was so unlike the countryside that surrounded Brother MacKenna's town. No brown northern hills here, their outlines made uncertain by drifting mist, no quick-running trout streams; but instead there were deep bogs, flat fields and heavy trees, slow rivers and canals, cottages on the English style planned by lords whose days were gone, a

slow-moving slow-speaking people. Some writer had called it a
sighing country.

'What do the people here make out of the novitiate?'

'We're not here long enough for them to know exactly what we
are. We have so little contact with the world.'

'Griffin the gardener,' said Brother Hanlon, 'told Brother Kehoe
that most of the locals think we're the children of parents who came
down in the world.'

'That's because they see us out in ordinary laymen's clothes.'

'And sometimes in the grounds in our tatters at outdoor works.'

'Griffin and the beegonyeeas.' They laughed with charity at the
way Griffin the gardener sung-sang the name 'begonia.' A little lost
in the intimate domestic twists of the talk, Brother MacKenna
meditated on what he had read of the father founder: a Latin man who
had never walked this clinging Irish soil, who could never perhaps
have imagined such dark golden autumns. His early ways had been in
white Italian sunshine. His mind had been turned towards God by the
poverty of vivacious brown running children, chirpy as birds, lively
as lizards. Then in some red eastern island, opposed by gods whose
names clanged like bronze, he had given his life for Christ, an
example forever to his followers. From above the chapel door his
face looked down at his men, officers, sergeants, privates, raw
rookies, from an octagonal portrait. Of the original of that portrait the
Order's official biographer had said: 'The face is that of man in the
fifties, with kind compassionate eyes. Evidently he has suffered, yet
remains steadfast and serene, ready to suffer more if necessary to
uphold his great ideal.'

What had all that to do with an old Georgian house abandoned to
decay in Irish woods by an Anglo-Irish nobleman whose Countess
had taken the Catholic cross; a house rescued from decay by
scholarly quiet men who taught in Irish schools, preached mission
sermons from pulpits in Irish churches? Jesus Christ, yesterday,
today, the same forever, linked up these sullen fields, the sea of
young conifers, the white Italian places, the struggle against carven
idols, the indoor and outdoor works, the death by torture and the

headsman's axe. One God. One world to be saved. One eternity in which all ages and places were drops in the ocean.

'Brother MacKenna's deep in thought.'

'Where will we walk to, Brother Hanlon.'

'What about the rock? Across the heath to the Rock?'

'It would be a fine day for the Rock. It's cold but it's clear.'

'Brother MacKenna would find the Rock interesting.'

Subjecting will and judgement with little perceptible effort, Brother MacKenna agreed. In history books and guide books he had read about the Rock. Five miles away the flatness of the land was broken by a line of low saw-tooth hills, one of them made distinctive by the square massive walls of a ruined castle. Seventeenth-century wars had stormed around that rock: Cromwell's men; the soldiers of Don Eugenio back from Spain, gallant Owen Roe; the clansmen of a warrior chieftan swooping down like eagles on the fat flat planted people.

They came at a cross on the main south road. Outside the whitewashed pub at the corner a dozen country boys played pitch and toss. One of them tentatively touched a cap as the novices strode past. Another sniggered. One snigger touched off another, the united sniggers swelled to a laugh, sparks in dry grass meeting in flame.

From memories of school debating societies, Brother Flynn said: 'The laughers have it. The cap-touchers are out.'

'To be esteemed a fool for Christ's sake,' said Brother Hanlon. But with his healthy red cheeks the smile on his mouth and behind his glasses, he didn't look like a martyr or a man of sorrows.

Brother Flynn said: 'The third degree of humility.'

'And the worst of it is,' said Brother Hanlon, 'the yobs don't even know how to play pitch and toss.'

'They all grew in the bog.'

'I knew a man who was a bank clerk once down here who said the only problem in his life then was distinguishing between his customers and the cows.'

'Charity, brothers, charity,' the anima, rapidly learning the vernacular, reproved.

'Ex ore infantium,' said Brother Flynn, and they were all laughing as they topped a rise on the wide south road and saw the heath undulating away towards the south. 'The high skies are over Ireland,' Brother MacKenna quoted, filling his lungs with a wind that blew from a far Atlantic, over Kerry, Limerick, and rich Tipperary, beyond there, where the south road dropped again over the horizon, 'and the lonesome mornings with birds crying on the bog.' The skies were high all right, standing up blue-grey and straight. But it wasn't bog. Dry short-grassed sandy heath, clumped with whins, dotted with sheep, netted by hedgeless roads, a house here and there, a golf club, the white railing and empty grandstand of a racecourse. On the main road cars ran north and south, drivers stepping on it to make the most of the open spaces of the heath, nothing like them except in France or on the plains of Mayo or the Curragh of Kildare. Half a mile away a man in white breeches exercised a young horse, circling him rapidly at the radius of a taut rope. One lone cyclist met them, free-wheel humming with the joy of the slope and the sailing pressure of the south-west wind. They cut across the grass, and the ground was dry and springy as rubber under their feet. They talked of the ways of the novitiate, of the simple fun that life there could offer, of the major villa, which meant summer holidays spent under relaxed discipline within the novitiate, of the long retreat which meant thirty days of almost unbroken silence. They talked about great days ahead in the houses of studies, humanities, philosophy, theology, or later in the schools or on the missions. They didn't talk of homes and people left behind because Brother MacKenna was new from the world, might feel homesick, might suffer the black melancholy pleasantly known as novitiate blues. On the golf-course four men in plus-fours and a young blonde woman in a tweed skirt moved jerkily, silhoutted against the sky like figures crudely scissored in cardboard. There went the world in all its glory, all its folly, golfing country doctors and bank clerks, their women, whiskey and cocktails in the club-house. Oculis dimissis the three Brothers talked of the Magnov's quiet sense of humour, his knowledge of the works of Newman. They said a silent pater and ave in the cold little empty church that seemed, for the shelter of a few trees, to have backed away from the open worldly windiness of the heath, horses, golf, fast cars on the main road. They crossed a bridge over a small stream and Brother Hanlon dissertated on watercress; the Irish word was biolar. On a narrow road, rough with loose stones, they commenced to climb. By a white cottage they left that road and went up through the crumbling outerworks of the ancient strong place. Around heaps of lichened stones, islanded in the grass, shaggy goats with curving horns bounded angrily from their approach.

'Do you remember, Brother,' the angel asked, 'what James Stephens wrote about goats on Howth head?'

Brother MacKenna remembered. He quoted as they climbed. 'You're going to be an acquisition in the novitiate,' Brother Hanlon said. 'Poetry on tap. MacKenna for poetry. Guinan for birds. Sadleir for stars. Cashman for jokes. O'Briend for ferns and flowers.'

'Hanlon for cress.'

'Flynn for fervour.'

'The Abbot Murphy for mortification.'

'Naked rolls in nettles. Up to the neck all night in the lake.'

The wind blew with fury. The heath was the world. But the Rock was boyhood, older than the world, than golf, or cocktails or racecourses, as old as Eden and as free. Restraint was gone. Jackdaws screamed from crannies in crumbling towers. Rules of modesty forgotten, the Brothers screamed back at the jackdaws. Adam in Eden had lived without rules.

This was the Rock. Below they saw heath, bog, fields cleaned of harvest, and woods in the distance, dark, decaying, falling into winter. High above those distant woods, like the masts of ships in harbour, rode the Californian cedars that had once been the main avenue of my lord's estate. Once, for the visit of an English king, that avenue had been softened with crimson carpet. Now grass grew rank on it; the cedars dropped their dead, the silence of the woods soaked the air. A side avenue led under russet beeches to the house of holiness.

Sheltered from the wind by a wall that had stood against wars, they ate their lunch of brown bread and butter, and small apples.

'What do you think of the Rock, MacKenna?'

MacKenna thought of the Rock and the vanished soldiers, of the golfers and the running horses, of the holy house, the face of the father founder, of the years ahead, and his home and the world behind.

He was happy. He was also lonely and cold and afraid.

V

'We eat in messes of four,' Flynn had said, 'even though we all sit at the same T-shaped table.' The mess of four used the same milk jug, sugar bowl, slop bowl, salt, pepper and mustard. One mess of four at dinner on the day of the walk to the Rock consisted of MacKenna, Barragry, Hanlon and Flynn. Barriers were down. Tongues were free and lively. Two great chandeliers, relics preserved from nights of dances, tinkled with light. Animae, like chickens from their mothers, were slipping away from Angeli. Tomorrow they would wear their own feathers, their own dark gowns. The table was pleasantly stocked. Lay brothers joked as they served the food. A grand atin' ordher, glory be to God. It was the feast of the father founder's martyrdom, red vestments at Mass, for the Order an exclusive double of the first class, for the novices an extra long walk, three extra courses, and talk at table. A century since, the Italian man had gone up a red road to the happiness of heaven, and logically, for men working hard towards heaven, the centenary was a day for joy. The blood of the martyr refreshed them for the uphill journey. His example inspired them. The saints of the Lord flourished like the lily, and precious in the sight of the Lord was the death of his saints.

Over the soup Barragry said: 'Brother MacKenna and myself haven't exactly met. But I think I know something about him.'

'Must be his elbow action when he does his teeth in the washroom.' That was Hanlon. 'He nearly broke my glasses yesterday.'

'No, this was about poems.'

'I remember the letter you wrote me. It was a change from the usual rejection slip.' It had been a kind whimsical letter and signed with a flourish: James Barragry, assistant-editor.

Breaking in from a neighbouring mess of four, Brother Guinan snub-nosed, thick-spectacled watcher of birds, said: 'I also knew Brother Barragry in mundo.'

'In the days of our flesh,' said Brother Barragry with mock solemnity. The talk of the world that was gone ended there. There didn't seem to be much point in Barragry saying 'How's your sister,' or in Guinan saying 'How's your brother.' Brothers and sisters, fathers and mothers, were well in the world, could be prayed for and occasionally seen. 'Did you enjoy your first long-table walk, Brother Barragry?'

'Wonderfully. My first taste of real austerity. I'm blisters to the knees, brothers, to the knees.'

A lay brother serving the first meat said to Brother Flynn: 'Oh! Brother, we miss you in the kitchen.'

'New blood now, Brother Molloy. New hands here. New novices full of fervour to keel the greasy pots.'

'Speed and efficiency,' Brother Molloy said, drawing out the first word to the length of a dozen vowels, and all the second-year novices within hearing laughed.

There, thought Barragry, goes a novitiate joke I still have to find the meaning of.

'Where did you walk to, Brother Barragry?'

'East the road to Ballyroan.'

'Even here in the jungle Brother Barragry already knows his cardinal points.'

'My dear,' said Brother Barragry, 'before you were born of either water of the Holy Ghost, a newspaper sent me to Ballyroan to interview a certain famous writer who lives there. You know, pictures and all, famous author back home from Cannes in favourite chair with favourite pipe pats head of favourite Alsatian while busily dictating next best-seller.'

Three messes of four were hushed with respectful interest: what does he look like? What does he talk about? Were you really inside that house? Is it true he is genuinely, in spite of his books, a practising Catholic?

'He's a fat man who practices drinking, smoking and growling about his neighbours.'

'Brother Barragry's blasé.'

'Well – I've come here to learn simplicity.'

'Where did Brother Guinan walk to?'

'Special favours for Brother Guinan on account of his high advance in virtue,' said the man of the birds. He had a pleasant vibrating resonance in his voice, and the easy rounded accent of the wealthier districts of South Dublin. 'I travelled by two-wheeled velocipede in the company of the Magnov and Brother Beadle to the Catholes.'

'Brother Beadle,' Barragry absently said, 'is no Bumble. His name is Kelly and he comes from Limerick.' Every three months one novice was chosen to act as a sort of bursar to the other novices. Deep down in Tipperary the calm happy silent chanting Cistercians joked that a bursar risked his soul for the good of the community.

'Why to the Catholes? It's too cold to swim. Anyway that river's full of mountain springs, as cold as ice.'

'Birds, dear brother in the Lord, birds. The Magnov wished to pick my brain. Mountain birds.'

'To pluck your brain.'

'Birds on the heather. Birds in the hazel glen below the Catholes.'

'Tweet tweet tweet.'

'My chain snapped and I had to walk the last two miles.'

'Rewards of vainglory.'

Brother MacKenna, bewildered, listened. Their talk was the talk of young men who came mostly from the same city, from the same two expensive and rather exclusive schools conducted by the Order, from the same football teams and debating societies. Photographs had already appeared in school annuals with captions to say that last year's school captain or scrum-half or prize essayist or gold medallist for debate had entered the novitiate. They knew each other's mannerisms and background. They tossed words at each other with enviable casualness. They had turned their backs on a common world. But somewhere along the table there must be novices, who, like himself, came from slow-moving provincial towns or quiet country places. Their faces had not yet for him separated themselves from the background of black gowns, nor their voices from the babel of tongues set loose for a long-table feast-day. Or perhaps it was that he had not yet adjusted himself to the tempo of novitiate talk, when talk was allowed; and for the present found himself more at home when silence settled over the house and he was free to think of the how and why, the where and when. At that laden long table, listening to laughter and easy charitable talk, he was suddenly lonely for Frankie, for Killyclogher woods, the hilly streets of the old abandoned town. He wrenched his thoughts away from them to listen and to learn about other places: about Ballyroan where the writer lived, where the canal went by aqueduct over the river; about the Catholes, out of walking distance and beyond the flat land, where the young river came leaping down over sheer limestone slabs. That sounded like his own country. He wanted suddenly to see the Catholes, the cataracts, the deep pools, the hazel bushes, to go immediately away from the table, the constraint and the permitted conversation.

'In the village,' Brother Guinan said, 'Master Cannon tried to fix my broken chain.'

'And failed?'

'And failed.'

'Ours should not talk with externs.'

'Master Cannon is only half an extern. Don't we teach catechism in his school as part of our training in teaching the young?'

'Have you finished all your experiments, Brother Guinan?'

The experiments meant teaching the catechism to children in schools, going down the mine which, in its turn, meant spending a month with the lay brothers in the kitchen, walking seven miles to a muddy neighbouring town to visit the sick and to preach short sermons to the paupers in the workhouse. Shadows of medieval mendicant friars fell faintly across those activities. The spirit was the same even if the trials were not so severe. Brother Guinan said: 'I still have Donohill to do.' Donohill was the muddy town, containing the workhouse with its paupers and incurable sick, as a rotting turnip might contain a festering lair of worms.

'I'm in Cannon's with Brother Nangle,' Hanlon said.

'So we know,' said Flynn, 'where the scholars object to the fact that Nangle doesn't use Gillette.'

'That was fun,' Hanlon said. Barragry braced himself for another novitiate joke. From the beaming smile and in the gentle voice of saintly Hanlon it came inevitably. 'You see when Nangle was teaching he heard the sniggers in the back row. When he wanted to know what it was all about they wouldn't talk. So he picked on the ringleader and sent him up to the master for impertinence. I wasn't impident, sir, says he, I only said the skewdent wanted a shave. And the poor master himself hadn't shaved for a week.'

Brother Flynn said the master had been to busy to shave, couldn't, in fact, be bothered shaving because he spent all his time reading and talking about Father Tom Burke's Refutation of Froude.

'Nangle says he can't be always shaving in order to satisfy the connoisseurs in the village school.'

Brother Molloy served tipsy cake. 'Had trouble there myself yesterday,' Hanlon said. The noise of voices swelled. Spoons cracked down on sweetplates. 'Over the question of whited sepulchres and what was inside them. Clay, says the scholar, clay.'

'Oh – fair enough,' said Barragry. 'That's as good as the boy in the Dublin school who said that the two great English martyrs were Bud Fischer and Tom Moore.'

'Or the wee boys in the north,' said MacKenna, 'who always in the Confiteor said Blessed John the Blacksmith, and the Holy Imposters Peter and Paul.' Two messes of four laughed encouragingly, because Brother MacKenna was coming out of himself, making jokes and that – however feebly and remotely – concerned the dear and abandoned homeland. All through the tipsy cake they talked of the north and the small number of novices that came from the north to the Order; and how had Brother MacKenna managed to come in contact with the Order.

'Reading,' he said, thinking it as good a reason as anything else, ashamed to mention the monstrance rising like a flame above the old town. 'Even reading what non-Catholics had to say against the teaching work done by the Order. Then I heard a mission preached by

Father O'Regan and some young Australian priest who was here on a visit.'

'The Magnov says Father O'Regan's sermons have brought scores to religion.'

'It's his fat cheerful face,' said Barragry.

'Coffee,' said Brother Guinan, 'and who'll sing the first long-table song.' For it was long-table custom to have songs over coffee and ginger biscuits, hard as slates, and slabs of cake called yellow peril spread with viscous red or yellow jam that came in heavy earthenware jars. At the top of the T-shaped table the fathers stood up, then the novices stood up and grace was said in sonorous Latin: Confiteantur tibi Domine omnia opera tua et sancti tui benedicant tibi. Then away from the boisterousness of youth the fathers, preceded by the grey-headed Rector, went to have their own coffee, and some of them, for health reasons, pipes, in a quiet parlour that overlooked the cobbled courtyard at the far end of the house. Feast or no feast, there could seldom be fusion between fathers and novices. The young must be tested before they could join the fit and few. In the silence as the fit and few fathers left the refectory, the rain could be heard lashing the great bay window. MacKenna was depressed with montage memories of flat sodden fields, dripping woods, rain flowing on the great stones that littered the rock, rain hissing around tyres as cars went north and south where the land's noblest road bisected the shelterless heath. Far away above the noise of the rain he heard a train whistle, a voice from another world, as lonely and as fit to create loneliness as the cry of the curlew. Guinan heard it, too, and sent his mind flying with the whimbrels, the seven lonely whistling birds in whom lived on, tradition said, the souls of seven Jews who had helped Roman soldiers to nail Christ to the Cross. Birds and the Saviour: the robin trying in mercy to draw the nail from the pierced hand, wearing forever the red blob of the precious blood; the sparrow with his chittering telling the Jews where Christ knelt in Gethsemane, and carrying forever God's curse. Was it the oyster-catcher had covered Him with seaweed by the Sea of Galilee so that his enemies couldn't find him? Or had the seven ominous whistling birds been whimbrels or curlews or widgeons or plovers? The train whistle ended. The noise of rain was lost again in the clamour of young voices.

Brother O'Brien had been a doctor in the world. On the day he entered the novitiate he had driven his own car to the bright blue gravel before the house and there abandoned it to his sister. He stood up now, a smooth-skinned stout man, bald above the temples, and sang about Burlington Bertie from Bow. One voice only, Barragry muttered, remembering a singing pub on the Dublin quays, pints flowing, pressed down and flowing over, symbols of the Lord's generosity, joxers straining their mufflers and tonsils and rending the rafters with sustained agonised elongated maudlin syllables: Caaan I forget yoooo, when every night reminds meee. No longer, he thought, should every night remind me. Life's new now. The road's clear ahead. How many men in this room have uneasy memories; or does the man who primarily turns to religion as to a refuge, who's running away from something or somebody, exist only in Barragry and in romantic novels?

Brother Cashman, olive-faced as a Frenchman, and always laughing, sang that it was his delight on a shining night in the season of the year. Viscous jam softened in the heat and flowed like wine. MacKenna remembered an Ulster Orange Song:

> *And when we arrived there in Aghalee*
> *The brandy it flowed like the Rhine ...*

Would it do to sing Orange tunes here in the house of holiness on the feast of an Italian saint, to open the mouth and bellow as Frankie would do walking to Killyclogher woods or to the bridge of initiation and discovery:

> *Oh, you Protestant heroes of Ireland*
> *Attention to what I write down ...*

Brother Madden with a voice soft as rain and turf-smoke, a man from Maam Cross in faraway Galway, sang about Kathleen and Saint Kevin in Glendalough: not Tom Moore's sad sentimental dirge, but the coy Thadyish song that saw a saint pushing a pursuing woman into a deep lake as matter for laughter and jammy spoons hammering on plates ...

> *You're a mighty fine fisher, says Kate,*

'Tis you that knows well how to hook 'em.
But when you have landed 'em nate,
Shure you want a young woman to cook 'em.

Brother Nangle, face still smarting from the unaccustomed razor, kept the fun going by reciting Queen Victoria's after-dinner speech at the Viceregal Lodge in the Phoenix Park in Dublin ...

I'm thinkin' there's a slate, sez she,
Off Willy Yeats, sez she,
He ought to be at home, sez she,
French polishing a pome, sez she,
Not writing letters, sez she,
About his betters, sez she,
Paradin' me crimes, sez she.
In the Irish Times, sez she ...

Minds crowded with jostling images – a stout queen slaughtering the queen's English, a medieval anchorite pushing the woman who loved him to a watery grave, a crouching poacher on a shiny night, a spiv called Berty who rose at ten-thirty – they walked in silence to the chapel. They prayed in silence until distractions died and there was only the altar and the rain on the windows. In silence, in single file, they walked through main hall, along the book-lined passage and past the conference room. To the left in a parlour the fathers, secluded as gods, still chatted over coffee. In silence down a stone stairway, along a stone basement passage to the boot-room. In the boot-room a few probationers, unnerved perhaps by the sudden return of silence, perhaps unable to forget the fat queen or the fishing saint, giggled as they changed from house-shoes to outdoor shoes, as they slipped on trench coats that diminished their gownless nakedness.

Along a curving stone-floored passage dedicated to Saint Francis of Assisi. A small lamp burned before a statue of the Umbrian saint. They filed silently through a low doorway and up concrete steps into the dark rainy night, yew trees swaying, cedar branches rising and falling like the gesturing arms of wizards. Then Brother Beadle, who was no Bumble, but a Kelly from Limerick, said Deo Gratias, and they broke file and ran, novices tucking skirts of gowns into pockets to keep fringes dry and set legs free for running, to the tin-roofed ambulacrum. And the ambulacrum was a long shed where novices walked on wet nights for their final recreation before what Brother Nangle called the four last things: not death, judgement, hell or heaven, but evening meditation in the chapel, supper in the refectory, the litany of the saints in the chapel, and then bed. At one end of the shed there was a green-robed, bearded, croziered, mitred image of glorious Saint Patrick herding the snakes from holy Ireland. At the other end Saint Aloysius Gonzaga in a blue gown spotted with five-fingered golden stars turned a pallid immobile face towards the iron girders of the roof. Between the two statues, and in groups of three, novices and probationers walked and talked. Barriers were down. Angeli and animae were no more. Tomorrow morning for Mass the former animae would wear the gown. All the brogues and accents of the island of Ireland came together in the ambulacrum, thirty voices gabbling all together and even in their gabbling praising the Lord; because to work and to pray and even to smear jam on yellow peril or ginger snaps, was, if the intention were pure, also to pray. O ye whales and all that move in the waters, bless the Lord: O all ye fowls of the air, bless the Lord.

Thought Barragry, remembering from Spenser the aged woman who kept the house of holiness: Dame Caelia men did her call, as thought from heaven to come, or thither to arise.

Sixty feet thudded on the hollow plank floor. Sadlier from Cork, whose brother hurled for that county, perched a battered black hat on the upturned face of Saint Aloysius.

And Dame Caelia had been the mother of three daughters who were well upbrought in goodly thewes and godly exercise. The two eldest of the three, explained Barragry to Guinan and the shaven Nangle, were most sober, chaste and wise, and their names were Fidelia and Speranza. He suppressed the lines that described them as virgins, that said that though spoused they yet wanted wedlock's solemnise. After all, he thought, smoothing his crisp wavy red hair with bony hands, I'm a late vocation, a grown man, and I've lived in the world beyond the pines, the bogs and flat fields, beyond the Huguenot town. Here I walk mainly among the innocent, boys of eighteen, straight from school and holy homes to the sheltering womblike walls of the holy house; and every night should not remind me. But Caelia's third daughter, he said, who was faire Charissa, was lincked to a lovely fere, which meant husband, and by him had many pledges dere, which meant a full nursery. Nangle who hated razors and Guinan who loved birds doubled with laughter as Barragry compared Dame Caelia's residence to the novitiate. It was easy to laugh in a quiet world. Barragry would be a godsend – a mature man, solid, experienced, confident, who had weighed the world and found it wanting.

Rain hammered on the ambulacrum's iron roof. Rain lashed the windows of the ancient house. Brother Beadle, hollowing thin jaws, blew a whistle, said semper Deo gratias. After that the only sounds were the rain, wind in the yews and cedars, red oaks groaning in the wood beyond the ambulacrum, house-shoed feet on corridors, creaking of kneeling boards in chapel, the house-bell rung by Brother Beadle, dividing the day's last silent hours.

VI

Litany of the saints still echoing in his ears MacKenna pulled the cold sheet up to his chin, lay flat on his back to ease each weary aching muscle.
Omnes sanctae Virgines et Viduae,
oráte pro nobis.
Under another cold white sheet Barragry grimly thought that it was a good idea to enlist together the prayers of the virgins and the widows.

MacKenna waited for Flynn, the senior novice in his camerata, to say semper deo gratias and switch out the light when the last bell rang.
From sudden and unprovided death,
Deliver us O Lord.
At the other side of MacKenna's white curtain, long-nosed Sweeney, a stammerer and clumsy, undressed slowly, was still fumbling, heavily breathing. Knocking against his jug and basin, when the light had gone and God had been forever thanked. Whiteness of curtains glimmered slowly out of the darkness. It

wasn't raining any more, but the rhythmical movement of great trees stirred by the wind could be heard. The earth was breathing. Thirty young men asleep in God. Twelve fit and few fathers asleep in God. Ten lay brothers and ten lay brother novices asleep in God. Sixty-two saints.

I'm supposed to go to sleep with my mind soaked in the matter prepared for my morning meditation.

But it was difficult to keep out of his mind the image of a monstrance above a town, of a rock above woods and flat land, to banish from the ears echoes of the babble of long-table ambulacrum voices, accents of all Ireland.

What, now, was my composition of place, the picture that, according to the Ignatian method of prayer, should control the imagination, draw it to holy things, prepare it and the other powers of the soul to converse with God? Imagine you are in the holy house of Nazareth. The poems I remember about that should aid the imagination. Alfred Noyes, for instance:

> *To watch the longlegged camels swaying*
> *Up the twisted street ...*

Or Rossetti:

> *Unto God's will she had devout respect*
> *Sublime simplicity of intellect*
> *And supreme patience ...*

Sir James Marchant, an Anglican almost on the threshold of the Church, had made an anthology about the Madonna. Chesterton had devoted his pen to her as knights used to devote their swords.

> *And men looked up at the woman made for morning*
> *When the stars were young,*
> *For whom, more rude than a beggar's rhymes in the gutter,*
> *These songs are sung.*

Poems, poems, poems and prayer. Swaying branches, living trees loved by the wind in the deep wood that led down to the lake. Up one tree, as he had walked out three mornings ago saying his beads, a squirrel had gone, quick as a snake, red as a ripe horse chestnut. Frankie had known about squirrels. Frankie might lie with Delia in Killyclogher woods looking up at the sky and at squirrels through the light blonde lacework of Delia's hair. Frankie had been, probably still was, a naturalist, and to Frankie he had written a poem never submitted to Barragry:

Now and henceforward I wish you
The strange things a bug-addict likes:
Abundance of everything crawling
In slimy, green, still-water dykes;
Sand-fleas and land-fleas, provided
The animals know their own place;
Lady-birds, grasshoppers, beetles,
Lizards and newts ... and newts ...

He couldn't remember any more. His memory crawled with all the colours of all the creeping things discoverable by turning back to the roots of the deep grasses of glossy June meadows. All a long long way from the holy house at Bethlehem. Laughing at himself, rocked by the rhythm of the wind, he fell asleep. Obdormivit in domino. The saints of God all over the house relaxed in their beds.

TWO: RORATE COELI DESUPER

I

Once a week it was permitted to talk to the world by writing a letter home. For other letters a special permission was necessary, a taking of one's place, between suppertime and the last recreation, in a queue in the corridor outside the Magnov's door. The door was a double one; first a cold expanse of wood coated with white enamel paint, then a red baize affair that moved slowly on stiff hinges and brushed against the bare wooden floor.

'Come in, Brother. Sit down, Brother.'

It was a large shadowy room packed to the ceiling with shelves of spiritual books. In one corner a screen concealed bed and washstand. In another corner a green-shaded reading lamp shed light on a scrupulously tidy desk. Beside the desk was a prie-dieu facing the wall, and on the wall was nailed a crucifix of black wood with a startlingly white figure of the crucified. In the shadows behind the green light the Magnov sat.

'Come in, Brother. Sit down, Brother.'

The charity of Christ was here, but Christ had never sat fortified behind an oaken desk, never sat gently smiling beyond a barrier pool of green light, never had had to be approached across a wooden floor that was mountainous with knots and as slippy to house-shoes as a rink to skates. MacKenna found it unnerving. His gown kept getting entangled with his knees as he walked from door to desk. Sit down uneasily in the chair facing Magnov. To make matters worse, the chair rocked slightly, one leg shorter than each of the other three. Fold gown over legs. Feel like a young girl in her first evening dress.

'Could I have special permission, Father, to write to Francis McLaughlin. He was my best friend at school.' High wind in Killyclogher woods: the leaves would be down now, the burn brown and swollen, the high hills sodden, the town more often black than any other colour.

'Certainly, Brother. We mustn't forget our friends. We leave them for Christ's love, but they go on living in the world and they like to hear from us. Write to them for their sake, not for our own. And never neglect the weekly letter to your parents. Some good novices write the most edifying letters to their people. Saint Paul himself couldn't do better. As it's my duty according to our rule to read those letters, I'm seldom short of matter for mirth. Beware of being too edifying, Brother. It's a well-intentioned fervour to which the young are very prone.'

'Yes, Father.' Then wryly: 'I don't think I'm in much danger of that.'

'You seem to have been reared sensibly, Brother. Some good novices will be well rewarded in heaven for the edification they give. But often they can be a trial to lesser mortals like ourselves. However, if we never have more severe trials we'll go easily through life.'

'Yes, Father.' Omnibus omnia. All things to all men. Saint Paul and the Magnov. If Brother Begley who lives all the time in a sort of rapture were here now in this chair the Magnov would look out through his green light and see into Begley as easily as he sees into me. He would also set Begley at ease with soothing understanding words.

'You find the life here not too strenuous, Brother?'

'No, Father.'

'You northern people are blessedly adaptable. It's a good quality to have when you join a regiment of guerrillas like ourselves. You never know where you may be next: in China learning Chinese or teaching hic haec hoc in Cork City.'

'Yes, Father.' Survey the world from Cork to Cathay. The idea had a lift in it, an inspiration.

'Anyhow – write to Francis, your friend. He's named after which saint?'

'Saint Francis Xavier, Father.'

'A great guerrilla for God, Brother.'

'Yes, Father.'

'Good night now, Brother, and pray for me. Remember I'm always here. It'll be easier coming to see me when your muscles get more accustomed to the springs on that baize door.' Behind the green light a head slowly nodded dismissal, a gentle smile made less embarrassing the journey back across the humps and ridges of the floor. Brother Barragry said he always felt like backing out of the room the way people did in Persia, where it wasn't reckoned right to turn your seat on a man you should respect.

Next day in the free time after the recreation that came after dinner (no talk at table now, but reading aloud by one novice in a rostrum: a page of À Kempis, a chapter of Patrick Campbell's history of the Jesuits, a brief menology life of one of the Order's holy men) he sat alone in his camerata and wrote to Francis, his friend, wrote to the world he'd left behind him. Francis might be christened after God's greatest guerrilla, but at that exact moment he was probably petting Delia's clever bony fingers in the dark at the matinée in the old town's one cinema. He wrote carefully because every word would pass under the Magnov's wise eyes. Brother Frawley, a burly black lad whose duty it was, among other things, to supply fresh water to the three or four roach in a small concrete pond near the ambulacrum, resented that censoring of letters, called it, bluntly, espionage. Brother Flynn, listening to Frawley, had remained, as a second-year novice should, discreetly and charitably silent, abstaining from pointing out that a good religious surrendered will and judgement in all things, short of sin, became the staff in the blind man's hand; that obedience could move mountains or make the dry stick planted in earth burst overnight into flower. The good religious did not thus reprove his brother.

'By this time you probably think I've been taken up to heaven in a flaming chariot. I haven't, though. My feet are solidly on the earth ....'

Not on the earth, but on the worn waxed floor of a quiet camerata. White curtains were drawn back and tied neatly around iron poles. Beds were neatly dressed with fringed white quilts. Flynn and Sweeney were not using their forty-five minutes of free time in order to write letters. Flynn was poring over books in the ad usum library, a selection of sound spiritual books intended especially for the use of the novices and shelved at one end of the house's topmost corridor where the lay-brother novices had their dormitory. Sweeney in one of the washrooms was scrubbing his jug and basin to the required whiteness. Chewing his pen, MacKenna could hear, going from him down the corridor the clink of some other novice's delph, the tap on linoleum of the hard heels of house-shoes.

'You'd like this place here, Frankie. It has woods that would remind you of the forest primeval, a lake with islands, and boats that we can use in the summertime when we have our villa – that's our holiday, and interesting places within walking distance. There's a rock with an old ruined castle on top of it. The other novices come from all over Ireland, Galway, Wexford, Dublin, even from Beare Island in Bantry Bay. They're very decent fellows. They're full of information about birds, bugs, trees, flowers, fish stars, everything, not, of course, forgetting books. Barragry, who used to be Assistant Editor of the *Bugle*, is here. You may remember he took a few poems of mine. He's a late vocation and a tower of strength to scaldies like myself.'

The sky beyond the wood and the lake, the western sky, was white enough to outline the dark bodies and arms of the trees. The still unseen water would be phosphorescent with the last light of a winter evening, and if the house had been completely quiet he might have heard the bitter complaints of the marsh birds and waterfowl. Up above the tree-tops the clouds had gathered, steel-blue and threatening. The wind promised snow.

'It isn't, of course, the right time of the year to appreciate this low-lying countryside. But we look forward, like poor old Shelley, to the spring that will follow the winter. Maybe you might get a chance to come and visit me then. We're allowed visitors here and they're well treated and well-fed and shown the beauties of the grounds around the house. So come and have a look. Save up the fare. Most of the old Lord's estate is under government forestry, but the Order kept some woods and parkland and a walk around the lake. After all, a religious house needs privacy.

'The life we live isn't exactly what I expected it to be. We don't do much study, only a little Latin, and only spiritual reading. But I'm discovering writers I never heard of before. The Abbé Fouard, who's written a two-volume life of Christ and good books on Saint Paul and Saint Peter. Archbishop Goodier has written a fine devotional life of Christ. Then there's Pourrat with a great three-volume work on Christian spirituality, Père Raoul Plus, a very up-to-date French Jesuit, Father Gallwey, Saint Francis de Sales, Saint Alphonsus Liguori, even Bossuet and Bourdaloue, Father Faber, the Oratorian who knew Newman, and others. The autobiography of Saint Thérèse of the Child Jesus is a delightfully human book.'

Was that too edifying? Would it set Frankie scratching his poll or the Magnov smiling? He re-read the paragraph: 'The life we live isn't exactly what I expected it to be ...' He stopped. He was aware then that the camerata was cold, that the town and Frankie and his people were far away, that he was alone in deep silence. He had heard second-year novices joke about novitiate blues: the reaction that followed when the novely had worn off; a mixture of homesickness, despair of perseverance, accedia or the noonday devil that had sent even cenobitical holy men restlessly from their desert cells to watch the African sun and hope for the break in the monotony caused by the day's one frugal meal. What did Pascal say about learning to live in one room? The Cistercians bound themselves by a vow of stability, on top of poverty, chastity, obedience and conversion of manners, to live always in the one monastry. But even the best and holiest had suffered from that mixture of tedium and temptation. Father Willy Doyle had advised young neophytes despairing of perseverance: every time you feel like quitting and going home, wait at least for the next meal. Hold on then from mealtime to mealtime, like a man swinging up a wooded hillslope by clutching from tree to tree. Was there a demon coming from the darkening woods into the cold camerata to overwhelm him with despondency before years of silence, study, prayer, abnegation, community life, uphill pulling towards the high hilltops of the spirit? The books on his table, the crucifix, the prayer printed on a red card were cold and unreal. Almost secretively he pulled out from under the table the red

rubber-padded wooden kneeler. Kneeling, crossing himself
elaborately, kissing the cold metal crucifix, he prayed: 'Remember, O
most gracious Virgin Mary, that never was it known that anyone who
fled to thy protection, implored thy aid, or sought thy intercession,
was left unaided.' He said three times: Sacred Heart of Jesus, grant
me perseverance, and asked himself: do I want perseverance for
God's glory, or only because I would be afraid and ashamed to face
back into the world?

But to work was to pray and even to write a letter, if the intention
was pure, was to work. In our house, said the rule, idleness which is
the devil's opportunity should have no part. So he sat up again to
finish his letter to Frankie.

People in the world, even those possessed of the world's goods –
Barragry would never pass that phrase – had their own troubles,
despondencies, family cares and responsibilities from which the
religious was set free. And how much greater was the reward, the
incorruptible crown, the religious strove for. The good religious,
Saint Bernard of Clairvaux had said, and Petit had the words on his
table written on the back of a holy leaflet where MacKenna had seen
them one day when he was sweeping camerata four, lives more
purely, falls less frequently, rises more quickly, walks more
cautiously, enjoys peace more securely, dies more confidently, is
purified more quickly and rewarded more richly. A proud boast. But
you couldn't accuse a saint of pride or boastfulness. What he said
must be true. Those eight points by Saint Bernard added up to
something it was surely worth fighting for.

He wrote: 'But strange as the life is, one can be very happy here.
The old town seems far away but not forgotten. Say a hail Mary for
me now and again that I'll persevere.' He almost wrote: 'Now that
I've put my hand to the plough I do not want to turn back.' But he
thought better of it. Frankie would say: Mac must think he's in an
agricultural college.

After some hesitation he added: 'Remember me to all our mutual
friends,' and saw the mutual friends, or some of them smiling and
nodding at him around the decorous white folds of Flynn's curtains,
tied around their upright iron post and swelling out slightly like an

evening dress on a slender girl. There was Frankie's laughing Delia.
There was the flash of the shiny prominent teeth of the red-headed
girl at the bridge. There was Geordie, nicknamed the Duke of
Saxe-Coburg, who had been in the war, who worked in the flour mill
and lived with a woman he wasn't married to. There was the
brown-headed girl at the other bridge whose educative efforts had
been thwarted by Brother Higgins the Stiggins, and MacKenna's
guardian angel. Frankie's grandmother said that the boy destined for
the priesthood could never lose his purity the whole way. There was
the Snifter Hannigan who would join the British Army as his father
had done before him. There was Freddie Atcheson, the burly
shoemaker, in whose cellar-like workshop he, Frankie, and four other
boys had once tasted methylated spirits and talked smut with a
shawled tramp woman and a Punjab peddler ....

But Sweeney stumbled in among them, scattered them, Sweeney
clumsily carrying spotless washstand, jug and basin. Down the
twisting wooden stairway from the ad usum, Flynn came
heavy-footed, sat down at his table to read his red-backed life of
Saint Peter Canisius. MacKenna addressed the envelope, but didn't
seal it. The Magnove would look at it before it went out through the
pine woods and the Huguenot town to Frankie and the world.

In the hall outside the refectory Brother Beadle rang the bell to
call the novices to the chapel for evening meditation.

The weekly letter to his mother was not such a trial. She was so
proud of him. She saw him as a boy in a white gansey. She heard his
vocation, his call, more distinctly than he heard it himself. It was a
gentle voice saying come, talking over a low hedge to her son
walking the road of life. It was a friendly greeting over a wooden gate
where country people learned to pass the time of day. So he wrote
simply to say he was happy and to tell her:

... that he rose at five thirty-five a.m. ('What do you think of that
and all the trouble Pop and yourself used to have rooting me out for
eight o'clock Mass?')

... that he was in good health, never better, eating well, sleeping
well, warm at night, wearing his heavy underwear for the winter.

('You'd be amazed at the good obedient boy I've become. Obedience is one of the great principles we live by here. Like soldiers in the army we do what we're told, only unlike soldiers there's no danger we'll ever be ordered to shoot our fellow men. We're soldiers of Christ.')

... that the other novices were the best fellows in the world and she'd love every one of them, that they came from all sorts of homes, rich and poor, town, city and country, and two had been educated at public schools in England, but that nevertheless they all lived together like brothers.

As he wrote that he thought to himself: behold how good and how pleasant it is for brethren to dwell together in unity: like the precious ointment on the head, that ran down upon the beard, the beard of Aaron, which ran down to the skirt of his garment: as the dew of Hermon which descendeth upon Mount Sion. But he didn't write that down because she'd think he's taken leave of his senses. He told her instead that:

... the novices did housework, washed dishes, swept and polished, studied to learn humility. ('You'd laugh to see me sweating at the business end of a polishing squeegee. We keep the floors as slippery as convent floors. You remember the commotion when Father Phil Doherty dislocated his hip on the floor of the Loreto convent.')

... that the novices also worked in the grounds around the house, hoed paths, weeded flower-beds, sowed flower, clipped hedges, kept the place tidy. ('Many hands make light work.')

... that when they worked outside they wore old tattered clothes that had passed down from generation to generation of novices, and were kept in an attic room called the leper colony, because some witty novice had once maintained that the place was bug-infested ....

... that when they played football they wore not togs, but the same ragged clothes. ('We call ourselves the flying scarecrows.')

... that they prayed a great deal, meditations morning and evening, examen of conscience twice a day, litanies at night, mass and benediction, beads in the morning walking in the grounds. ('We have a special examen beads, eight or nine beads on a double string. We pin it inside the jacket and pull a bead every time we commit the fault we're concentrating on eradicating.')

Would she think that silly? Concentrating on eradicating? Perhaps the letter was long enough. So he hoped that all were well at home and praying for him. He didn't write: pray for me that I may persevere. That would alarm her. She had never heard of novitiate blues. She would not be able to imagine how anyone trusting in God and putting the hand to the plough could ever turn back.

In the world Barragry had always regarded letter-writing as the most distasteful form of work, and he had never considered that to work was to pray. Having no parents alive to write to, he wrote every week with the utmost brevity to his elder brother, a lawyer who drank too much. That was a Barragry failing.

'Everything fine here. I pray hard that all publicans see the light and that nobody sells you inferior malt. Wine, the scripture says, rejoiceth the heart of man. My regards to all our friends.'

He knew coldly, almost callously, that those regards would never penetrate the barrier of silence between himself and the thing, or person, he had fled from. You couldn't, even in the world, tell an elder brother everything.

II

The little red-backed meditation books supplied to the novices as a basis for their morning meditation followed the story of Christ round and round the liturgical year. To the Romans forever and ever and in all places Saint Paul encouragingly wrote: it is now the hour for us to rise from sleep for now our salvation is nearer than we believed. The night was past and the day was at hand and the novices, clothed in the armour of advent light, went out in groups of four to gather Christmas holly. In the dripping sodden woods the only remaining colour was in rust-red bravely-clinging beech leaves, in polished crimson berries peeping from prickly glossy-green holly bushes. The exercise of sawing and hatcheting, of chipping with murderous knives, was welcome release from the heightened austerity of advent

days. Into purifying preparatory flames the Lord's angel went down
to the furnace with Azarias and his companions, and in the canticle of
the praising children miraculously preserved from the sting of the
flames, the holy house welcomed the coming of Christ. During
Advent there were no long walks, no occasional talk nor jam nor
biscuits nor slabs of yellow peril with after-dinner coffee. The
discipline was taken in the cameratas on four nights of the week
instead of two. Chains bit into forearms on four mornings instead of
two. The senior novice in each camerata chanted; de profundis
clamavi ad te Domine. The other novices responded: domine exaudi
vocem meam. In the curtained privacy of his cubicle MacKenna
swung right-handed, felt the whipcord bite into the bared flesh of his
right shoulder. Frawley, deep in novitiate blues, seeing life as an
endless chain of buckets of water poured into a concrete pond to
refresh stupid-eyed moveless roach, wryly belaboured his pillow and
joined in the chorus. Barragry, in the course of one night's penitential
exercises, set all the novices in his camerata giggling by an especially
sonorous, mournful, meaningful intonation of domine, domine quis
sustinebit.

With Donnelly from Armagh, Sadlier from Cork and Kelly from
Limerick, MacKenna pulled a handcart heavily laden with holly
down the avenue to the village. "Tis our privilege every year,'
Sadleir said, 'to put up the holly in the village church for poor Father
Robert.'

'Have they no altar society in the parish?'

'They haven't the nails to scratch themselves. Too lazy. Too
stupid.'

The hollow under the imitation Lourdes grotto was filled with
concave glass intended to simulate water. Beside the baptismal font
the dead countess slept in carven marble. In the cold church the four
novices wreathed lamp standards with holly, cleaned the tubes of the
tall Mass candles, fixed flowers in vases, changed altar linen. Red
letters on white cloth said: Gloria in excelsis deo. In the organ loft
jovial Donnelly touched his fingers skilfully along the keys of the
harmonium. In the world, or halfways into the world, his uncle was a
bishop and Donnelly had been a cathedral chorister, as good as reared

in surplice and soutane, a natural priest if ever there was one. He played the missa de angelis gloria, and then, rubicund face crinkling with mischief, irreverently in God's house, he played the ranting tune of an old Gaelic ballad. Settling the last wreath of holly on one of the lamps that guarded the sanctuary gate, Kelly from Limerick said: 'Donnelly is a disedifying divil.'

Sadlier said: 'A born vandal. Didn't he eat half a dozen apples out of the stock the poor Protestants had in the church above for harvest thanksgiving.'

'Give thanks properly, Donnelly said,' said Kelly, 'by showing the Lord you appreciate his gifts.'

'King David ate the loaves of sacrifice.'

'The Lord's disciples nibbled the ears of corn.'

'On the Sabbath, at that.'

The ballad tune still danced from the organ loft. The words that went with it said that the people in the world were always contriving to gather and make store of gold pieces, always thinking on the shortness of life and how they'd soon be stretched under a flagstone; that neither landlord, duke, nor king would have a penny with them and they going under the sod, so all things considered, the wisest way for a man to be was to be alway leppin' in drink. 'Donnelly's way,' said MacKenna, 'of saying, "Lay not up for yourselves treasures."'

'Father Robert, God help him, will be scandalised if he hears us.'

'Father Robert'll think it's a hymn.'

'An Ulster hymn, played by Donnelly. Confraternity men to the fight.'

'Here he is.'

'Donnelly?'

'Father Robert.'

It was Father Robert, and he did think it was a hymn. The music ceased, but from the organ loft, above the open door above the coloured stall of wilting Catholic Truth pamphlets, above the sleeping marble countess, Donnelly's red face grinned down, behind the parish priest's back, at his embarrassed brothers. Donnelly's body inclined forwards in the mockery of a bow.

MacKenna had never before spoken to Father Robert. He had heard of his gentleness, his simplicity, his love for the Order men who had taken the deserted big house and brought, he said, a powerhouse of prayer into his parish. He had pressed forward the negotiations that had left the Order in possession of the place and set the powerhouse humming. Once a week he smoked, sipped coffee, chatted with the fathers after dinner in their parlour. Twice a year he walked and talked with all the novices after long-table dinners. Every night he prayed that the special privilege of dying in the Order's habit might be his. For tradition said, and Father Robert and others believed it, that to go so clad to the gate of heaven was to be certain of a welcome. Barragry, when he heard that, said: dying put on the weeds of Dominic or in Franciscan think to pass disguised. But Barragry was old, unenthusiastic, ready to joke about anything. Father Robert was, as Barragry knew and readily admitted, a simple saint. He said: 'Brothers, I recognise Brother Donnelly's touch.' Perhaps he wasn't so simple. His asthmatic voice re-echoed from every corner of the cold quiet church. He smiled at the three. His rimless glasses glistened so that his eyes were invisible and his large shiny false teeth joggled on unsure foundations. He said: 'Music, while you work,' and they listened to the sound of Donnelly's steps descending the dusty hollow wooden stairs from the organ loft.

Father Robert in the lead between Kelly and Sadleir, Donnelly and MacKenna in the rear, they walked down the nave and out of the church. A net guarding the door against summer flies and not removed for the winter hung brown and dusty and a little disturbed by the wind. The wind ruffled Father Robert's snow-white hair. He walked stiffly, rheumatically, small paunch bobbing, white hands resting on the arms of Kelly and Sadleir. 'Father Master, brothers, has given me permission to ask you in for a cup of tea.'

'Good. Good,' said Donnelly unashamedly.

'Oh nothing up to the standard of your monastery, Brother Donnelly. You take the vow of poverty. We poor secular priests keep it.'

'The circulars,' Donnelly said. He and the priest laughed like old friends. Petit, the rigid bright Latin scholar, or Begley, the placid mystic, or Foley, the pale ascetic, would have been disedified by Donnelly. But Sadleir and Kelly, ex-provincial school footballers, the slowly settling residue of abnormally active boyhoods, didn't mind. 'God forgive you, Brother Donnelly. You're the image of that high and mighty episcopal uncle of yours. Jesting at an old man's waistline. Wait, wait until you're my age.' He puffed with the effort of walking, laughing and talking all together. 'I remember your uncle now, when we were in Dunboyne together ....' Along the path to the priest's house they listened to memories of Maynooth. That path was sheltered by what Hanlon claimed was the country's best beech hedge, crisp coloured leaves rasping in the wind. The tea the priest's housekeeper made was strong and sweet. They drank from large flower-patterned china cups that opened out like dowdy rain-battered roses. Father Robert's books, and in his prime he had been a noted moral theologian, lined the walls of the room they sat in. Firelight glinted on tall black bindings secure from dust behind glass doors, and on a long mahogany table. Firelight burned scores of golden spots into the silver on the sideboard. MacKenna meditated on comfort combined with quietude. The housekeeper was a buxom motherly woman, a link with home and the flowery warm appetising smell of baking scones. In the holy house now the camerata windows were open, the radiators were turned down, the white curtains twisting round their poles with the cold wind from the sleeping bogs. Sipping their strong tea, listening to Maynooth memories, the four novices felt the power of the contrast. Donnelly found it amusing, but then Donnelly found everything amusing, even harmoniums in Catholic churches, even apples, cabbages, turnips piled for harvest thanksgiving in Protestant churches. The world, for the greater glory of God and the greater amusement of Donnelly, was one huge joke. Kelly and Sadleir placidly envied Father Robert his fire, his easy chair, his books, the strong tea and rich fruit cake, and possibly, the decanter hidden there in the sideboard, rich with amber fluid from the bishop's bottle, nobody knew his drop like a good Irish parish priest.

But then, MacKenna thought, fortifying himself against homesickness and the thought of cold wind in the cameratas, he has a lonely existence. The country priest is a solitary man, short of congenial company, exposed overmuch to the shocks of the world, lacking the security and environing charity of community life. Doesn't Father Robert want to go to God wearing our habit? Each man to his own vocation. I'm glad I chose as I did: community life, silence, strict rules, no holidays at home, poverty, chastity, obedience. Think of the young secular students home on holidays playing football with country teams, swimming and golfing at seaside resorts, the odd one, as the world knows, spending more time than for his own good he should in female company. A man must be strong to live like that, to be in the world and not of it. Another phrase there that Barragry wouldn't stomach.

But to stand against temptation, to persevere, I need the wall the Order builds around me. Ordo est dux ad deum, order is the guide to God and all things that come from God are ordinated, set in order, ordinata sint omnia a deo. A ghastly word: ordinated. Barragry would wrinkle his ex-assistant-editor's nose. But the translation of the Ignatian spiritual exercises does say something about the de-ordination or re-ordination of one's life. So ordinated would pass, and damn Barragry. Et omnia a deo ....

'Goodbye, brothers, and thanks and God bless you. The infant Jesus will bless you for everything you've done for me.' Genuinely there were tears in the old man's eyes. 'Pray for me, brothers.' The whole long sharp battlemented beech hedge dryly rustled. 'Remember I belong to an Order as well. The order of Saint Peter. The oldest order in the Church.' Through his tears he laughed after them. They laughed and waved their hands, the wind flapping their gowns. Donnelly's left shoe was burst and his little toe showing. Above them the village sprawled along a broken-backed hill, squat houses ruled by the high oblong of the pub and the long low oblong of the schoolhouse. The skewdent, said the sniggering pupil to the bearded schoolmaster, needs a shave.

With Frawley, Curran and Sweetman, Barragry helped to decorate the refectory. White morning mist washed like a sluggish milky sea around the trunks of the bare trees in the wood that went down to the lake. The glass of the great bay window ran with slimy snaily rivulets. For the purposes of greater efficiency, the four holly-hangers had permission to talk essential talk. Curran, tall and sallow, his enormous tight-skinned forehead angled like a balancing rock above a face that ran to a point at the chin, perched high on the top of a ladder, religiously saying only the essential things.

'Now, please, Brother Barragry, hand me the tacks. Now, please, Brother Frawley, the end of the twine.'

Sweetman, benign, sandy-haired, with stooping shoulders, was more indulgent to the possible pre-Christmas homesickness of first-year men. With Frawley, the brusque and discontented, he chatted above the hullabaloo that had preluded departure from the world, the talks with relatives, the farewells to friends, the purchasing of the long list of necessary clothes. 'Up and down Grafton Street I was dragged.' He talked sideways through barely opened lips. Poor old Abbot Curran aloft on the masthead mustn't be disedified. Like convicts on the exercise ground, thought Frawley, talking the way old lags talk. 'Up and down Grafton Street, fitting on things everywhere, feeling like a fool, excessive humiliation in cloth shops, my aunt on one side of me, my mother on the other.'

Barragry old-lagged: 'The third degree of humility. To be a fool for Christ's sake.'

For Christ's sake, Frawley thought, and then, ashamed of himself, remembered he was no longer a rowdy footballing schoolboy.

'We had tea in Fuller's,' Sweetman whispered. The clink of delph, the sound of voices came from the scullery that opened off the refectory. Brother Molloy was leading operation washing-up. Down the mine with the lay brothers a man could talk almost as much as he liked. 'Fuller's was stuffy with wealthy old ladies and wealthy young ladies. The air was dizzy with perfume. Myself in the middle of them like one horn on a unicorn.'

'Brother,' Barragry reproved. 'Brother.' On top of the ladder Curran – who had overheard – remembered a ponytrap drive with his mother to a small West Cork seaport town. In the dark musty little shops there was leisurely talk, neighbours bethanking God that Ma'am Mrs Curran your fine son is called to follow a higher way. Afterwards in the darkness they drove slowly home. The trap's lamplight fell on roadside grass, on grey lichened drystone walls, shone like bronze on the pony's chestnut flanks, swaying rhythmically as the beast pulled uphill against slopes rough with loose pebbles. The bulky precious parcels packed the trap. Brown parcelling paper rustled. Springs creaked. His mother hadn't a word to say.

'Bought my own clothes,' Barragry said. 'Had to pay for them too. Left the world without a sigh. Overdrawn. Holy poverty, how are you. A runaway vocation. A moonlight flit. My bank manager will remember me, and I hope, pray for me.'

Frawley sniggered. There was a comfort in Barragry. He didn't seem to disapprove silently and in charity and patience of everything one said. He didn't walk around rigid with piety like Curran, or Begley, or Petit, or Foley. It must feel fine to have reached manhood in the world as Barragry had done, to have worked on newspapers, signed cheques, had a bank manager. My mother hoarded every penny for those blessed clothes. She bought them in Talbot Street, too, not in Grafton Street except for that nonsensical long-tailed Chesterfield suit which nobody here seems to wear anyway, except when walking on the experiment to preach to the paupers in a workhouse. There's sense for you: on with tailed coats and off to the poorhouse. In Talbot Street the shops didn't stock such objects. She hoarded every penny and never in her life had tea in Fuller's. If it wasn't for the thought of the sacrifice that flummery had cost her, I'd be at home again long ago, although God knows I'd be as well at home looking for a job, as in this place pouring buckets of water over half-dead fish, beating my pillow, so as to share in the shindy, with a wee whip. It's hard to see how carry-on of that sort could be regarded as giving your life for Christ, or preparing for priesthood or advancing in the spiritual life or taking up your cross or anything else. Feed my lambs, water my fish, whip yourself, meditate in frozen cameratas for an hour on end, kneel down at what they call a quarter of charity while your brothers, moryah, stand up and tell the Master of Novices what they consider your rough corners are from the point of view of community life. We aren't allowed corners, not even in the way we speak or read aloud in the refectory or kneel in the chapel.

Ours shouldn't this. Ours shouldn't that. Ours shouldn't be individual human beings at all. Seems I'm all rough corners. Father, I think Brother Frawley speaks too loud at recreation. Loudly, dear Brother, loudly. Father, I think Brother Frawley is over robust on the football field and inclined to disregard the ne tangas rule. Now, how could a novice, or a cherub for that matter, play football and yet observe a rule about no body touching another body. In the garden where the opened tomb was, Christ said noli me tangere to the advancing Magdalen. Father, I think Brother Frawley takes the stairs two at a time. Father, I think Brother Frawley breathes too heavily in the chapel.

Quarter of charity, my Frawley foot. No quarter, more like. Before I entered or, as they say, when I lived in the world I read a book by Maurice Walsh called: *And No Quarter*. That was the Covenanters' battle-cry: Jesus and no quarter. No quarter at the Q.C.

Sweetman whispered to Barragry: 'He's going back to Dublin today.'

At a small table at the far end of the refectory one of the fathers from a Dublin house meditatively ate his breakfast. That morning he had ended his annual eight days' retreat. Spiritually refreshed, he was going back to grapple with the world. The monastery's V-8, driven by a lay brother, would carry him to the Huguenot town and the Dublin train. He was a slight, gaunt bespectacled man with shiny black hair sleeked down at two or three angles, like dark conflicting tides, on a narrow head. He was a noted scholar and lecturer.

Frawley muttered: 'I wish I was going with him. What do you think, Barragry?' Sweetman smiled sympathetically. Curran hammered home the last tack. Barragry said: 'Brother, I'm not so sure.' And he wasn't so sure, for reasons he couldn't talk about to Sweetman or Curran, or Frawley: reasons that had nothing to do with holly-hanging in the refectory of a holy house.

Twelve months ago to the day he had sat warm with her in the smoke-room of an old-fashioned hotel. Barragry the bold, the monk with a past, the late vocation, the broken heart, the soul surfeited with the world, the melodrama, we have sinned so get me to a nunnery, Heloise and Abelard. But seriously, though, do I want to see her again? Could she ever understand what I have done and why I have done it? She has not, as they say, the faith. She has not the sense of sin. Does my vocation just appear to her like cold-blooded desertion, the effect of satiety, of being too certain that she was in love with me? I could never manage to make clear to her what I meant. No tears from her, just a clenching of the fingers, a pale face, an uncomprehending quiet stare. What we have done, she almost certainly thought but wouldn't say, we have done together, and deeds and a death bind us together as one person, just as securely as lovers who live completely in the approved daylight are bound before an altar by vows and prayers.

'I'll miss you when you're gone, Barr. It was very pleasant.'

'All of it?'

'All of it. Even that.'

Even the panicky journey to London, the intrigue, the fear of detection, the growing realisation that something irrevocable had, in sordidness and secrecy, been done. 'Even that,' she said. She hadn't for a moment lacked courage. He had weighed evil against evil, decided which was the lesser and she had accepted his judgement. 'If you feel you must go, you must.'

'I know I must.'

'I can't understand.'

'You must understand.'

Does she now meet and drink with the men I left behind me, the men from the mountain, the men from the hut? Do they say: Poor Barragry, the best of us have a kink, and look at her and wonder: God above – was he mad to leave that behind him, to go and lock himself up in a holy house.

The hut on the mountain had certainly not been a holy house. They had named it the stinking pit after the picture Beauchamp had painted, but it had always been summer up there, air fresh from the heather, long evenings rowdy with song, days rich with the feeling that every meeting with her was a new, thrilling discovery.

Every spring Barragry, Beauchamp, Kennedy and Wilkes, a journalist, two bank clerks, a teacher, moved out from their flats in the city to the mountain hut. There they lived a community life, not

fearfully worried about the greater glory of God. Every morning
Barragry, who didn't have to rise early, could sensually sink deeper
into his mattress, his stinking pit, and wickedly enjoy the
discomfiture of the other three. They shaved, groaned, cursed, ate
hurried breakfasts, called names to Barragry, struggled into clothes,
raced down the mountain to catch the train to town: 'Barragry, you
blackguard, enjoy your pit.'

Then Beauchamp, with a Beardsley twist somewhere in mind and
eyes and fingers, had painted the picture: Barragry bloated in bed, his
face hideously carbuncled; the room peopled with the coloured
monsters of his supposedly foul imaginings. There were strutting
lascivious hens that were half-women, little fat green leering boys
with drooped eyelids, bulls blowing flame from pallid human
buttocks, men with heads of dragons, hunchbacked naked dancing
girls, goats humped like dromedaries. A wonderful fantasy. Fun from
Beauchamp and good fun, too, though it could never take its place
among novitiate jokes. Actually his imaginings as he rested in bed
had never been foul, for when Beauchamp, Wilkes and Kennedy had
gone, she would come quietly up the mountain to see him. When she
was there the sun always shone. That was the summer before guilt
and secrets. The old green seat outside the hut, creaking under their
weight in a sheltered corner, was a bed of asphodel, roses, anything
wonderful two lovers could think of, sun-soaked resilient clouds.

The scholarly holy father wiped his lips with his napkin. He piled
plate, cup and saucer together, carried them to the scullery, went his
way to Dublin. Frawley's eyes, defying custos oculorum, followed
him. Far across the bogland a train whistled. Barragry held the ladder
while Curran carefully descended. Sweetman swept fragments of
holly from the refectory floor.

With a great care, Nangle, MacKenna and Barragry elaborated
their new joke, not a stinking pit joke, but a good novitiate joke about
the shrine of the shaking shepherd. At recreation after dinner, they
walked across the football fields towards the lake. For the first fifteen
minutes they talked Latin, obeying the rule, suffering as Donnelly
had once said from mental diarrhoea and acute verbal constipation.

Underfoot the short grass was inert, crushed by winter, crisped by white frost. At the iron wicket gate that gave on to the path by the lake-shore the fifteen minutes of Latin ended with a heartfelt Deo Gratias. 'There I was,' Nangle said. He squeezed his way through the gate. 'There I was with my handiwork completed. In the corner under the stairs a crib what would do credit to a master craftsman.' From dry reeds by dark cold water a swan suspiciously watched them. The tails of their gowns flapped like dark batwings in the cold wind. 'The swan,' MacKenna quoted: 'has leaped into the desolate heaven.'

'That swan,' Nangle said, 'has done no such thing. Anyway, give over poetry and hear about the miracle.'

'Nangle,' said Barragry, 'has been vouchsafed a vision.'

Every year the crib was built under the stairs near the door of the chapel. The smooth stone wall was masked by thick dark paper rumpled to simulate rocks. Until midnight on Christmas Eve a heavy curtain concealed it from view.

'Behind the curtain,' Nangle said, 'it was half-dark. I might as well have been in a cave. Guinan had left me and gone to clean the Mass candles. And then it happened.'

'What happened?'

'One of the shepherds moved.'

'Moved?'

'And nodded his head. He shook for fifty seconds.'

'The shrine,' said Barragry, 'of the shaking shepherd.' It was a long long way to the stinking pit. 'Millions of the faithful come every year to see it. To touch the hem of the outdoor works clothes of the venerable Brother Nangle, only saint, so far, to be during his lifetime, raised to the altars.'

'Petit,' said MacKenna, seeing the square jaws, the owlish spectacled, the pious determination, 'would think that was blasphemy.' Fraternally charitable, they meditated on Petit, who with Begley and Foley lived among the angels, in the chapel nodded heads in fervour, went up, as less intense novices said, in smoke. 'Petit,' said Barragry, 'would think it blasphemy to go wrong in the wee rhyme about the Latin prepositions that govern the accusative case.'

'Last week,' Nangle said: 'I was working under him at outdoor works, hoeing the blue gravel. Talking compulsory Latin. Opera, sez he, frater Nangle, hic sez he, or words to that effect and pointing to a place behind Begley. My Latin isn't perfect.'

'You'd have puzzled Pliny.'

'Pliny puzzles me. We can't all be scholars. Sez I: Frater Petit, post fratrem Begley. Retro, sez he, frater, retro. Only the charity that binds us kept me from slicing his holy head with the hoe. Retro.' They halted at the door of the boathouse. Guinan, Lacy and Lagan went by, gowns flapping in the other direction, talking in Irish about Birds. 'What,' asked MacKenna, 'shook the shepherd?'

'Must I confess. Can I not stand by my vision?' Barragry opened the creaking boathouse door. Raised for the winter from the water the two long boats lay like captured, killed lake monsters. 'The shepherd was shook by a relic of old decency. The only flea-bitten Persian cat her dead and sainted ladyship left behind her. He was sleeping between the wall and the black paper. He turned in his sleep and rumped the shepherd. But for a moment I thought: Heights of sanctity, contemplative prayer, after aridness and the dark night of the soul, Brother Nangle is vouchsafed a vision. You know I'd been doing my evening meditation out of the Abbot Marmion's *Christ, the Life of the Soul*, The higher way. Petit and myself. And one day in the ad usum I read two pages of the revelations of divine love of Julian of Norwich.'

'Smoke. Pure smoke.'

'Marvellous and solemn,' Nangle quoted, 'is the place where the Lord dwelleth, and therefore he willeth that we readily answer to his gracious touching.'

'Smoke. Worse than Father Faber.'

'Worse than Mother Mary Loyola.'

'Madden calls her Mother Mary Lie Over.'

'Madden comes from Galway.'

'When Father Master was giving a retreat a nun told him she read Father Faber because he was all sunshine. Father Master said moonshine, dear Sister in the Lord, moonshine.'

Their laughter drummingly echoed in the boathouse, went out over dark water towards a wooded island. We now possess, Barragry knew, another novitiate joke, In its own way and against its own background it's not such a bad joke. In the back bar of the Dolphin it could stir up only a polite pitying smile, but in these contemplative woods it will remain effective because here the world and the ways of man are pristine. What jokes did Adam in Eden tell in the evening, when gardening was done, to set Eve laughing? Not jokes about fig-leaves. Not jokes about the boss prowling all morning around the garden. Here in these Eden woods for years to come the story of the shrine of the shaking shepherd would live, passed on from generation to generation of novices. In time even a crib statue of a shepherd might be called a Nangle shaker. The slop bowls on the refectory tables were called Crowleys after a novice of some former time who had been, because he detested cold tea, particularly given to using them. He had later taken his hand from the plough and, back in the world, was a successful politician. Possibly his surest claim to immortality would be in the name he had given to receptacles for dining-room slops. Chesterfield suits, too, were called Donohill suits because they were worn only when novices on experiment walked out to visit the sick and to preach to them tyro sermons called extraordinary tones.

This is a small anonymous world. We know one another and know that we differ from one another. Uniformity of rule and custom could never make Petit exactly like Sadleir, nor Guinan exactly like me. Yet viewed by the world beyond the trees we must look remarkably alike. A novelist writing about us would scarcely need to label the little snippets of dialogue that novelists must use to avoid boring their readers by long stretches of description, or philosophising. When I get back to the world I'll write a novel about this place: the lake and the trees, the seclusion from everything, even newspapers, the prayer, the charity, the peace, the blues, the noonday devil, the fear for perseverance, the long corridors the high rooms that like myself remember the world, the leper colony with its tattered suits of clothes, the one room where the white, ancient, naked statuary of dead days has, for the sake of decorum, been decently stored away.

When I get back to the world?

That stopped his philosophising. So easily he had accepted as a truth that here he was living a dream, that his real life was out there, that inevitably he would return to it. Should he feel blues now and pray for perseverance and consult Father Master or Father Socius about his vocation? Other novices did so. But other novices were younger, and, strictly speaking, had no previous existence to remember.

In the distance a warning bell rang for the end of recreation. They walked back through the bare woods. They talked about the walnut trees that ringed the croquet court. Hanlon, who knew about hedges and trees, also knew about croquet. They talked about the American watercress planted to keep the lake water fresh, and, like rabbits in Australia, increasing and multiplying until there was more cress almost than water. The paths were damp between the trees. The air was cold.

'In the summer Father Rector wants the lake dredged.'

'He's having a special dredger barge made by a carpenter in the town.'

'Lovely work for the villa,' Barragry said.

Through cheerless Advent woods Nangle and MacKenna looked forward to the villa. Barragry looked forward to the next meal. At this time of the evening the boys would be in the back bar.

In his camerata Brother O'Brien, who had been a doctor in the world, was solemnly darning his socks, his spectacles balanced on the tip of his nose, his face placidly happy. There are late vocations and late vocations. There are men and men, and women, and holy houses, and stinking pits, and the world. There was Edmund Spenser's house of holinesse, its dore fast lockt for it was warely watched by night and day for feare of many foes. If people in the world, said Father Willy Doyle, only knew the happiness to be found in religious life they would burst down the doors to get in. Actually the door of Spenser's house opened to a civil knock and there stood the porter, an aged syre, all hory gray, with lookes full lowly cast and gate full slow. Wont, he was, on a staff his feeble steps to stay. He was hight Humilta.

From a volume by Mother Saint Paul, Barragry prepared the three points for his evening meditation.

The right porter didn't open the door for me. I never laid eyes on poor spavined humility hirpling on his staff. Red-eyed remorse ushered me in. Or was it a green-eyed pride in my power to feel a remorse that left her untouched? Spenser's wayfarers following old humility went in stouping low, for streight and narrow was the way which he did show. Inclining his body to Mother Saint Paul, Barragry did his best to follow them.

'Father, I think that at recreation Brother MacKenna talks too much about books.'

'A scholarly complaint, dear Brother Donnelly. Brother MacKenna, unlike so many men from his stern part of the country, is devoted to the muse. We all learn from each other. We must not, though, force our interests on others.'

'Yes, Father.'

Another voice said: 'Father, I think Brother MacKenna makes too much noise in the camerata.'

'A serious thing, Brother. True silence is more than a mere matter of not speaking. Still, we're men, not mice, nor ghosts.'

'Yes, Father.'

On his knees on the conference room floor, his back to his brothers in Christ, his eyes on the pedals of the harmonium, MacKenna was inwardly contorted with laughter. The Magnov was a delight. He agreed and disagreed, he soothed and then suddenly he pinched.

Nangle was forever buzzing with ideas for brightening up the quarters of charity. Suppose you upped and said: Father, I think Brother Barragry robs too many banks, or Brother Furlong keeps too many empty whiskey bottles in his locker, or Brother Guinan shoots with a catapult at the high candles in the chapel, or the Abbot Lagan scribbles naughty limericks on the books in the ad usum, or Brother Lacy slips down to the kitchen every night when the house is asleep. Would that shake the Magnov out of his smiling charitable calm? Or would he simply say: the good religious, dear Brother, should not be inordinately attached to catapults, empty whiskey bottles, banks, limericks, or the delights of the kitchen?

'Father, I think Brother MacKenna doesn't shave as often as he should.'

'Father Socius, Brother, has a large stock of the best razor blades. No religious need be deprived of the smooth joys of Gillette. We're not Capuchins, dear brothers. Some of the saints, we know, were not too particular about hygiene. When Saint Benedict Joseph Labre went to confession his confessor had to hold his nostrils. Still, for our work in the world a habit of reasonable neatness and cleanliness is essential. For God's greater glory. We don't want to be popinjays, of course.'

'No, Father.'

Back in his chair, his faults made known, MacKenna struggled to master the swelling inward laughter, to feel penitent, to feel that the quarter of charity – every voice, too, the voice of God – did genuinely involve intense mortification. Some novices did feel that way about this soft and gentle public recitation of peccadilloes. It gave Frawley gooseflesh, made him feel that the life of the community was a sort of suffocating frog-spawn quivering with prying eyes. Frawley got mortification out of it, and therefore merit. MacKenna got only laughs.

Barragry was on the floor now, the back of his neck long, thin, hollow, stained with the stubble of brick-red hair. What could one say about Barragry: Father, when he was in mundo he rejected four of my poems?

'And you, Brother MacKenna?'

Lacy had just said that Barragry was inclined to be cynical and had thus adroitly stolen the thunder of every other novice who might be asked to tell Barragry his faults, to help him to see himself as others saw him. What faults were the faults of brick-red Barragry? He was helpful, kind, wiser than others because he had a portion of a life behind him. Feeling as tall as Tom the Steeple, MacKenna stood stammering, blushing as brick-red as Barragry's hair, unable to pick a hole, to find a fault, unable to articulate. Somebody sniggered. The Magnov said: 'Brother Barragry has been made perfect in a short

time. Consummatus in brevi. When he was in my Latin class years
ago he had as many faults as many of us. I distinctly remember the
day he smeared my chair with Seccotine. A clear case of sacrilege.'
Brothers in the Lord laughed in the Lord. Barragry's shoulders shook
with laughter. There was a hole in the sole of his right house-shoe.
Was that a fault? Barragry thought: If she saw me now, the
impeccable Barragry, sinless and beautiful star of the sea; poor old
MacKenna, gentle poet from the black Northern hills, unable to find
a brother's fault.

Stammering hopelessly, MacKenna sat down. There were more
ways than one of getting mortification from a quarter of charity. Why
couldn't he find a fault in Barragry? Did he admire him too much?
Was that a particular affection for one brother above and beyond all
others, the inordinate attachment that the Magnov and the rule-book
warned one against? It disturbed the even tenor of community life. It
unbalanced the soul on its way towards God. Still, the Lord Himself
had a favourite among his chosen twelve. And the blues were less
bitter when Barragry was around being gently and amusingly cynical;
it was less necessary, because of Barragry, to run to kneel in the
chapel, fingers interlaced until they hurt, beseeching perseverance in
words that repeated themselves in an infantile way, being distracted
now and again by the rocking of the head of Foley, rapt up as usual
into some world of holy smoke. There was great comfort in the
presence of Barragry.

Still the rule is the rule: I must make my particular examen of
conscience on inordinate affection, I must ask the Magnov about it
when I go to confession, when I kneel on his prie-dieu, eyes fixed on
his crucifix, hearing his voice of wisdom from the shadows behind
his desk.

Right hand hidden under gown, he pulled down one of his examen
beads: a black mark. It was a fault not to find a fault in Barragry, not
to be able to help a brother to know himself.

Somebody was saying he thought, Father, that Brother Guinan
walked with his toes turned up and swung his arms too much. They
didn't seem fearful faults. Filing back across the dusky main hall,
Guinan walked ahead of MacKenna. He wasn't swinging his arms.

But he hadn't turned down those unruly unconventual toes. Guinan would walk that way through life, preaching and teaching, thinking happily about the birds of God. Had Guinan an inordinate affection for birds? Going, one step at a time, up the main stairway, MacKenna was able to smile at his own scruples about Barragry.

Outside the camerata window the woods were a menacing shadow. On MacKenna's table were two letters, both opened according to rule, one from his mother and one from Frankie. On Barragry's table one letter with two words printed on it: Good wishes. Nothing more than that. The past was dead. The world was no more.

Tomorrow was Christmas Eve. The heavens would rain down dew in men's hearts for the birth of Christ.

Drop down dew, ye heavens, from on high, and let the clouds rain the Just One.

At the back of the chapel Brother Donnelly, fingering the harmonium, was at his best. Around him the twelve novices who formed the choir raised their voices in the Latin of Rorate. O'Brien, Curran and the Abbot Lagan, had worked all Christmas Eve gilding and furnishing the altar for midnight Mass. Rorate coeli desuper et nubes pluant justum.

Be not angry, O Lord, keep not any longer our iniquity in Thy mind; behold, the City of the Holy One has become deserted, Sion is deserted, Jerusalem is desolate, the abode of Thy holiness and glory where our fathers were wont to praise Thee.

But not now, not at this moment, Foley raptly thought, head nodding, lips moving in prayer, Sion is not deserted. In every religious house in this land, powerhouses of prayer, midnight Mass is being read, voices of religious who have devoted their lives to God are being raised in sacred song. God's wrath must be appeased. Everywhere today over the world, even perhaps in secret in godless Russia and in the persecuted lands, Christmas Mass is being read. Voices would sing, to welcome the Christ child, the Gloria, the Adeste, the Rorate. The holy sacrifice of the Mass girdled the earth, went on continously round the globe for the whole twenty-four hours.

Over snowy country roads or great city streets or even over burning sands the faithful walked to bright resounding churches, to the miracle hidden in the tabernacle, the manger. Ne irasceris Domine, Foley prayed, savouring the words as if they were fruit, panting like the hart for the fountains of water, disturbing Sadleir from a pleasant distracting memory, cauda serpentis, of his brother's midget racing car. Sadleir's brother in mundo owned a garage. Ne irasceris Domine, ne ultra memineris iniquitatis ....

We have sinned and have become like men unclean, and like the leaf we have all fallen down: our iniquities as the wind have carried us off: Thou hast hidden Thy face from us, and hurled us down because of our iniquity.

Serving Mass for one of the missionary fathers in a small chapel on the first floor, Brother Barragry could feel the boards quiver under his knees with the singing and music passing from the chapel towards heaven. Distracted, worried about his own cynicism, he remembered a quotation from Huysmans, the hard old Huysmans, reformed naturalist or whatever he was: 'Now that it is my fate to live in this clerical world I must begin by throwing prejudice overboard.' Somebody should teach that to Frawley, poor chap, who thought he was living in the valley of the squinting windows. Barragry shook the sanctus bell. Holy, holy, holy. Who was he to criticise Frawley? Peccavimus, et facti sumus tamquam immundus nos, and who was more unclean than Barragry and had fallen more like a withered leaf, to be swept away on the roaring wind of iniquity? Where was the leaf that had dropped from the same branch? Did the iniquitous wind still blow outside this house, beyond these woods?

Look down, O Lord, on the affliction of Thy people; send Him whom Thou hast in mind to send; send forth the Lamb, Lord and Ruler of the earth, from the rock of the desert to Mount Sion, that He Himself may remove the yoke of our captivity.

At Christmas, Curran found the blues worse than ever. The added excitement, the lights, the long table, the extra fervour that some novices clearly enjoyed only depressed him more deeply. In Muskerry, where he came from, the country boys would savegely hunt the wren on Saint Stephen's Day, or if there was snow on the hills you could track hares for miles until keen cold air quickened the appetite for Christmas dinner. His mother, beads twined around her fingers, would quietly pray for him. The walls here around him were a prison. Vide Domine Afflictionem populi tui.

Be ye comforted, be ye consoled, O my people, your salvation shall come speedily: why are you consumed with sorrow, why has grief disfigured you. I shall save you, fear not, for I am the Lord God, the Holy One of Israel, your Redeemer.

Donnelly enjoyed the keys of the harmonium rising and falling under his lively fingers. He enjoyed the swelling sound, the lights, the incense smell, the twelve voices around him blended to unison by Donnelly, the choirmaster, the bishop's nephew. Was that vainglory? Was it a matter, if his fingers were free, for a tug at the examen beads? The idea amused him, inwardly, of course; he mustn't disedify by chuckling or smiling, by betraying the levity commented upon ninety times at quarters of charity. Donnelly, the levite, was a victim of levity. Rorate was the best of all hymns and after it came Tota pulchra es, O Maria, et macula non est in te quam speciosa. Hold on now; Donnelly mustn't play the wrong hymn and by disharmony set the Order and the church tottering, fissure the Rock of Peter to its base. Consolamini, consolamini, popule meus.

Donnelly was comforted and consoled. The long table would be a stunner. He would have a visit from his people, the bishop included, within a week. This was a day for tidings of great joy so let the heavens rain down dew.

III

Frawley was the first of the first-year novices to take his hand from the plough. 'Shot down,' said Barragry, 'over Alsace': and, indeed, the blue depression that followed Frawley's departure was not unlike the atmosphere Barragry had once felt in the mess of an Army aerodrome on a wet morning when two brother pilots had collided in mid-air above the field. The pilots, still alive, had sat silently eating, sharply conscious of two empty chairs, of rain on the square outside and on the hangars, of cooling metal fragments piled on the field.

One night Frawley was more than usually boisterous at the recreation that preceded the four last things. Next morning he was gone with no goodbyes said, no statement made by the Magnov. He had been swept away into silence and only one of his brothers had seen him go, not in a flaming sky-going chariot, but in the battered monastery V-8.

Short-taken early that morning, MacKenna had slipped out to the lavatory. The holy gown, God's uniform, made a useful dressing-gown. At a side window his custody of the eyes relaxed. He hadn't the strength of Bernard of Clairvaux, who, eyes cast down, never knew how many windows there were in the chapel of his monastery. Through the side-window he saw Frawley and a lay-brother lifting travelling bags into the car. The Magnov stood with them and gently patted Frawley's shoulder and gently shook his hand. Boisterous uncontrollable unconventual Frawley would bear back with him to the world the memory of that gentleness. For the rest of his life he would be free to gallop up stairs three at a time and nobody would remind him of it at a quarter of charity. He could be as rough as he liked on the football field. He need never again feed water to stupid roach in a concrete aquarium. Beyond the blue gravel the still dark woods steamed with rain. It was a depressing sight, a death-bed scene, a peep over a prison wall at eight o'clock on the morning of an execution, a reminder that one was mortal, liable to sin, subject to death. MacKenna's stomach was sick. Squatting on the lavatory bowl, he fingered the coarse cloth of his gown hanging on the back of the door, and prayed: Sacred Heart of Jesus, grant me perseverance.

Afterwards the brothers kept a silence, perhaps charitable, perhaps terrified, but certainly uncanny, about the passing of Frawley. His death to the religious life seemed to have touched even Petit, Foley and Begley with a sense of insecurity, to have forced home on them that perseverance did not depend on human strength unaided, but on humble prayer, obedience to the rule, on the circumfluent, all-powerful grace of God. Many were called, but few were chosen. But how did even Petit know he would be chosen? The prayers for perseverance redoubled. During free time the chapel was full of novices kneeling as rigidly as carven images. Observing the frisson that followed his one remark about the shooting down of Frawley, even Barragry was no longer cynical.

But hatted and Chesterfield-coated and on the cold January road towards preaching and consoling in the Donohill poorhouse, Barragry spoke about Frawley to his companions, Donnelly and MacKenna. They followed a frosty car-track through the oak wood called the clochar. In ancient Ireland it seemed, a house of holy women, a clochar, had stood there. Ancient Ireland's holy Christian people, Brigid in Kildare, Colmcille in Derry, had loved the oak groves; ancient Ireland's pagan druids had carried out their rites under the branches of the spreading oaks. In single file they tramped along a forester's path, through somebody's farmyard, through a breach in the estate wall, down a gravelled laneway, over a stile to the Donohill Road. Traffic had thawed parallel tracks in the thin ice. They walked in those tracks. From the decent Protestant church that topped the neighbouring hill a funeral bell tolled. Lunches of brown bread and butter, wrapped in old newspapers, and two green apples each, lumped awkwardly in their pockets. Once in a while a novice would break the rule and read those newspaper fragments, establishing for a moment a forbidden contact with the world of cities, aeroplanes, wars. The poorhouse was seven miles away. From dark fir groves on the bog below the embanked highway ghosts of medieval pilgrims, mendicant friars, wandering preachers, might, MacKenna thought, watch us pass.

Barragry said: 'Frawley's in Dublin now.' He didn't mean to unsettle Donnelly or MacKenna. He was thinking of Frawley's Dublin in relation to his own Dublin.

'Poor Frawley couldn't take it,' Donnelly said. 'Community life got him down. But he could always become a secular.'

'Like Father Robert. But not so gentle. Unless age would make him gentle, rub off the corners.'

Donnelly said: 'It's a high vocation. In many ways it's a harder vocation than ours.' Donnelly was a second-year novice and even though it went counter to his genial humility deliberately to edify, he had to try, now and again, to talk like that. This, too, was his extraordinary tone day, and folded in his pocket, exhorting or shaming him to higher thought was the short sermon the grey-coated paupers would hear from his lips. Overmuch dwelling on the Frawley tragedy was bad for novitiate morale.

Conscious of futility, MacKenna asked: 'Why do people leave?'

Seriously questioning, Barragry said: 'Why do people come? Do we know why we come? Do we know what we come to? Do we know what we leave behind?'

'Brother,' said Donnelly, 'we're supposed to have minds of our own. We can only hope and pray that God will guide them the right way.'

'Two years ago,' Barragry remembered, 'I went on a retreat. I was worried about something.' Something serious, he was about to say. 'The director came into the chapel to give us our first talk. He looked at us for a while. Silently, then he said: "Why in the name of Jasus am I here."'

On a high lumpbacked railway bridge frosty wind cut water from their eyes. The wind shrieked in the taut telegraph wires. Visible for miles, north towards Dublin and south towards Cork and Waterford, the shining tracks bisected deep brown bog. When MacKenna's blues were bad enough to keep him awake at night he could hear from his restless bed passing trains whistle, a sound lonely as the cries of bog birds.

'You can guess,' Barragry said, 'we were all flabbergasted. Bad language from the altar. God's name taken in vain the way a corner-boy would take it. A few elderly respectable exercitants were jolted up in their seats as if his reverence had just gone crackers and kicked somebody in the stomach. But then he qualified the startling statement. He said: "Words taken not from the gospel but overheard from one of you dear exercitants, on your arrival last night in main hall."' Donnelly laughed. Barragry was incalculable. 'Then on he went to tell us all about the meaning of a retreat, about the desire to find God and oneself in silence.'

'A cute idea,' MacKenna said. At an old mill by a small stream they had left the road, and took to the frozen towing path. 'But I often say that to myself now,' Barragry said. 'Why in the name of Jasus am

I here?' The wind rasped in dry thorn hedges. MacKenna could find nothing to say. Somewhere deep down in his back a gnawing pain reminded him of an ailment that had troubled his schooldays, a mysterious pain coming and going – kidneys or lumbago or wearing too tightly a leather criss-cross belt that had belonged to his father? – then vanishing, no doctor consulted, nobody told, a year ago and, he had thankfully thought, forever. Now like a hot knitting needle it stabbed him three times on the road to the poorhouse, then fled, a red imp scurrying away over the bog. Was Barragry also vulnerable, subject to blues? Was Barragry, the brave, the wise, the strong, was Barragry also afraid? Donnelly could have said semper. It was the one word a senior novice could use to check undesirable conversation, the first of three words that meant always thank God, and implied: curb the tongue, the frail instrument spoken of by James the Lesser, the spinner of idle words every one of which would have to be accounted for; curb the tongue, have faith, accept God's will, subject the will and judgement, be the stick in the blind man's hand. But Donnelly said nothing. He wasn't the semper sort and Barragry wasn't an easy man to reprove.

'The sense of security,' Barragry half-soliloquised, 'is the oddest thing. Every man desires it. Some Communists, I'm told, have it. I knew a New Zealand officer who had a lot to do with Russians during the war. Said you couldn't shake them. Impervious to all argument.'

'Chesterton,' MacKenna said, 'would call that the padded-cell mentality. No man except a madman can be proof against reasonable argument.' Nor proof against pain. The hot knitting needle was stabbing again, one, two, and then away, a red flash over the cold canal. Walking up a slight slope – for the duration of the hot-needle stabs it seemed like Annapurna – he rested his hand on the great icy lever of a lock gate. Over the half-door of the lock-keeper's house he could see a red fire, a real home, plates on the dresser, no rigid bells dividing the day, no over-aired corridors, no discipline, no chain, no quarters of charity, but amiable life unfettered by rule. 'Chesterton,' Barragry said, 'could be a confounded old ass.' Barragry knew this was no way to talk before men so much younger than himself, mere boys, but he couldn't stop. He wanted to hurt. He wanted to shock. The canker was eating him: Remorse about Remorse. A black Chesterfield coat could never armour him against memory. He said: 'I once gave a lecture to a community of nuns and found there what the New Zealander said he found among the Russians. Armour-plated against fact. Smiled at all argument. Were they in a padded cell?'

'You surely didn't talk facts to nuns?'

'That was their simple faith,' Donnelly beamed. 'Little children asleep in the Lord.' He was the only one of the three unaffected by the day's bitter cold. He wished to heaven, though, Barragry would quit this talk. Why did the Magnov, with smiling malevolence and the wish to mortify him, send him out on the Donohill experiment with novitiate's two littérateurs? Could he switch the chat to Palestrina or football or the examen of conscience? The semper word bubbled in his mouth like a tiny wet balloon, but he couldn't burst it into reproving sound. But Barragry, with delicate understanding helped poor Donnelly from the dilemma's horns. He spoke to the still canal, to the sodden fields that were there on a lower level than the water, to one square Roman house grey between gaunt trees. He said: 'Semper, Brother Barragry, semper. You're a disgrace to the Catholic Church.' Donnelly and MacKenna laughed. Barragry could always be depended on. A mile ahead roofs and a thin steeple stood up out of the level land. 'Compulsory Latin at night recreation,' Barragry said, 'is a wonderful thing.'

At ease again, Donnelly was ready to argue: 'Kills me. I'll never face theology. Just imagine debating in Latin.'

'Irish is worse,' MacKenna said. Sometimes on long walks novices for thirty minutes, never more, never less, according to holy obedience, spoke compulsory Irish. MacKenna spoke Irish badly.

'The other night,' Barragry said, 'Just before recreation I was with the Magnov. Long talk on journalism, the apostolate of the Press. A fine fire on his holy hearth. I was in no hurry to go. Stretch the legs, says I, and have the talk out until the dear brothers have hirpled through their stiff fifteen minutes of Latin. Siste perumper, quaeso, frater, or, stay a minute, I beseech you, Brother.'

'When I came first,' said Donnelly, 'I thought Siste Perumper was the name of some nun who wrote spiritual books, like Mother Saint Paul, or Mother Mary Loyola.'

'I wait for Brother Beadle's whistle from the Manresa walk to tell that Latin's ended. In English I can manage with little gusto, to talk stars with Brother Curran. But to talk about the stellae is utterly beyond me. Whistle blows. Out goes Barragry, fresh as a daisy and full of eloquence, only to find that that night English came first and Latin last. Very tiresome, I call it. Very tiresome'

For a long time MacKenna was to remember in moments of stress Barragry's whimsical intonation when he said: Very tiresome. Donnelly said: 'I bet the Magnov knew what you were at.'

'I suspect, dear Brother, he did. Fabius Cunctator himself wouldn't have been shrewd enough for him. The ways of the saints are not our ways.'

'Wise as the serpent, simple as the dove.'

'With your usual aptness, Brother MacKenna.' They walked by a huge half-ruined warehouse built where the branch canal ended in a square, now bargeless, harbour at the edge of the dismal town. 'You gave a top performance, Brother Barragry, yesterday at voice production. In the clochar, you took my mind and MacKenna's off Bell's elocution. Even Petit smiled.'

'One of my great moments. A whole smile from Petit. Why did I ever leave the music-hall?' To say or think 'Why did I ever leave' was to open the mind to serpents.

MacKenna mimicked Barragry's precise accent reading aloud a Bret Harte poem from Bell's elocution: Didn't know Flynn, Flynn of Virginia, lookee hyar stranger, where hev you been? 'Myself,' Barragry said, 'I prefer steady boys and step together. The patriotic touch. Resurgent Ireland on the march.' They stepped together along a muddy side-street. From the doorways of mean whitewashed houses people watched them, saluted them casually. It was an unhandsome town and their rule allowed them to see only the worst end of it.

Every morning between breakfast and beads, said silently walking in the open air or in the ambulacrum if it was raining, novices were encouraged to practise vowel sounds and read aloud on the twisted paths between the clochar's oaktrees. Their voices must, in that way and by reading during meals in the refectory, be prepared for the pulpit. Barragry had an ironic knack of picking on inappropriate books and reading them aloud with a strained Oxford accent. Donnelly said: 'Voice production helps me to let off steam. It's grand to shout.'

'Left, right, left right,' Barragry said with B.B.C. smoothness, 'Steady boys and step together. Wasn't he a blessed Irish patriot who put that copy of *The Spirit of the Nation* into the ad usum. It looks so funny cheek by jowl with Archbishop Goodier and Saint Francis de Sales.' MacKenna whistled softly the patriotic tune as he had heard it played in processions and on sports fields by spitting, puffing, fife-and-drum bandsmen.

'Ours, I'm sure,' Barragry said, 'shouldn't whistle party tunes. Although it wouldn't seem to matter what you do in this town. Did you ever see so much mud?'

Gratefully they left the muddy street to walk, by a sluggish river, along a black crunching cindery path. The town's main street, shops, carts, cars, gossip, lay over a bridge to their right. But the town, like the newspapers around their brown bread and the externs met on the roads, was the world and was no concern of theirs. MacKenna's left heel was skinned. There was gravel in his shoe. But he walked on, not like a friar keeping pebbles in his sandals to mortify the flesh, but because he feared if he bent down to mend matters the knitting needle would stab again as he tried to straighten up. The gates of the poorhouse were ahead.

IV

'In all our sufferings,' Donnelly said, 'we should remember what our Divine Lord suffered on the cross for our sins. Not only will that memory help us the better to bear our own trials but we will gain great grace by realising how much our Lord suffered for us, and by joining our sufferings to his sufferings and the sufferings of the holy martyrs who also suffered and died. We should say,' said Donnelly desperately, suffering himself, feeling like a martyr, 'Thy holy will be done.' To pad things out a bit he added: 'On earth as it is in heaven.' An old simple-minded man in Donnelly's congregation piously bowed the knee and crossed himself.

Standing on the stone floor a little to the rear of Donnelly (retro, Brother, not post, as Petit would say) Barragry thought like a sub-editor: Too many sufferings in that one.

Donnelly knew he couldn't talk for toffee. Diligently he had cribbed from books of sermons in the ad usum, passing over Bossuet, Lacordaire and Bourdaloue as just a little bit high for a poorhouse audience, finding most help in a shapeless badly-bound book produced by an Irish provincial press to enshrine the Sunday morning sermons of some country parish priest. The style wasn't so hot, but it was good plain meat thickly sliced from the haunch of the gospel. The great thing was, of course, to speak from the heart and let God do the rest. But why wouldn't God do something to make his tongue less like a pig's bladder, his hands less like the heavier weights of a wag-by-the-wall clock, his words less like distant boomings in a tunnel. The heart was all very well, but if his grey grim audience couldn't hear what he was saying, the grace of God would find itself working overtime. Wasn't there some story about Joseph of Cupertino, the saintly illiterate lay brother, being compelled by holy obedience to preach a sermon, and skilfully dodging the column by saying an aspiration aloud or repeating several times the holy name of Jesus, or something like that? But then Joseph of Cupertino was an exceptionally rare bird, liable to levitate when serving at table in the refectory, and to soar upwards leaving hungry and aghast brothers grounded and foodless. H.G. Wells had a funny story about a man who levitated, not from sanctity, but because he drank some rare Indian potion and, whoops, he hit the ceiling. You wouldn't expect H.G. Wells to know much about sanctity. Professor Alfred O'Rahilly of Cork, who had written the life of Father Willy Doyle, the Jesuit war chaplain, had called Wells a Cockney Voltaire.

Heavenly Father, he'd have to keep his mind on his tone – or on the old parish priest's sermon, written, perhaps, some peaceful morning to the accompaniment of birdsong in the trees around the

rural presbytery. Distractions were the devil. Literally, I suppose,
they're the work of the devil. Saint Ignatius advised one to diagnose
and conquer them by, now and again, tracing a distraction back to its
beginning, cauda serpentis, the tail of the snake. But you couldn't
very well indulge in snake chasing or charming while trying to
preach to forty paupers – the up-patients in a poorhouse – dressed in
grey suits and peaked caps that had buttons on the tops, and with no
money and no hopes.

'The winter is all around us now,' Donnelly said. His right arm,
more or less under its own steam, rose and fell like a stiff lever as,
somewhat unnecessarily, he indicated the environing winter. The
bare stone-floored shed into which the men had congregated stank of
Jeyes' Fluid. They had closed the double door on an open courtyard
where the soil underfoot was as black as coal. But the door fitted
badly and rattled in the wind and draughts came through like knives.
There were no benches to sit on. Winter was around them and in their
eyes and hearts, yet they were not on the defensive with any
suspicion of patronage. They welcomed their visitors. They found
even the infantile sermons, the pious leaflets and rosary beads
distributed – while nowhere on the level of a newspaper or a pipe of
free tobacco – were still a break in the monotony of possessing
nothing, having nowhere to go: 'Shure the poor brothers, God help
us. They're innocent young men. They'll be priests some day.'

'And in the winter life can be very cheerless. Yet even in these
January days the word of God teaches us to rejoice.' Barragry
thought: Holy God. MacKenna wanted to titter.

'Today, for instance, as we all know, is the second Sunday after
the feast of the Epiphany – the feast of the three wise men who came
from the East to see the Divine Child to show us how the ends of the
earth must come together to praise the Lord.' That flourish must have
given the old parish priest the pure white glow that could only come
from creative achievement. 'And what words today does the priest
read out at the Introit of the Mass. What words, dear men, but those
words of joy from the sixty-fifth psalm of King David' – a bearded
veteran in the congregation nodded gravely – 'Let all the earth adore
Thee and sing to Thee, O God. Let it sing a psalm to Thy name, O

Most High. And I, dear men, say with the psalmist' ... Donnelly's face was puce. '... praise the Lord and rejoice even in the winter of our days.'

'Dixit,' Barragry whispered. For the look of the thing MacKenna crossed himself and said Amen. 'Praise the Lord,' Donnelly whispered, 'and pass the ammunition. Rejoice ye saints that that's over. Do you think they'll tear me limb from limb?'

An arthritic bewhiskered cripple said loudly: 'Yes, yes; not a word of a lie.' The other men laughed, and talking and movement began in an easy friendly way.

The bearded veteran who had acknowledged King David shook Donnelly's hand. 'I'm eighty years of age, sir, and not of your persuasion, but we both worship the same God.' Then he added: 'I was a bugler in the Connaught Rangers.' He had round, apple-red cheeks and bright eyes. He had stood, he said, on the guard of honour when the Prince had visited the holy house, then my lord's mansion, and the red carpet was laid on the avenue under the high sailing cedars. He read his Bible every day and it had never failed him. Here's holiness, Donnelly thought, and felt seven times a fool. At the town's end, forever a pauper, was the veteran happy with his Bible, with his recollections of bugles blown, red carpet laid for royalty.

In the coal-black courtyard Barragry talked with a small square quick-spoken man. The other paupers nicknamed him the fiddler.

'You're from Dublin, Brother.'

'I am indeed.'

'Oh, the true jackeen. I'd know the twang anywhere.'

The Barragrys had never considered that they spoke with the true twang of the Dublin jackeen. 'Yes, indeed. You never lose the Dublin accent.' But the fiddler, a staccato person, had already lost interest in accents. He was cross-eyed. Towards two different points of the compass he looked disconcertingly beyond Barragry. He said: 'Tell me, Brother, do you know Tommy Behan, the weight-lifter?'

'No, I can't say I do.'

'From Cuffe Street. Decent people Tommy's people. Many's the pint I had with them.'

What would Petit say under such circumstances: talk about Dom Anscar Vonier or recite his Latin grammar runes about ante, apud, ad, adversus, circum, circa, citra, cis?

'No, I have heard of Tommy Behan. But we never met.'

Cuffe Street wasn't exactly Barragry territory. They went in silence seven paces over coal-black earth. Could this absurd spancelled talking across the unbridgeable gulf be regarded as the Christian act of visiting the sick, consoling the poor and the afflicted? He made another effort. He said: 'Poor weather today.'

'Aye, poor, poor. Brother, you wouldn't have a bob you could spare?'

'No. I'm very sorry. You see. We don't have any money.'

'Oh, no harm done, Brother. No harm done. But the nuns are a wee bit rough here if a man slips out to have a jar. They don't understand it, you see, Brother. They don't understand the thirst.'

'I suppose not. If I had it, you'd be welcome to it. But as it is ... '
His face was as brick red as his hair.

'I know, Brother. I wouldn't doubt you. God, I'd love a pint. Excuse the language, Brother.'

Holy poverty would mean that all through life things like this would go on happening. Poor people, genuinely poor or just touchers, would cringe up to you on the streets of Dublin and ask for alms when you hadn't a tosser in your pocket. The clerical coat and collar were sticking-out targets for touchers. Fools of laymen watching your flustered humiliation, while they jingled cash in their own pockets, would neatly judge you: the priests, it was easily seen, had no time for the poor. That was all part of the practice of the third degree of humility – to be esteemed a fool for Christ's sake – but in its own way it was as grim as the third degree practised by the American, and other, police. 'If I had it, you know you could have it.'

'I know, Brother. Shure, we're all poor. Tell me ...' and the eyes again angled around Barragry '... do you know Tommy Behan, the weight lifter?'

One of the holy nuns, in stiff white bonnet and blue voluminous habit, had taken the mild MacKenna in tow. The clerical hat in his hand felt as big and heavy as a pot of potatoes boiled for pigs. He walked with her up steps and along a metallically echoing stone corridor into a whitewashed ward where eight incurable men lay in eight iron beds. Then she left him suddenly and twittered, yes Brother, no Brother, away, leaving him islanded, isolated, marooned, solitary, awkward, and – hat in hand, alone with sixteen half-interested half-hostile eyes smouldering around him. She returned as suddenly, carrying on a white enamelled blue-rimmed tray surgical things that jingled even under a muting chequered cloth.

'Can I help you, Sister?'

'Yes, Brother. Just lift up the bedclothes.'

'This way, Sister?'

'No; higher still, Brother, clear off the bed-cage. The abscess is on the thigh.'

He saw bandages and a vast limb. 'Is that right, Sister?' His stomach somersaulted. 'Yes, Brother. Now, Brother, hold the tray.' She was a perky white-and-blue bird. He held the tray and he saw dropsy, the huge swollen limb, the oozing wound; and he heard the groans or snorts from the whale of a man mountainous on the bed. You read about dropsy in the New Testament, but you didn't imagine it in the least like this. New Testament dropsy was tantamount to a running nose. Then hobbling to his relief came the bewhiskered arthritic cripple who had capped Donnelly's tone with that odd grammar of assent: 'Yes, yes, not a word of a lie.' He said: 'Sister, Brother, I'll have the tray. Yes, yes, Brother, not a word of a lie.' His name was Pat Flynn and among his fellows his nickname was, of all things, Yes Yes Flynn. When the dropsical man's wound was dressed and the blue-and-white sister had twittered away he sat between MacKenna and a bed-ridden patient and told funny, but decent, tall stories. After each story he slapped a right hip that stood out like a buttress and said 'Yes, yes, not a word of a lie,' and 'As sure as my name is Pat Flynn.' He had power in the place. The nuns liked him. He never lacked tobacco. He seemed happy. He had probably no doubts about perseverance in his vocation. Could the knitting kneedle in the back be the arthritic twinge?

Donnelly sat, helpless and wordless, by the bedside of a man who had a weak heart, and a wife in a lunatic asylum. Let the earth adore thee and sing to Thee O God. 'She was the best woman, Brother, a man was ever married on. The constant care she gave to the house and the farm. Cooking she was and cleaning night and day. And in the harvest, Brother, or at the turf she'd do the work of two men. The children went away across the water and they're doing well. I never told them I was here.' A thin quivering hand pleated the bedclothes. A long grey louse crawled slowly over hills and down hollows on the coverlet. Donnelly watched it as a glistening jungle man, crouching and gripping the shaft of his spear might watch a prowling tiger. 'She prayed night, noon and early morning, and you know, Brother, it was a queer thing, but in the end the praying drove her astray. We lived three miles from the chapel, and go right, go wrong, work or no work, she took to going there twice a day on her bicycle.'

Down some quiet country road, Donnelly saw, dust spirting under the tyres, dust grey and heavy on June roadside grass, drooping June leaves, to pray in a quiet empty chapel, perhaps in Father Robert's parish, sparrows twittering outside pointed windows, to pray like novices in the blues, hands clasped so as to hurt each other, lips moving, head nodding slowly from side to side. To pray for what: perseverance in sanity, riches, good crops, healthy cattle, laying hens, the children over the water, the husband at home? To pray and pray and pray until something snapped. 'We found her wandering in the fields one day singing hymns and laughing to herself. I wondered how God could thole it and she so good.' The louse, striking a grey patch of quilt and acquiring camouflage, had disappeared. MacKenna would be capable of quoting about the swan leaping into the desolate heavens, about the wandering hawk soaring off into blue air, about the poet rising and twitching his mantle blue and setting off tomorrow to fresh fields and pastures new. Did the louse know he was only a poorhouse louse, a pauper louse? 'When the weakness isn't bad I'm driven over in a car to see her. The nuns are very good about that. I never tell her I'm here though, Brother. You see, everything failed when she left me. The cattle and the crops and everything. It's hard to fathom it all, Brother. Sometimes she knows me and sometimes she doesn't and they say she prays there all the time with long rosary beads swinging rattling from her like a nun.' The novitiate harmonium, the uncle the bishop, were as far away as Mars.

'Shure, maybe God that she prays so much to will give us all release before the children find out, and they doing well beyond in Philadelphia.'

Barragry gave three holy pictures to a bed-ridden ancient with long white whiskers, apple-red cheeks, lively cunning eyes. 'Twenty years in the States, Brother, piling up the dollars and now I haven't a ha'penny to call my own. Is Brother Matthews, the fairheaded fellow, with you today?'

'No. Matthews isn't here today.' In the kitchen in the holy house Matthews was helping the lay brothers. He would as it happened, never again see old white-whiskers, who loved Matthews' cheery cocky Dublin chat, his capacity for inventing tall tales about the racehorses his father had in Kildare stables. Matthews' father was, in fact, a secondary school-teacher, but tall tales never worried Matthews if they went coupled with laughter.

'How's that bay two-year-old behaving for Matthews' old man?'

Barragry lied: 'Won a race Saturday last.' A horse that lived only in Matthews' words was for the charitable sake of entertaining an old incurable invalid, suddenly real and thundering home to a photo finish. The whole novitiate knew of Matthews' imaginary horses. The dollars piled up in the States had been squandered in Ireland by rapacious relatives. 'Then one day, Brother, out picking blackberries, I reached across a dry dyke to grab a bramble and in I went on my seat. Bust up my back. What's that written on the leaflet, Brother?'

'It's French. It just says Sacred Heart of Jesus.'

'Sacred Heart of Jesus. My, my! And French.' It was hard to be sure that the old man wasn't secretly laughing at the visiting brothers, but genuinely enjoying and understanding Matthews, the inventor of horses. 'And what's the picture, Brother, above the French words?' It was a circular picture of Christ on the Cross, showing only the head, bowed and thorn-crowned, the bleeding face, racked arms, stabbed side. 'It's our Lord on the cross,' Barragry said.

'Sure. Well, fancy that. My old spectacles aren't so good.' From under his pillow he fished a pair of steel-rimmed oval-shaped spectacles, one lens missing. 'Sure I see. I see something like a man expanding his chest. Like Max Schmeling, or Jack Dempsey himself. I saw Dempsey, Brother, in Madison Square. There was a fighter.' Bending low over the leaflet, white-whiskers choked with laughter.

'The old heathen,' Barragry said. 'The old rip. He mad me feel like a pious girl.'

Will that embarrassment at the fact that I'm now supposed to be good follow me forever? How crippled I felt when I realised that I couldn't talk to that old man as I would have talked to him twelve months ago, as I would have talked to him if she had been with me: bawdy stories, perhaps, to set him laughing, money to keep him in tobacco. French leaflets, my sainted backside. In his time in the States that old fellow has seen more French letters than French leaflets. Nice thoughts for a neophyte. What in the name of Jasus am I doing here? This experiment, this relic of medieval mendicancy, this memory of saints who toiled in lazar houses, is meant as a test for the young and innocent, to show them suffering, to show them what the world can do to men. That old man saw me also as one of the innocent, made me feel a dirty hypocrite and I couldn't talk naturally to him, couldn't even, like Matthews, invent an amusing lie. To his holy brothers, Barragry said: 'He was laughing at me all the time.' They walked away from the poorhouse on the black cindery path by the black sluggish river.

'He knows Matthews is a chancer.'

'He takes the cowboy stories about the Kildare stables exactly in the spirit in which Matthews tells them.'

'Pleasant fairy tales.'

'To please an old pauper. It's a queer background for fairy tales.'

'Gruesome.'

'It'd make you think,' Donnelly said.

'If anything could.'

Mizzling rain, swept this way and that by weak puffs of wind, fell on the muddy town. The back of the frost was broken. 'Poor old shaky Horgan. Seventeen years there in bed clutching a medal of the Little Flower.'

'And shivering and shuddering all the time.'

'And the old fellow in the corner with the high nightcap on his head.'

'Groaning to himself about the graveyard'

'Under the cap there's a growth as big as his head again.'

'Oh, come off it. You're worse than Matthews.'

'Honest. The cap fell off one day and I saw it. I'll never forget it.'

'Semper deo gratias. I want to be able to eat my lunch.'

'I'm so hungry, I could eat a corpse.'

'Everyone to his own taste.'

'As the woman said when she kissed the cow.'

'Ours,' Barragry intoned, 'should not discuss amorous matters.'

Laughing, because they were young and the house of incurable disease, poverty and death could now be forgotten, they turned their backs on the muddy town, their faces to the towing path raised high above low fields and dim stretches of bog, luminous in places with silver-barked birch trees or flat pools reflecting steel-grey sky. They ate their lunch, brown bread and small sour apples, in the shelter of a lock wall. Water thundered down from one great wooden gate. Rain blew in wreaths and veils over the bog.

'A drop of hot tea now ...'

'Semper, Brother, semper.'

'We must learn austerity.'

'Haven't had a nettle roll since before Christmas.'

'Nettles will be better in the spring.'

'Poor old brother ass. In the world now he used to love tea with his brown bread. Sugar in it as well. And sweet cakes.'

'Father Willy Doyle loved sweet cakes.'

'He used to cut himself with a knife too, cut our Lord's initials on his chest.'

'And he a Jesuit.'

There was a munching silence. Then Barragry said: 'Each goodly thing is hardest to begin.'

'What's that?'

'Spenser the poet writing about Zeal. Zeal was a francklin fair and free in the house of holinesse. Spenser spelled it Z-E-L-E.'

'Wonderful, dear Brother. Could we wash this brown sawdust down with canal water.'

'But after the hard beginning when you enter the house of holinesse you see a spacious court, spelled S-P-A-T-I-O-U-S.'

'Main hall. Polishing novices. Squeegees.'

'No. The Leper Colony.'

'No. The refectory.'

'And Zele there to entertain you with comely, courteous glee.'

'That would be the scholar Petit.'

His arm out, as if gesturing a blessing over tumbling canal water, Barragry quoted: 'His name was Zele, that him right well became: for in his speeches and behaveour hee did labour lively to express the same, and gladly did him guide, till to the Hall they came.'

Donnelly wiped his fingers on wet grass. MacKenna tossed the newspaper in which his lunch had been wrapped into the churning spuming lock. 'And gladly did them guide,' Donnelly said, and MacKenna said: 'Lead on, Zele.' They pulled up black coat collars against the strengthening rain. 'Pilgrims are we,' Barragry said. 'Steady boys and step together.'

THREE: MANRESA

I

The year has put his cloak away, MacKenna read at voice production in the clochar. His feet felt like silk on a soft sandy path between brown still-leafless oaks. His cloak, he read, of cold and wind and rain. Never since that first white morning last autumn had he felt such a sense of exultation, of absolute sacrosanct detachment from the world. For a whole long week of freedom from the blues, of no regrets, of spiritual fruit and consolation, of meditations that, morning and evening, seemed to mean something, the knitting needle in the back had not stabbed. In bed at night on a spring mattress no longer young, he still had a breathless fear, the nervous memory of past pain, of bending his back and relaxing with the mattress as it sagged.

Ours, said the holy rule, if suffering from any physical ailment should prudently report the matter to that person in the community into whose charge the care of such things is committed, that for God's greater glory their health be preserved to praise and serve Him.

The words had haunted him for weeks. The person in the community to whose charge the care of such things was committed was Peesoc, Pater Socius, Father Companion of the Magnov. He was a small gentle-spoken man with large soft eyes behind round black-rimmed spectacles, with a pale face and hollow jaws indicating that, from his own experience, he would understand and sympathise with any talk of ill-health. There was nothing to fear from Peesoc. But suppose the knitting needle was something serious, not lumbago, but a rotting kidney, or a diseased bone? Suppose all his prayers for perseverance were to meet with the ironic reward of a return, feet first, on a shutter, via hospital, to the world that in these days of smoke and consolation, high on the mount alone with God, he no longer wished to see.

Petit overtook him, walking swiftly, reading with deep concentration a passage from Father Gallwey's *Watches of the Passion.* Three egg-proud hens cackled in unison from their nests in an enclosure beyond the clochar. An oak-tree, brown with age, but not too brown to be ready again to greet the spring with green leaves, bent down an arm over Petit as if to salute his flapping faded gown, his intense reading aloud of a book that neither Father Gallwey nor anybody else had ever intended to be read aloud. From another path, hidden behind azaleas, Donnelly and Curran in varying dialects bellowed vowel sounds. Knitting needle or no knitting needle it was funny The year had put the knitting needle away; and no bird nor beast, MacKenna read to restrain his laughter, but joins today his song or jargon in his strain; rivulet, stream and spring today wear, as splendid livery, spangles of silver filigree; the year has put his cloak away, his cloak of cold and wind and rain.

The bell rang for the end of voice production and the beginning of indoor works. MacKenna prayed an ave for the Magnov of some past time who had hadded to the ad usum the book with that Charles d'Orleans Rondel: le temps a laissie son manteau, de vent, de froidure et de pluye.

In the stone-floored high-vaulted bootroom he and his brothers put their gowns away, grabbed brushes, dusters and squeegees, to make the holy house beautiful as spangles of silver filigree.

That day at dinner he, while his brothers ate, read, very nervously, for the first time from the rostrum in the refectory. The preliminaries were nerve-racking. He had a good voice and he knew it, but his vowel sounds were as God made them and as the Order, preferring a sort of uniformity in pronunciation, could never tolerate them. He had listened when other novices, exposed in the rostrum, while spoons rattled on plates and soup was eaten, were repeatedly corrected by Peesoc. 'No, Brother, the word is not as you pronounce it. No, Brother, this way. Please, Brother.' And a nervous brother novice, meaning no harm, would be unable to restrain a splutter of agonised laughter. Crucifixion any day of the week would be preferable, or cathodes through slit trouser legs and the sizzling hot seat.

'Frater MacKenna hasn't read yet in the refectory.'

'Frater MacKenna's name, to his sorrow, is up on the works tabella for next week's reading.'

'You lose free time and some recreation too. You have to eat at second table dinner.'

'It's a woeful job.'

'The À Kempis and menology's the worst.'

'Bloody I calls it.'

'Brother! Bloody! Semper, Brother.'

'Semper your foot.'

Every day over the soup the menology told the deeds and good habits of some holy man of the Order, missionary or teacher or lay brother, who now rested with the Lord.

'Don't worry. Brother Beadle will show you the ropes.'

'Brother Beadle Houlihan from Kilkenny. The greatest slave-driver we ever had as beadle.'

'Qui vos audit me audit. Even the voice of Brother Beadle is the voice of God.'

'Brother Houlihan's a Norman type.'

'Is the Lord then a Norman type?'

'From Brother Houlihan and reading in the refectory.'

'Libera nos domine.'

'Prayers are requested for Brother MacKenna's special intention.'

Erect in the rostrum, feeling like a man in the dock, he opened the À Kempis. His fingers trembled. One had to read so slowly that breath seemed to strain along from word to word like wire drawn from one telegraph pole to the next. Garrick or Kean or Olivier would have faltered had they looked across footlights at an audience unfolding napkins and settling down to soup. Over fifty bowed heads he looked in silent supplication to the crucifix on the wall behind the Father's table.

'You'll certainly feel a fool for Christ's sake. You'll have your third degree.'

'When the cross Father Campbell was Peesoc years ago he was such a horror for correcting readers that one afflicted monk threw the martyrology at him.'

'Et alibi aliorum plurimorum sanctorum martyrum et confessorum.' The Latin martyrology every day ended the reading thus resoundingly.

'It landed in some lay brother's soup.'

'I suppose that novice lost his vocation.'

'He wasn't mortified enough.'

'He's a secular now. In America.'

'Monks are always throwing books in America.'

'Always writing books too. About monastic silence.'

'There was one poor man who read about Saint Ambrose or somebody flaking off into the desert with his missus under his arm. His MSS., you know.'

'Don't be so obvious, dear Brother. We do know.'

'Brother Cashman pronounced antipopes the way you pronounce antipodes.'

'Great fun for all.'

'Except the reader. Pity the poor reader.'

'Pity the poor little goldfinch, sitting on top of the tree.' To console MacKenna, Thomas of Kempis from his monastery of Zwoll enabled him to read to the unfolders of napkins: Truly a lowly rustic that serveth God is better than a proud philosopher who pondereth the courses of the stars and neglecteth himself.

Very sound, he could imagine Barragry thinking, as he spooned oxtail upwards towards lean jaws and expectantly opening lips, very sound.

That day the menology told of a holy father who had preached among the Eskimos and died in the end, full of years and merits, from frostbite.

From the tail of his eye he could see, beyond the menology and the bench where a lay brother ladled soup, into the small service kitchen attached to the refectory. Rumbling like the guns of Malplaquet, a wooden lift ascended from the underworld, from Avernus, from the main kitchen, from the mine. The first meat was on the way, steaming, fragrant, rich for the bench and the knife of the lay brother. With the first meat the main reading began.

'It follows,' he read out as if he was saying oyez, oyez, hear ye, hear ye. He felt like Big Ben striking. On a huge white tray the first meat was borne by Petit and Curran, both for the time doing their service in the mine, to the altar of sacrifice. 'It follows in the life of Saint John of God by Norbert MacMahon. Chapter Four. Apostolate of the Press.' Three plates balanced on his left arm and one in his right hand, Brother Molloy was making off up the floor towards the Father's table. 'His thirst satisfied,' MacKenna read about the days when John of God was an itinerant seller of books and met on one of his tramps a ragged poor child, and befriended the child and knelt down by a wayside fountain to drink, 'he felt sufficiently refreshed to resume his loads, but first he looked to see if the child also wished to drink. To John's amazed eyes, the child was a different being to the dusty little boy he had borne on his shoulders. A radiance shone around him, and in his hand he held a half-opened pomegranate, surmounted by a cross. Addressing himself to the startled man, the child uttered these mysterious words: "John of God, Granada shall be thy cross."'

At the word pomegranate he stumbled heavily. Pomegranates he associated, anyway, with *Tanglewood Tales* or with a small green book of stories by Oscar Wilde. Why should a mysterious child by a Spanish fountain display to John of God a half-opened pomegranate surmounted by a cross? But down the long masticating refectory Peesoc, for Brother MacKenna's benefit, pronounced clearly and humiliatingly the syllables of pomegranate. Scarcely seeing the words, MacKenna read on. He had rehearsed it so often that he was startled to find he could read passages by heart while his eyes wandered down the white cloth between the parallel lines of black gowns and eyes cast down. While his brethren refreshed their bodies he thundered, that their souls also might have their food, about the wanderings of a Spaniard, not Gil Blas, not Don Quixote. Granada shall be thy cross. What would Barragry think about that chapter on the apostolate of the press?

Years from now he might be reading in the same stiff stylised way against the clatter of knives and forks made by the guests in some of the retreat houses run by the Order. Second meat was on the way. He read: 'How many of us have the courage of Saint Sebastian? Do we not rather drag ourselves along in a cowardly attempt to compromise between God and the world, between heaven and earth ... between God and the creature.'

'Repeat, Brother, please repeat.' Peesoc knew some other way of pronouncing creature. Of all the accursed words, too. But then Nangle had been hauled up for not calling a coquette a cokette. 'As if, Brother MacKenna, ours should know that a cokette has no queue.'

The memory of Nangle braced him against the prospect of the worst horror or all, the huge unwieldly Latin martyrology, telling in scarlet and black the virtues of the saint of the day. He would stumble awkwardly, his quantities were bad, through the booming words when dinner was over, the servers withdrawn, the scullery door closed, the whole long refectory deadly quiet. His brethren, fingers knitted over refolded napkins, eyes on the tablecloth, would sit back stiffly in their chairs. Every time he sat back like that in the refectory and drew a deep breath the chair's hard wood hurt his right shoulder where the discipline taken, as in the cubicles in the cameratas they cried to God out of the depths, had cut and wealed his flesh. On every right shoulder along the table was the same mark of the scourge: a small token pain self-inflicted because of all Christ had suffered for us, a sign, a memento. But deeper down in his back was the threat of the more serious pain. It wasn't stabbing now. Yet there it was like an animal lurking in a dark cave. It was as mysterious as the devil.

The unease, the illness of spirit that could not be accounted for, was the prompting of the devil. Could the unaccountable ache in the body come also from hell?

Sunlight through the great bay window made Barragry's hair like bronze. The tinkle of water as Guinan, Donnelly and Curran angled carafes over tumblers tempted MacKenna's parched tongue. Christ in the desert, Christ on the Cross, had known thirst. Accept this thirst in union with the holy thirst.

Accept everything: pain in the spine, sweat now on palms and forehead, hopeless floundering among Latin words as big and cumbersome as rocks, the humiliation of being corrected, of standing like a mute by the rostrum while the community filed out to recreation, the sense of ashy bitter unworthiness. Accept everything in return for the gift of perseverance, for the grace of advancement in the spiritual life, of living and dying in the holy habit, of the company for all eternity of Christ and His saints. Abandon everything, even the wish to write poetry, in order to gain everything.

Ahead, like a haven calm between sheltering cliffs, he saw the gliding flow of the et alibi aliorum plurimorum sanctorum martyrum et confessorum. All ye confessors and martyrs help me to make the haven without shipwreck.

When the door had closed behind the last novice he sat down to second table dinner. The lay brother Molloy sat by his side. As yet he had not spoken more than six words to Brother Molloy. He would get to know him, and the other lay brothers and lay brother novices, when he went down the mine. There was comfort about Molloy's square white capable hands. Black hairs sprouted on the backs of his fingers. Could monks who didn't have to study or trepidantly look forward to the high-perilous calling of priesthood, Cardinal Manning's book was called eternal priesthood, suffer from such ghastly blues? Brother Molloy, for God's glory, humbly cooked and carved. He didn't seem worried about perseverance. Under a haystack of coal-black hair his broad white face was always easy with smiles. He certainly wasn't pushed about poetry.

II

But MacKenna genuinely was worried about poetry. Walking to a country school, not the village school but another school five miles away beside a Norman tower and almost in the shadow of the castled rock, where novices also went to teach catechism, he mentioned his worries to Barragry. Petit walked doggedly between them, the tails of his gown tucked into his pockets. A haircut from Brother Sadleir, novitiate barber for the month, had left Petit like a fugitive from a chain gang.

'Of course poetry's a distraction,' Petit said. 'Later on in the houses of study it would be all right, with the superior's permission, to bother about poetry.'

'But couldn't the mind go to God through poetry,' MacKenna said. 'The mind's ascent to God by the ladder of created things.'

'I was wondering,' Barragry said, 'who was always pinching Saint Robert Bellarmine's treatise out of the ad usum library. It's the only book there after *The Spirit of the Nation* I get any creature comfort from.' At the crossroads they looked south towards Tipperary and Limerick. Rising and falling like a surf-rider, a great grey car came speeding towards them along the undulating land, swept past, klaxon horn blaring, a young blonde woman at the wheel. They made no comment. 'Bellarmine was after all,' Petit said, 'a saint.'

'But Gerard Manley Hopkins,' Barragry said, 'was encouraged to write the Deutschland poem by his superior.' That car in an hour would be running down the quays into Dublin, going rapidly through the late afternoon lull that preceded the teatime rush. He could have stopped it and sent a message: O motor motor flying east go to her underneath her eaves and tell her tell her on a midland road you met a redheaded man in a ragged gown who is beginning to know himself as he never did in the world. Petit said: 'At that time Gerard Manley Hopkins was a professed Jesuit father.'

'I haven't yet handed up the old notebook I used to write poems into. It's not that they're good poems. But I hate parting with them altogether.'

Petit said: 'But that's attachment to a creature. Just as much as if you were attached to ... to ...' He stopped there. The mention of creature had conjured up images that shouldn't have anything to do with the conversation of novices.

'To whiskey,' Barragry suggested. He was enjoying himself. 'Or to running dogs or to little girls.' In the silence that followed, the guillotining word semper was unspoken but still as noticeable as the Norman tower pushing up a ruined grey head above surrounding sycamores. 'From here to Limerick,' Barragry said, 'the country is lined with those towers. The Normans were great builders.'

Petit, the formidable, said: 'Not so good as the Romans.' His left shoe-lace had come unloosed, but he was too determinedly absorbed in his own talk to pay any attention to the fact. 'If I were you, Brother, I'd ask Father Master about the poetry.'

'A good idea,' Barragry said. 'Brother Petit, your lace will trip you.' His foot on the low parapet of a bridge over a small stream, Petit said sideways as he bent to fasten his lace: 'After all, if we don't interrupt the novitiate training in prayer by studying, there's no reason why we should do so by writing poetry.'

'We don't,' Barragry said. 'Only MacKenna does. It's his little devil.'

'Of course, poetry has been written for God's glory.'

'I've heard so,' said Barragry. 'I've heard so.'

Serious, intense, narrow-minded Petit, the formidable Latin scholar, the solid man of prayer, was still a child and no match for Barragry's banter. 'It doesn't matter, anyway,' MacKenna said. 'Not for the sort of poetry I write.' Rooks rose squabbling from the tower's top. The small stream meandered weed-fringed through reviving meadows. The hedgegrows had taken their first brush of young green. 'All the way from here to Limerick must be pleasant,' MacKenna said. 'I was never farther south than where we are.'

'I was on a funny job once in a village in Clare,' Barragry said.

There were things he could, and could not, tell them about that queer job in the Clare village. He could and did tell them about the local correspondent, impoverished for something to write about to the Dublin papers, who invented for the sake of three-ha'pence a line a whole reafforestation scheme on waste ground beside that village; parish enterprise, communal effort, walls built, land drained, trees planted, Ireland free and prosperous, the parish priest in the lead planting the first tree, nothing like it, bejasus, since the Tennessee Valley Authority. Then one city news editor thought the story should be more fully written about in a human feature with photographs of trees, walls and toiling men. So down came Barragry complete with cameraman, by bus to the village and charging the paper for taxis –

Petit could ponder over the morality – to find two stripling Scotch firs withering to death from dust at the corner of a main road. The parish priest laughed uproariously: 'Shure, Pether do have to write to the papers about something or he'd starve. Man, though, but he do have the imagination. It runs in that family. His grandfather storytelling could root you in your chair half a day.'

A huge square castle stood up above that village. All along the road from Limerick the Normans had built in every second field. 'This country,' the photographer said, 'is lousy with castles.'

'Cromwell slept in every one.'

'Who with, I wonder.'

He couldn't repeat that dialogue to MacKenna and Petit. The schoolhouse was in sight now. Children played in a dusty walled enclosure. He couldn't repeat the stories the photographer told over glasses of port wine in the village pub. The stout was flat. The whiskey looked dangerous. The village was as dead as a vault. Nor could he tell how as they sipped sickly sweet wine a young woman came into the pub, on her way driving to Dublin, to slake her thirst with a mineral. The village was no longer a dead dusty place. It was all of a sudden exciting and musical. The rooks at the top of the great square tower were positively singing, were cutting on the air, too, the pattern of a sable dance. Looking now at another castle and other rooks he felt weak and sick. O motor motor flying east. That was the first time he had met her. Things happened that way. Remorse could end nothing. It could only lead to remorse about remorse.

'Working on papers,' Petit said, 'and going about the country like that must have given you a great knowledge of people.'

'It did indeed. One met all sorts.'

Knowledge of all sorts about all sorts of people, about the young woman who laughed over her mineral at the cameraman's disgruntlement with port wine, Norman castles, Cromwellian fables, dusty supine villages. She offered them a lift back to Dublin. They spent two days on the journey idling by midland lakes and by-roads and small lost towns. In a dark valley he showed her the ruined walls of what had once been a medieval town and the rock where Ireland's last hermit had lived. What had he fled from? What had he sought?

With a free week-end ahead Barragry and the cameraman were in no hurry back to the office. He couldn't tell Petit of the knowledge a man gathered wandering in the world, of the morning the cameraman had whispered to him before she had come to the breakfast table: 'Lucky bastard, Barragry. I don't know how you get away with it. Not a chance she'd wander into my room.' She hadn't wandered. She had walked deliberately, her mind made up. 'I always make up my mind on the spur of the moment when I want to do anything. I never did anything like this before.' He knew she hadn't.

'A good training for the missions,' Petit said. 'Getting to know every part of the country.' O my America, my newfound land.

MacKenna's hand was on the gate of the school playground. He said: 'If I show my poems to the Magnov they'll kill him. They're not good enough even to be distractions.'

Down in deep woods trying to pray one knew how prayer itself could be pride, how remorse could be pride, and saying: 'What we did we did for the best,' and 'You must understand that I must do this,' could be blind blind selfish pride. MacKenna, perhaps, was thinking that poems were pride. Petit might, with all his dogged wearisome holiness, think now and again that his ante, apud, ad, adversus, his rebuking retro, frater, retro were aspects of the sin that had brought Lucifer down.

'Yes, do show the poems to the Magnov. Tell him I published some of them. That'll shake him.'

'I'll tell him you rejected most of them.'

The running children went before them to the school porch. They were ready for fun and the Brother and the catechism class. Young fellows in long black gowns asking you questions wasn't like school at all.

Waiting in the corridor outside the Magnov's door, MacKenna thought shall I burn my boats, shall I burn my books, will the Magnov laugh at me, me and my poems, poems God help us; if I tore up these scribbles would the pain in my back go away. They may be scribbles but I like them, not out of literary vanity, but nostalgia. They remind me of things: the white strand in the Rosses of Donegal written about by me in desperate verse as the place of parting where emigrants waited in famine days for boats to carry them to the masted vessels; my fit or fancy for Chesterton enshrined in a woeful imitative ballad about Ponder's End and Surbiton and Putney, places I've never seen; my effort to write two epics, no less, one about Barak and Deborah, the other about Saint Patrick on Slane and Tara; my patriotic poem when Barnes and McCormick were hanged in Birmingham – two men dead in Birmingham, two men hanged for Granuaile; my calf poem about the week girl I ground in Latin, with a shattering penultimate line about a thing called a Sacred Flame.

'Should I remember those things,' he asked Barragry.

'Why not, dear Brother. They're part of your soul. You'd be so much less if you denied them. At the worst they can only be funny. You're a lucky man if your worst memory only leads to a laugh.'

Nangle came out. Curran went in. The double door closed sibilantly behind him. Nangle knelt down at the prie-dieu before Our Lady's shrine. He looked comically ghoulish in the blue light. What worry had he just carried to the Magnov? Or what had the solid Curran on his mind? I wrote a poem too about Tommy who died when we were at school, and about W.B. Yeats and about Samuel Johnson, and a poem, that Barragry liked, about men leaning against a street corner. There's life there, he said. I suppose Barragry's a good judge. Myself, I preferred the one about Yeats, but I'm glad I never showed Barragry the one about the sacred flame. What would the poor girl have done had she known I was writing a poem about the golden secrets in her heart, no less, and a silent shrine wherein I hoped to find my name engraven? Told her mother probably. She failed her exam, anyway. Either my grinding was as bad as my poetry, or she just couldn't learn Latin. She should have had Petit to run her through Allen's Latin grammar. He couldn't have wasted his time flattering beauty's ignorant ear.

His palms on the cover of the notebook of poems were perspiring. Would Curran never come out? Curran probably had the Magnov involved now in some unending harangue about Abbot Marmion's *Christ the Life of the Soul,* Curran's favourite book. He was scarcely confessing to his ghostly father that he suffered from distractions caused by adolescent memories that had crystallised into atrocious juvenilia. Could I slip away now and flush the stuff by degrees down the lavatory, my poems, nostalgias, memories, temptations?

The Magnov didn't look up, didn't smile when MacKenna entered the room and walked across the floor through shadows towards the circle of green light and the chair that wasn't steady on its feet. Saints in heaven, he'll throw me out on my ear. In green silence, he's writing a letter, holding the pen almost perpendicularly. The paper's thick crisp paper that crackles as he folds it into the envelope.

'Seal that for me, please, Brother.'

'Certainly, Father.'

'Sit down, dear Brother, sit down.'

'Yes Father.'

To sit down, to seal the envelope, to steady the rocking rattling chair, to balance my book of memories on my knees: no contortionist ever worked harder.

'Thank you, Brother.'

He smiled all right but in an absent-minded way.

'Brother, you look well. Always smiling.'

Was I smiling, or was it my facial nerves writhing in panic?

'Natural frivolity, Father.'

'Not necessarily frivolity, Brother. Just good spirits and good digestion. Your health is good?'

'Yes, Father.' He wouldn't yet mention the knitting needle in the spine. The rule said to report such matters to Father Socius. He would, some day soon, if the thing didn't go away, obediently do that. 'Good digestion and good spirits, Brother, are things to be thankful for. It's bad to be too serious and not to be able to digest your food.' He addressed the envelope. The nib squeaked and scratched. He read the address carefully. The silence seemed to drag on for minutes. He said: 'Brother Curran has decided to leave us.'

'Brother Curran, Father.' The chair rocked. The room rocked. MacKenna's guts were water. Curran the solid man. It couldn't be. Who then was safe?

'Overstrain, dear Brother. Too serious. Affecting his health. No help for it. He has prayed and tried hard for a long time. Vocation is a strange gift, Brother. Some of us persevere and some do not.'

'Will he become a secular, Father?' What else could one say?

'Perhaps, Brother. Who knows? He'll fill his place wherever he goes. It was a pity to lose him. God's ways are mysterious.' He tapped the smooth desk surface with a bone paper knife. 'Don't mention this to the other novices, Brother. Some of us incline to alarm at such events. Poor Brother Curran will be gone in the morning.'

'In the morning, Father.' That tapping knife, indecently white as the belly of a fish in green sea-cavern light, held his eyes, mesmerised him. He wanted to, but couldn't look up at the priest's face to ask: Why, Father, should you think I wouldn't incline to alarm? 'Yes, Brother. And now, what did you want to see me about?'

'About poetry, Father.'

'Poetry. A pleasant topic.'

'Is it right, Father, to use poetry as a help in mental prayer. For the imagination. In the composition of place.'

'Well, of course, Brother, a lot depends on the poetry. What poetry were you thinking of?'

'Rossetti, Father, Dante Gabriel.'

'I assumed it wasn't Christina, Brother. Dante Gabriel wasn't the worst. Devout, but flowery. Any particular poem of his?'

'The sonnet about Our Lady, Father.'

'This is that blessed Mary pre-elect God's virgin.'

'Yes, Father.'

'I wouldn't be too carried away by it, Brother. You know the purpose of prayer isn't just to have nice thoughts.'

'Yes, Father.' Tap, tap, tap, the white knife in the green submarine circle. 'Father, I write poems myself.'

'So Brother Barragry tells me. Quite good too.'

'Is it a distraction to think about them now or to keep poems already written? I have a book of them.' He had, too, between sweating palms, that unfortunate book; pray God the Magnov wouldn't look at it: the Sacred Flame, the inner shrine, to find engraven there my name.

'Very little harm, Brother, unless you actually make a distraction out of them. Don't let them get in the way of your indoor or outdoor works.'

'No, Father.'

'Shelley, I'm sure, would have been useless with a squeegee waxing the floor in the main hall. Francis Thompson, I feel, would never have been a success on the blue gravel scuffling with a hoe.' They shared a laugh. 'For the novitiate, Brother, I'd confine myself, if I were you, to comic verse. From troubles of the world I turn to ducks. Things like that. Or the ballad of the shrine of the shaking shepherd.' The knife had ceased tapping. The Magnov was smiling normally. Brother Curran's passing had been accepted as God's will. 'Brother Nangle favours me with some of his fantasies.' For MacKenna then the room, green light, surrounding shadows, writing desk, prie-dieu, crucifix, the bed behind the screen was all happiness. The holy house was home and all who lived in it one family, and Nangle was the comical child that could always draw laughter from its parents. 'Many good religious have written poems. Father Hopkins, the Jesuit, for instance.'

'Yes, Father.'

'Gerald Griffin the novelist did, I know, tear up manuscripts when he became a Christian Brother. But then he was a morbid man and inclined to rush to extremes. Avoid extremes Brother. Only the saints can afford them. Be gentle and prudent and obey the rule. It's there to guide us to God.'

'Yes, Father.'

'Good night, Brother.'

Lord God, get me up quick from this rocking unstable chair, get me out through the double door with this asinine notebook before I explode with the realisation of my own folly. Per Christum Dominum nostrum.

'Oh by the way, Brother.' MacKenna's hand was on the inner door.

'Yes, Father.'

'I'm sending you to the kitchen tomorrow, to Brother Molloy. I think you call it going down the mine.'

'Yes, Father.'

'You'll enjoy it, I think. Most novices do; lovely greasy pots and pans.'

'Yes, Father.'

'Brother Barragry will descend with you, and Brother Bob Barnes. You'll have a high time talking literature. More suitable, perhaps, for a novelist than a poet.'

'Yes, Father.' Their laughter met in the shadows in the middle of the room. 'Good night, Brother, and God bless you; and pray for me.'

'Yes, Father. Thank you, Father.'

Barnes was next in the queue outside the door. He was gently reared. He wouldn't like the pots and pans.

Alone in candle-light in a corner of the chapel Curran was praying, elbows on bench, shoulders hunched. MacKenna looked at him for the last time. He wanted to touch him, to say something, to break the silence with words of sympathy.

I was the last novice, too, to look on Frawley.

III

In that great vault of a kitchen my lord's cooks had once prepared a meal for a king. The wide chimney place was still there where little half-cooked boys had once turned spits over scorching golden pyramids of burning peat. And tall men go by, MacKenna remembered, and their clothes the colour of burning sods. Poetry was no distraction here. It steadied the mind in the dinnertime hubbub. Rattling trolley carrying food to the lift, the measured tread on the floor above as the community entered the refectory, the rush and bustle of Brother Molloy, and his sing-song chant: speed and efficiency. Brother Barnes' lips moved in despairing aspirations as he pared parsnips or peeled potatoes. He had been reared in a quiet home in Waterford by a maiden aunt whose favourite reading was illustrated books about the King and Queen of England. The spit boys were gone forever. A King had passed that way once, walked on the floor above. The great fireplace, cold now and antiseptically clean, housed incongruously a cream-coloured electric cooker large as a Russian tank.

At one of the four kitchen sinks MacKenna, now gowned in a white apron, washed plates, and Barnes, aspirating continuously, sighing his soul upwards to God, dried them. In the remotest and dankest of the chain of sculleries Barragry and a lay brother novice emptied refuse from pots and pans into a bin for the monastery pigs. Later they would carry the bin down the long stone corridor, past the baths and the bootroom, across the cobbled courtyard to the farmyard. On the surface of the bin discarded fruit floated in crimson juice. 'Marvellous pigs,' the lay brother novice said, 'to be getting all that. Many's the Christian hasn't the like.'

'And why not, Brother O'Rhattigan. Good religious pigs. Many's a Christian isn't much of a Christian, but pigs is pigs.' Every stoic, said poor old Emerson, was a stoic, but in Christendom where is the Christian.

In the mine the rule of silence didn't bind one so strictly. Barragry's apron was black and greasy. Sunlight slanted through the high barred scullery window. Crimson to the elbows with the blood of the broken fruit, he thought of the gentle Squyre, hight Reverence, of mild demeanure and rare courtesee, who, in company with humility, had a receptionist's job in Spenser's House of Holinesse. Humility should be at home here by the pigs' bin. But where did Reverence fit in? In Spenser's poem Reverence led the world-weary wanderers, first before all the fair lady Una, to meet Dame Caelia, mistress of the house, busy at her beades. Dame Caelia, heavenly woman, embraced Una, called her a most virtuous virgin who had wandered through the world now long a day and had come at last to haven.

'Think it over, Brother, during the Long Retreat,' the Magnov had said to him. 'Your trouble, as much of it as you've told me, seems serious. Don't rake in dead embers, though. Thin bony men like you are often overscrupulous. You made a general confession before you came here?'

'I did.'

'Accounts were settled then in the eyes of God. You believe that.'

'I do.'

'There's often a secret vanity in returning to worry about sins forgiven. A danger too.'

Remorse about remorse. 'But if what we've done hurts somebody, marks somebody? Can we excuse ourselves of all obligation because we've had absolution?'

'Restitution. You're a grown man. You must think that out for yourself. Give it the benefit of the Long Retreat. The Ignatian exercises catch everything in their net. We'll have a very good Jesuit here.'

'Should I make another general confession?'

'Only since your last one. Ad quietam conscientiam. The sacrament is meant to soothe us with God's forgiveness, not to torment us. You feel now that it might be right for you to go back to the world.'

'I'm not certain.'

'To your obligation. You feel you're not free.'

'Yes.'

'Every man born is tied to the earth by some rope. Charity cuts the moorings. The main thing is eternity and the skies, not the hangar, not the brief life of the flesh. My metaphors are awful. You think you're unworthy?'

'Yes.'

'A sound feeling if sincere. Remember the devil's favourite sin.'

'The pride that apes humility.'

'Which of us is worthy? To call God down from the skies. To drink his blood. To put his body on the tongues of the people. You're probably now such a villain as you think. Many men have pasts. Many saints have had pasts.'

A talk with Father MacGrath could have its resemblances to a sharp cold shower bath. 'When you came here you thought then that was the right thing to do.'

'That's true.' That was remorse.

'Now you're not certain.' This is remorse about remorse.

'Pray Brother. Ask for guidance. Men can be swept this way and that by every wind. Go down into the cave of Manresa with Saint Ignatius. He's a good companion for hardheaded men. We're changeable creatures, Barragry.'

O'Rhattigan and Barragry carried the laden, overflowing, red-running bin to the piggery. Softly Barragry quoted: So few there bee, that chose the narrow path, or seeke the right: all keepe the broad high way, and take delight with many rather for to go astray, and be partakers of their evil plight, than with a few to walke the rightest way.

Tilting the contents of the bin into a huge odorous iron tub, fleshpot for the pigs, he said sternly to O'Rhattigan: 'O foolish men, why hast ye to your own decay.'

'Decay's right, Brother Barragry. Pigs are wonderful eaters. The mixtures they like!' Pale blue prominent eyes goggled with wonder. Blond hair clipped close stood up in little bristles and sweat beaded a freckled forehead. Brother O'Rhattigan looked at home in the farmyard. Swinging the lightened bin between them, they walked back to the scullery. The clochar's iron oaks were bubbling with young green.

'I love trees,' O'Rhattigan said, 'and timber. Do you know the best wood for coffins is mock-elm?'

'Good Lord. I never did.'

'Sure as you're there holding the other handle of the bin. I was apprenticed to an undertaker. It's a queer job.'

'Somebody has to do it.'

'Somebody has, I suppose. You worked with books and wrote for the papers. That'll be useful to you in your studies.'

Feet on the floor above, then on the stone stairs, indicated that the novices were bound for the bootroom and recreation. 'We'll be late for second table dinner.'

'Divil the fear, Brother Barragry. I was never late for a meal in my life.' Under a high spouting scullery tap O'Rhattigan sluiced gobbets of pigs' food from round strong arms. 'Working with books and studying is the best way to work.'

'I'm not so certain.' Could a canto of an Elizabethan poem send a man to the cloister or did it need a leg broken on Pamplona's walls, a blinding light on the road to Tarsus?

'Sill, it was working with an undertaker sent me here.'

'How come?'

'We opened a grave, you see. There was trouble in it. Some old fellow slipped rat poison in his brother's gruel. So, long after, we opened the grave and took up the coffin. The wood was as good as new.'

'Mock elm?'

'The best ever planed. But when we took off the lid. Reach me the towel, Brother. The pigs bin itself wouldn't be in it for a mixture maxture. Things floating and all.'

'There's the dinner bell.'

'We've pucks of time. I thought to myself then, Barney boy, what's the use of working, anyway? Death ends it all. Save your soul's the only thing.'

'So you came here.' Bright light on the road to Tarsus. Broken leg on Pamplona's walls. Father Rodriguez writing on humility invites me to consider my body as a load of dung, but how could that gay thought induce humility, for it I am dung so's the Pope, so's Rita Hayworth, so was Helen of Troy and the man who broke the bank at Monte Carlo. Complete balls, as a man could say if he was in the back bar of the Dolphin.

'Sometimes I regret it now, Brother. There's great fun in the world too if it wasn't for death putting an end to it all. Take a look at that, Brother.' While O'Rhattigan buttoned on his gown Barragry looked. It was a snapshot. On seaside sand, rocks behind and a hill with white houses, a laughing girl in a bathing suit tailor-squatted. She was well-made. 'That was at Kilkee on a holiday,' O'Rhattigan sighed. 'She was the girl friend. She said she'd enter a convent. But yerra, I don't know. It's hard to say.'

'It's hard to say.'

They walked along the stone corridor to the narrow stairs that led up to the refectory scullery. Should I laugh now at myself or at the lunacy of all of us thinking we've conquered the world, thinking we're elect and chosen? Or should I weep soft sentimental tears for O'Rhattigan's simplicity? Or should I rip this gown off my back and race out of the house down the long cedar avenue where a lecherous king – mentioned in *Ulysses* for his fornicatory capacity – once rode in his coach, wheels soft on red carpet; down through soft deep grass to the old broken shell of a coaching inn on the Dublin Road? A green bus or a lift, perhaps, in a passing car and Barragry, Barragry flying east forgetting his futile effort to edge in among the saints.

MacKenna and Barnes came, struggling into gowns, from the kitchen. Barnes looked flustered. He had smashed three plates. On his knees, arms extended, he would tomorrow in the refectory confess his fault to his brothers. He would appear and sound extremely funny. He would remember a quiet Suirside house, Victorian furniture, pictures of royalty, talk of country occasions, where smashed crockery was something deep down in the basement in the maid's private world to be compensated for by weekly deductions from the maid's pay.

IV

O'Rhattigan's simplicities were full of surprises. He represented an extremity in the novitiate: a rugged rural character with a good deal of impulsive superstitious sanctity in him. The things he said could corrugate with laughter the even movement of what Barragry, when no lay brother was listening, called the life below stairs. How, dear Brother MacKenna, do you find life in the servants' hall?

Under the tall beech trees behind the Lourdes grotto O'Rhattigan said to Barnes: 'Brother, I was in Waterford once at a football match?'

'Rugger.'

'What's that, Brother?'

'Rugby football.'

'Oh, save us, not at all. That's only played by Protestants and bank clerks. It was Gaelic football, to be sure. Jump high and kick hard.'

'The Croke Park stuff,' Barragry annotated. 'Brother Barnes didn't go in for that.

'It was a grand game too. Great catching. That's the secret of victory. Midfield men who have hands and who can rise.'

Barnes was puzzled. 'They'd look odd without hands.' O'Rhattigan to demonstrate tossed a pine cone in the air, and agilely, and with a most unmonastic whoop, leaped after it, then, face red, eyes brightly protruding, beamed on Barnes: 'You see what I mean, Brother.'

'Clearly, Brother, clearly.'

'There was a man in that game could leap like a white trout. I remember him well. It rained in the evening, too.' From the Lourdes Grotto they walked down the fringe of the deep grapery wood to the walled garden. Jays screamed from the branches. A squirrel shone for a second like the twist of a golden coin.

'I met a man in an eating-house after the match. In an eating-house on the quays. He was a bread-server to trade. Made good money, too, on commission, at a good clean job. And who did he turn out to be but the man who played the great game.'

'The white trout,' MacKenna said.

'Man, he was cheered that day to the echo. His name was McMonagle. You might know him, Brother Barnes, and you from the same city.'

Barnes, his fat, olive bespectacled face flushed with the embarrassment of knowing how much Barragry was relishing his inability to cope with O'Rhattigan's ingenuousness, said No, no, my goodness no, he didn't think he knew McMonagle the white trout, the prosperous bread-server. 'You may have seen him once or twice,' Barragry said, 'serving bread as was his wont.'

MacKenna said: 'The Barnes never ate less than cake.' Through a low narrow gateway they entered the garden. Within the high walls where the sunshine was trapped and concentrated it was as warm as summer. They followed the slow-spoken gardener through long hothouses, took from him fruit and flowers reluctantly given. 'I do hate touching the flowers, brothers. They do look so lovely hanging. But I suppose that's the way.'

'No omelettes,' Barnes chirruped, 'without breaking eggs.'

The gardener looked at him as if he was a greenfly. He said: 'That's the way, Brother. That's the way.' In the days of the dead lord he had been a young gardener snipping flowers or plucking fruit for the bosoms or lips and white teeth and tender palates of noble beauties. The holy fathers had kept him on although they knew he didn't go to Mass, had coloured memories of a past in which he had reputedly been a gay young man, although they felt that his soul burned when he saw a black habit. You couldn't get a better gardener. Working for God, however, unwillingly or indirectly, might melt his plum-stone of a heart. 'I know Barnes can't help it,' MacKenna said to Barragry, 'but he always does set me thinking about the brothers below stairs and the scholars, ourselves, in the upper clearer air.'

'The head does the work of the head, the hands the work of the hands.'

'I know it's not a matter of class distinction. Things like that are left behind in the world. But look at Barney O'Rhattigan with his bathing beauties and mock elm coffins. And then look at Brother Barnes with his talk of dear old ladies and the Queen and goose for dinner at Michaelmas.'

'When he asked Nangle if his people had goose for Michaelmas, Nangle said his people hadn't kept geese.'

'But I mean what could bridge the gulf between Barney and Barnes?'

'Bridging gulfs are you, like the best newspaper in the land? The gulf, so to speak, has been bridged, hasn't it? They're here together in God's garden.'

'Are you being unctuous or cynical?'

'Charity makes them brothers.'

'Charity, then, can do all things.'

'So we're told.'

'I'm sure McMonagle was the bread-man who supplied the Barnes household.'

'O'Rhattigan and Barnes met so, in the world. At one remove. The ways of God are wonderful.'

'And consider the other lay brothers.' Apart from their brethren, who had followed the gardener to the far end of the long hothouse, MacKenna and Barragry considered the men who did the work of the hands.

There was Brother Fergus, who in the world had been a cook, and now, for God's glory and the community's health, was a better cook than ever.

There was Brother Madigan, who had been a boxer and now, since boxing ability was no longer required, tended the community's livestock.

There was Brother Hazlitt, flat-hatted, bent double with age, supporting himself, Donnelly said, by simultaneously leaning on a stick and tugging his coat-tail. Grey locks hung down to hide his jaw bones. He was in charge of the farm, and his old eyes were sharp enough, they said, to see the grass growing. Nobody knew what he had been in the world. It was so long ago there was a chance that he had forgotten there had been a world. Over sixty or seventy years he had known all the great men of the Order. Barring some extraordinary accident, he was pretty sure of perseverance.

There was Brother Jackson, bald, middle-aged, a late vocation, and still in his novitiate, who had been a photographer with a special burning artistic interest in child photography. He had know Barragry, the journalist. Looking at his brown shrewd eyes, that had so often through lenses marvelled at the beauty of God's children, Barragry frequently wondered how much Jackson had known about Barragry, the journalist.

There was Brother Molloy, of course, with dark hair, broad white face and kind awkward ways; and Brother Shaw, small, neat, with polished red cheeks, and a destiny in the foreign missions, a past in which he had helped the world to keep french-polished its more valuable pieces of wood; and Harry, the postulant who wanted to pray perpetually, who had doubts as to whether or not he shouldn't have been a Cistercian. Harry would hardly last. 'How do we know he won't last?' Barragry said. 'How do we know who'll last?'

'Oh, Foley, Petit, Begley, for certain.'

'You'd have said Curran for certain. It's a queer business. Begley has a defect in his speech that may come against him in the pulpit. Apparently we have to be without blemish of body like ancient Irish chieftains.'

'Purity in our hearts. Truth on our lips. Strength in our arms.'

It was an uneasy unreal conversation. It went over boundaries to crash in on what the novitiate called forbidden topics, but there was nobody there to check it with a *semper deo gratias*. The hothouse air was silent with unseen threat. MacKenna thought fearfully: Why did Barragry mention blemish of body? A burning needle in the back is a deadlier blemish than a halt in the speech.

Barragry thought wryly: Purity in our hearts. What is purity? Am I pure now? Was I impure then? Was she impure?

MacKenna said: 'I feel a fool when I do the spiritual reading for the brothers, out loud, in their community room, about Portuguese martyrs in Goa, of all things.'

'Brother Molloy loves it and Barney the mock-elm man. The tortures give them a laugh.'

'They seem to know so much more about it than I do.'

'The rule's the rule. We're supposed to do their spiritual reading out loud. I suppose once upon a time lay brothers couldn't read. Tradition's a great thing.'

'Harry all the time looks vacantly up at the barred window, at the glimpse of lawn, and the blue gravel. Thinking of Cisercians chanting in Mellross.'

'That community room was once the butler's room.' Through dripping steaming air they walked towards the reluctant gardener and the gatherers of fruit and flowers.

'Still, oddly enough I feel more at ease down the mine than I did upstairs.'

'Break in the monotony. So do I. Perhaps we should have been lay brothers.'

'We have no time to think.'

'And more to occupy the body.'

The body. The body. The body. Why does some demon drive Barragry's tongue to talk so much about the body? With me the sting in the flesh does not mean what it is normally taken to mean. It's a sharp stab in the back and an accompanying fear of the ineluctability of the moment when I'll face Peesoc and say: Father, I'm afraid there's something wrong with my back. What exactly, Brother? Oh, nothing serious. I'm sure, Father. But I just thought I'd mention it. Perhaps you'd better see a doctor, Brother.

Once those words had been spoken anything might happen. So work, work, work, wash dishes, scrub floors, read to the brothers, forget about pain, and kneel at night at litanies, mind and body numb with weariness. From the morning watch even until night let MacKenna hope in the power of the Lord to deal with pains and premonitions. So sharply swing the discipline and hope that a mortificatory cut on the right shoulder may draw out the pain lurking and gnawing within. When he lay down at night in his cubicle in the camerata, among other novices with whom he didn't, according to rule, speak while he was down the mine, he was oppressed with a deeper sense of loneliness. I am out of humanity's reach. The train whistle beyond the deep woods had never sounded so desolate. I must finish my journey alone. He tried to ease his fears by thinking of the walled garden, the odorous hothouses, Barragry's crisp voice, about a joke Nangle had made about the Abbot Smaragdus, so called Nangle said, because he was always at the jampot at night in the refectory scullery. His body shaking with silent laughter – no proper way to prepare for morning meditation – awoke the crouching pain, and taut with agony he listened to the smooth breathing of his sleeping brothers. Deliver us, oh Lord, from pain, from all evil, from all sin, from sudden and unprovided death, from the snares of the devil, from anger, hatred and all ill-will. From the spirit of fornication, from the scourge of earthquake, from plague, famine and war, from lightning and tempest, deliver us, O Lord. Through Thy baptism and holy fasting, through Thy Cross and Passion, through the coming of the Holy Ghost, the Paraclete, deliver us, O Lord. Libera nos domine. Libera nos domine. Set free from deep pines a train whistled eastwards. He imagined the drumming sound of wheels, welcomed their rhythm into his throbbing pain until that rhythm drugged him into tired frightened tear-stained sleep.

V

For two years of her life she had awakened every morning to excitement and expectation. Even when she had gone to London on what Barr had called their secret mission she hadn't been weary or depressed. She had been afraid, but not weary, nor depressed. It was different when you were doing what you did with somebody, for somebody. The handsome young steward who carried her bag below had edged, with ingratiatory ideas, into her cabin. Almost pressed up against him in the confined space, she had laughed at him pleasantly. Poor fellow, poor fellow, poor would-be glamour boy tormented with visions of Camb and liner cabins, if you only knew the secret Barr and myself have between us. But now for an autumn and a bleak winter and the beginning of another spring the mornings had been different. She had changed the furniture in the room as part of her effort to wipe out the past. She had wiped it out too from everything and everywhere except her own soul, except that marked spot on the wall a foot to the left of the gas-fire. Popping a champagne bottle, the fine celebrations there had been when the secret mission was over and the sky clear again, he had cut his finger and wiped it there on the wallpaper. She scolded him for carelessness, kissed and bandaged the finger, drank champagne with him, gave and took love in that room.

I should have known that, bright morning preluding a day of tempest, the clear sky was threatened by deeper clouds, loneliness, abandonment.

Put out the milk bottle. Make sure the key's in my handbag before I slam the door. The landlady keeps a duplicate key. Perhaps she's afraid I might have a man hiding under my bed all day long.

On the floor she tapped on Julie's door, heard the sweet, precise little voice inviting her to enter, took the invitation, saw Julie arising tousled, cheeks a little flushed, from the nest-like security of her virgin bed. Two books of advice for young married couples lay demurely side by side on the bedside table. Julie, the joys of holy matrimony a brief bright week ahead, was borrowing from the travelled eloquent wisdom of Monsignor Fulton Sheen, no bloodstains on the wall, no secret missions to London, everything open and above-board, everything moving visibly, as happily as birdsong, in the daylight.'

'You're early, darling.'

'You're late.'

'Heavens.' A peep at the wrist-watch, the tiniest wrist-watch imaginable, a present from the gauche youth whose privilege it would be to ruffle the nest. 'I am late. Jim'll be waiting. And we had a date at that furniture place.' On the landing the telephone rang. 'Do answer it, darling. It's bound to be Jim.'

'You answer it. He'll want to talk to you, anyway. I'll make some tea.'

Through the doorway as she made tea she could see little Julie, all innocent in slightly disarrayed pyjamas, on tiptoe to the telephone, all tousled curls and eagerness and excitement, and don't move, Jim darling, don't stir, drink coffee, read the papers. I'm coming. I'm coming. I'm coming. If Jim could only see to the other end of the telephone line. What bliss awaited him striding out towards manhood hand in hand through the mystic wood with a famous American preacher.

Jim would wait patiently enough in a coffee-shop – he didn't drink – while Julie dressed meticulously, walked out in all her lovely innocence to disturb uselessly the thoughts of young men in 'buses. Together she and Julie would go down town as they had done so many mornings since they had first taken flats in the same building. Julie had known about Barr as much as Julie could be allowed to know or could comprehend about such things. Suspecting something, and not knowing what exactly it was, she had disapproved, but had in the end approved when she heard of Barr's last fatal decision: 'Darling, I know it's hard for you to understand because you're not a Catholic. But if he feels he must go, then he must. It'll be better for everybody in the long run.'

Oh, Barr, Oh, Barr; and poor little Julie, who on the strength of an engagement ring and two books of good advice sees herself as a settled Catholic matron, the world well conquered, children growing up in the love and fear of God.

Jim was waiting, patiently. Beauchamp, the painter of the stinking pit, sat with him, his sallow face rigid with impatience. Beauchamp did drink ('just one pint now before I go home to my aged mother' – and then he'd remain drinking pints for hours) and didn't like coffee-shops, and regularly with effort he barely restrained himself from admitting that the youth and fey innocence of Julie's tinkling slender-wristed approach to Jim troubled his nerves. With Barragry, Beauchamp had shared once a certain amount of cynicism. Because of that he had found it harder than most people to sympathise with what Barragry had done.

'I understand. You don't,' Beauchamp had said to her. 'I am or I was a Catholic. I know that in this country most of us live on the verge of the cloister. The cloister and the pub. But Barr should not have gone off like that. It was panic. It was weak-minded.'

'He felt he had to go.'

'I've often felt I should go to Canada or New Zealand. But I've never gone. There are things that hold me here. Friends: men and women. My aged mother.' Long languid hands gestured with expressive precision. The smooth slow voice sharpened and quickened almost to indignation: 'I have my boat too on the bay. If I were to go, how could my boat live without me?'

They walked with Jim and Julie through the long shop, air heavy with coffee smell, to the bright spring streets. They watched Jim and Julie walk away from them, hand in hand. 'Cantering off to purchase pos and plates and things. All the properties of happiness.'

'Beauchamp, you're disgracefully unkind. Even Barr ...' She stopped there. Barr was no longer to be compared with the living.

'My dear child, Barr would have said exactly that, would probably still say it from the tomb where they have laid him.'

Extracting two coppers, as delicately as if they were golden guineas, from a waistcoat pocket, he purchased a newspaper, meticulously folded it, said: 'For my mother. She takes an avid interest in world affairs. Will you indulge in a drink, my dear? Just one. My good mother will have my lunch piping hot.' They turned a corner out of the crowd and the sunshine. He said: 'I was about to marry once. But somebody advised me against it.' He was taller than

Barragry. He was horse-faced. He had black sleeked hair. 'She wanted to live in England. I wanted to live here. So we parted.'

'You can't have loved her very much.'

'Inexpressibly, I tell you. But I loved Ireland more. Savouring the nuptial rites with her, I'd always have thought, like Sarsfield on the field of Landen, Oh, that this were for Ireland. It would have come between us. Also there was always my boat.' They went by a narrow street parallel to the quays to the hotel bar that had been Barragry's favourite drinking place. The furniture was old-fashioned, not antique, just rickety; tables and chairs didn't match; on dark walls quaint framed verses praised the joys of a good pipe. She knew his fantasy was feigned, was meant to raise her morale. Then over the first drink he was serious: 'I wouldn't give up, my dear. I'd go and see him. He was possessed. Candidly, I believe, he was possessed.'

'I couldn't. I wouldn't have the courage. He'd hate me.'

'I'll go with you. I'll drive you there.'

'You'd have to write to the people who run the place. You'd have to make arrangements.'

'Oh take them by surprise. Shock tactics. They're only priests. They're good Christians. They won't throw you out.'

'They might. He might refuse to see us.' The last time he was here, she remembered, he sat slumped on that low sagging couch, a glass of yellow ale untasted on the table before him; and afterwards he had told her what he intended to do. 'He wouldn't refuse to see us,' Beauchamp said. 'I know that countryside well. I'll drive you there.'

It was curious, typically curious of the curious Beauchamp that he should try to force her into this because she knew, and he knew she knew, how gladly he would have stepped into the shoes – if shoes was what she meant – of the absent Barragry.

But then how curious Beauchamp was with his boat on the bay, his aged mother, his interest in meteorology and aeronautics, his quaint satirical artistic talent, his gargantuan dock-labourer's pint-drinking powers that went so oddly with his immaculate appearance, affected manners, languid voice. Behind all his oddities there was somewhere a deep concern for his friends, a zeal to see justice done even though his own cherished secret desires might thereby suffer. She sipped gin and lime and said: 'It would be interesting to go there.' Never, she knew, would she have the courage to enter the house where Barragry had shut himself away from her and from the world; or was it just from her? If he wanted her he would come for her. Too clearly he had shown how he wanted to forget her and all that had ever been between them: secret missions, love, spilled champagne, blood on the wallpaper, pride in shamelessness, shame, reproaches, kisses and bandages, remorse. Still, it could be no harm to go and look at the place, and from a distance to glance across fields or peer through woods and imagine, within hearing of the bells, the way of life he had preferred to her, the lineaments of the other woman.

'I'll go,' she said. 'Thanks, Beauchamp,' she said, 'for the offer.'

'Ah, a pleasure, my sweet.' He shot back stiff white cuffs. He raised a black pint aloft and looked at it fondly as if it were the choicest, rarest, most delicate wine. 'To you and your wishes.'

She thought: To Barragry and his wishes, odd as they are. For what he wishes, even if it means a world without me, must be what I wish, must, must, must be what I wish.

Beauchamp sighed with pleasure in his black pint. His ivory white cuffs resettled well below the prominent knobs of his wrists. 'One last quick one for what we call the road. My poor dear mother is still keeping the frugal luncheon hot, my dear, piping hot.'

VI

They ran from the world to the hot red desert. They lived on bread, coarse herbs, water, and found space and peace for prayer. They followed God's footsteps over the sands and, also in his footsteps, attempted the high hills of cloud and vision.

Patrick Of Ireland on a wet Ulster mountain minded sheep for a pagan and talked to God in the mist and rain or in green corners under leaning rocks where he and the sheep sheltered from Irish weather. Kevin of Glendalough found a hole in a rock above a black gloomy Wicklow lake, hid there to pray and, they say, tumbled young

Kathleeen, who followed him, down the cliff into the water. What Saint Nicephorous did I can't remember, but Benedict, I know, abandoned licentious Rome for the desert mountains of Sublacum, forty miles away, and there in a barren hideous chain of rocks, with a river and a lake in the valley, found a cavern now called the Holy Grotto, then almost but not quite inaccessible to man. His nurse Cyrilla, who loved him dearly, followed him thirty miles to Afinum.

And Marcarius the younger, a confectioner of Alexandria, in the flower of his age forsook his confections and went, via the Thebais, up the Nile to sixty years of prayer and penance.

And Simeon Stylites, who should be if he isn't the patron saint of steeplejacks, erected a pillar six cubits high and lived on it for four years; ascended then to a second pillar, twenty-two cubits high, for another ten years; and going higher still and higher spent his last twenty years at a height of forty cubits. But, balancing there on his perch, we must remember that his heart was all humility and he would have descended like a peppered widgeon if he had been compelled to by holy obedience. At the foot of the pillar, Theodosius the Cenobiarch heard and heeded the lofty airborne wisdom of Simeon and found also his cave, his diet of coarse pulse and wild herbs.

'Never ate pulse in my life,' Nangle said to Barragry. They walked the lake walk with Donnelly two days before the Long Retreat began. 'I always thought pulse was something you felt. And as for wild herbs, absint, as Saint Paul says.'

'And the other Saint Paul, or one of the other saints of the name, who had been the first hermit, was only twenty-two years of age when he entered the desert. Previously he had experienced in the Lower Thebais in Egypt the persecution of Decius, whose game was, in A.D. 250, to kill the soul and not the body. To which end – as was it the learned Cassian, a favourite character of Guinan, relates? – Decius had a soldier of Christ who had already triumphed over other tortures stripped naked, rubbed all over with honey, laid flat on his back in the broiling sun so that any flies, wasps, bugs, fleas, moths and beetles in the locality might enjoy themselves sucking, creeping, stinging. Decius was good to insects.'

'I never think of it,' said O'Brien, who looked after the two skeps in the clochar, 'without some fellow-feeling. Was Decius, the devil, the first entomologist?'

And yet another Christian who defied Decius, who was kind in his own odd way, was bound by silken cords on a bed of down in a delightful garden and tempted by a lascivious woman. Thus bound and helpless, he spat in her Egyptian face, having first bitten off his tongue to give power to his spit. His bleeding tongue, like the pain in MacKenna's spine, was a sharper thing than the sting of concupiscence.

'Father Rodriguez,' said Barragry, 'doted on such anecdotes. How neatly he inlaid them into his three volumes of spiritual treatises.'

'Should we (aspiring religious) laugh at Cassian,' Petit wondered, 'or even at the Abbot Smaragdus, or at the young exorcist, too fond of his own family, who was put to shame when the devil in the demented one called out: Mama, Mama.'

And Paul and Anthony, hermits all for heaven's sake, embraced in the desert while an obliging raven, carrier for manna, dropped them a loaf. When they had discussed and eaten the loaf and refreshed themselves by a bubbling spring, they passed the night in prayer.

'The saints first learned in solitude,' Sweetman read in the refectory on the day before the Long Retreat began and the visiting Jesuit was there sitting beside Father Rector, 'to die to the world and themselves, to put on the spirit of Christ and ground themselves in a habit of recollection and a relish only for heavenly things, before they entered upon the exterior functions even of a spiritual ministry.'

It was all very well to joke about Decian persecutions and confectioners transmogrified into hermits, but the chill truth was that the way to God was through silence, humility, solitude, prayer, mortification, renunciation, the realisation – O'Rhattigan had it perhaps when he saw greasy fluid in a reopened mock elm coffin – that the world itself was a desert. God had gone hungry in a desert. From the age of twelve to the age of thirty God in humility had planed rough wood and worked as a carpenter with His foster-father.

And Francis de Sales, suave stylist, had known deserts of aridity, walked over them from perfect tranquility and peace of mind to the brink of despair. So bitter was his desolation that it gave him the yellow jaundice and he could neither eat, drink nor sleep; but he found ease when in a church dedicated to Stephen, protomartyr, he prostrated himself before a statue of the Mother of God.

And Brigid the nun of Kildare found peace among the quiet oak woods, where a tall round tower, in a flat land of stables and stud farms, still stands to mark the holy place.

The day before the Long Retreat began the exercitants moved to one wing of the house and the non-exercitants to the other. For thirty days each group would have its own beadle, its own notice-board, its own way of life. The exercitants stood on the edge of the deep silent desert with Paul, the first hermit, and John the Baptist, and Kevin on the way to his cave in the glen of the two lakes.

And Romauld, who founded the Order of Camaldoli used, when young and hunting in the woods, to cry out when he came to an agreeably peaceful spot: 'How happy were the ancient hermits who had such habitations. With what tranquility could they serve God, free from the tumult of the world.'

Donnelly would be Long Retreat Beadle for the exercitants.

They could write him notes, but couldn't speak to him, couldn't speak at all except to the Magnov, and the Jesuit who would direct the Retreat, and except on the two repose days that would come to ease the nerves and lessen the tension of continual silence. About the wing of the house reserved for the exercitants there was a special atmosphere. The woods moved closer to the walls, became deeper, more silently curtaining. They were green now. They were the walls of a cave or the surrounding desert sand or the steep below-the-cloud-line slopes of Thabor.

And talking about the mixture maxture in the mock elm coffin, didn't Margaret of Cortona turn to God when she saw the dead putrefying diseased body of one of the gallants who had loved her? The extraordinary austerities with which she punished her criminal flesh soon disfigured her body. Many a lover has lain with thee, Patrick Pearse wrote about Saint Mary Magdalene, but the shuiler, the tramp man, Christ will welcome thee.

And Saint Cunegundes, Empress, daughter of Sigefride, first Count of Luxembourg, to prove to her husband that she hadn't dabbled with other men, walked barefoot and unscathed on red-hot ploughshares. And Saint Abraham, a man of Mesopotamia, fled from his bridal night to a cell two miles from Edessa, where his friends, after a search of seventeen days, found him at prayer. The bride's private thoughts are recorded in no martyrology.

Et alibi aliorum plurimorum sanctorum martyrum et confessorum.

So that it wouldn't seem a great thing for O'Brien the ex-doctor to abandon his car on the blue gravel, nor for Barragry to abandon a woman who wasn't even a bride, nor for MacKenna to abandon Frankie and a humpy town and poetic aspirations, nor for Donnelly to turn his back on his uncle the bishop and his chances of advancement as a secular priest, nor for any young fellow, fresh from school and practically unsoiled, to choose a life of discipline and prayer. The walls of their cave were lovely with the green of spring. The birds sang like mad. In the night beyond the woods a train wailed to tell them the world was a sad place. One night they had their first lecture of the Long Retreat. After litanies a last bell rang and they were in the grotto of Manresa helping Ignatius, limping Pamplona soldier, to watch his devoted armour. 'Man was created for a certain end,' he told them over his sword and armour. 'This end is to praise, to reverence, and to serve the Lord his God, and by this means to arrive at eternal salvation.'

Think over that now. There's matter for a lifetime's meditation. The first truth is: 'I come from God.'

VII

Where was I a hundred years ago? Saint Ignatius encouraged Barragry and his brethren to think. I was nothing. If I look back a hundred years I see the world with its empires, its cities, its inhabitants: I see the sun which shines today, the earth on which I dwell, the land which gave me birth, the family from which I sprung, the name by which I am known: but I – what was I and where was I. I was nothing and it is amidst nothingness I must be sought.

But now I exist.

The chapel with four seats full of recollected retreatants had never seemed so still. The Jesuit father, his back to the tabernacle, sat at the top of the altar steps, his notes before him on a small table. Those notes were his way, learned from prayer and experience, of using the spiritual weapon given to him by his Spanish father founder. They were based on the sparse dry unliterary sentences of the Ignatian spiritual exercises. They could be arranged and adapted to suit all people and all occasions: a thirty-day retreat for contemplative nuns, a week-end retreat for city 'bus conductors, a series of mission sermons in a crowded city church or in some cold draughty church on the side of a mountain. They were the sword and armour Ignatius had kept vigil over.

My name I won't find, MacKenna thought, if I look back a hundred years, for our genealogy can't be traced beyond my father's father, who left the County Antrim in a hurry.

But the Barragry name, Barragry knew, had been in the Dublin burgher class for two or three centuries, small solid shopkeepers in the Coombe progressing to bigger shops in the city centre, then to medicine and the law and more ample houses near Dalkey above the bay. Two Barragrys of that branch now remained, one a neophyte (how funny) with memories of a woman, the other a boozy misogynous barrister. Where had the woman been a hundred years ago? On her way through infinity to a sleepy dusty village where two men drank port wine? Where was she now? Back in the nothingness where she had originally belonged? Did God send her to that village or could God send one a person with whom in happiness one could wound and affront God by sin?

The second truth was: I belong to God. The third truth was: I am destined for God. After that the three affections were sorrow for the past, contempt for creatures, love of God.

It rained in the afternoon when, gowned and coated, the exercitants walked abroad for recollection. Over the bogs beyond the sleeping pockmarked lake the sky was dark and lowering, no higher than the tops of the trees, but away towards the town with the cooling tower the darkness was disturbed by a thundery red glow, sunshine struggling vainly to break through. Donnelly had never been so deeply in the blues. The noise of non-exercitants at recreation in the ambulacrum made him remember a day at school, his companions' voices clear as bird-calls from the football field while he had been held back to stew Greek he had floundered in during class. The sense of isolation was similarly overpowering. Sorrow for the past, he thought, and prayed, O God, Thou knowest my foolishness, and my offences are not hidden from Thee, my secret idea that life as a secular would have been simpler, less severe, my passion for (inordinate attachment to) the harmonium, my flippancy, the protestant harvest thanksgiving fruits greedily eaten, my craving on walks for cakes to sweeten the palate, for hot tea to wash down dry brown bread, my sickening fear that the studies before me will leave me with a benumbed broken head.

All those that go far from thee, the psalmist prompted Barragry, shall perish. Thou hast destroyed all those who were disloyal to thee; but it is good for me to adhere to my God. Between clipped wire-corsetted yews beaded with midland rain Barragry walked with the singing sinning Jewish King, ancestor of Jesus on the mother's side. King David was a one to talk. Is it good for one to adhere to God merely because destruction is the penalty of non-adherence? And what about Bathsheeba, glimpsed at her ablutions, two more small ports and a mineral for the lady who's driving; and what about her husband sent to the wars, on a secret mission to London, to his death? Barragry couldn't remember what, after David's repentance, had become of Bathsheeba. But who hath known the mind of the Lord; for even if the King sinning with Bathsheeba, singing with his psaltery, made him sound revengeful, vindictive, wasn't he better by a long shot than one of the two surviving Barragrys? The Lord destroyed only the disloyal. Barragry abandoned the person who loved him most. You couldn't contemn a creature, oh soldier from Pamplona be your age, who had risked everything, disgrace, to be esteemed a harlot for Barragry's sake, who had risked death itself for your sake. The whirring starlings were in flight again. In sodden reeds by the puddled lake-walk the swans were nesting, proudly savagely sitting on shapeless piles or rubbish. Barragry walked as far as the boat-house and back. Hands muffed in the sleeves of his coat, he gripped his fingers together until the knuckles cracked. He walked rapidly, splashing as carelessly in puddles as a child might, his head bowed in the mizzling rain. Beyond that steaming wood, that quaggy bog, the world was, and the world was one person: a solution to his problem, or just a temptation, bite out your tongue and spit it in her face, chase her as Thomas tun-belly Aquinas chased the bad woman with a red-hot poker. But she was a lover and had been beloved. She was, perhaps, a devil in fair human form.

Oh God, he was degenerating into the sort of monk you read about in stories about Abelard and Heloise; he was the cloister and the boudoir type; he was in Tolstoi's Kreutzer sonata mood of the man who has had too much of a good thing; he was flying from sin, but still, like the ragged children in a Bistro advertisement, appreciatively sniffing the fleshpots.

'Fleshpots, my ainted arse.' He stopped dead by the boathouse. He had heard his own voice talking to himself. Did that violate the holy silence? A younger more imaginative novice might have thought he had heard the mockery of the devil speaking from the damp leaves or the deep boggy lake. A heron flapped out from behind the wooded island they called the priest's island. The demon in the form of a grey bird.

It's high time the holy Brother Barragry began to laugh at himself. Do what the Magnov said: Listen to Ignatius, pray, think, be a grown man, be humble, let God decide. Think with Ignatius about your purpose on earth, about death and judgment, heaven and hell; stand with him and look, as if you were looking at living coloured pictures, at the mysteries of the life of Christ. Represent to yourself two vast plains; in one, near to Babylon, Lucifer assembles around him all sinners; in the other, near to Jerusalem, our Lord is surrounded by all the just. Jesus has one standard, Lucifer another. Which will you follow? Where will you ask the airline people to drop you: Babylon or Jerusalem?

Run up a wall, Barragry. What's Babylon to you? Babylon and Jerusalem meant something to Ignatius; to you they could only be comic symbols; and standards and banners and badges are matters for

pious confraternities or orange processions or football finals. If
Beauchamp or your boozy brother could only read your mind now.
Life isn't as simple as two standards, or two teams, one playing for
Babylon and Beelzebub, the other for Jesus and Jerusalem. The mind
of Ignatius, remember, had much of the crass simplicity of the
soldier: take this side or that, take a sword, a banner, a gun, a drum, a
bugle, let Lucifer or who likes take the man who stands swithering in
the middle. God, what thoughts for a neophyte! This, with a
vengeance, is what you might call resisting grace.

Give it up, Barragry, give it up. Look at the lake, look at the
swans. Look at the wooden jetty over there overhung by the bending
branch of an old oak. Close your eyes then and see it when warm
days have come and the strain of this long prayerful examining
silence is over, and the water by the jetty is porpoised with the clean
bodies of novices, temples of the holy spirit, happy in trudgeon,
side-stroke, crawl, happy in the Lord. Smell the musty smell of the
boat-house, all the boats but one still up and waiting for the
relaxation of the villa. Be patient for a while. God is for ever. The
world if in the end it claims you again can well afford to wait.

He walked back towards the house by the path that edged the
sodden playing fields. A great rain-pool circled one goal, and two
gulls, blown from the sluggish river beyond the bog or from the canal
country, walked, foraging grenadiers, on the rim of the water. 'No
carrion for ye there. This is holy ground.' Saint Barragry, to break the
holy silence, addressed himself to the birds. Doric and sharply
outlined and apparently leaning forwards towards him from its slight
hill, the holy house stood up above the cedars on Saint Joseph's walk.
Petit, Murphy, the Abbot Lagan, non-exercitants, all walked, talking
together and full of purpose, towards the grapery and the garden.
They wore coats over their gowns and would have looked like many
skirted members of the Sanhedrin if it hadn't been for incongrous
cloth caps borrowed from the leper colony. A few exercitants paced,
black statues striving to walk, in rain-moistened reflection: creatures
belong to God, are for God through the medium of man, all creatures
assist me in meriting the possession of God, bless God in the name of
all creatures like the children in the furnace in the Book of Daniel,

grieve for having sought happiness from creatures and say with Ecclesiastes, Saint Ignatius and William Makepeace Thackeray: Vanity of vanities and all is vanity. Resolve to Love God alone.

The creature rain coagulated on a graceful branch of the creature cedar, dropped with a splash on Barragry's stiff rain-resisting red hair. Learn indifference with regard to creatures. Nevertheless, he wiped away the miniature pool. Unholy hands planted those cedars in landlord days, so it can be presumed that the deluge on my sainted skull was the work of a tree demon, the same that set mad Sweeney, ancient Irish King, forty-second cousin of Simeon Stylites, skulking and poetically staving in the branches, in places normally reserved for birds. To make himself laugh, he thought of the naked pagan statues, my Lord's prized ornamental creatures, in disgrace forever in there in a locked room. Suppose the devil that lives in stone and marble, tempting sculptors to fashion lascivious shapes, gave them life some warm night during the Villa and they were to parade the house, breathing marble succubae, or to bathe in the lake, under the oak bending above the wooden jetty, heating the water forever to a temperature detrimental to purity, capable of raising blisters on the bodies of novices when the bathing began. Beauchamp could draw that. It wasn't easy to laugh in the silence and mizzling rain. Thin blond wavy-haired Brother Keown passed him, his beads in his wet fingers, his face distraught. Wet Friday, fish for dinner, Latin recreation in the ambulacrum were, Nangle said, the three greatest afflictions a man could endure. Even the thought of Nangle wasn't funny or of Sadleir's battered hat on the upturned nose of Aloysius Gonzaga. So he fell back on his favourite distraction and thought of bitter Penaunce with a yron whip who in Spenser's holy house was wont every day to discipline the pilgrim knight, while sharp remorse his hart did prick and nip and sad Repentance did his blamefull body in salt water sore embay. If he could only see remorse and repentance as jokes, then the citadel would be saved.

But when he stooped to put on his house-shoes in the bootroom he still wasn't laughing.

Deep in recollection in the rain on a path that ran between the grapery trees and the high grey wall of the garden, MacKenna fell heavily and made a poem. It was a bloody awful poem, but what better could you do on a wet day in the middle of a harrowing long retreat, wearing a coat and a cap that didn't belong to you, and bogged to the neck in a spiritual desolation that would have given Charles Atlas, let alone Francis de Sales, the yellow jaundice. In the poem he gave the Lord thanks if for today he (the Lord) sheltered MacKenna and kept temptation far away. Temptation included also the needle stab in the back. He was afraid to say so much in words. The dripping trees might hear and tell Peesoc. But he was exultant in the knowledge that since the retreat began he had not suffered a single stab. If he didn't have spiritual consolation, if he hadn't soared or levitated or melted into ecstasy or the gift of tears, then he had at least physical comfort and freedom from fear. Furthermore, in the poem – it might be a good prayer even if it wasn't a good poem – he confided in the Lord that if he was sheltered for the day his heart with glee would, free from fetters, bound towards Heaven and Thee and that then the sound of soft-sung angel music would enwrap him round. Sheet music descending like manna to make celestial cellophane bed-clothes.

Lacy, tall, darkhaired, palefaced, wearing the novitiate's most respectable raincoat, crossed his path at right angles, walked on rapidly, his beads swinging, eyes cast down, lips moving. Petit, Murphy, the Abbot Lagan, hushed their voices as they overtook him and burrowed through the garden gateway into the dryness and warmth of the glass-houses. One must not disturb the recollection of the exercitants.

The time that's past, MacKenna composed – meaning the time since the first white morning when the great-tit had squeaked from the tree in the grapery – has drenched my soul with hidden joy. The hidden joy was opulently described as that slumbrous, tranquil, undisturbed roll (of waves not of drums) which could not cloy, and also as creeping, round, green waves no gale could annoy. From a swaying fir branch a cascade of water descended, missing him by a few feet. The liquid waves also laved the leeward side of a sea-flung harbour mole. That was the end of the second verse.

Through the mizzling rain came the sound of the warning bell for the day's third lecture to precede the day's third meditation. He walked faster. On the paths netting the green slope that spread out from the wide refectory window recollecting retreatants came to life, accelerated, shook rain from shoulders like dogs drying themselves after a swim, converged towards the Assisi passage and the dry boot-room. On his prie-dieu in the camerata he shared with Donnelly and Keown, MacKenna – it is to be regretted – finished his poem. One couldn't meditate all the time. One couldn't meditate anyway, with Keown fidgeting as if he had the itch, and Donnelly, even though he was as solid as a rock, breathing with heavy distracting regularity. So he told the Lord, in verse number three (What price the psalms, the canticle of canticles, or the blythe hymn of Ananias, Azarias and Misael, cool as pear melbas, in the fiery heat of the furnace!) that what shivering shadows leaned aslant the way that he must tread, could not uphurl this surely-fashioned day to plant instead eternal shades of gloom and faith found dead. No, he composed, and if he hadn't been kneeling stiffly, his hands locked together, he might have managed a gesture, in the room, dim-vaulted, of eternal life there gleamed the ray, twin-shaped, of hope and doom. It wasn't, he felt, in his very best manner. Donnelly, clearly going up Thabor like a grey hound up a hare-haunted hill, was nodding his head slowly from side to side. The rain had strengthened to a downpour. The wind battered it against the window at his back. There was an unnatural darkness in the room. A fine time it would be to meditate on hell, to represent to yourself the length, the width, the depth of hell, to ask of God a lively fear of the pains of hell, to think of it as the winepress of the fury of the Almighty under which he would trample and crush his enemies. Papa gets tight and wrecks the house. Think of the society of the damned, nothing like it in the dungeons and galleys of human justice, of the torment of the damned in the imagination, the memory, the understanding, the will, in sight, hearing, smell, taste, touch, in the knowledge that the torment will go on for ever, for ever the company of the devils, for ever devouring flames.

Keown behind me there thinks that this meditation will go on for ever. I can't see him, but I know he's on one knee, his shoulders slumped, his head in his hands. He's heard so often about that at quarters of charity. He was reared too easily: one handsome son in a houseful of gay sisters who treated him like a toy.

Slithering down from Thabor for a moment, Donnelly stood up and switched on the light. Later on in the retreat, when they had worked their way around to the consideration of hell and kindred formidable topics, the meditating would be done in darkened cameratas, shutters closed against wind sound in branches, against birds and the light. Catch the imagination. The Ignatian method was thorough.

The fourth verse of his poem tormented MacKenna's imagination like a sin that had to be confessed. In for a penny, in for a pound. He'd have scruples about it, anyway. He might as well finish it.

So for that day, Creator, he asked Thee to grant Thy grace, to preserve in truth what Thou preservest in life before Thy face; and he called Thee: Eternal Ruth. Always critical of his own efforts he considered that he was right down to the level of a prayer by Sybil F. Partridge, set to music by Blanche Ebert Seaver and unctuously recorded by the Athlone tenor John Count McCormack on H.M.V. Record D.A.929 to sell at five shillings and ninepence, to the effect that: Lord, for tomorrow and its needs I do not pray. Dismissing that thought as even a more wily twist of the old serpent Distraction he asked Thee, Creator, to set free our souls from graving bands (whatever they were) and to smooth life's moving sands, and also, while Thou wert at it, to set free Thy race, flung from the charnel-house of sin and shame, with snow-white hands.

He laughed at himself then. He spluttered and pretended to blow his nose. His mind set free, like a goat rid of a spancel, cleared all obstacles with one goat-bell-jingling bound. He saw spring up in the Sperrin Hills beyond Gortin, streams brown and full, trout-fishing soon to begin on the Strule, the Camowen, the Mourne, Drumragh, Derg, Owenkillew, Glenelly, on the wide Foyle itself. Frankie would come to see him after the retreat. His parents wouldn't come. His mother had written to say her clothes weren't good enough. She was nervous of the long journey.

'But we pray for you night and day,' she wrote. 'Your name is in the holy rosary every night, and in the catena, the chain of prayer of the Legion of Mary, that we say with the rosary.'

'I give out your decade myself,' she said.

FOUR: ALLELUIA

I

Sunlight dancing around them they descended the mountain on Easter Sunday morning. I arose and am still with thee, alleluia! Donnelly chirruped quietly to himself, as he bent over the washbasin and spat, in unison with Lacy, pink carbolic fluid on to white chipped porcelain. The Long Retreat was over, and Donnelly, Alleluia! and praise the Lord, had survived, his head still stubbornly unbroken. Lord, thou hast proved me and known me, thou hast known my sitting down and rising up. In the free time after breakfast the novices making beds, cleaning teeth, emptying slops, moved more lightly on their feet, more rapidly, dancingly, alertly than ever before. On the long walk later in the day, and the sun glorious above them, retreatants and non-retreatants, brothers all, would fuse together again, the separation and the great test over, glad together that only once more in their religious life would they have to go through the Long Retreat. I arose and am still with thee Donnelly prefaced his half hour's reading of his life of a saint, and he opened the stiffly-bound book and read about Saint Gerard Majella: 'When writing to his holy friend, Mother Mary of Jesus in Ripacandia, he speaks of the tabernacle as a prison of love, carcere di amore, and addresses the prioress as prima carceriera, head jaileress.'

'I'm in jail,' Keown had said to Donnelly, shattering the holy silence, on that ghastly wet afternoon during the first week of the retreat. 'I'm in jail. I might as well be in jail. I can't stick this place any longer.'

Keown hadn't come down for dinner. Donnelly, heavy with his beadle's responsibility, had walked up to the camerata to find Keown's curtains drawn. Keown fully clothed and lying on his bed, his fair hair ruffled, tears in his eyes. 'Fed-up to the teeth, Brother.

Fed-up to the teeth. I couldn't bear the thought of facing those holy Marys at dinner.'

With a shock Donnelly realised that they were talking, in whispers; but in the quiet camerata with the whole community below in the refectory, the whispers seemed as penetrating as screams. Far far away Sweetman's soft voice read from the rostrum.

'We should write what we have to say, Brother.'

'Oh! feck writing. We're not deaf and dumb. What did God give us tongues for? I'm going home.'

'Come down and eat, Brother.'

'What for? To look at Brother Petit picking his nose for his pleasure. The only pleasure he allows himself.'

'Brother.' It was difficult not to laugh. 'You're not sick?'

'Sick. Sick. I've nausea from boredom. I'm going home, Brother, I've had it.'

'You must see Father Master.'

'I've seen him. He can't keep me here. Nothing can keep me here except manacles and irons. Long Retreats. Meditations. The discipline. That silly chain. Hell. Heaven. Purgatory. Limbo. The two standards. The third degree of humility. Quarters of charity. Obedience, dumb and blind. Lives of starchy saints. That's no way for a man to live.'

'Brother, I can't argue with you about all that. If you don't accept it, you just don't accept it and you'd be as well off at home. But a good meal's a good meal any day of the week. We all get browned-off at times. So do people in the world. It's not easy to go against our nature.'

'It's not easy for me, anyway.'

'You're not the only one.'

'Oh, most of you like it.'

Should one laugh at him or shake him: the spoiled curly-headed brother of handsome sisters. 'I like my food, anyway,' Donnelly said.

'So do I. But I just can't face that refectory, Brother. I'd scream. I'd fling my soup at that Jesuit. Himself and his holy father founder. How do they do it? How do they keep it up for a lifetime? Have they any blood in their veins?'

'They eat well. They must be full of blood. They strike me as reasonable men.

'Who wants to be reasonable. If that MacKenna looks pale and poetic once again I'll hit him. And that stick of a Barragry with the special pair of hedge-clippers the Magnov gave him.'

'They have their own troubles.'

'What right has he to have a special pair of hedge-clippers?'

'He's older than most of us.'

'And that Petit, the Latin maniac. And Begley, wagging his pious head like a golliwog. I'd sooner starve than look at them.

'I'll say you're sick. I'll send you up some food from second table.'

'God bless, Brother Donnelly. You're human. You won't comment on it if I dodge the discipline tonight. I've had enough of that too. I'm going as soon as I can get packed. As soon as this frigging wet weather comes to an end. Janey, I'd love to be going to the pictures in Dublin. With a girl. Holding her hand. Eating caramels.'

Later in his scholastic life Donnelly read the Russian Goncharov about the Russian Oblomov, who wouldn't get up out of bed, and understood Keown a bit better. But Oblomov wasn't there that wet day. Saint Ignatius himself knew, and so did Saint John Nepomucene, his patron, who was fecked over a bridge or something in Eastern Europe, know, and so did our own Italian father founder, who had great devotion to Saint Ignatius, know, that it was no cinch of a job being a Long Retreat beadle. There you had Keown acting like a baby, shoulder-blades imbedded in his bed, and the good smell of food and the decent sound of sensible eating so close to him. Those sounds increased attractively as Donnelly, hitching the front of his gown so that he wouldn't trip and fall, walked down the stairs. There was nothing, thank heaven, against holy perfection in being fond of your food. He had the dirty job now of stamping up the whole long refectory to whisper to the Magnov that Keown wasn't well. The Magnov knew what was wrong with Keown, so it would be no word of a lie, yes! yes! not a word of a lie, whispered the workhouse arthritic, simply to say that the little ninny, heaven look down easily on my uncharity, wasn't well.

Then there was Barragry, et tu Barragry, who was old enough to have sense enough, berserk with boredom in his camerata and using his la-de-da hedge-clippers to snip the fringes off his bed quilt; and MacKenna looking pale but not poetic. MacKenna was pale because he wasn't well. That was another bother for brother beadle. Should he burst in on MacKenna's privacy and write to him: Brother are you ill? Or should he talk to Peesoc? Then there was Kelly, that unrestrained divil, as depredating as a Tipperary goat, making a mess with a slasher of six young saplings Father Rector had planted on the lake walk. Silence drove fellows to that. A year ago Kelly had been cutting and slashing with a hurley stick and thus steaming off the animal energy now dangerously compressed inside him. And Lacy had no wearable socks and Sweeney no tooth-powder and Furlong wanted his shoes half-soled, and Barnes was ready to cut his throat because of spiritual desolation and told Donnelly so in spidery antique handwriting; and Oh! Domine, Domine, isn't it aptly the Cistercians talk of the bursar risking his soul for the good of the community? I might as well be running a factory as doing a long retreat. Hell to the chance too, until all this is over, of laying a paw on the harmonium.

There now is the refectory, a mile long if it's an inch. Father Master's ear awaits the beadle's whisper. Sweetman in the rostrum in his saintly way will pause briefly in his reading to allow me to whisper. Everybody, eyes holily cast down, will know what I'm at, and wonder what's wrong with Keown. Who would, Oh! who would be a brother beadle?

As it happened, Keown lasted nearly as long as the Long Retreat. He was gone on the Wednesday before Easter, taking the wet weather with him; off, Donnelly hoped, to caramels in cinemas per omnia saecula saeculorum. His absence was naturally noticed. The Magnov forewarned Donnelly, but it was Flynn the heavy-footed, now beadle for the non-exercitants, who carried the travelling bags to the front steps and the boot of the V-8. MacKenna realised it with a shock when he saw the rolled blankets, the slipless pillows on the stripped bed. The other exercitants sensed it in the air. It trebled the strain of the last few days of the retreat. It was all the more horrible because you couldn't talk about it even if you wanted to. Commandos creeping sooty-faced in perilous silence towards an enemy installation on a bristling coast might feel that way on hearing a thud, a hiss of expiring breath, knowing a comrade dead, his unseen killer somewhere. You couldn't stop to discuss it. There was danger in sound. Every man had to watch every shadow, and terrifyingly alone to look out for himself.

Then suddenly the strain snapped in laughter. A non-exercitant typed the Order of the Day for the exercitants, ended his typing every day with initials in rubrics – L.D.S. which was Laus Deo Semper, which meant, in spite of wet Fridays and blues and brother bludgeoned back to the world, that God was always to be praised. An unfortunate mistype swung over to Mammon and read L.S.D. from the quiet, recollected, frightened gathering around the notice-board Barragry's bony finger pointed to the typical trivial novitiate joke. In a strained silent world anything was funny. The cameratas seethed with half-suppressed laughter. Beadle Donnelly vastly grinned. Nerves pleasantly relaxed and all of a sudden the sound of alleluias, they were coming down the mountain dancing back from the desert, a special morning recreation to look forward to as they had sliced, for their long walks, their luncheons of brown bread.

The slicing was done at the refectory carving table. There were biscuits today and red apples, and jam if you felt like it, because Christ was risen, as He had promised, the stone was rolled away, the tomb empty, death's sting drawn, the long retreat over. Across the bread-and-biscuit-littered table retreatants and non-retreatants eyed each other with silent holy jubilant expectation. They were one again. Donnelly couldn't stop grinning. He was no longer a beadle. He would, for benediction, be back to his harmonium: Guinan's red apples escaped through a hole in the pocket of his gown, hopped like live things along the polished floor. Everybody tittered. Guinan, toes turned up, stalked the errant fruit with affected caution. They might have been red delightful birds.

Spring possessed the grapery. The sun possessed the world. Lovely little midland roads invitingly opened before them: twisting luxuriously between deep quilted hedges, straggling like tinkers across the heath, humping like delighted friendly dragons over canal bridges, crossing the sluggish pike-infested river, tailing off into bogland that under the sun would smell like wine, winding around grey shattered Norman towers, ending helplessly at rusted sagging gates, opened now only for passing cattle, on overgrown avenues leading to abandoned country houses. Sweetman on a walk had discovered one such mysterious stranded wreck. He would walk there today with Flynn and Lacy and show them the decayed walled garden where fruit still reddened for departed planters who would never return to pluck and bite and savour. Some day a religious order might buy the house.

They could walk all day or loll in sunshine on whinny banks by small streams. The rule now allowed them to sit down in the open air. They'd come home tired, gloriously hungry, and kneel before dinner to examine their consciences with an expertise acquired from a deeper knowledge of the Ignatian method. The long table dinner would be, apart from the Christmas dinner, the year's best. Afterwards they would fuse with the missionary fathers, hear from their experienced lips maxims and anecdotes that would set them exultantly looking ahead to the great work to be done when their own two years of hidden life were over. Father Robert would be there, his rubicund face and restless false teeth all aglisten with joy. The visiting Jesuit would be there. He was one of the biggest men the jays had. Next week he would be in Rome consulting with the Jesuit father general.

Truly Christ was risen, alleluia! and if the world only knew the happiness of religious life there wouldn't be a door in one sound piece in any ancient holy house in – but not of – the world.

II

Barragry hadn't straddled a bicycle for two years. He said to the Magnov: 'I'm full of fear for my calves, Father.' Lagan and Matthews, cycling down the avenue ahead of Barragry and the Magnov, laughed. Matthews loved bicycles. In their own way they were horses. Matthews was happy. Lagan was happy because he loved boats and had just had his orders from the Magnov to prepare the boats for the coming summer, to go also with a lay brother to the

Huguenot town to see how the work was going on the raft for dredging the jungle of American watercress from the lake. An island man from Bantry Bay, knowing in the ways of things that floated, Lagan had planned the raft. It was something quite new in naval design. It was to be called the 'Queen Mary,' and Nangle had suggested that at the launching Barnes, who knew about kings and queens, should smash a bottle of Lourdes water over the prow, if they could find out which end was the prow. If it floated at all, Nangle said, let the credit go not to Lagan from beyond Bantry from beyond Adrigole, where in the stone clefts of the West Cork mountains the people lived by instinct, but to holy Bernadette, the Pyrenean maiden and Our Lady of Lourdes.

The great beeches lining the avenue on the hill above the village were delicate green clouds, alive with wind-whispering, soaked in and dripping with sunlight. You felt you could grasp in handfuls the odours from the marshalled ordered firs and pines. They seemed to have grown determinedly since last autumn, defying winter's negation, sucking the stored strength from the good Midland ground. The rides between them and underneath them seemed longer, more mysteriously shadowed, more startlingly splotched with sunlight. You could wander down there alone and walk, perhaps, into another country. 'How far is it to the Catholes?' Barragry asked.

'Twelve miles.'

'Uphill?'

'Mostly. After Ardpatrick.' Ardpatrick was another town, a main-road with no old Huguenot houses, but with a mill, a jail, a new white hospital, a prosperous business life. 'Saints preserve us,' Barragry said, considering his calves and the uphill push.

'You can free-wheel on the way home.'

'After tribulation you promise me great calm. I'm almost certain to get a puncture on the way home.'

'Brother Barragry's a Jonah.'

'You mean a Jeremiah.'

Hatless, grey-headed, quiet, his smooth forehead raised to the sunlight, his face smiling praise for sunlight, for lovely odours of grass and trees, the Master deftly pushed his pedals. A young man in the world, he had for speed and the corruptible crown risked his neck at Brooklands. Now he rode with his disciples, at ease with them in their frivolity.

On a bench outside the village pub a bearded tramp slept in Easter sunshine. The Magnov dismounted for a moment to deliver a bundle of Canadian newspapers sent by Father Minister to the old lady who lived, secure behind green wooden railings and privet hedges, in the house across the road from the pub. The scrape of his foot on gravel awakened the tramp, who sat up, raised solemnly the hat that shielded his eyes from the sun, then lay back again to his slumbers, his alleluia duty to God fulfilled. Left feet resting on the road's grass margin, hats on handlebars, right feet poised on pedals, the three novices waited until Father Master had exchanged civilities with the old lady. She had once lived in Calgary. They were curiously silent when the Magnov wasn't with them. The thought that they were specially privileged in being with him on this run to the Catholes, the cool rock pools in the young river in the high hills, to swim with him in the dark water, made them nervous.

Does he want to come to grips with me, Barragry thought, about the canker that's gnawing out my innards? Not even Saint Ignatius and the Long Retreat could kill that canker.

Does he want to tell me, ever so gently, Lagan feared, that I give too much of my attention to the vanities of boats, to the prospects of the dredger I designed?

Does he want to tell me, Matthews wondered, that he knows of the lies I told, about my father's imaginary horses, to that old codger in the workhouse ward.

The Magnov was clearly resisting an invitation to tea. From the whitened doorstep he slowly retreated, smiling, shaking his head. The Lord Himself couldn't have been more gentle. But how splendid it would be, Barragry hoped, if he yielded, if we could see the inside of the house, the inevitable knick-knacks and whatnots, the polished lino on the floor, the cat, the sewing machine, the chrysanthemum offering hospitality to a strayed fritillary. There might even be a canary or a whistling chatty parrot. I'd like for a break in monastic monotony to peep into a corner where life would be as even as the ticking of an old clock, no regrets for the fleshpots, no hankerings for the high hills nor for caves in the red desert. I'd like to see life again, not drink, not jollification, neither excitement nor sin, but quiet people living in an easy world that makes its own rules, needs no bells, no imposed pattern. Guinan, who's a mathematician as well as a bird-watcher, worked out the number of bells we respond to in a two years' novitiate: some fantastic, incredible, astronomical total; for works indoor and out, for Mass, meditation, meals, spiritual reading, litanies, conferences, examen of conscience, beads, voice production, free time, for our rising up and also for our lying down. I've always abominated bells, telephone bells, the bells of Shandon that sound so great on the pleasant waters of the River Lee, sleigh bells in the snow and the tintinnabulation of the bells of Edgar Allen Poe. At heart I must be the average domesticated man: pipe, warm bedroom slippers, one female voice saying darling the meal is on the dining-room table. Perhaps the Magnov in his time felt like that too, and the little old lady at the door of her village home, the walls destined soon to be wreathed with rambling roses, might be as severe a temptation for him as a lascivious sun-browned Alexandrian hip-swaying harlot for a desert father, or for me Barragry the bad, a motor flying east to Dublin with a blonde girl at the wheel.

The Magnov fumbled and foothered with the latch of the wooden gate. From the concealment of the doorway the old lady stepped into the sunlight and bowed to the three novices. In unison, like cavalry men, they swung feet to the ground and returned the salute. Barragry savagely skinned his ankle agains the cotter-pin, surveyed the dear dame dimly through a puce blur of pain.

They topped the hill beyond the village and free-wheeled by the decaying estate wall towards the main road and the heath. 'She's a saintly old soul,' the Magnov said. 'Her brother was one of ours in Canada. He died there. He was a most active devoted man.' The thoughts of Matthews dwelt on Canada and on far-away missionary places, on wide lands where horses could run wild. He had imagined horses for an old pauper's pleasure, but, for God's greater glory in remote parts of the world, in Kenya, Rhodesia, or Burma, as he had read in the missionary magazines, God's priests lived like cowboys in the saddle. Then the heath was ahead of them, as wide as Canada. The inevitable man in white breeches swung the young horse on the radius of rope. The clumped furze was golden. On the skyline to the west a line of seven horses went trotting for exercise. The south-west wind leaned heavily against the holy cycling men. Barragry groaned and stood up on his pedals as he pushed and Matthews and Lagan most uncharitably laughed. The Magnov's hat blew off, perched like a sable bird on the exact centre of a formidable circle of furze; and Barragry, glad of the chance to dismount, retrieved it.

'Brother Barragry's most mortified.'

'He loves to roll in the furze.'

'Better by far than nettles. Much more merit.'

'The Barragrys always were a stiff breed.'

'That's what the Long Retreat does for you.'

Like a honey-smeared martyr strapped naked on an anthill the Magnov smiled and said: 'Thank you, Brother Barragry. You're active for your age.' The slope of the road again in their favour and a hummock of green land sheltering them from the wind they singingly free-wheeled past the white gates of the Golf Club. Three women in slacks, burdened with bags of niblicks, mashies and putters, strode off for their eighteen relaxing, husband-escaping, gossipy, girl-against-girl contests. 'Dear Brothers, what we escape,' the Magnov said. 'How stern they look.' Laughing, they left the heath behind them and cycled three miles through rich farmland to the busy main-road town. Cars going east and cars going west met them and overtook them. This road was the world. This was the first town Barragry had actually entered since his flight to the desert.

'There's many a man in there,' Matthews said, 'would be glad to be out here cycling with sore calves, pushing against the wind.'

'Sick and in prison,' Lagan said. 'I don't see how you could be in there and not be sick.'

'Nor how you could be really sick' Barragry said, 'and not be, so to speak, in prison.' The new hospital on the edge of the town was a bright, white, cubical, flat-roofed, wide-windowed marvel of modern architecture. The grey grim jail, designed for another purpose, had been built in another period.

'In Britain and the States now,' Matthews said, 'they have prisons without walls.'

Lagan said: 'That's the sort of prison I'd opt to go to. There'd be no holding you if you felt like fresh air. A fair field and no favour.'

'What would that place look like,' Barragry said, 'if you took the walls away?' They looked at the formidable hideous walls, the thin barred windows, the gate that seemed as if it had never been opened, never could be opened. 'It's another sort of community life,' the Magnov said. 'If a man accepted his punishment for the proper motive he could walk out of that gate a saint. The chaplain there tells me that the instances of sanctity within prison walls are amazing. You know, dear brothers, in the world we live in it's only the sinners get publicity. A few years in the confessional will teach you the world is full of saints. Full of saints, brothers. Claudel said the world was crying out for saints. But then Claudel never heard confessions. The police and the newspapers aren't interested in saints.' The brothers cycled in respectful silence. The Magnov hadn't spoken for a long time. He had quietly pushed his pedals, and, oculis dimissis, watched the ribbon of road reeling backwards. 'We could pray for those who are in prison,' he said. 'They must be very unhappy or they wouldn't be there at all.'

The town was around them, as lively as cricket chirrups. Nobody in the town seemed in the least impressed by the proximity of hundreds of sinners, cut off from society, expiating in cells behind bars and stone walls, caged because of their sins more securely than wild beasts in a zoo. What a load off the taxpayers, Barragry thought, but didn't say, if they were exhibited like caged wild beasts, cages labelled with the Latin names of their various crimes, to be gazed at by the curious who were prepared to pay sixpence at the turnstile.

At a street corner seven loungers, peaks of caps shading eyes, absorbed the sun. A high shiny silo dwarfed the church steeple. A black and yellow fingerpost told you how far it was to Dublin, and to Cork and Limerick. They cycled through shadow under a railway arch. Children, clustered around the lever-handle of a spouting iron pump, respectfully paused in a splashing game to salute the clerics. At the gate of a field bright with bunting, crowds were coming together for a hurling match; a half-dozen hurlers already on the field swung white ash sticks and limbered their muscles. Three miles beyond the town the climb commenced: up first by switch-back roads, streams brawling in wooded hollows, then up to dry fields and banks of flaming furze. By a lonely mountain cottage they stopped to drink cool water. The man of the house filled their cups from a white enamelled bucket secure in a shady corner on the flat stone at the door. The woman of the house led two flaxen-haired children, shy as wild deer, out from the shadowy kitchen and the whole family knelt for the holy father's blessing. Afterwards Matthews and Lagan talked of the strong faith of the Irish country people. The Magnov and Barragry were silently sucking in the lively mountain air. Miles to the left the highest ridge rose, dark at first with conifers, then bare and rigid with exposed ribs of rock. One mountain track alone crossed that ridge and went on through loneliness to drop down again to rich flat land by the Shannon shore. The river burst out from somewhere between the conifers, leaped down from cool pool to cool pool, was captured below the Catholes by the reservoir that supplied the busy main road town, the hospital, the grey prison. In four secluded corners behind banks of furze the Magnov and the novices, regarding the rules of modesty, stripped separately. Lagan, tough as an islandman's oar, was first into the water. Matthews followed him, recklessly clambering down rocks, plunging clumsily in, coming up with puffings and roarings at the shock of the spring-cold pool. The Magnov had thin hirsute legs and a comically old-fashioned bathing suit, but his dive was as sharp and decisive as the slash of a knife, and when he surfaced there was no gasping, no blowing. 'Come on, Brother Barragry. It's most refreshing.' Barragry poised himself on the edge of a rock. The last time he'd dived it had been into warm swinging salt water and he'd been in mixed company. Below him in the river there was enough sanctity to turn the water into holy water. In the foam pattern dizzily widening out from the rapid above the pool he saw his whole life. He sensed, but could not define the future. Matthews shouted: 'Come on, Barragry. Be mortified.' Matthews somersaulted in the pool. Lagan pulled himself up to a rock, rubbed water out of his eyes. The Magnov was methodically circling the pool using a breast stroke that was strong and orderly as an ascetic meditative life.

III

The furze lost its glow and the sky darkened as they free-wheeled back down the mountain. Barragry didn't get a puncture. The hurling game was over, the main road crowded with cars, cyclists, walking people. A thirsty throng waited the blessed moment of the opening of the public-houses. 'Cannier boozers are already in by the back door,' Barragry said.

'Brother Barragry remembers the fleshpots.'

'The pint pots.'

'Ours may not consume pints in public.'

'Nor in private, I fear, dear brothers,' the Magnov said.

'At the most, a bottle of stout by doctor's orders.'

'Father Minister's health bottle popped in the kitchen yesterday.'

'Ascended like a fountain in the sight of the Lord.'

'A week ago, by mistake, Brother O'Rhattigan served Father Minister's bottle to the missionary father who lectures every year to the total abstainers.'

The Magnov laughed. The total abstinence missioner had been outraged. There was a suspicion that Brother O'Rhattigan's faux-pas had had some guiding mind behind it. 'We should have had a photographer present.' At the jail gate they heard far away the first distant rumble of thunder. 'They won't get wet in there, anyway,' Matthews said.

'A slight consolation.'

The clouds leaned down ominously. The rock was theatrically unreal, outlined against a last fragment of bright sky. 'We'll be soaked.'

'Oh ye of little faith.'

'Brother Barragry's fault. His faith failed before his fear of punctures.' They cycled faster. The countryside was breathlessly quiet. Cycling ahead, Lagan and Matthews discussed the various odd and often unworthy motives that brought people to the religious life. 'Brother O'Brien says he really came here to write a novel. He says never in the world could he find a novel to please him.'

'God tempts us all with the bait He knows will attract us.'

God's a cute codger, Barragry thought. What fly did He take me on: the red butcher of remorse, or the mayfly of brief pleasure, or was the bait just our old friend, the worm that dieth not? Perhaps He hasn't taken me yet. I wanted peace once. I thought I must make expiation. Now I don't know what I must do or what I want. Matthews called back: 'Brother Barragry, I saw you reading *Christianus.*'

'You did indeed.'

'A very sound writer, Dom Anscar Vonier.' From the book by the Benedictine, Vonier, Barragry had that morning transcribed into his notebook a paragraph about Christian repentance. To the rhythm of the push of the pedals the ideas jerked through his head: the peculiar spirit of Christian repentance is to live by the conviction that, however great the havoc wrought, things can be made right in the most complete manner. Could a woman be made virgin again? Could a death shabbily, secretly contrived, be changed into growing increasing life? But the learned Vonier pointed out that a sinner could feel true sorrow and still lack the persuasion that everything could be made right. Man could be truly contrite but also convinced that the wrong done would be eternally an incurable wound in the spiritual world. But that wasn't the Christian way, for Christianus penitens was also sperans, his sorrow full of faith in a power that could build up everything that had been pulled down. For one sinner doing penance in that way the angels rejoiced in heaven. Well, up above that black sky it looked as if the angels in heaven were by no means rejoicing. They suspected that Barragry, no Christian according to Dom Anscar Vonier, was out and about, and they were ready for him with a deluge which, the Magnov also being abroad, would drench indubitably both the just and the unjust.

Over a cottage half-door two women looked out at the dark threateningly hushed afternoon. Hens drooped feathers, tucked in heads, waited nervously in dusty places under wayside bushes. A crowded bus overtook the cyclists. Coloured scarves and jerseys fluttered like flags from its windows. It carried homewards singing shouting supporters of football teams. Lagan and Matthews still discussed Vonier's Christian man, but in his gaudens or joyful state, not in his mood of hopeful penitence or penitent hope. The Magnov interjected the occasional, quiet, sapient remark.

How does he thole all the callow things we have to say about books on the spiritual life? If he only saw the notebook I write striking passages in. In its own way, it's as funny as MacKenna says his book of poems is. Why, a month before I entered I was solemnly noting down some of the more blasphemous meanderings of George Moore on the Essenes and the Resurrection of Christ. Georgie Porgie and Anscar Vonier are queer bedfellows, if bedfellows is what I mean. Because some learned German thought Christ was an Essene and had a cataleptic trance instead of a real death. George thought so too, and wrote away about the Essenes. What could George know about life in a holy house, or what did I know about it when I wrote down in my notebook what George had made Manahem say to holy Paul about the simple life of the brothers?

It was a strictly regulated life. So is ours. Bells, bells, bells. Each brother had his own work. So have we. Those who had power as soothsayers and wonder-healers went forth among the people. We have our missionary fathers. And the Essene prior said: 'Once a man enters these doors his past is dead to him and to his brethren here.' My own past, living on in me, makes nonsense of my being here at all.

The Magnov said: 'How quiet you are, Brother Barragry.'

'Pondering the sky, Father.'

'Like the learned Thales, the Ionian sage.'

'Who fell down the well while looking at the stars. I was watching the road too, Father. The sky's nearly as low as the road.'

'Our Easter sun didn't dance for long.' Now's the time to tell him. Lagan and Matthews are out of earshot. But how to phrase it? I'm going, Father, or Father, I've no vocation and I never had, never will have, or Father, I must return to the world, or I can't stick it, or I'm finished. Am I finished? Wait, said Father Willy Doyle, until the next mealtime.

The Magnov said: 'The novices always look forward very much to the Easter Long table.'

'Relief from the Long Retreat, I suppose, Father.' You'd think he was reading my thoughts.

'Father Robert is a most popular figure at fusion.'

'He's a saintly soul.' God above, I couldn't go on for the rest of my life talking like this. I'll out with it now. Or I'll lag behind and slip away at the next corner and cycle through rain and thunder to Dublin. For every man that legged it from the fleshpots to the desert there must have been another who sprinted the other way, glad to escape from God, relieved at no longer having to hoist himself towards heaven by his shoe-laces. The hound of heaven, I suppose, would, like a trick dog from a circus, cycle after me: deliberate speed, majestic instancy, and a celestial three-speed gear.

Raindrops pocked the road with circles as wide as pennies. Dust spirited like smoke puffs. The black sky was a metal furnace. The water was boiling.

'We must find shelter.'

'Father,' Barragry said. But the Magnov was leaning heavily on the pedals, speeding ahead, stealing the lead from galloping Matthews. The old saint was as tough as a gad. The first sheet of rain struck them. The furiously pedalling priest, not turning his head, shouted down the fury of the tempest: 'Any port in a storm.' The port happened to be a crossroads pub, apparently closed and lifeless. But through an open gate you could see ranks of bicycles in the backyard.

I might as well leave it now till the next mealtime. It's a long time since I entered a pub.

Big countrymen, black pints in hand, crowded the bar. The day being Sunday, the windows were respectfully shuttered. Shuffling in the shadows, the big men doffed hats, lowered pints, and made way for the shepherd and his three sheep.

'The weather's ruined, Father.'

Another voice said: 'God's good, Mickey. Don't be always complaining.'

'A dreadful day, Father.' They gurgled into their pints. Smiling obsequiously, a tall bald publican lifted the counter flap, led the Magnov and his men over an uneven flagged floor, between rows of red-ended barrels and by the foot of a narrow linoleumed staircase into a low-raftered kitchen.

'Were ye at the game, Father?'

Smiling with the smile of one of Christ's suffering saints the Magnov said: 'No; we were swimming in the Catholes.'

'Swimming is it? Cold days yet for that, Father. The boys here don't wet themselves till June's well in. Barring them that's very hardy. 'Twas a grand game too.'

'Were you there?'

'No. More's the pity. 'Tis hard to leave the business on a Sunday. But the boys beyond give me all the news.' A small four-paned window, deep in the wall streamed with rain. The only light in the kitchen came flickeringly from the great hearth fire. Figures leaped at you from old family portraits, then were sucked back as suddenly into the shadows. Plates on the dresser, furniture of old dark oak reflected the red light.

'You'll be comfortable here, Father, I hope, until the tempest passes.'

'Thank you very much indeed. We were glad to escape the rain.'

'It came like all of a sudden, Father.'

'It certainly did.' In a dark kitchen behind a bar crowded with shouting men and with three tender novices in his care and talking to a slieveen of a publican, the capacity of the Magnov to be, after Saint Paul, omnibus omnia was nervously strained.

From deeper shadow under the stairs came the rustle of a newspaper, came a long shock-headed lout of a fellow uncoiling himself from a low chair, nodding and mumbling civilly to, but rapidly evacuating before, the clerical visitors. Civilly as he shambled out of the kitchen he handed the Sunday newspaper to Lagan. How could he read in there in the half darkness? Cat's eyes: a line every time the fire flickered. Lagan held the newspaper as if it would bite him. He had, if not the flesh and the devil, certainly the world and all the distracting pomps thereof between his neophytical finger and thumb. 'That's my son,' the publican said, not exactly with pride. Most sons of publicans went for the priesthood. This one clearly had other ideas. The force of the contrast between his ursine offspring and the clean young black-clothed men with their white shirts and black ties, each one of them the makings of a priest and a great glory and honourable expense to his people, momentarily stunned the publican into silence. From the doorway he said humbly: 'Would you touch a drop at all, Father?'

'No thank you very much.' Barragry's tongue was arid with memories. Wouldn't I half touch a drop of it if I had the chance? His coat was wet on his bony shoulders.

'Or a drop o' tea itself. Nelly the girl will have the kettle hot in a minute.' No one of the chosen people entertaining a passing prophet or an incognito angel could have been more hospitably considerate.

The Magnov pondered, then visibly relaxed. The brothers were as wet as he was. They were young. They hadn't for a long time sipped tea by an open fire, hadn't warmed themselves at anything less inhuman than a radiator. Lagan gingerly placed the newspaper on the kitchen table. The Magnov said: 'We'd all be grateful for a cup of tea.'

Nelly, the girl, would draw no young man away from his celibate sacerdotal calling. She was ancient, fat and greasy, was shapelessly bundled into a sack of a slovenly apron. When, as a girl, she had rolled behind whins on the heath, her lovers had worn whiskers and strong watch-chains weighted with pendants. 'Not a styme of light here,' she grumbled. Still grumbling to herself and apologising vaguely to the Magnov, she lighted the long oil-lamp swinging on chains from the ceiling. The mellow radiance gradually gathered strength, defining every angle of the little room, enabling Barragry to read with sly devilment the headings on the newspaper that Lagan had cast from him. On the page, visible where the paper lay on the table, there was a column by a man he knew, a popular columnist who, in a great car, coloured cream and maroon, and accompanied by a photographer, scoured the country in search of the unusual. Suppose for fun that cream-and-maroon car now pulled up at the door; suppose the columnist and camera man came in. Could Barragry under such unusual circumstances have special permission to talk to externs? Would the columnist write: 'Yesterday in a midland pub I met by chance my old friend, Barragry, once a journalist, and now a clerical student.' What would the columnist think looking at me here in my holy strait-jacket and listening to our stilted talk?

Nelly, the girl, left the door open behind her while she went searching for the best china. Rain drummed on the tin roofs of outhouses. The pub noises grew louder. A voice, thick with porter, said: 'Bejasus it was a powerful puck. Your man Timmy's the best hurler going today.' There was an embarrassed laugh, then a long meaningful silence. So here we sit, being trained to lead the world to God and the world can't even talk naturally in our presence. At the moment Barragry hated the Magnov. At the moment he knew he shouldn't be there, dressed in black, being a dilettante in the ways of God. The Magnov was close to him; Matthews and Lagan sat at a distance between the swinging lamp and the red fire. He said: 'They have their own community life, Father, out there in the bar.'

'We're gregarious, Brother. We like to get together either to pray or drink porter.'

'Hermits, Father?'

'Are exceptions, dear Brother. And not necessarily welcome phenomena.'

'But hermits have been saints.'

'Quite so, Brother. God's grace can make hermits saints and courtesans saints. But then secret drinkers are hermits in their own peculiar way. And, with your experience, I think you'll admit that the pint-drinkers outside are on safer ground than the secret drinkers.'

Thunder rolled over the heath. It wasn't easy to outflank the Magnov. His quiet smiling adroitness was something to marvel at. It forced a man back into good humour. The thunder growled nearer. The club-house on the golf links would be crowded now with drinkers of another sort, on another level of community life. Barragry laughed. If Matthews and Lagan could hear him now, they'd be shocked at his audacity: 'Why can't we go out and talk naturally to them, Father?'

Outside in the bar a voice began to sing: Oh dear, what can the matter be, three old ladies locked in the lavatory. Then hissing, warning, reproving sounds stilled the imprudent singer.

'But we can, Brother.'

'Yet their talk would be stilted and unnatural if we were there. Even as it is there's a curb on their tongues.'

'The tongue, the apostle tells us, is a frail instrument. No harm to curb it.'

'But don't they resent the fact that our being here cripples their talk?'

The thunder was over the house now, was taking echoes from tin roofs. A startled dog barked furiously in the darkened bar. Nelly, the girl, covered with a cloth the kitchen's one mirror. 'The lightning's a terror, Father. Not though that I'd have any fear with yourselves under the roof.' She bent to unhook the bubbling steaming kettle. Lagan and Matthews, ecstatic at the prospect of tea, leaped to help her. 'They'd resent it much more,' the Magnov said, 'if I went out and over a pint helped them to sing about those three tragic old ladies. They'd feel we'd been false, not only to ourselves, but to them and to something bigger than the lot of us put together.'

'But how are the priests to win the people if they're partitioned off from them.'

'There are all sorts of priests in all sorts of places. In fashionable churches in London, tents in the Algerian desert, caravans in France. The hail-fellow-well-met priest who can take his whiskey can do a lot of good. But, Brother, he has no easy vocation.'

I'm being a bowsy, Barragry thought. I'm discontented myself and I'm trying to let off steam by this idiotic carping argument, lacking the courage to tell this man that I'm a misfit, that I resent the way of life because I'm not able to follow it. The ropes and cables holding the Barragry balloon down to the moorings at the hangar are too strong.

'Wouldn't you imagine, Brother Barragry, that it might be better to feel that we're not a match for the world than to feel that we're too good for the world.'

'I'd imagine so, Father.' There was no point in arguing further. The Magnov was settled as securely in God's world, in the world of holy houses, as the rock in spite of rain and thunder, was rooted in green midland ground, and out of that security he spoke, and Barragry meant as much as the rain on the outhouse roofs. Courteously, from Nelly the girl, the Magnov accepted his cup of hot tea. 'Out there now over the pints,' he said, 'there might be a saint or two.'

'That could be, Father.'

'There must be a lot of holiness in the world. The Sunday newspapers tell of horrors.' How well he knew I was slyly reading the newspaper on the table. 'Novelists pick on the horrors because, God help them, they must have stories. It's easier, say, to tell stories about Christie, the strangler, than about Matt Talbot, a poor ignorant Dublin working man who was very holy.'

The Magnov sipped his tea, assured Nelly the girl that in heat, sweetness, and strength it was to his satisfaction. The rain on the tin roofs eased until the loudest sound was the sound of water pumping from a spout, overflowing from a barrel. In the bar the publican was quietly talking, gently holding the attention of his customers, a Magnov in his own way, in his own community.

'We're meandering, Brother Barragry,' the Magnov said. 'Where is all this talk leading us?'

Up Thabor or back to Dublin, on to the mission fields in the footsteps of the Italian father founder, or back to Egypt, to find a job again, meet a woman, properly rehabilitate oneself, properly make restitution?

'The trouble with late vocations is they're so receptive I'm inclined to ramble on. I taught you Latin when you were a boy.'

'I remember.'

'I was younger then myself. Most of my novices here are still boys. All now except O'Brien and yourself, and Petit. Petit was never a boy.'

'He's very earnest.'

'He'll be a good priest with God's help. I'm still a sort of a schoolmaster, Brother Barragry.'

'I suppose so, Father.'

'They come to me all hope and ignorance and good intentions. Some can't last it out. But whether they persevere or not they all move on from me.'

'When they leave you, they're well equipped for the future.'

'I hope so, Brother. God is good. One does one's best. But I work with imponderables, with incalculables. Mother Janet Erskine Stuart, the Great Sacred Heart nun – I must have her life and letters by Maud Monahan read in the refectory. Do you know what she compared the spiritual life to?'

'No, Father.'

'The material on the weaver's loom. The weaver sits behind it, working away, never sees the pattern, the design, until the work is complete and perfect.'

'Is God the weaver?'

'No; each man weaves his own pattern out of the material supplied by God. My trouble is that I have to train the young apprentices.'

'You do it well, Father.'

'Thank you, Brother Barragry. Heaven forgive me the vainglory, but I rather like appreciation from an old crust like yourself.'

Lagan and Matthews had overheard the tail end of the talk. The shepherd and the three sheep laughed together a community laugh. Returning daylight shone through the clouds and drying panes, quarrelled with the pale lamplight. The Magnov said: 'Pray for me, brothers.'

Once again he assured Nelly the girl that the tea was the loveliest he had ever tasted and he said to her the cup that cheers but not inebriates, and Nelly, who didn't understand, laughed heartily and then quietly knelt for his blessing. They thanked the publican and, avoiding the crowded bar, went out by the backdoor, picked their steps across a puddled yard to the road and their bicycles. Hens sheltering in a car shed clucked dismally. The rain was a fine mizzle. The green land steamed. The outline of the rock was vague in drifting mist. Matthews and Lagan cycled ahead, free-wheeling along a rough wet by-road.

'You're still worried, Brother Barragry,' the Magnov said. 'You're still not happy.'

Stones bounced from the wheels with the force of bullets. Between puddles and loose stones steering was hazardous.

'Take it easy,' the Magnov said. 'You've all your life yet. Don't rush things. Promise me that.'

Under the dark sky and after the rain the first furze blossoms were radiant. 'You won't be held here against your will.'

'I know that, Father.'

The sky cracked and a watery sun shone. By a deep sandpit they topped a rise in the road. Away east was the wide plain: poplars, steaming woods and fields, farms, roads, railways, towns, the world. Away east were Wicklow hills, faintly blue, barely visible, and north of the hills lay Dublin.

IV

Behind the grapery trees the evening Easter sun was going down in triumph. The leaves were still dripping, but the rain had only varnished their green; the rain had only made the birds sing louder. Birds and novices knew it was Easter and God was alive, alleluia! and summer and villa and visits from relatives were on the way. That evening Easter sun, barred behind the grapery trees, was by no means in prison. His beams illumed, as Guinan said, the tall vases of spring flowers, the coloured quivering jellies, the glass ware, even the mushroom soup and the first and second meat on the year's second-best long table. Father Robert's face was a sun in itself. Die now, it signified, and go straight to heaven if heaven itself and all its high courts could be any improvement on this. Gowns once black but now faded to green and frayed and patched, and worn to teach the novices humility or, more bluntly, to knock the notions out of them, shone now like the raiment of archangels, alleluia!

'Thank God the Long Retreat's over,' Lacy said. 'As long as I live I'll never forget the walk I had with Kelly and Feehan on the first repose day. It rained. It rained. We sheltered in an old broken-down hayshed and munched our brown bread.'

'Miserably munched,' said Nangle, 'miserably munched.'

'Kelly wore a black oily sort of a raincoat that stank. Kelly was gay. Not even death and hell and Saint Ignatius could keep him down. Feehan – weren't you, Feehan? – was morose.'

To his first meat Feehan said: 'I read the newspaper was around my lunch. It was the only sin I could think of. It was a piece of the financial page of the *Irish Press*.'

'Mammon,' Kelly said. His mouth was full of meat. He swallowed and said: 'Did you ever see anything as funny as Barragry and his special hedge-clippers?'

'The hedges here will never grow again. They'd be afraid.'

'Topiarist,' said Barragry, 'is my middle name. I should have been a labouring man living in a roadside cottage, clipping my hedges into queer shapes, elephants, crowing cocks, to frighten passing horses.'

Instead of examining his conscience before dinner, Barragry had read his notebook: George Moore on the Essenes and the cataleptic Christ, Anscar Vonier on Christianus repentant, and Uncle Tom Cobbleigh and all. What the hell was the use of examining a conscience in which he could find always and only the one scruple, the one irritating jagged fragment? His notebook of select quotations did, at least, make him laugh. In that way it had a sanative value.

'Poor Keown,' Donnelly said. 'Saint Ignatius shot him down.'

'Eschew the semicolon,' O'Brien said. He was talking to Guinan about literary style and the writing, for God's greater glory, of novels. 'I saw it, incredible as it may seem, in one of those manuals about writing. Eschew the semicolon.'

'I have always,' Guinan said, 'eschewed semicolons. My mother told me so. Never speak, she said, to strangers or semicolons.'

Lagan said: 'I spem a change of cameratas now the Ignatian ordeal is over.' To spem meant, if you knew your elementary Latin grammar, to hope for or to forecast. It was a word in the vocabulary peculiar to the sequestered life of the holy house.

'Pray God,' Begley said. 'I hate the place I'm in. There's a hole in the floor beside my bed. I'm always waiting for a rat to pop up his head.'

'Brother Begley,' Barnes twittered. 'A most mortified man and afeard of rats.' From mess of four to mess of four, all along the long long table the words ran on. 'I want no change of cameratas,' said Madden, the Galway man. 'There's a radiator in my cubicle I can tap for hot water when I want to shave,' Petit said: 'Semper, Brother. Semper deo gratias.'

'Semper my foot. You wait, Petit, till you've a man's beard. That'll try your virtue.' Madden had a chin like that of a Gascoigne braggart.

Donnelly was teaching MacKenna, whose back after the long Easter walk was hurting him, the words of the Irish hymn to Saint Brigid, the nun of the oak grees, the sun goddess, some said, the nun of Kildare.

> *Help us bright Mother, be always listening to us;*
> *O holy Brigid, spouse of Christ,*
> *like the seagull on the wave.*

The words, said Donnelly, were done by Doctor Douglas Hyde. Head close to MacKenna's head, defying the rattle and clash of table utensils, Donnelly hummed the music and thought lasciviously of the harmonium.

The Magnov was telling the Jesuit Father and also Father Robert that the villa excursion, the one occasion in the year on which the novices boarded a bus and travelled a distance from the novitiate, would be to the Cistercian Abbey at Mellross.

'You're not afraid of turning them into Cistercians.'

'Those white habits are seductive.'

'No; I'm not afraid,' the Magnov said. 'I'm not afraid. Times I'd like to be a Cistercian myself. The chant. The silence. The stability.'

'We,' said the Jesuit father, 'will all be Cistercians in heaven. Here and now, somebody has to work.' The three priests laughed. Two of them knew that the third didn't mean what he said. The Jesuits and the Cistercians were great friends, were brothers. So were the Jesuits and the Dominicans in spite of their different angles on Aquinas. But brothers could enjoy a joke about each other, could have their friendly rivalries.

'Did you hear the joke,' Father Robert wheezed, 'about the Jesuit, the Dominican and the Franciscan arriving together at the gates of heaven?'

They had heard it. But they listened patiently and laughed holily. Father Robert was a saintly soul and God was risen, alleluia, and the Easter sun, now smothered by the grapery trees, would rise again tomorrow morning and make another day in which to serve God.

FIVE: VILLA

I

'I'll be there with you soon,' Frankie wrote. 'See and have the band out, or at least have the novitiate choir ready to sing the ecce sacerdos magnus, or whatever you sing for distinguished visitors.' MacKenna and his brothers stood silent in dark rows in the conference room and waited for the Magnov to come. It was the time of the day for reading letters, if you had any to read. Barragry snatched the moment to read a few lines out of his favourite volume of Vonier. Petit had a letter from his mother, but for mortification he had postponed the opening of the envelope and instead read, lips quietly moving, out of the novitiate book of rules and customs: ours shall and ours shall not. Donnelly had enough letters in his fist and in the pockets of his gown to do credit to a film star. A touch of some skin ailment had spared him for a week from the thrall and boredom of shaving, and his solid, swarthy chin was black with soft stubble that undulated when he smiled like delicate shrubbery in a summer wind.

The summer too, was warm around and inside the house. Even the chill stone corridor by the boot-room and the baths felt the influence of mellow lights and currents of air perfumed in ripe hayfields. The sun was bright on grass, trees, on ranked flowers in full flowerbeds, on the arm of the lake glittering in the distance; the windows of the conference room were wide open; the villa was due to begin tomorrow. In the long bright evenings when the novices had gone, not too willingly, to bed, they could lie and listen, with varying degrees of restlessness, to the perpetual moan of the doves in the grapery. If your mind wasn't grappled to the matter for your morning meditation, you might even remember shadowy country roads, calls of young people alive in the warm evening world, sunset on old roofs and steeples.

'Met your old man yesterday,' Frankie wrote. 'He's in the pink and your mother's fine too, but she still doesn't feel able to face the long train journey. Killyclogher woods are at their best now, and there never was a better season for the trout-fishing. All your old pals out that way miss you very much.' If the Magnov had really gone to the trouble of reading that epistle – he might have had, because the envelope had at least, unlike the envelope around Petit's letter from his mother, been opened – he could never have understood that trout-fishing meant Delia and Frankie rolling on warm Killyclogher grass. Smiling to himself, the Magnov never opened Petit's envelopes. Why deny Petit the pleasure of mortifying himself by carrying his letters about for days unread?

But Frankie was a daft devil to write things like that to somebody in a religious house. MacKenna permitted himself a twinge of annoyance, then had scruples because he might be adopting a pharisaical attitude towards a friend who, living by the ways and lights of the world, might yet be closer to God than any novice in the room. Then in holy horror he read the next bit of the letter:

'Jinny Campbell has gone away to Liverpool to the same sort of job her sister, Mary, got two years ago.'

Thanks and praises be to the holy father founder the Magnov didn't know the left-handed extra-marital story of the gay sad girls referred to. Mary Campbell, finding herself with a baby and with no father to account for it, had slipped off to Liverpool for more privacy than her own small town would afford. Now her sister Jinny had followed her unfortunate footsteps. Some families were like that. MacKenna had once kissed Jinny. The sun outside was a furnace. What would Petit say if he knew? Under his breath MacKenna aspirated: 'Sacred Heart of Jesus, in Thee I trust.' If Frankie's letter was as bad as this, then to have a visit from him would be positively to leap into the jaws of death, into the dangerous occasions of sin. Yet Father Master always pointed out that visits from relatives and externs, like the letters written to them, were not for the benefits of the novices, but for the edification of the relatives and externs. If he felt worried about what Frankie might say, he could always take another novice with him as a socius; and for healthy religious exercise they could row a boat on the lake, around the wooded priest's island, around Lagan's monstrous barge, launched, with difficulty, yesterday, past the jetty with its crooked overhanging oak, along the far shore where dry resinous regularly-planted woods gave way gradually to deep tussocky trackless bog. Frankie would love the place. His talk would be all about botany.

The Magnov's shoes creaked across main hall, along the dark book-lined passage. From far away in the world, Killyclogher woods behind him, the burn brawling down from the mountains, Delia blonde and lissom on the grass, Frankie fired his last shot: 'Brother Higgins asks to be remembered in your prayers. He's as fond of his tea as ever and he still goes walking on the railway line. The Belfast express nearly did him in some time ago. Snifter Hannigan, like his father before him, has joined the British Army. See you soon, D.V., your old pal, Frankie.'

Kneeling, facing the harmonium, around which Donnelly and his choir practised, the Magnov prayed: 'Come, O Holy Ghost, fill the hearts of the faithful.' Behind him the novices knelt and prayed that the Holy Ghost would be with them for the holidays, that he would bless their rising up and lying down, the lake water they would swim in, and fish in, and row on, the courts, orange and green, they would play tennis and croquet on, the bus that would take them south to Mellross to visit the chanting Cistercians, the special holiday books they would read, books more profane than Vonier Pourrat, Rodriguez, Scaramelli, Père Plus, Father Peter Gallwey, or Mother Saint Paul, books, in fact, by Chesterton, Belloc, Arnold Lunn, Ronald Knox and Monsignor Fulton Sheen.

'For nearly a year, dear brothers,' the Magnov said, 'you've lived a life of great concentration. I'm talking now mainly to the first-year novices, not to those second-year veterans in virtue whose good example sustains us all.' At that expense of the second year, the first year laughed. 'You've lived a life of prayer, meditation, spiritual reading, manual work, regular examination of conscience. Following a regular pattern all the time as very few of us, except I'm told, American millionaires, ever do in the world. None of us are every likely to be millionaires ....' Second and first year laughed together.

'Or saints, dear brothers. Millionaires seem to live on charcoal pills and saints don't go in much for luxurious feeding. Father John Sullivan used to feast on crusts out of the ashbin. Didn't Francis Thompson say that Saint Ignatius was one of the world's great dyspeptics? I know a most estimable father in our English province who lives almost entirely on his pipe. No stomach to speak of.'

Petit, a born chronic taker of notes, was scribbling something in his little brown book. Under gently-drooping eyebrows the Magnov favoured him with an understanding smile. 'But I'm rambling, brothers. What I did mean to say was that now we're about to get our first little period of relaxation. We should be careful not to run wild, not to kick over the traces altogether. We have our holidays here in community and it has been said that we lose in that way by not getting any change of air or scene. But on the other hand I think it has proved that a holiday like this cements the sense of community life that's so important for our work. For the next few weeks we won't hear so mnay bells, but we should pay attention to the bells we do hear, and try to avoid unpunctuality. On villa you'll find that the strain comes in being in time for lunch or dinner. It's easy enough being in time for meditation when we haven't our own rooms and the force of example is pushing us on. At least we're safeguarded from the temptation a good religious I know succumbed to later on in life when he had his own room. He leaped out of bed to answer the caller's benedicamus domino and then leaped back again to slumber away the hour of mental prayer. He also possessed two pairs of black silk pyjamas presented to him by a convent of nuns, the dear women. He reformed, though, you'll be glad to hear.'

Guinan was clearly glad to hear. The thought of those black silk pyjamas had set him off into an uncontrollable fit of the titters.

'Make your examen of conscience regularly,' the Magnov said. 'Don't be late for meals. Enjoy yourselves. Only remember, on holiday or not, you're still learning to be members of a religious community. Say your beads. Help your brothers to enjoy themselves. Keep the silence when it should be kept. Don't scamp the preparing of the points for morning meditation. I know I sound like Polonius to

Laertes, dear brothers. Enjoy the sun and the fresh air, and God's delightful birds. Brother Guinan will help you all there.'

Tears running down from under his thick-lensed spectacles, Brother Guinan, with an effort that strained his ribs, ceased his hysterical tittering. Black pyjamas, eh, black pyjamas, and let us bless the Lord and thanks be to God and back to bed to meditate. Hermits, as Wordsworth said, are contented with their cells. Bravely Guinan responded to his Master's gentle rebuke, bravely returned his smile.

'Enjoy the trees, the lake, the boats,' the Magnov said, 'the swimming, croquet, tennis and so on. You're all young and active. And don't forget the Queen Mary now on her maiden voyage towards the far bog. Brother Lagan has designed a unique ship.'

The whole house laughed. Gratefully Guinan relaxed his tense ribs and laughed with them. How much sweeter it was to laugh in community, to be gregarious, than to titter, like a hermit, alone. But oh, black pyjamas on a pious monk and the villa coming and the great red box of the Queen Mary rocking, if anything so clumsy could be said to rock, above the crawling watercress on the lake water. Lagan had moored her on the far shore, mooring ropes twisted around a grey broken-nosed stone statue of Diana. Oh! who in days of sin had wickedly broken the nose of the queen and huntress chaste and fair?

Past her broken nose, over the bulky Queen Mary, over the lake, Diana disdainfully stared to where, tangled in bushes at the clochar's foot, Actaeon forever struggled helplessly against the fell and cruel hounds of his desires.

Shepherd and sheep knelt again and prayed the Holy Ghost to bless their joy. In the pocket of his gown Guinan had a book about birds specially loaned to him by the Magnov for the villa. It had everything you wanted to know. It had glossy coloured pictures of every bird described. It was a beauty.

II

The conference room became something like a club-room. On the long yellow blistered tables holiday books, even magazines, were scattered in a way that Barragry said was almost symbolic of dissipation. 'Next thing we know we'll be taking *The News of the World.*' Brazenly beside the solemn ancient wheezy harmonium stood a glossy frivolous piano, almost like a woman breaking the rules of clausura, venturing hussylike into the penetralia of a building reserved for chaste meditating males. On wet days – and as it happened there were a few wet days – Donnelly sat down beside her brazen ladyship, and, while the mournful harmonium stared him reproachfully, seeing in him a brand gone back to the burning, he fingered lively ragtime and led his brothers in profane, but not irreverent song.

'Brother, have you read Chesterton's *The Resurrection of Rome.*' That was Petit. Donnelly strummed the melody of 'Home on the Range': Sadleir aped Bing Crosby.

'The Jesuits are doing wonderful work in China.'

'Yes, I read that in their magazine, *The Rock.* Some very interesting articles.'

'They say one of their big men is friendly with Madame Chiang Kai-shek.'

'Trust the Jesuits.'

'Did you read the pamphlet, *Those Terrible Jesuits*, by Father Daniel Lord?'

'They can afford to laugh at the accusations that are made against them.'

'If they weren't doing great work those accusations wouldn't be made.'

Donnelly strummed the music of 'Marching through Georgia.' 'Reach me *A Bonfire of Weeds,*' said Sadleir, 'by J.B. Morton. Dr Strabismus (whom God preserve!) of Utrecht. It's a funny book. I'm on my holidays.'

On sunny days the grassy slope around the ambulacrum was littered with drying togs and towels. 'The place is like a cheap seaside resort.'

'But we've no bathing beauties.'

'Except Petit.'

'Or the Abbot Lagan. He'd sweep all before him at Folkestone. Diana Dors wouldn't have a chance.' For a shimmering second a long-haired girl, cool in a bikini, but hot as a harpy, swooped down between high trees to hover over holy grass. Florentius, the evil Subiaco sub-deacon, seeing that not even with poisoned loaves could he kill the body of the holy Benedict, laboured what he could to destroy the souls of his disciples; and for that purpose he sent into the yard of the Abbey seven naked young women, which did there take hands together, play and dance a long time before them, to the end that by this means they might inflame their minds to sinful lust. 'Semper, Brother, Semper,' Begley said to Guinan, who had compared Lagan to Diana Dors. But flat on his back on the grass under the great translucent beech trees by the Lourdes grotto Barragry laughed at Guinan and Begley and welcomed the sylph-like vision of Dors, the beauty queen, as an ease for strained nerves. Hadn't Barney below in the basement a snapshot of a girl tailor-squatting on the sands at Kilkee?

'I was once a judge at a beauty show,' he said, and God's truth he had once sat in the seat of judgement in a ballroom where the air was gritty with the influence of inferior perfume. With his memories of that event he set the crew laughing until Guinan forgot his momentary annoyance with Begley's prompt reproof. Six shy girls, awkward on high heels, spavindy poor girls, not one of them could walk like a queen, hobbling around the waxed floor, the cynosure of many mocking eyes, each girl holding in her hand a numbered card.

Then Barragry harshly hushed the laughter: 'But, brothers, it was degrading. Those poor silly girls. And the whole thing was just to push the sales of some inferior cosmetic. They walked round and round like cattle at a show. You'd see better slushing down the North Circular Road on the way from the cattle-market to the quays. They must have been exceptionally humble. To be esteemed as cattle for the sake of somebody's face powder. They couldn't have looked less like haughty beauties. They were hoping for something.' The prize-winner had gone to Hollywood for a screen test and had come unpublicised home and the newspapers knew her no more. A month after the contest the pouting blonde who had come third had been killed in a drunken car crash.

The brothers grouped around Barragry were embarassedly silent. In a raspy way he could turn the tables on you as neatly as Father Master. The white back of the grotto Virgin shone between the boles of the beeches. Then Donnelly, quickest to recover, said: 'The judgement of Paris was nothing to the judgement of Barragry. He's just admitted he wouldn't know the difference between a cow and a beauty queen.' Pretentiousness, sententiousness were blunted against honest Donnelly. Above their laughter the brothers heard Lacy and Furlong calling them from the tennis courts. They saw Barnes and Hanlon, mallets on shoulders, moving towards the grapery and the croquet lawn by the walnut tree.

'Barnes looks happier with a croquet mallet than with a mattock.'

'Hanlon will kill him. Hanlon is a croquet demon.'

In the world, Barragry had been a good man with a racquet. Lacy, tall, with magnificent agility and reach, had been a schools champion player, and together they tussled on the courts while brotherly voices, studiously and mockingly edifying, twitted them with vainglory.

'The corruptible crown.'

'Who'd have thought the old man had so much bounce in him.'

'Fifteen love. Thirty all. Deuce. Your van. My van.'

'You won't find those words in Rodriguez.'

'Nor in the venerable Cassian.'

'Did Mother Saint Paul play tennis?'

'Mother Janet Erskine Stuart rode to hounds.'

'When she was a Stuart. Not when she was a nun.'

Hanlon was a demon at croquet, cheating like any criminal, ready at the twist of a ball to lose his cherubic smile, to fly into a temper, expostulate, relapsing into an Ulster accent as broad as the spreading River Foyle. 'The villa, I spem,' Flynn said, 'will wreck the spiritual life of Hanlon.'

'When all other wiles failed, and tempter lured him to destruction because of his inordinate lust for triumph at croquet.' And one day when the grapery trees were motionless in the bright heat, the birds hushed to occasional lazy chirpings, Hanlon swung his croquet mallet as Kelly would swing a slasher or a hurling stick, sent the ball soaring from the lawn to burst like a shell in the wasp's nest under the walnut tree. Brothers, gownless, coatless, Madden with his sleeves rolled up to display brawny, hairy, most unspiritual arms, fled like savages laughing in some jungle sport. It didn't matter about coats, gowns or sleeves, for even the rules of modesty had been relaxed and you could sensuously seek ease in the cool lake water by the jetty under the leaning oak. The path to the oak tree and the place where the novices stripped wound around little bays of the lake, cut through dense clumps of glossy sticky azaleas. All around them the deep ranked woods of fir and pine offered tantalising forbidden shade from the heat. Except on walk days, the deep woods were out of bounds. Away from the croquet lawn Hanlon was his own man again, saintly lover of trees, tall, dreamy, head too big for his body, pink-cheeked, saucer eyes blinking short-sightedly over the rims of his spectacles. Sunning between swims on the sloping grass, his brothers twitted him about his passion for mallets. 'His grandfather was a blacksmith.' His grandfather had, as it happened, been a blacksmith brawnily swinging his sledge in a crossroads smithy, within sight of the green rounded glacial hills called the mountains of Pomeroy. Perhaps something ancestral stirred electrically in Hanlon when he swung a mallet, and the green monastic lawn became a dark smithy, shadows crouching away from the red point of the forge, a horse stamping, air scalded with the reek of hot iron. But between the water and the trees no atavisms perturbed him. He said: 'You can almost hear the trees breathing.'

'Imaginative, Hanlon.'

'No; it's true. Listen.'

The novices listened. A wind rustled down the long arcades, shadowed and lined by conifers. The wind rippled under the lake water. Beyond the priest's island oars rattled. 'Under those trees,' Hanlon said, 'the ground's covered with a carpet like dry silk. Only really heavy rain can ever get through there. A fire in there would sweep the country. 'Twould catch the heather too in the bog beyond.'

Donnelly cheerfully suggested: 'Let's put a match to it.'

Clad only in a skirt of a towel he blissfully absorbed the sun. He was the hairiest novice in the holy house. 'Donnelly, the pious pyromaniac.'

'Ye shall be salted with fire,' Donnelly said, addressing himself to the woods.

'The forestry men are panicky about picnickers from the town. They had a fire two years ago.' Hanlon climbed slowly down the ladder into the water. He wore spectacles when he swam. He said: 'Brother MacKenna, I'll race you to the barge.'

Thirty yards from the tip of the rickety jetty the red Queen Mary proudly rode the water. Lagan, builder of ships, had let his imagination loose. The result was a huge oblong box, twenty feet by six and standing four feet above the surface, balancing on no keel, but upon the extent of its own base and on six pointed peninsulas made of planks that projected from that base. The idea was that novices, long bent graips in hands, would crouch on each peninsula, rip up the superfluous watercress, toss it into the hollow of the vessel. Complete with cargo, the monster would be towed and poled to the far bog shore and the retting cress scattered as an offering on the ground around Diana's feet. 'Just as well for Diana that her nose is broken.' The small amount of dredged weed already on board stank noticeably. Swinging up to one of the peninsulas, Hanlon said: 'Reminds me of an iron tonic. That black liquid should be grand for the blood.' He beamed at the viscous pool in the bottom of the barge. The red timber was painfully warm to the touch.

Still puffing and spluttering in the water – Hanlon was a powerful swimmer – MacKenna said: 'We should bottle it and sell it. Made by the monks of Buckfast. After all, our Order has no special wine.' Holding to one of the six wooden projections, he kicked his heels lazily in the water, enjoying natural freedom, remembering swims in the cold deep pool in Killyclogher burn. In the rocky bed of that mountain stream there were springs by the dozen and even on the hottest day in summer the black water had an Arctic ascetic pinch. Here, within sight of the holy house, the water in the lanes between the weeds was lukewarm from its own quietness, from the direct sun, from the surrounding brown heavy bog. The essence of the weeds gave it a faintly greenish tinge as if it were dense with disturbed sediment. Yet it was ease and liberty, it evoked fast-racing water bursting over rocks, it was as unmonastic as a day spent mitching from school. You could never imagine Saint Aloysius doing the trudgeon or the great Saint Teresa, or even the Little Saint Thérèse, frolicking in a bathing suit. Irreverent thoughts, villa or no villa. He crawled on to the barge and sat down beside Hanlon. Voices of brothers drifted to them across the water. Behind them the deep bog, grey Diana its faithful mutilated sentry, fringed too by conifers, not young forestry trees but old gnarled veterans planted by landlord's men, was sultry as Orinoco jungle. Guinan, now dressed, was slowly poling towards them in a flat-bottomed boat.

'Brother Hanlon. I never had such a fine holiday in my life.'

'In the world one never had such good company.'

'It's amazing how the brethren can relax.'

'Relax in the Lord, Brother. Relax in the Lord.' Flat on his back, Hanlon eased himself to the full of his length along the hot red timber of the rim of the barge. He said: 'Even Begley and Petit are new men.'

'The Magnov was right about the villa helping the community spirit.'

'Strikes me the Magnov's always right.'

'O'Brien has permission to set night lines for pike behind the priest's island.'

'The deep side over by the bog must be alive with pike.'

'Later on in other houses the monks go away for villa to seaside place. Or to the west to polish up their Irish.'

'More restful to stay at home.'

'Brother, the Cistercian spirit is creeping in.'

'Just now I'd take the vow of stability like a shot.' They lazed undisturbed in the sun, nostrils now accustomed to the odour of decaying weeds. From the boat Guinan called to them, poled closer, leaped to the barge and slipped, and then it happened. There was a sharp crack and Guinan, wet to the knees, white in the face, was holding up his left hand and saying: 'Look at my thumb.' It was bent sideways at right angles.

'It's broken.'

'Give it to me,' Hanlon said. Guinan, eyes blind with pain, obeyed. Hanlon, the saintly, the croquet fiend, the lover of trees, the blacksmith's grandson, had a curiously commanding way with him, had long strong hands that closed gently, firmly over the injured thumb and pressed until it cracked again, and Guinan cried out through clenched teeth. 'As good as new,' Hanlon said. 'It was only out of joint.'

Guinan, breathing heavily, one tear on his left cheek, waggled his thumb. 'It works. Brother Hanlon, I never knew you were a bonesetter.'

'You never know your brethren until villa time. I never knew Curran could stab fish until this time last year.' There was a chill awkward silence. The sunshine was unreal. The red solid barge was fragile. Curran, dead to this life, would never again in saintly fashion, like the monk in the ballad seeking the fish that had swallowed the philosopher's stone, use his spear in this summery lake.

'Poor Curran.'

'He broke his head.'

'I wonder where he is now.'

'I heard in a letter from the world that he was going as a secular for the French Mission.'

'There's great work to be done in France. They get very few vocations.' Silent on a barge on a lake in the Irish Midlands three innocents thought of faraway France. Then they talked of tomorrow's excursion to Mellross, the great central event of the villa, a journey through the world to another holy house.

Crowded together in a bus and dressed in their long-tailed poorhouse suits, they were driven down the avenue, through the village, across the heath on towards the south. Father Robert, happy as sixteen, came with them. They passed through towns and villages and felt a little shocked with unexpected unfamiliarity at the sight of people walking on pavements, entering or leaving shops, waving from roadside houses. Father Robert came away without his pipe, and they halted in the first town while Sweetman helped him to buy a suitable replacement. 'What does Sweetman know about it?' Sadleir growled. 'Let me in there and I'll sample all the pipes in the shop.'

They saw the tall-towered monastery, solemnly medieval, a startling contrast to the landlord's oblong Doric relic in which they themselves sought God. They saw the white-and-black robed monks – 'mere clerks we are, but we're mobile' – the visitors buying holy objects from the lay brother in the Repository by the main gate. 'Some of them come here to be cured of the drink.'

'The second,' Barragry said, 'was an Almner of the place: His office was the hungry for to feed, and thirsty give to drink; a worke of grace. He feard not once himself to be in need.' He added: 'The monks try to work them gradually off the whiskey.' His brother, with some temporary success, had once tried the cure.

They kissed the Abbot's ring and discussed his exact ecclesiastical status. They knelt in the cool high-roofed monastery church and heard behind a screen the solemn Latin chant. Petit said afterwards: 'Rather slovenly.' They saw monks digging and mowing, bending in the fields and the gardens, and two monks who were plasterers stood high on a scaffold pointing the bricks in the wall of the guesthouse. Their skirts were tucked up, their heads shaven; they wore huge nailed boots. 'At least,' Kelly the slasher said, 'they're doing something. Not just getting nowhere scuffling with a hoe.'

'But the work we do is meant solely as a mortification.' That was Begley.

'It is too.'

They saw the library and the long common dormitory. 'A shocking racket here,' Donnelly said, 'when they're at the discipline.'

'Don't they lambaste each other?'

'Semper, Brother, semper.'

'Relax. You're on villa.'

They discussed the sign language the monks used and the one orange they were allowed to eat on feast days, and the austere facts that they ate no meat and used their tongues only a few times of the year, for half an hour at a time. 'Heloise,' Barragry said, 'wrote that we shouldn't aspire to be more than Christians. What does meat matter one way or the other?'

'Heloise was a lively girl.'

'You won't find her in the ad usum.'

'She wasn't a patch on Mother Saint Paul.'

'Or Mother Mary Lie Over.'

'Anyway, the monks are as tough as nails living on nuts and greens.'

'Like Bernard Shaw.'

Sweetman, who had a Cistercian cousin, was allowed to visit him, and in their brief talk the cousin said that he didn't really care if he never spoke again. Over lunch the voluble Barnes marvelled at the news.

'How on earth do they stand it? All the time.'

'Lose power of their tongues after a while,' Guinan solemnly assured him.

'The muscles in there decay.' He indicated the exact muscles.

'Not really, Brother Guinan.' This would go out in the next letter to the old ladies among the magazines and the glass-cased chiming clocks.

'On my solemn word, Barnes.' Behind thick lenses, Guinan's eyes were dark, assuring circles. 'There's a surgeon in Dublin made a stack cutting dead tongue muscles out of Cistercians. They use them for shoe-laces.'

Kelly said: 'There's one in Limerick that cuts the feet off nuns. Did you ever notice nuns have no feet?'

To his mess of four, Barragry told how once for the press he had visited a new monastery when the monks, with bell, book, candle and chanted prayer, were electing their first abbot. Through the room where the pressmen sat at lunch a procession of shaven supplicating singers swung backwards and forwards with metronomical regularity. Like clockwork figures the respectful visitors stood up, sat down, stood up, sat down, lunch cooling on the table, until finally one seasoned trouper said, 'Oh, Damn the crooners,' and went on sitting and eating. Barragry's listeners laughed. The word, as it happened, had not been 'damn'.

Then once again they listened to the chanting of the hours and Father Robert, puffing like a chimney, led Hanlon and Sweetman into some part of the monastery where they shouldn't have been. They were led out again by the smiling Sub-prior, who stayed with them until the bus was ready and the engine purring.

Dusk blurred the outlines of house and hedge. In a village by a quiet stream a fisherman cast his fly. While the bus was stopped for petrol, they could hear the tick of the reel, distant shouts of playing children, the barking of dogs. In a roadside pub a woman lighted an oil lamp and as the bus swept past they heard one burst of boozy singing. The world, it's work done, was settling down to everything, from domesticity to devilry. Guinan it was that commenced the yawning.

'Never so gloriously tired. It was a whale of a day.'

Father Robert, recalled to his college days, sang in a quavering voice, and to the Magnov's saintly embarrassment: 'This is the end of a perfect day.' Donnelly had the giggles.

The lights were up in the towns. When they passed a well-known commercial hotel Barragry had an insane wish to stop the bus, to rush into the girl at the bar and say: Do you remember me? Certainly Mr Barragry. It's so long since we've seen you. What'll it be? She couldn't call him Brother Barragry. To his horror, he found there was sweat on his face and his nails were dug into his palms. Beside him Guinan yawned and stretched luxuriously, and said: 'Saw a queer stonechat today at the back of the monastery.'

They had seen towns and main road traffic and girls in bright summer frocks. Fleetingly they had revisited the world. They had talked with monks and the bus driver. From his white gate Father Robert waved goodbye. Under the trees the avenue was in deep darkness. They were at home again. What'll it be, Mr Barragry? What'll it be? Though thy sins be as scarlet, you'd feel better after a large whiskey. Vonier's repentant Christian shouldn't want a woman, shouldn't see tantalising visions of amber liquid in delicate glasses.

The holy house was there as they left it. Nothing had changed. The villa would continue tomorrow. The last prayers were said. The white curtains were drawn. Silence returned. Mournfully the world called to them in the whistle of a train passing east away beyond the dry silky woods.

III

'I went out with him yesterday in his boat,' little Eddy said, 'after mackerel.'

Beauchamp said: 'We enjoyed an excellent day's fishing.'

'Fishing. Fishing. It was unholy slaughter.' Little Eddy was Beauchamp's closest friend, the short, excitable necessary contrast to all that languid length. He had russet curly hair; and bushy eyebrows and a small moustache that were lighter by a shade. 'We had the good fortune,' Beauchamp said, 'to fill the bag.'

'He filled the boat. We met a shoal or a school or something. In with the hook. Out with the fish. Smack its skull on the gunwale. Throw it on the pile. Blood and guts all over the place. Half-dead fish flapping all around us. We were up to the arse in mackerel. He wouldn't stop. It was brutal. There should be a society to prevent the like.'

She said: 'The Miraculous Society for the Prevention of Cruelty to Mackerel.'

Leaning forward from the back seat of the car little Eddy spluttered between the head of Barragry's woman and Beauchamp's lean right jaw: 'One hundred and forty-seven bloody mackerel. Bloody was right.' She had curious arrangements of freckles around the corners of her eyes.

'One hundred and forty-six,' Beauchamp said, 'and one whiting.'

'You should have seen the glint in his eye as he butchered them. He put them in a sack, like turf. Seven little girls on the quayside said: Give us a fish, mister, and he gave them one each. Generosity, how are you? He could have fed the poor of Dublin for a week. He could have founded a fishmeal factory and given employment to hundreds.'

'My revered mother has a distinct fondness for mackerel.'

'Surely to Christ she didn't eat the whole one hundred and thirty-nine.'

'My mother has unsuspected capacity.' Above their laughter at the image of a most respectable suburban lady displaying her capacity before a mound of mackerel, topped by one solitary whiting, the girl said: 'There's the last of the city.' A filling station, a half-built hospital drooped away behind them and the south road under sunshine beckoned them ahead. At Red Cow Inn they drank their first drink and their second at Roche's of Rathcoole, and in the quiet bars the drinks took exceptional savour, a taste of summer morning coolness, of a day or two rescued from routine. 'Barr's at his orisons now. I'm sure he'd love a jar.' She sipped sherry and said nothing. A passing motorist in for a quick one eyed her with appreciation and thought, because he was a horsy man from the Curragh, in terms of long-legged thoroughbred bay mares and wondered where she picked up the two queers: the tall one with the accent, the short one with the splutter and the moustache. Those tall calm beauties often picked their friends like that: used them as a bodyguard. He finished his drink and left. Little Eddy gave a coin to the juke-box, and obediently the bearded Burl Ives sang about the Idaho State Fair.

In Naas of the Kings they had their third and fourth drinks, their fifth in Newbridge, and their sixth by the round tower of Kildare. 'Beau,' she said, 'where do you put it? All those pints?'

'But, they're delicious, so refreshing, such a steadying influence.' A blob of black porter had stained his radiant white shirt.

'They satisfy his blood lust when he's not slaughtering harmless fish.'

'I suppose, Beau, one hundred and thirty-nine mackerel would give you a thirst.' The six small pale sherries had misted her eyes. It was too early in the day and she wasn't much used to drinking any more. The champagne age was dead and done with, and once you had looked with Barragry on the stuff when it was bubbling there was no pop in drinking with anyone else, man or woman. Today, though, should be different because Beau and Eddy were – weren't they? – good news, they had known Barragry so well, they were all going to the country where he was still alive, and the road ahead to that place went now easily downhill to a wide, wooded, well-rivered plain. Oh Beau, drive faster, drive faster. Eddy, with no driver's responsibility, with six small whiskeys under his belt, slumped back in the seat and began to sing. Wine mist in her eyes tinted bogs, trees and flat fields with something of the radiance of the Spain the wine had come from. But five miles further on the warmth had gone and the mist, and with naked miserable clarity she knew: just the country where he exists, not where he's still alive. We'll see nothing today but an imprisoning house, a block of stone as expressive as a tomb where young men study to die to life. They try to twist their characters all the one way so that, until the day when the clay is mercifully shovelled over them, they'll be like stunted sapless bushes blown and bent one way by a sea-wind. I might as well get tipsy tonight. It's the custom of the country to come home drunk from a funeral.

'Some nob lives in this town,' Eddy said, 'in that big house by the river.'

'He is, I'm told on the very best authority, an author of best sellers. While I myself am not acquainted with any of his notable works, they are the favourite relaxation of my good mother. Our friend Barragry once interviewed him on behalf of the curious readers of a newspaper.'

'I don't remember,' she said.

'O woman stately as the swan, that was before your time.'

'Oh,' she said. There had been a time before her time, before champagne, before the bloodstain on the wallpaper, before the trip to London. The present, this quiet town, the red-leaded farm carts, the unshapely monument in the square, the holy mausoleum in the woods ahead, were all after her time. One hand on her shoulder, one hand on Beauchamp's shoulder, Little Eddy hoisted himself: 'Shall we have a drink here, Beau?'

'And, Edward, why not? It's your round. Just one drink, and for the driver a modest soothing pint of plain porter.' So they drank in a cave of a room at the back of a tottering house. To get to that room they walked through a shop with bacon to one hand and boots to the other. In the shadows Beauchamp groped for his black pint and said suddenly, soberly, seriously:

'Will you go to see him when you get there?'

'No.'

'Please yourself. It's not impossible.'

'What's the use?'

'You might shake him back to sanity.' Eddy, embarrassed, walked deeper into the shadows and down an echoing flight of wooden steps to relieve his feelings and his kidneys in a back-yard thronged with greyhounds. Beau said: 'Excuse me. It's not my business, I know. I may seem like a devil's advocate, being a Catholic and all that. But Barragry should not be there. He has as much vocation for the religious life as I have. He never had. He never will have.'

'How do you know? He went, didn't he? He's there isn't he?'

'I know. I've seen holy people. My dear mother's holy. Incidentally, she didn't eat the mackerel. She hates fish. I ate thirty. She cooked them. I gave one hundred and nine mackerel away to various fish-loving friends of mine.'

She laughed. She said: 'Who ate the whiting?' In the shadows it was possible unseen to wipe tears from her face.

'I've known people like Barragry who'd cut off their heads for remorse. Vanity. Remorse is nonsense. Help the living and be cheerful about it. God can look after Himself. Remorse is rot.'

'Remorse,' she said. 'What do you know?'

'Nothing. Nothing. Except that I feel if Barragry ever becomes a priest he'll be a bad one. And nobody, not even a heathen like myself, wants a bad priest. The good ones can be bad enough. Some of the good ones don't know how bad they are.' He sucked his pint; its meniscus of white froth shone phosphorescently at his thirsty mouth. He said: 'I'm a wonderful moraliser. I should have been a cleric myself.' Relieved and rebuttoned, Eddy slowly came back with the deliberate stride of a Western gunman entering a hostile saloon. 'A bloody greyhound,' he said, 'nearly bit me where the wound would never have mended.'

'Greyhounds, I'm told,' and Beauchamp, noisily as the last departing bath water, ended his pint, 'are full of hydrophobia, rotten with rabies. He didn't scratch you?'

'It was a she.'

'Oh, I see. She couldn't resist you.'

'Ladies present,' Eddy said. He bit off the end of his whiskey.

'The lady likes it.'

'All ladies should.'

'I mean the talk,' she said. Laughing tipsily, they walked out again between the bacon and the boots. The woman behind the counter, their money safe in her pocket, eyed them with disapproval. It was a relief, though, to turn to talk that was unbalanced a little with bawdy references, blown away to burst like bubbles, meaning nothing, being neither good nor bad, neither dirty nor clean. 'Over the bog road,' Beauchamp said. 'I'll frighten your wits and unsettle your guts.' Perilously they bent and twisted out of the sleepy end of the sleepy town over what Eddy said was the most awkward canal bridge in Ireland, and then the deep bog was before them, brown and purple, vast as savannahs, drowsy under the sun. Far away two men in dark pants and white shirts worked at a turf bank. The unfenced road went high on a causeway above the bog, the bumps on its surface swinging the car this way and that. It was the shortest way to the Huguenot town, but no buses and few cars went that way. There were no houses for a bus to serve, and the woeful surface, the patches where the soft bog had subsided, bringing the road with it, would have deterred any motorist except Beauchamp. Somewhere beyond sobriety, he laughed as he drove and lifted his hands from the wheel and sang in a high falsetto, snatches of 'O sole mio.' The wind, gathering power across the flat bog, roared in at the open windows. Two high white clouds spun like blown bog-cotton across the blue sky. Would he hear about it now if Beau made a mistake and we pitched down that banking, turning over, and over, bursting into flames? No; he wouldn't. They don't even read the newspapers. In a month perhaps a letter might tell him the news and he could pray for my soul and go on forever being vainly remorseful, being, as Beau says, a bad priest. How does Beau know who would or would not make a good priest?

The swaying lurching movement ended. They were back smoothly on the main road. 'It's over there,' Beau said. She saw the white belly of the cooling tower, its wide mouth lazily puffing upwards white clouds of steam. 'No; far to the left of the tower. To the right of the gazebo of a monument on the hill, where the high trees, my dear, stand up above the new plantations.' She saw the high sailing

Californian cedars. 'It's a lovely place over there in the woods,' Beau said. 'Quiet as a cloister. I suppose that's how it should be.' Between solid old grey houses he drove more slowly, to pull up at the door of the town's one hotel. 'Lunch first,' he said, 'and then.'

'To the woods. To the woods,' Eddy said. He hitched up his pants. He said: 'I need another drink. That bog-road was hell. Your round, Beau, the fisherman.'

Frankie was waiting in one of the parlours. Feeling exceptionally sacrosanct in one of the less-frayed gowns worn when visitors were received, MacKenna walked down the stairs, moistened forefinger and forehead at the holy-water font, said briefly in the chapel the prayer to the Holy Ghost: Enkindle in them the fire of thy love. Stepping across the polished floor of the main hall towards the parlours he felt how the wearing of house shoes did to some extent make a ninny out of one, left one at a disadvantage, before more solidly shod externs. He might as well be wearing pyjamas or football togs for some formal dress occasion. Slowly, nervously he opened the parlour door. It was a long way to Killyclogher woods, the fishy football pavilion, the sun-warmed grass of the railway bank, the great angelic boots of Brother Higgins striding from sleeper to sleeper on the Belfast line. Frankie would be changed, would look at him over a dividing wall or between bars. Frankie, in fact, his back to the door, was gazing out of the parlour window at woods and grass, doric columns, stone lions, blue gravel. He turned quickly. He seemed to have grown since – so long ago it seemed – he had left MacKenna at the railway station and had stood in silence, a puzzled, embarrassed member of the farewell party. His skin, never too healthy, seemed more than usually pimpled; but the shambling stoop-shouldered walk hadn't altered, nor the untidiness of the light blond hair, nor the slow grin, given its own peculiar character by a slight cast in the left eye. He said: 'Mac, you look fine. But you should wear a big long pair of rosary beads.'

'We wear them in our pockets.' All shyness went with a handshake and the first words spoken.

'I thought you'd have long beads, trailing down, rattling when you walked, each bead as big as a billiard ball. You know the pair my old aunt had that she got from a Nazareth nun. Gosh, this is a lovely place.'

'Did you have anything to eat?'

'Had a snack at the hotel in the town. A very quiet place except for three people, who got there in a car just as I was leaving.

'Dinner's at four-thirty here. Second table dinner. You can eat in the refectory or here in the parlour.

'I'd like to see the refectory.'

'You can only talk to Brother Barragry and myself. He has special permission to join us.'

'Sounds a bit like jail,' Frankie said cheerfully.

'Oh, no; just rules. The novitiate rules are meant to teach us, train us ....' Then he blushed and Frankie laughed and MacKenna, caught by the infectiousness of Frankie's laughter, heard wind in green woods, saw himself again idling along summery Ulster roads. They descended the stone stairs to the boot-room where the ninnyish house-shoes were discarded. Brother Molloy's voice could be heard echoing along the cool stone-flagged corridor from the distant kitchen; but otherwise the great rectangular house was as quiet as a tomb. The other novices were at the lake or at croquet or tennis. 'No squalling children,' Frankie whispered. 'No radio. No gramophone.' He was a little awed. Barragry waited for them in the courtyard, pacing the hot cobbles, peering through sun-glasses at a page of the Abbot Marmion that he could not find stimulating.

They walked first of all through the farmyard, saw clean byres and piggeries and hens meditating, for higher efficiency, in separate coops; eremitical hens. 'Your mother would be glad to see you looking so well, Mack. She said she'd be here soon to see you. And your brother too. I'll be able to tell her you don't lack fresh eggs.'

'We eat well,' Barragry said. 'Our one carnal consolation. After all, we've given up the world.'

Had Frankie been a novice, he'd never have kept the ne tangas rule, for he waddled rather than walked, bumping again and again against Barragry and MacKenna, or, to emphasis his words, catching

MacKenna by the elbow, resting a hand on his shoulder. MacKenna embarrassingly felt like a sensitive maiden in the neighbourhood of a pawsy man. Yet it was gratifyingly clear that Frankie and Barragry liked each other; and although their might be comic references to Brother Higgins, the stiggins, there could, in Barragry's presence, be no talk of Delia, no jests about the good jobs the Campbell girls had found in Liverpool. First visits, other novices had said, were always a strain, always evoked nostalgic memories of a world abandoned; and ended, when the visitors had gone again through the curtaining woods, in the most abysmal blues. But this was going to be a happy day.

It'll convince Frankie, and myself, that I did do the right thing when I made up my mind to be a priest. When I told him what I intended to do, I remember that Frankie looked as if I had just stunned him with a blow behind the ear.

They walked down the grapery to the boathouse. From the croquet lawn, where Hanlon was vigorously swinging the ancestral sledge, came roars of laughter. 'You all seem to have a fine time here,' Frankie said. 'There must be some wonderful trees and shrubs in this wood.'

'You'd love it, Frankie.'

'And I thought you were astray in the head when you said you were entering.' As a guileless remark from the lips of one fresh from the world, that was passed over in Christly silence. 'Now I think 'tis myself that's astray in the head. Breaking my neck and disembowelling my father's purse doing medicine with a lot of hooligans in Queen's University, Belfast.' He filled his lungs with the air of the grapery. He said: 'This is the place for me.'

'You should enter,' Frankie and Barragry laughed then. They understood each other. 'I'll think it over,' Frankie said. 'There are a few impediments in the way.' For a threatening moment Delia, blonde as the sunshine, peeped laughingly at them from behind a screen of lime leaves; then she was gone, gone, a nymph vanishing in pagan woods. 'Every young man should come here for a while,' Barragry said. 'Like compulsory military service. Teach him to appreciate the world.'

Why did Barragry have to say things like that? Begley or Petit might have been less unsettling companions on a day like today.

'In Thailand now,' Barragry said, 'every devout Buddhist at some time or other does a stretch in a monastery. He shaves his scalp and eyebrows and wears a saffron robe.'

'Brighter than the mourning clothes you fellows wear. As bright as a loyal Orange sash.'

'We're not Orangemen. We're not Buddhists, thank heaven,' MacKenna said; and, thank heaven, they were at the boats and Barragry, who was a good oarsman, would find something else to talk about. They rowed twice around the lake. They saw the stiff, forked sticks on the swan-trodden, swampy edge of the priest's island where O'Brien had set his lines for pike. Broad hooks somewhere in the dark water lacerated the thighs of pleading-eyed frogs. 'If O'Brien was a Buddhist,' Barragry said, 'he wouldn't do that.'

'He'd be afraid that in his next existence he might be a frog.'

'More likely O'Brien'll be a pike, quiet, green, ravenous.' They climbed aboard the Queen Mary and climbed off again more hurriedly, for the stench of retting weeds was strengthening in the heat. 'Ozone,' said Barragry, and Frankie said, 'Like a lint dam,' and told them how a young horse-woman he knew had been thrown when her horse shied at the stink from a muddy dam where flax was retting on its way to become linen. Delia, MacKenna remembered, had been a great girl for riding horses, for parading the town in jodhpurs to cause susurrus and a movement and a craning of necks among the street-corner turtles.

'We'll have to blow up the barge soon,' Barragry said.

'With Lagan, the maker, on board.'

''Blow up with the brig.'

A dozen or so novices were splashing in the water around the jetty. Frankie, the visitor, and his two companions didn't, because they couldn't, join them. But they rowed around and around the lake until the novices had emerged, towelled themselves, clothed themselves and departed for the examen of conscience that preceded first table dinner. Then they rowed in under the overhanging oak to inspect the crazy wooden structure that the workmen of an ancient earl had built. After that they rowed once again around the lake. Great trees leaned out over deep dark water. Lagan's barge had made only a slight impression on the tenacious weeds. The novices on their knees in the holy house were silently scrutinising their consciences and around the one lonely boat the great quiet of bogs and woods came so awesomely that the sounds of voices, the creak of oars were faint, pathetically futile, were mocked both by memories of a worldly past and by the rank stenchy force of green, growing, voracious life.

They walked back to the holy house by way of the football fields. From the yew-lined walk dedicated to Saint Joseph, they looked down the slope at the shining lake. In the holy house a warning bell rang for second table dinner.

'There's somebody down there at the jetty,' Frankie said. He had amazingly sharp eyes. MacKenna could see nothing. 'In the bushes beyond the big oak. I thought I saw something move.'

'It couldn't be one of the brethren. They're all in the house. And externs don't come in there.'

'There are all sorts of notices,' Barragry said, 'saying private and no trespassing. We must keep the world out.'

'Well, you couldn't have trippers all over the place. What would happen to our recollection?'

'Probably forestry people,' Barragry said. But then with better eyes than MacKenna had, he saw three people appear for a moment on the lake shore, and then vanish again into the trees: two men, the flash of a girl's coloured dress. 'Trippers sure enough,' he said. 'Petit told me that one day he saw two cyclists, girls, wearing shorts, out on the blue gravel.'

'They must have lost their way.'

'Perhaps,' Frankie suggested, 'they were interested in architecture.'

Laughing at nothing in particular, they led Frankie into dinner. Frankie bore himself bravely in the silence and listened to the reader with a grave attention that made MacKenna want to giggle; but rather than disedify an extern he made the heroic effort and restrained himself. After dinner they showed Frankie the old tunnel that went most of the way from the kitchen to the walled garden. It had been bored in my Lord's time so that guests would not be disedified by a glimpse of scullions basely wheeling in barrowloads of roots and vegetables. Frankie loved the garden. He talked about gardens and growing things all the way back to the parlour, where they had tea together and a brief visit from the Magnov. On the steps between the two stone lions, while they waited for the V-8 with Brother Molloy at the wheel, they made jokes about Frankie's love of flowers and plants, said that he had already one of the qualifications of the good novice.

Dusk was already darkening the clump of oaks beyond the blue gravel. Homecoming rooks were squabbling above the clochar. They shook hands. MacKenna and Barragry stood talking on the steps until the sound of the car had died away towards the Huguenot town. Then in silence they walked through the house, knelt for a moment in the chapel, went to join their brothers at evening recreation in the ambulacrum. Has he gone back spiritually refreshed, Barragry wondered, has he left MacKenna completely at peace? The cawing rooks were unreal, the visitor from the world, the day on the lake, the trespassing externs, the flash of colour from a girl's dress. Barragry was irritable with unrest.

In the ambulacrum, Madden e'en at the foot of Gonzaga's statue which all the while looked holily upwards at the girded roof, was showing the brethren a ferret the aged Brother Hazlitt had bought to keep the rabbits under control on the farm. 'Brother Hazlitt,' Donnelly said, 'should be lively enough to catch the rabbits without a ferret.' Flynn, to Petit's disgust, said: 'We'll have rabbit now every day for dinner.'

MacKenna didn't know if he had or had not the blues. He kept his mind away from Frankie and his homeward journey. The train would soon whistle away beyond the woods. Thank heaven, anyway, he had no pain in his back.

'I know the way well,' Beauchamp said. 'I've shot ducks and grouse around here.'

In spite of the sobering effect of his lunch, Eddy was still extremely tight. He said: 'God Almighty, do you ever think of anything but killing? Grouse, pheasant, mackerel, even ducks. Poor little bunny rabbits, too, with white tails.'

'They don't call them tails.'

'He keeps a diary of his dreams,' Eddy said. 'Beau, the brutal, keeps a diary of his dreams. I saw a page of it once. I'll quote you a sentence.'

'A man's most innermost thoughts are no longer, my dear, secure from the prying eyes of the world.'

'Just one sentence. Big handwriting in red ink. It said: I am in a corridor killing cats. Now what could that mean?'

'That Beau dreamt the night before that he was in a corridor killing cats.'

'Why cats? Just think of it. In a corridor killing cats.'

'My dear mother was frightened by a cat shortly before my auspicious nativity. It's all in Freud, Edward.'

They left the town by a narrow road that squeezed out of the main street between two high-gabled houses. In the sunshine a high grain-elevator shone like silver. 'It's only a few miles now,' Beau said. She looked dazedly ahead as the car bumped over another high canal bridge and from the momentary elevation, saw brown bogland away ahead to the mysterious edge of the trees. The carping chatter of Beau and Eddy sounded very far distant. 'There's a legend hereabouts,' Beau said, 'concerning the mallards that were tamed by the monks with whom dear Barragry's now an apprentice.'

Somewhere in those woods, Barragry, an apprentice monk, had hidden himself from her.

'Like Eddy, this tender-hearted intoxicated humanitarian, the monks don't shoot ducks. Their lake and the land around it is a bird sanctuary.'

'One up for the monks,' Eddy said.

'Their holy Father Rector makes a stack out of bird photography. Proceeds in aid of the foreign missions to Borneo, to natives who kill each other, not to talk of birds.' The trees closed around them, trees of mature plantation high enough and dense enough to make two warm walls that muffled the noise of the engine, to make a roof that latticed the sunlight.

'But this flight of mallards, you see, were so tame they came when the monks whistled. They were religious duck subject to holy obedience. They'd been trained to eat bits of bread from the hands of holy men who wouldn't know one end of a gun from the other. Two sportsmen in the town behind heard the glad news.' Beauchamp drove slowly through a narrow arched gateway, saluted the woman at the door of the gate-lodge, swerved on to the wide grass margin to make room for a laden haycart. 'So in they sneaked, this way, guns at the ready, the back way into the estate, through the woods to the lake, the way we'll go. They whistle. Down come the ducks. Perched practically on the gun-barrels, I'm assured. Bang, bang, bang, a fine bag and the monastery knew the mallards no more.'

'A tale of horror,' Eddy said, 'and you love it, you ghoul.' In mock agony he covered his face with his hands, and Beauchamp recited: 'From troubles of the world I turn to ducks.' she looked ahead down the narrow dusty switchback road, once a private way through a great man's fields. They noticed her quietness and made no comment, but they laughed and talked more boisterously, not knowing whether they were behaving like wise men or like callow inhuman schoolboys. Then on one side of the road the trees fell away and the neat sunny fields of Brother Hazlitt's farm delighted the eyes. Beyond the fields there were younger woods and above their deep green, high light-green beeches proud on a hilltop. 'Here's the place,' Beauchamp said. He parked the car by a gate and, crossing a stile, they went, Beauchamp in the lead into the trees. 'Look at him,' Eddy said. 'The last of the bloody Mohicans.'

'Deerslayer would be more appropriate, wouldn't it?' She said; and Eddy and Beauchamp, with a false laugh that went eerily away under the branches and rebounded more eerily from tall straight tree-trunks, welcomed her escape from quietness. Pacing behind her, lifting his feet drunkenly over crackling twigs, Eddy said, 'In all the best novels, I'd be supposed to admire the lithe grace of your movements, the easy sway of your buttocks under your ...'

'Skirt,' she said quickly. 'Well, do you?'

'I certainly do.'

'Thank you, Eddy.'

Beauchamp said: 'Thank God I'm here to protect you.'

'You snatched the words from my lips, Pathfinder.' Halted for a moment, his foot resting on a fallen tree-trunk left alone and forgotten to rot with all that new life growing up around it, Eddy was guzzling whiskey from a naggin bottle. 'A day in the country does us all good,' Beauchamp said. 'Eddy loves the fresh air. Pass me the bottle, plainsman.'

'Here y'are, Hawkeye.'

She said: 'With either of you I'd feel safe in the African jungle.'

'Thank you.'

'Thank you.'

'Perhaps, my dear,' Beauchamp said, 'you over-estimate our power of restraint.' He raised his hand for silence. Birds murmured sleepily in the heat, in the deep trees. The sound of their steps was muffled by the droppings of the pines. Beauchamp went forward stepping theatrically on tiptoe, his arms extended like the wings of a huge thin bird. He said: 'Two holy novices told the court that in the course of their after-dinner walk they heard a woman's screams issuing from the woods. They reverently crossed themselves, said the prayer to the Holy Ghost, Veni Sancte Spiritus, tucked up their skirts and ran to the place from whence the sound proceeded. There they observed a young woman being mercilessly ravaged by two men. On the ground beside her recumbent form was an empty naggin bottle which had clearly contained, to judge by the puce fumes still exuding from it, a quantity of enamel polish that Irish publicans, who have all got sons in the priests, sell to unfortunate laymen, under the appearance, not of bread and wine but of whiskey. The two holy novices told the court how they averted their eyes from this immodest scene lest the sight of the young woman in her semi-nude state might come between themselves and their religious vows, not to mention their sleep o' nights. Later they heard that a dead and mutilated ...'

A flutter and crash, thirty yards away in the undergrowth interrupted him. He dropped to his knees, a dead branch rifle-wise to his shoulder. He was a boy again, he was Hawkeye the fearless scout drawing a deadly accurate bead on a pesky fleeing hostile Iroquois

Indian. From each of his jacket pockets protruded the neck of a naggin bottle. 'There he goes,' he said tensely, sternly. He was a frontiersman whispering warning out of the side of his mouth. 'The first of those varmints I've seen this moon. A monkish scout. Swinging his machete. Naked as nature.'

'He has rosary beads for a loincloth,' Eddy said. She giggled idiotically at their antics. She said, 'Oh, stop. It's a bird or a badger or something.' Bending down, she plucked the naggin bottle out of Beauchamp's right hand pocket, uncorked it, tasted with a shudder the neat pungent liquor. 'Girl,' said Eddy, 'doesn't know a bird from a badger.' He tossed an empty bottle away from him. It struck with a thud against the soft pulpy flesh of a decayed lightning-riven oak that stood monstrously white among the new trees. 'Reminds me of my days in Tibet,' Beauchamp said, 'my first visit to the grand Llama. Sentries behind every Himalayan rock.' He strode on past the riven oak, stepped like a stork over a trailing wire fence, crossed a forestry ride, then plunged again into the trees. He had an unerring sense of direction. As she followed she sipped more whiskey, sipped it now with pleasure because the initial shudder was over. Eddy had produced and uncorked yet another naggin bottle. 'If the forestry men saw us,' Beauchamp said, 'they'd arrest us for running the risk of setting the woods on fire.' Eddy shouted: 'Whoopee.' The echo, like rings made by a smooth pebble on calm water, died away, bound by bound in the long aisles under the trees. 'Fire,' Eddy shouted. He tossed handfuls of dry pine-needles over the head, over Beauchamp's head. He was a drunken wedding guest scattering confetti. 'They'd burn like a bloody bonfire,' he said. 'A day in the woods, by God. A day in the woods with a lovely woman. Look at the swaying movements of her what do you call 'em.'

'Shoulder-blades,' she said, and 'Thank you Eddy,' and 'Beau, how do you know where you're going?'

'My nose, my dear. I can smell water.'

'He needs water for his whiskey.'

'Hush,' Beauchamp said. He dropped to his hands and knees, crawled out of sight into the undergrowth. With difficulty they followed. Fallen pine-cones bruised her palms and knees. Eddy, crawling behind her, made snarling noises and pretended to gnaw her unstockinged calves. Deep in the undergrowth Beauchamp stood up and beckoned them to his side. They stood close together. She picked pine needles from her hair. On a level with her breasts, Eddy's hot breath blurred the air with whiskey fumes. 'Look, my lovelies,' Beauchamp said. With strong arms he parted fir branches and they saw the lake. A crazy jetty ran out to a placid blue-green mirror of islanded water. Sloping ground studded with trees went from the far shore. Above tufted branches they saw the square shoulder of an eighteenth-century house. She held the whiskey bottle to her lips; she sipped from it several times and looked into peace and found her eyes misted with tears that she savagely rubbed away, then savagely gulped whiskey until she coughed. Beauchamp patted her shoulder gently. He said: 'I'll scout around to see if we're observed.' Crawling on his belly around an azalea bush, Eddy said: 'I see black men in the distance.'

'Mau Mau, I'll be bound. Or black spots on your drunken eyes.'

'Wait, wait. Keep down now. Mustn't let 'em see us. They're hell altogether for white women.' She stood alone, the curtaining fir branches fallen again to cut her off from the lake of peace. Looking blankly into deep green, she heard Beauchamp and Eddy crawl away from her, as stealthily as left-footed alligators. She finished her naggin bottle, not tasting the whiskey, not coughing, feeling only a dead drugging heat.

'All clear,' Eddy called. 'The Mau Mau are back in the bush.' Behind a clump of azaleas, they found a hidden sunny corner, where Beauchamp and Eddy killed the contents of the last surviving bottle. She felt hot and angry and no longer on the verge of tears; and lying on her stomach, supporting herself on her elbows, she saw the green bright ground gently rocking with an alcoholic rhythm. 'We should send a drop of this up to Barragry, the poor bastard,' Eddy said.

Beauchamp reproved: 'Edward. Language.'

'Oh, sorry, sorry. But just imagine, in there saying your prayers or whipping yourself, or something, on a day like this.'

'My dear Edward. They're not flagellants.'

'They do that. You can't deny it.'

'Their souls benefit thereby. Consider what you do for the sake of your body. Drink, fornicate; and the little benefit you get.'

'I don't fornicate.' Eddy tossed two pine cones from him to drop plop-plop in the still water. Deluded by the sound a dozen silly perch broke the surface. Quietness returned. Beauchamp dozed. The trees were motionless in the heat. Eddy said: 'Jesus, I'd love a swim.' Beauchamp mocked: 'Three hundred days' plenary indulgence. How reverently Edward employs that distinguished name.' She soothed her hot forehead in the grass. Perhaps he had stood here or undressed and dressed in this sheltered spot when he came swimming, and squeezed lake water out of his togs on these blades of grass.

'Ned of the Hill, you can't swim here.'

'Why not?' she said. 'I'll swim.'

'Do you see the notice that says private? Think of the poor monks.' A swing of Eddy's right arm sent a corked empty naggin bottle bobbing far out in the lake. 'I should have written a message for Barragry,' he said, 'and put it into that bottle, saying we were here, but that we heard him at the discipline and couldn't bear to disturb him.'

She said, less to Beauchamp than to the ground that Barragry might have touched, to the entire circling earth on which he and she still lived: 'So if I wanted to swim who's here to see me?'

'Eddy and myself. You haven't even a costume.'

'I've bra and pants, haven't I?'

'My dear, I hope so.'

'They're not as revealing as a Bikini. You can close your eyes, can't you? You can look the other way.' She was more than a little drunk. She was burning with misery, with a desire to plunge into the cool blue-green water, because of a certainty Barragry had been there.

'Out on the lake you could see from the windows of the house. In pants, my dear, and brassière. Think of the monks. Of their somewhat susceptible feelings on the question of unclothed women.'

'I'm thinking of them.' She wanted to beat the ground with her fists, except that, even as a child, she had always been afraid and ashamed of hysteria. 'I'm thinking of them.'

'I declare to me God,' Eddy said, 'if you go in there the way you said the water'll boil, steam, hot geysers, the Yellowstone park, sulphur and brimstone, the Bikini mushroom. That's bloody good, isn't it, Beau? The Bikini mushroom. I mean, you know, Bikini atoll, and then.'

Beauchamp said: 'I know.' He was curiously sober.

'Let it boil. Oh, let it boil,' she said.

'The mallards are dead,' Beauchamp said. 'We shan't even have roast duck out of your experiment and I shudder to think of the rank nature of the fish resident therein.'

'No mackerel,' Eddy said.

When she rose to her feet she was proud that she didn't stagger. With no attempt at concealment, she paced the lakewalk until she found a corner sheltered even from Eddy and Beauchamp. Haven't I as much or more right to swim in those waters as any of the holy men who live under one roof with Barragry? Through the branches of her shelter as she stripped she could see the high Grecian corner of the ancient house. Her fingers, as she undid zips and fasteners, were tingling with mischievous, sacrilegious joy. Eddy and Beauchamp had turned their backs on her and studiously they watched the distant house. Was that modesty or disapproval or just a precaution against the coming of a monk or two upon a sight no monk should witness? A loose plank on the jetty wobbled and rattled under her feet, but Eddy and Beauchamp did not turn to look at her. Not even when they heard the sharp clean splash of her body in the water did they take their eyes away from the holy house. Easily, lazily, luxuriously she swam halfways to the monstrous red barge, and swimming back again she closed her eyes and sensed Barrgary swimming by her side in the sanctified, secluded water.

Afterwards, Beauchamp spoke to her, standing to his full lanky height, tossing to her over green branches an enormous linen handkerchief to use as a towel:

'Enjoy your swim, my dear.'

'The sky didn't crack,' she said. The water had been colder than she expected. She shivered as she squeezed water from the pants and brassière and spread them to dry in the sunshine. She was sober and a little ashamed. 'That handkerchief of mine should be a sort of relic now,' Beauchamp said. 'Holy water wiped from such pleasant places.'

'Beau, you're a blackguard.' She laughed, even though her teeth were chattering. Beauchamp understood why she had done it, and was trying to put her at her ease. Eddy said: 'I want a drink.' They went back through the woods. Diaphanous cloth clung damply to her body. She didn't look again towards the holy house. She had done all she could to level it with her curse. To warm herself, she ran, Eddy and Beauchamp lumbering after her, along a forestry ride.

After dinner they sat in the hotel bar and drank until midnight. When she opened the door of her bedroom her feet were unsteady and her head as full of noises as Prospero's island. She looked out of the window at great trees clearly outlined against the pale darkness of the brief summer night. Thinking of the house now holily asleep in the heart of deep woods, she choked with loneliness. Drink did no good. Defying the sanctity of the place by throwing her body into the water of the private lake did no good. In the next room Eddy and Beauchamp still talked, still drank, too. They'd brought a half-bottle with them from the bar. Why bother any longer? Why any longer torment oneself with memory? Ten to one Barragry had already forgotten, had found his own peace in his own peculiar way. Why continue to preserve what was no longer worth preserving? A wise woman would join the two men in the next room and drink herself stupid, and perhaps, divide between them Barragry's unwanted leavings. Eddy and Beauchamp were laughing now. Her hand was on the knob of her door, but a hardness somewhere in her, a mad unholy hope kept her alone in her room. Couldn't her desires, the warmth of her body, the loneliness crying out from her to the woods and the night, the hot branding mark she had made on the holy lake, prove as strong as any mumbled half-intended prayer? She locked the door, carried the key to the window and flung it into the darkness. It dropped soundlessly on shadowy lawn. She wasn't worried about the inconvenience the loss of the key would cause in the morning. She was a witch in the night tossing a metal charm towards the bed of the man that, against God, she wanted. Beauchamp and Eddy were still talking when she fell asleep. The tinkle of bottle against glass followed her into forgetfulness. She sank down and down to the smooth sandy floor of a crystal lake. Under the bright water Barragry dressed like a Buddhist monk and Beauchamp feathered like a Mohican chief danced around each other in solemn slow motion. Mackerel, large as salmon, went stupidly by in shoals, but Eddy was nowhere to be seen.

IV

The sun had burned Barragry's skin. In the half-darkness of the camerata, white curtains glimmering around him, he lay awake listening to the even breathing of Sweetman, Flynn and Guinan. His cubicle was nearest to the door. He hadn't undressed, and under his shirt his shoulders throbbed painfully with heat absorbed yesterday and the day before, when, after swimming, he'd sunned himself on the grassy edge of the lake. The curse of red hair was that your skin hadn't the oily ability to absorb heat, health and brightness, without afterwards suffering form lobster-red irritation. Oh, I'm restless from the sun. Where are the points that should be in my head, ideas gently, holily sleeping like seeds underground to burst out to flowers and fruit under the blessed fertilising influence of morning meditation?

It so happened that, not for the first time, he hadn't prepared any points. He'd sat, fair enough, for fifteen minutes with a meditation manual on his table, but his thoughts had been all of summer woods, sunshine on grass and leaves, and – he had to admit it to himself – of the distant vanishing flash of a woman's coloured dress. I am poor Brother Lippo by your leave, Browning's errant Lippo hopping over the wall from Spenser's holy house to dissertate to night-watchman at an alley's end where sportive ladies leave their doors ajar. Flower o' the quince, I let Lisa go, and what good's in life since.

When he put his jacket on again he had no fully-developed intention of going out of the holy house. He wasn't a schoolboy any more and playing truant didn't seem fair to Sweetman and company asleep in the Lord nor to the Magnov nor Peesoc still probably praying or reading. But signs and symbols led him on like crooked, devilish, beckoning fingers. The sun, great blazing pagan God, heated skin and blood, set the mind seething; the coloured flash of the nymph on the fringe of the woods did the rest. The pale rectangle of window at one end of the corridor suggested warm summer darkness that was but the dawn of day – how bloody poetic he was feeling – and cool dewy fields, perfumed hedges, silent white byroads, and all the rest of it. Let me out, let me out; what in the name of Jasus am I doing here locked in like a child in the nursery and the pubs not closed yet? No grown man could be expected to sleep in a white bed on such a night as this when Barragry with house-shoes in his hand stealthily tiptoed down stone stairs, along a flagged passage to the boot-room. In the weak light that seeped in through two barred windows – he couldn't switch on the electric light – the place could have been a medieval dungeon. Ghostly coats dangled from hooks. Their owners dreamed of God. Outdoor boots, and did those feet in ancient times, were rowed in iron racks. In the Assisi passage by the stronger light from a glass-panelled door, he studied the walks and recreation tabella. Each holy brother's name was printed on a slip of white paper, the paper was pasted on a small sliding block of wood, the blocks inserted into a slotted notice board. Pull out your name when you go out, push in your name when you come in, was the rule of the house, one small part of holy obedience. Petit, returning from that day's last recreation, had forgotten to restore his name to its proper place. Barragry smiled at the thought that Petit, too, might be out in the night woods speaking rhyming rules of Latin grammar to the boles of the trees. Slowly, in ironic accordance with the holy rule, he pulled out his own name. Fra Lippo Lippi, tempted by lute strings, laughter, whifs of song, slim shapes and upturned faces in the Florentine street below the window of his cell had had to make shreds of curtain, counterpane, coverlet, all the bed furniture, to descend perilously by rope ladder to his night of life. Here there was no such need for acrobatics. The thin door that opened from the far end of the Assisi passage to the sloping lawns at the back of the house wasn't even locked. A paradise for burglars; but why should a burglar wish to break into a holy house unless he'd read what Father

Willy Doyle of the Society of Jesus said about the happiness of the true religious, unless he wanted to steal a holy habit in which to die and go disguised before God?

Three steps from the door he was hidden in the shadow of a line of yews. Saint Bernard never even knew how many windows there were in his monstery chapel. It wasn't likely that any father or brother would be sitting pensive at his casement watching the night. Still, he had to be careful. A sick cow in the farmyard, and, perhaps, the unsleeping ante-diluvian, Brother Hazlitt, perhaps one of the lay servants could be prowling around. From the shelter of the clochar's trees he looked at the farmyard. He sniffed rich odours of bedding and manure. A horse stamped, a cow rattled head-chains, but there was no light, no other sound except the chug-chug of the donkey engine that said to the holy house: let there be light. He went on quietly, walking on the grass margin to avoid crunching gravel, or rolling pebbles. The short grass was wet with dew. Furtive things rustled in the shadows, somewhere a small animal cried shrilly, a bird stirred and squawked on a branch above him. He came to a wooden stile, saw a road ahead dazzlingly white and bright after the darkness of the clochar. One foot on the stile, he stopped to think: suppose when I return the thin door is barred, what then? Attempt a window? A lot to be said, when you think of it, for Lippo's rope-ladder of monastery bed-clothes. I don't want to be locked out, detected in a daft escapade, esteemed a fool for Christ's sake or anybody's sake even for the sake of one free night spent living like a man. I don't want to be drummed out of the holy house, Humilta, the hoary gray door porter – see Spenser – footing me one final one in the seat as I step down between the two stone lions. My mind isn't clear yet. I haven't made my choice. Leaning against the stile, he laughed hysterically at the idea that a religious with a genuine vocation should be out nightroving like a college boy looking for girls.

He didn't, now that he was at liberty with a free foot and a fellow for it, know where to go. But the road was invitingly ahead, must somewhere touch on life, externs, some fragment of the world. The night was young. He walked on, cheerfully kicking up the white dust. The woods fell back a step. The night stirrings of the furred and feathered creatures were friendly fairytale sounds. This was the way a man should meditate, walking on his own in the darkness not perched uncomfortably on a prie-dieu in a room, yclept camerata, with pious beardless boys disturbingly breathing all around him.

With the tense delight of a hunter he watched for the signs the world would give him that it was still alive. Half a mile from the holy house he came to the building where the forestry men lived. It was grey and square like a piece of poor law architecture sullen in ugliness at the end of a provincial town. It was gloomy and forbidding except for one lighted uncurtained window that shone across the narrow road. Even without approaching he could see into a room, bare as a dayroom in a police barracks, where four men sat card-playing. A fifth man, heavily built and gum-booted, stood shaving at a mirror above the mantlepiece. He walked on. No use in standing like a ghost looking enviously at men still alive. You couldn't stamp in from some place beyond the world, and, without a red cent in your pocket, offer to take a hand in their game. The trees, a taller older growth now, crushed in again around him. The thickening darkness matched his mood of depression. A young couple passed him, bundled together on one lampless bicycle. The man spoke to him. Country people were friendly. The girl was laughing. The music of her light happy voice died away into the trees. A hundred yards ahead the bicycle was abandoned by the roadside. A high humped railway bridge lifted him up out of the stifling woods and he saw the lights and the bulked irregular silhouette of the Huguenot town. Behind him in the velvety darkness of the wood, the couple who had abandoned the bicycles were now, possibly, at their ease on the deep pine needles.

Leaning on the cool stone parapet of the bridge, he watched the town. It was alive. It was a challenge and a threat. He was a little afraid of it. It was one thing to cycle through a town with Matthews, Lagan and the Magnov, or to go in a bus, surrounded and buttressed by holy brothers and the security of community life. It was another thing altogether to walk into a town alone, by night, playing truant. What could he do in there? Whom could he talk to? He was a stranger, a vagrant, a pauper, a ghost. For half an hour he lost the power of movement. The woods were dead. The interminable railway tracks were dead. Then a man carrying out a white enamelled bucket stepped out from a cottage half hidden in bushes at the foot of the slope below the bridge. He filled the bucket at a roadside pump. In the quiet night the splash of water might have been a torrent, the creak of the bucket's iron handle the scream of machinery. For a while the man stood by the pump whistling and calling for a dog that didn't, as far as Barragry could see, respond to him. Then casually he urinated into the ditch, untroubled by any communal rule of modesty: ours shall not. Barragry wanted to join him, to stand beside him relieving the bladder every bit as casually, and chatting sideways over the shoulder about the affairs of the country and the world: coursings, wars, tractors, football matches, film actresses, local instances of assault and battery, the iniquities of priest or publican. Holy Anthony himself was no more strongly assailed by visions of the Queen of Sheba, her vesture of gold brocade divided by flounces worked in pearls and jets and sapphires and clinging like a sheath to her Marilyn Monroe body, than Barragry was then tempted and shaken back to life by that vision of easy, earthy companionship.

He moved towards the man, too late. He heard heavy boots crunching away from him, heard one last whistle and one last call for the wandering dog, then the chill iron finality of a clicking latch. He couldn't knock at the door of the cottage and say to the man: Look, I'm a monk out for the night. I saw you pissing on the side of the road and I thought it would be a change from cenobitical conversation to chat with you about greyhounds or the Fordson tractor. My name is Barragry, and I come from Dublin. I'm one of the better sort of people, even if in the world I did work for a newspaper. I meditate regularly and use the discipline twice a week, perfunctorily, and, odd as it may seem, I was some time since smitten with a vague idea of becoming a priest. I take size sixteen and a half in collars and I abandoned a mistress to the tender mercies of the world. Now, tell me about yourself, and would you have a bottle of stout in the house or a drop of malt itself, barley blood of the gods? Being holy is thirsty work.

Automatically he passed the cottage and walked on towards the town, depressed for a moment with the sense of his isolation. For one night he was a refugee in a strange country. But with every step his spirits revived. He had been in towns before. He wore an ordinary unclerical shabby suit. Nobody could guess that he was a truant aspirant to the altar of God. He hadn't a halo round his head. When he came to the town's first low white cottages he was walking rapidly and in high good humour. The night air, he decided, sniffing like a connisseur, was lively as wine. Back now in the cameratas in the holy stillness the atmosphere would be unpleasantly warm. In spite of what they said about the odour of sanctity, the bodies of the just confined five or six together in one room on a warm night affected the air much as the bodies of worldlings did.

A puff of dishwater stench from a slimy vennel perturbed him momentarily. He pressed on. Children still played on the rugged ill-lighted side street. From three open doorways he heard the same radio programme, recognised the annoucner's fruity voice. He was childishly amazed to realise that the night was much younger in the world than it was behind him in the holy house in the woods. That was one of the things you forgot when immured in your desert cave: the world lived late, lay late in the morning, seldom meditated, laughed and suffered with more abandon, had the recklessness about its own affairs that should really characterise the children of light.

Seven cars were parked outside the town's one hotel. The bar windows were still lighted, the door still hospitably and legally open for the passing stranger. His tongue was dry with thirst. But he couldn't risk the hotel bar because you never know what old friend might be travelling that way and stopping to drink there. Moreover, he hadn't a penny in his pocket. Holy poverty. It'd be easier to manage a free drink in an honest tavern. Tonight he'd be a genuine scrounging mendicant friar, battening as a Barragry had hitherto never battened, not a phoney mendicant as he had been when he'd walked to Donohill to listen to Donnelly telling the paupers to rejoice in the Lord. A stray dog sniffed at his heels, then abandoned him contemptously. Loungers at a corner didn't even turn from their talk to look after him. Three girls passed scattering chatter and laughter to the night, and the odour of cheap perfume; drawing whistles, cluck-clucking noises from the loungers. He walked the length of the town and back again, read the posters outside a cinema and felt that he had defaced every image in the chapel. He stood by a lighted shop window where bicycles, radio sets, prams, gramophones, were mingled in magnificent confusion. There was a public-house across the street. He liked the look of it.

Three big men went in through the front door leaving a horse and spring van outside, reins wrapped around a telegraph post. As the door closed behind him he heard enviously the shout of welcome from the drinkers within, then one authoritative voice, the publican's voice, rising inexorably above the din to restore order. Silence. Somebody played a melodeon, then somebody sang. One voice only, and beery, dewy-eyed appreciation from listening men. From a side door half hidden in the darkness of an entry came two old tottering men – what heavenly fun if one of them should prove to be Brother Hazlitt. Out on the street they buttoned heavy coats as carefully as if a gale had been blowing, steadied hats on heads, went their way, placing their feet cautiously as if they distrusted the steadiness of the pavement. The side door, then, is the door for me, for monks and policemen and drinkers outside the legal hours. It opened into a dark unevenly-flagged passage that led to a room behind the bar. The warm smoky air was as solid as a wall. He stood for a moment at the door until he could distinguish objects from environing shadows: two barrels of draught with quart jugs to catch drippings from the taps; a door to the right to the select and empty room, a door straight ahead to the gents; the shoulder-high hatch to the bar where the light and the singing was, and at the hatch a tall bewhiskered drunken man, his old eagle face bronze in the square of lamplight. From the bar a girl's voice said: 'Shall I open the door for you, Mr Harte?'

'No. No.' Then, without turning his head and with a suddenness that surprised Barragry, he said: 'This gentleman here will look after the door. One before we go, Kate! Just one.'

'You've had enough, Mr Harte.' The unseen Kate had a warm contralto voice.

'But, Kate, this gentleman has only just come in. Parched with thirst. What will it be? For the first time he turned towards Barragry, who thought: The Barragry luck; my brother always said we instinctively met the right people. He could have danced a jig. He wanted to order something outrageous, something gargantuan: a cooper of stout, a bottle of malt. But instead he said modestly: 'A pint of stout.' Temperance in all things. Be a mortified monk. I'm not a novice for nothing. Anyway the walk to the world had given him a thirst.

'Have a glass of whiskey?'

'No; a pint.'

'Have a glass. It's turned cold to-night.'

Kate's contralto said: 'I'm roasted alive.'

'You're young, Kate. And well upholstered. We'll compromise,' he said to Barragry. 'Have a glass and a pint.' Fra Filippo Lippi compromised with the best grace in the world. His hand trembled as he reached towards the drink. Someone in the bar was wildly dancing. He didn't know which drink to grab first, but he chose the whiskey and coughed and spluttered heavily over the first sip. 'Not well enough christened, son.' The whiskered benefactor pushed towards him a tumbler of water and he helped himself, a little hazy in his memory about the exact amount of water he used to take with his whiskey. 'Thanks,' he said. 'It's just that I've been on the dry for a long time. I'm not used to it.' Suppose I revealed my halo and was levitated and this old fellow realised for what a monument of mental prayer he was buying a drink, none of your cup of cold water either, but the liveliest juice that could be squeezed out of the barley. He was clearly a lonely man who wanted somebody, anybody to drink with. Our holy father founder forfend that he should expect me to buy a drink in return. What aspiration should a good novice make in such an unwonted crisis? What would Father Willy Doyle do or that more than ordinary boy, Stanislas Kostka, or that Franciscan high-flyer, Joseph of Cupertino? Here's an excellent composition of place for a meditation on the marriage feast of Cana: the dark passage, the old man's face in the square of lamplight, the dripping barrels, the jugs, in the bar the revellers calling for more wine. Kate said: 'Ready now, Mr Harte, I'll open the door.'

'One more, Kate. One for the road.'

Blessed Martin de Porres defend me.

'No! No! One more would be for the ditch.'

'One drop. I won't be a minute. I'll knock it back.' Towards Barragry he echoed: 'Knock it back.'

Saint Jude patron of hopeless cases persuade her to put him out before my poverty is exposed.

'One more, Mr Harte, would knock you back.'

Saint Jude came to the rescue, Kate, his winged messenger appearing suddenly, but with no accompanying nimbus of roseate cloud, from the door that led to the jakes. She certainly was well upholstered. She looked as warm as her voice had sounded. Her face was circular and boyish and crimson with heat, her short blonde hair puffed out as if it had recently been washed and intended never again to take life lying down. Red pullover sleeves shot out like cylinders of flame from the armholes of a blue overall. She was as far away from the holy house as from the silent unreproaching woman he had abandoned to the world. 'Now, Mr Harte,' and took his arm while Barragry, to give Saint Jude a helping hand, rapidly opened the door. He had the half of his pint to finish, could drink it at his leisure and look through the hatch into the bar, into the red heart of the world. He could offer up his morning meditation or the merit acquired by his next bout of the discipline for his aged benefactor. He walked with the warm barmaid while she armed and mothered the old man as far as the pavement. The light had gone out in the windowful of prams and bicycles. The three laughing girls went back up the street. They looked after the old man as he walked away. The odour of Kate was not the odour of the three giglots with the cheap perfume, but a combination of the musky odour of a healthily perspiring body and the odour of a woman who worked to the elbows in ales, wines and spirits.

'Poor old Harte,' she said. 'He'll be got dead some night. And he the best man hereabouts to breed boxer dogs.'

'Has he anybody to look after him?'

'Oh, he lives with a widow. An old landlord's widow. They've stacks of cash. What the two of them do together only the Sacred Heart knows.' If he knows, Barragry thought, it certainly wasn't one of the things He revealed to Saint Margaret Mary Alacoque. After this night, could he ever go back and kneel without itching among the innocent and the good? How many miles from Babylon back through the woods to the house of holinesse? They walked back to the side-door of the pub. Kate folded her arms and took her time, her shoulder brushing against him as they walked. Compared with the heat and din of the bar, the night air must be sweet. She said: 'I never saw you here before.'

'I never was here before. I'm just passing through.'

'It's a good place to pass through.' Inside, in the dark hallway, he knew she wouldn't have objected to a cuddle and the idea sharply touched him with a panic that should affect only the virginal, the chaste, the devoted, the untouched. My life in the woods, so, has made its mark on me. He fled for refuge from the thought back to the red hatch and the end of the black pint. In the bar a wild-headed tinker man was dancing, waving his arms, singing in an execrable drunken voice: 'Don't let the stars get in your eyes.'

'Stars in his tattered ass,' Kate said. 'Members of the itinerant classes. There's the level of our select customers. Or drunken husbands from the mill spending all their money on drink and gamecocks and their wives going to Mass in rags. Will you have another drink?'

'I haven't the price of it.' He hadn't meant to say that.

She surveyed him cannily: 'Don't tell me you're another itinerant.'

'No. Not exactly.'

'You don't look it. Those tramps always have money. Although where they get it only the Heart of Jesus knows.' She had a high opinion of the omniscience of the heart of Jesus. Abruptly she walked away from him, vanishing through the door that led to the gents, and reappearing behind the bar. Like those stout Parisiennes who apportion paper to squatting males, she had no inhibitions about being seen in a place designed exclusively for the use of men. Then to his amazed delight she placed before him on the hatch another glass of malt and another pint. 'Pay me when you're passing through again.'

'Thanks a lot.'

'Don't mention it.' A backward nod of her head indicated the white-headed publican busily pint-pulling, casting the odd irritated glance at the dancing tinker. 'I suppose you have your own troubles.'

'They seem less with these drinks before me.' O ye whales and all that move in the waters bless the Lord: O all ye fowls of the air, bless the Lord, and down the hatch.

She didn't bother him any more and with an odd feeling of chagrin he knew that his brief contact with the world had come to an end. She pulled pints, poured whiskey for the rowdy men. The dancer, exhausted, sat down on a high stool, mopped his brow, drained an entire pint before the applause for his efforts had died down. She crossed the counter to collect empty glasses and join intermittently in a game of darts, displaying a remarkably skilful underhand throw and an uncanny capacity for striking the double one. One of the tinker men pinned a ten-shilling note to the centre of the board, and, to billowing cheers, she pierced it five throws out of six. High on a shelf above a row of dusty bottles an enormous stuffed cock pheasant cast a benevolent eye on the whirling world and said: I am above and beyond you; once I was the proudest bird in the deep woods, but now I'm immortal, under my feet the dark wine of Portugal, and a brass plaque making immortal also the noble man, friend of a lord, whose gun killed me. Dance and drink and pray, pitiful sons of misery. I am a bird. I am a legend. I am a god.

Two large ones, two pints, and I'm getting drunk. The cenobitical life leaves a drinking man out of practice. Will she or won't she look around to bid me goodbye? If I stand here too long, it'll look as if I'm hoping for another free drink, and yet, and yet it seems uncivil and mean to slip away silently, ungratefully. Oh, plump and body-odoured mockery of all the tall tales of bearded scrawny desert fathers tempted by the sinuous lascivious queens of Sheba, cast down upon me thine eyes of mercy so that I may be released from this warm corridor and given the grace to take the dark road back through trees to perseverance in my vocation.

But the patroness, he silently aspired to didn't turn to look at him. She'd dismissed him as she'd dismissed old Harte westering home to his boxer dogs and the landlord's widow to do what only the Sacred Heart of Jesus knew. The cock pheasant on the shelf winked knowingly at him, clearly intimating: I know you for what you are and where you come from, Lippo Lippi, leaper over walls. Go back like a good boy to your woods, where I was once winged, wild and happy, mortal and a mere bird. He took the hint. The night air was chilly after the smoky smelly heat of the bar. The loafers were gone from the corner. He walked fast, the drink already dying in him, his mind unpleasantly numb. There were only three cars now outside the hotel and its doors were closed and all but one window dark. In the morning he'd have to use an extra quantity of that hideous pink tooth-cleansing powder to kill the smell of liqour. He was detailed to serve Peesoc's Mass in one of the side chapels and to receive Communion too. For a hermit not contented with his cell, there wasn't, he supposed, any sin in slipping out at night to cadge drink in a pub, nothing momentous enough to come as an obstacle between himself and the white body of God.

From a shed beside the cottage where he had seen the man comfortably urinating a dog barked at the sound of his passing footsteps. The whistled-for wanderer, it seemed, had come home again. It comforted him a little to think that somebody, even a dog, was aware of him in this empty night world. The bicycle was no longer where the courting couple had left it on the roadside. The noises in the woods had a sharper sound, azure and awakening with the promise of morning, no longer brown and slumberous and furtive. Away east beyond Dublin the sky seemed brighter. It would be comical – wouldn't it? – if he walked blithely up the clochar to find the inmates of the holy house responding to the arousing words: benedicamus domino. That was the worst of having no watch or, rather, of having, in due submission to holy obedience, surrendered the worldly watch at the end of the period of probation. Only on walk days were watches temporarily released, one to each senior novice in a walk group; holy poverty, holy poverty. Father Minister, a blithe literary character, a great admirer of Chesterton, had once at fusion told the novices of a day in a house of studies when he had set out cycling with his fellows. In his saddle-bag he had had as a special feast-day treat, a pot of jam to smear on their brown bread. 'And at that time, brothers (Great Chestertonian billows of the giant laughter of Christian men), my cousin, same age as myself, was a parish priest, and my brother the managing director of a firm.' Barragry had laughed with the other novices, but he had not genuinely been amused. Holy poverty was fair enough for a boy out of school who'd never had a damned thing to call his own, barring a cricket bat or a hurley stick, or football boots; never a cheque-book, nor a car, nor needless to say, a living breathing woman.

When he walked up through the clochar, the house was still asleep. There was no light, no sound in the farmyard. The narrow door into the Assisi passage was still on the latch. He pushed home in his name on the tabella and – why not do him a good turn? – Petit's name too. Carrying his house-shoes in his hand, he went quietly up the stone stairs. On one landing he was startled by the noise of falling waters as somebody pulled a lavatory chain, and Petit, gown over pyjamas, eyes cast down in recollection, crossed his path. Had Petit seen him? Would Petit realise that he had been night-wandering? Would Petit think it his grim unpleasant duty, as the rule enjoined, prudently to inform the superior of a brother's lapse, to the end that the erring one might in charity be brought to a knowledge of his ways? Night-wandering, if not what the world would call a sin, still is a fault in a religious – a tort, a misdemeanour, a bit of a barratry, or embracery, but nowhere on the level of arson in a naval dockyard. It should, I imagine, be mentioned in confession, but not to the Magnov, no, not to the Magnov. Seal or no seal, I couldn't face him with that story. I'll go, *ad quietam conscientiam*, to one of the missionary fathers who come and go like nomads, who rest for intervals in the wing up the long curved corridor that passes the parlours and the infirmary.

Easing his bones on his bed, he knew with a shock of finality that he didn't give a monkey's damn what Petit saw or realised or told. He knew too that he'd never bother his foot telling a confessor about the two large malts and the two pints. He had recovered from remorse.

V

'Tomorrow,' O'Brien said, 'no more villa.'

'Do you think will there be any pike on the hooks?'

'You're bloodthirsty, Brother MacKenna.'

'But you're supposed to catch them, aren't you, O'Brien?'

'The Magnov thinks fishing does me good. He considers it a fine amusement for an old man. He lets me set lines for pike for the same reason that made him present Barragry with the de luxe hedge-clippers.'

'Barragry's a different type of old man.'

'How? In what way?'

'He's sharper. He's harder. He's not so much at rest.'

'You mean he's not so lazy.' O'Brien's heavy spectacles were slung perilously low on his nose. His hair showed quartz-like flashes of grey, but the skin of his round contented face was young, smooth, creamy, and never betrayed stubble. 'Barragry at least did clip the hedges. But I've never caught a single pike. I like the boat, though.' The way he rowed, easily, gently, like an old man coaxing a grandchild, showed that he liked the boat. He was as placid as the peace of God, as the evening all around them, as undisturbed as the dusky trees drooping over ebony moveless water. MacKenna sat in the stern, the tails of his gown tucked into the pockets of his jacket. The oars faintly crinkled the surface between the boathouse and the priest's island. 'Are you sorry the villa's over, O'Brien?'

'Brother, all things end. That's the will of God. I suppose we would get dissipated and relaxed if the villa ordo went on all the time.' Lazily pulling on, or leaning on, the oars, he looked the picture of perfect relaxation, no line nor ridge nor angle nor jut of asceticism noticeable in him anywhere. They nosed the boat under trees to touch the fringe of the island, mud and sodden grass marked by the toes and the droppings of birds. They inspected the five lines strung carefully over resilient forked sticks.

'No. No pike.'

'The pike are not together at the rising of the moon.'

'O'Brien, what a ghastly pun.' Waddling around the marshy little island and looking for all the world like a fat amiable goose, O'Brien seemed happy that he hadn't caught any pike. Three of the five brutal hooks were completely bare. 'The pike ate the bait.'

'Let us more charitably prognosticate, MacKenna, that the frogs got away.' O'Brien had a weakness for words and phrases from the treatises of the Venerable Father Rodriguez. 'Only holy obedience compels me in thus wise to lacerate the creatures.' He tapped one of the hooks with his forefinger, then tossed it unbaited into the water. MacKenna, amused by O'Brien, laughed until he choked and bent double, then abruptly ceased laughing and straightened up slowly. Voices sounded far away on the croquet lawn. The wood pigeons moaned ceaselessly. O'Brien and MacKenna were the only two novices near the lake. 'Anything wrong, MacKenna?' O'Brien was looking at him curiously. 'No. Nothing, thanks.' But there was something wrong. The knitting needle was there again, relentlessly, viciously returning to put an end to days of physical content and spiritual consolation. 'Are you sure?'

'Quite sure, thanks.' There was a terrifying alertness in O'Brien's way of looking at one; there was knowledge too, a quick perception that didn't seem to go with that placidity, that easy acceptance of the rule, of poverty, chastity, obedience, silence, community life, of, as Nangle said, fish for dinner, a wet Friday recreation in stilted Latin in the ambulacrum, and outdoor works with the dynamic Petit. They walked back to the boat. MacKenna thought miserably: O'Brien was a doctor in the world he knows there's something wrong, he may even guess what it is, he may know what I don't know. O'Brien said: 'I've one more line on the Queen Mary. It's a sort of island now, too. There's so much rotten weed in it, it'll never be moved from where it is.' He pulled slowly across the darkening lake. Curlews cried from the deep bog. He said: 'It's just as well Lagan entered religion. He'd never make his way as a boatbuilder. And look at that forest of weed. Undisturbed, serene.'

'Like yourself.'

'Thank you, MacKenna. I'm a weed, but not a water one. I'm the ivy on the old sunny wall. I'm a parasite in paradise.' The weed was green and cool and in places lipped out of the water so that it seemed wonderful that the oars were not lost in its coils, nor the slow boat grounded on its thicker, stronger clumps. 'We can write off the Queen Mary as a weed-killer.'

'We could drain the lake and give all the novices bill-hooks and let Barragry loose with his clippers.'

'That'd be killing work on the back,' O'Brien said, and MacKenna didn't speak again until the bow bumped against the stinking barge. A cloud of flies rose before them. 'Pestilential,' O'Brien said. 'There's my line. The frog will be asphyxiated.' It may have been the sudden ascent of the black buzzing army, or the fact that one tail of his gown escaped from a jacket pocket to trollop around his feet, or it may have been the memory of how Guinan had similarly missed his footing that made MacKenna miscalculate the distance between boat and barge. For an instant he swayed backwards and forwards, levitated, and then, not trusting the evidence of his senses, plunged seat foremost into the weedy water. It wasn't at all like going in deliberately in a bathing costume, or in your pelt into a cool pool in a burn. O'Brien said: 'Man over-board.' He stepped on to the barge and helped his sodden brother out of the lake. 'At least you nearly died in the holy gown.' The flies too fierce to be routed by any splash were returning. The pike hook was bare. With astounding speed, O'Brien pulled back to the boathouse. Standing in the boat, MacKenna squeezed water out of his gown and jacket, and wondered did a novice who fell into the lake have to kneel in the refectory, arms extended and confess his fault. Already he felt the creeping cold around his legs and back, and in the boathouse he was seized with a shivering fit that bent him double. O'Brien helped him to stand straight again. They trotted up the grapery wood. 'Dear Brother, if I may advise you, I'm older than you, you won't mind, I'd see Peesoc.'

'I'll dry out in a while.'

'That wasn't what I meant. The wet will do you no harm. Many waters cannot quench charity. Fact is ...' O'Brien was puffed. He didn't trot well. 'Fact is, your ducking might provide a new novitiate joke. Add to our store of holy mirth. The mortified MacKenna cools the flesh in the lake water. Or, stunned by the smell of the Queen Mary, MacKenna took a plunge. But what I meant was: is there something wrong with your back?'

'Oh, it's nothing.'

'That could be. There's no harm in finding out for certain. What's it feel like?'

'A sharp shooting pain. Like a knitting needle.' At the croquet lawn they found Hanlon, Barnes and Flynn gathering up mallets and balls and sorrowfully saying farewell to the villa. 'You should see Peesoc,' O'Brien whispered hastily, and then they were swamped by the laughter of the brethren rejoicing at MacKenna's bedraggled condition. O'Brien said nothing more. But that made no difference, for the inevitable had, in the fullness of time, come to pass: the knitting needle had been mentioned in words and had so taken on a new malevolence. The tumble in the lake had been willed, and so had O'Brien's kindly advice, and, hidden there in his body, something was wrong and the holy rule would have to be obeyed.

Dressed in the gown he had worn on the day of Frankie's visit, and in his long-tailed Donohill poorhouse suit, he knelt to pray at the blue-lighted shrine in the novice's corridor. On his first morning, he remembered, some novice had knelt there, his face cadaverous and intense in the odd blueness; but he couldn't remember who it had been: Curran or Frawley, or Keown, who were gone, or Petit, Nangle or Barragry, or any of the others who were still strong in the Lord. On that first morning he hadn't, of course, known the people nor the world they lived in, and in so short a time their ways and their world had become so familiar to him, so dear too; and here in the blue light before God's Mother, footsteps above him of novices at the shelves in the ad usum, noises from the chapel where Brother Sacristan Madden, and Guinan, his assistant, were cleaning the tall Mass candlesticks, it was all dear and beloved in a heartbreaking way that he was afraid to try to understand. He tried to pray. Peesoc's door was only a few paces away. He said three times: 'Heal me, body and soul, for the conversion of sinners.'

What am I trying to do: get around God? Fix my back and I'll forever be your hired man. I'll be your sweetheart if you will be mine.

He found himself trying to rehearse a possible beginning for his talk with Peesoc, but no wise phrase came to him.

Let it be. Let the Lord open the lips, the Holy Spirit infuse the wisdom, mould and eject the words.

The good Donohill suit, smelling of camphor, the unfrayed visiting-day gown, made him feel as if he was arrayed for a sacrifice.

He stood up with effort. His legs were cold and stiff. Peesoc said: 'Do come in, Brother. I had been wanting to see you.' That was the way with Peesoc. He always made you feel welcome. He wanted always to show you that you hadn't disturbed him. He had too, been wanting to talk to MacKenna about a matter that had nothing to do with tumbles in the lake, nor pains in the back: a matter slight, irrelevant, as far away as the moon from the granite moment when MacKenna would have to say: 'Father, I'm afraid there's something the matter with my health.'

SIX: VALE

The day MacKenna went to Dublin for his X-ray the Magnov sent
O'Brien and Barragry along with him. Brother Molloy drove them to
the station along the road Barragry had walked on his night jaunt to
see the world. Where now was the man who'd pissed and whistled
for the dog? There, anyway, was his cottage, white and lively in the
bright morning, the door open, smoke puffing up from the chimney.
Or what would Kate the plump dart-player be doing now, or ancient
Harte who bred the boxer dogs? The Sacred Heart alone knew. What
would Kate say or what odd amazed expression would come on her
round face if she could see me sailing by in all the glory of clerical
black hat and tails?

At the station Brother Molloy said: 'Don't have a worry, Brother.
Everything will turn out all right.' Barragry and O'Brien were buying
the tickets. 'You remember the little prayer you had on the leaflet
when you were down the mine,' Brother Molloy said. 'You wrote it
out for me and I learned it off by heart. Let nothing disturb thee.'

'I do indeed. Saint Teresa's prayer.'

'Let nothing affright thee,' O'Brien said behind them. 'You aren't
the first holy monk who went to Dublin to see the doctor, and came
back alive, too. Brother Hazlitt, they say, had gallstones once.'

'Back in Parnell's time,' Barragry said. They were talking and
laughing about Brother Hazlitt ('When will he die and give us a
feastday?') when the train pulled away from the platform and Brother
Molloy, solid, friendly man, from the deep woods and the shiny silo,
from the white bellying cooling tower and the comical conical pimple
of a water tower. MacKenna was drowsy already. O'Brien watched
him quietly. Drowsiness and weariness too often overcame him now
in the early morning. He closed his eyes and thought of the morning
woods they had motored through, looked down the cool arcades, felt
metronomical flashes and splashes of sunlight soothing his tired eyes.

His back wasn't hurting him. He thought about Brother Molloy and Saint Teresa: Let nothing disturb thee, nothing affright thee, all things are passing; God only is changeless. Patience gains all things. Who has God wants nothing. God alone suffices.

Barragry was flying, flying east. Landmarks he knew moved back towards the west. He didn't see them.

Two nights ago the Magnov had said to him: 'The doctor in the town diagnoses something the matter with Brother MacKenna's spine. I'm sending him to Dublin for an X-ray.'

'I hope it's nothing serious, Father.'

'I want Brother O'Brien and yourself to go with him. O'Brien knows his way around the Dublin hospitals. You can handle the purse. You know your way around Dublin.'

'I should, Father.'

'You'll be a useful guide in the world too, after your recent experiences.' The Magnov was laughing, actually laughing, his head back in the shadows that surrounded the pool of green light in which he wrote and read. So Petit, eyes cast down, had seen the return of the prodigal from the pint pots, had guessed the truth or some of it, had obeyed the rule and informed the superior, to the end that a brother might, for God's greater glory, be made conscious of his fault. But the Magnov was laughing still, head in the shadows, laughing. He wasn't saying: Depart from me, ye accursed. His laughter made it all the harder to find anything to say by way of explanation.

'Oh, I know, Brother, the strain is more severe on you than on the others. Yet I honestly think that the best way to ease the strain is to follow the rule. The grace of state will come. It's very human to feel the need of a night walk and a breath of fresh air. The summer woods are at their loveliest then. Summer? Why, autumn's on the way. I saw brown leaves yesterday. Autumn gets more beautiful as you grow older.'

'Very melancholy, Father.' Thanks be to whichever saint was the patron of night-strollers, night-watchmen, poachers and burglars, the Magnov knew nothing of Kate and Harte, and the two pints and the two large malts. Petit's brotherly imagination couldn't sink to such sinful things.

'Normally, such a serious breach of the rule could lead to expulsion. But I know you, Brother Barragry. I've some idea of your problem. I taught you when you were a schoolboy. Even if you do elect to return to the world, this last year could still have been a part of God's plan for you. It could mean a lot to you, and the people you know, in the time to come. But do please, Brother, take your time. Give the Lord a chance. Don't panic into a decision. I know I can trust you.'

'Thank you, Father.'

The Magnov's parting shots as novices turned at the door to say good night were a notable feature of novitiate life: 'And, oh, Brother, if you feel like a walk at any time in the future, do please, let Brother Hazlitt know. He has a two-barrelled gun in the farmyard. Father Rector is beddy about his food these days. Like Saint Ignatius, he's one of the world's great dyspeptics. I know he'd love game for breakfast.' He was laughing agian. He was even – oh, holy father founder look down on us – he was actually whistling; and the tune, well and clearly whistled, was: It is my delight on a shiny night in the season of the year.

A town went westwards, a flat town of big hotels and horse-breeders with a great college where men of another religious order, serving God under another rule, taught wisdom to the young.

You see, you couldn't be angry with the man. Nor, when you thought it over, could you be angry with Petit. According to schoolboy standards, he was a sneak. According to adult worldly standards, he was an informer, a stool-pigeon. At best, according to the ways of the world, he was something like one Communist shooting another for the good of the Party. But no worldly standard applied here. Petit had almost certainly prayed like bedammed about the business, had suffered from scruples, tortured himself, put extra vim into his whacking with the discipline, pulled the chain on his wrists a notch tigher, and in the end, for the sake of a brother's soul, Petit had squealed, in obedience to the holy rule.

That very morning at breakfast Barragry had found himself sitting opposite Petit. He had looked at Petit's eyes, veiled and downcast behind thick-rimmed spectacles, at his uncouth red hands reaching out for bread. Barragry had felt no antagonism, no resentment. He knew that Petit was a brother to be loved like sweet ointment flowing down somebody's beard; and, although you wouldn't think it to look at him, Petit was like to the dew of Hermon which descended upon Mount Sion.

Did the fact that Barragry felt brotherly love towards Petit, in spite of all, mean that Barragry knew he was eastwards bound for the world, and so didn't give a tinker's fart about what went on in the woods? Or did it mean that he had learned more of the ways of God than he thought he had and that having learned so much he should stay to learn more?

The three novices didn't talk much. Monastic silence went with them and there were, moreover, two externs in the carriage: a fat heavily-breathing man who dressed and looked like a lawyer, a thin-faced mousy-haired teenage girl. MacKenna tried to read. With the Magnov's permission, he had brought with him from the ad usum Francis de Sales' treatise on the love of God. But the old book had been stiffly rebound in the novitiate bookbindery, and could only be held open with difficulty. The pages were yellow and frayed at the edges, the translation was stilted and archaic. It hurt his hands, his eyes and his head; there was no consolation in the words of that sweet saint. He put the book aside and read instead from a pamphlet called *Christ Consciousness*, written by some Dominican friar and sent to MacKenna from his own humpy town by a pious gossip of his mother. It told him that Christ was a high mountain, the summit of which soared up into the godhead: 'Springs gush forth all around us: we should not stop at these streams which come from Him (that would be self-indulgence), but we should go to the mountain itself....'

With the pamphlet open on his knees, he saw through blurred eyes the old uneven town, the hills all around it, and streams gushing forth from them. Mullaghcarn mountain itself would be Christ, and the sky above Gortin the Godhead.

To the rhythm of the wheels he remembered a hill-billy song, and quietly moved his lips to the words. Barragry and O'Brien would think he was making aspirations. When the north winds blow an' we're gonna have snow an' the rain an' the hail come a-bouncing, we'll build a hut where the buffaloes go, way out on the mountain. He wasn't sure if he had the words correctly. The effort of memory cleared his eyes and he saw again the Christ-conscious pamphlet, his likewise Christ-conscious brothers, the thin girl conscious of her bony knees and modestly covering them because the carriage was full of the makings of priests. He saw the road that ran parallel to the track, the same great road that bisected the heath where he had walked joyously on taut turf with Angelus Flynn and Hanlon the croquet fiend. Would Flynn lose his anima and be like a guardian angel going back empty-handed and forlorn to report his failure to God? A fleet of heavily-laden turf lorries moved east. The legal gentleman wound his watch. MacKenna fell asleep.

When he awoke Barragry was reading to O'Brien out of a notebook: 'I want to become rather than to know. If I raise myself, I raise the world so much, and if I fail I drag others down also.'

O'Brien said: 'Not bad for an old pagan.'

'Who was it?' MacKenna asked.

'Ah, Brother MacKenna, back with us again.'

'A slumber did his spirit steal.'

'Tired eyelids upon tired eyes.'

'It was A.E.', Barragry said. 'This 'ere's my famous spiritual notebook.'

'Spiritual my pants. Writing down clipes from an old Rathmines windbag.'

'He did his best.'

'So do we all, Frater Barragry.'

'Let me read,' O'Brien said, settling his spectacles, snatching the book: '"I can have no friends outside those who are in earnest about life, in terrible earnest ...." He underlined that bit. He thought a lot of himself, the old boaster with his thick woollen socks.'

'He was a poet like MacKenna.'

They wrangled nonsensically, pretending a good humour and inconsequence they could not feel, because the city and the radiographer were not now far away. They looked at MacKenna with the eyes of worried elder brothers. He couldn't help them to pretend, because his very knowledge of their intentions put a lump in his throat. They were generous, they were kind, and a feeling in his bones – yes, literally a feeling in his bones – told him he was going to lose them. They would be priests, collared for life, Nangle said: he didn't know what he would be. Listening to their nonsensical argument, he seemed already to be drifting out of their lives. 'The Liffey,' Barragry said, and they saw the river, still unspoiled by the city, winding between deep-grassed fields, bending under leaning grey willows. 'Cheer up,' Barragry said. 'I know there's a lot to be said for holy poverty, but I've the purse here, and, for God's greater glory, I'll stand you both a decent lunch.'

Caught in the pandemonium on the platform, it was hard for a moment to realise that the quiet holy woods were only fifty miles away. The world was a bewildering place. Only Barragry seemed at home in it, but then this was Barragry's town. 'My appointment's at three,' MacKenna said. He felt cold and sick.

'You've pucks of time.'

O'Brien asked Barragry did he want to see his brother. 'I've permission. But I'd rather not. He's probably busy just now.' He would probably be busy sluicing away the dust of a forenoon's legal work. 'I may telephone him before I leave.' They walked out of the station. A boisterous wind came up the quays and MacKenna was acutely conscious of the insecure way his hat balanced on his unkempt hair. He should have had one of Brother Sadleir's drastic coiffures before venturing out to face the world. 'A taxi,' Barragry said. It wasn't in keeping with holy poverty, but MacKenna could be a sick boy. 'I know a nice hotel.'

When MacKenna had had his X-ray they walked to a neighbouring city church to make their examen of conscience. It was a dark, gritty place, noisy with worshippers coming and going. It was so much easier to pray in the novitiate chapel. Children on their way home from school rattled around the stations of the Cross. On marble steps at the sanctuary gates a charwoman was at work with a scrubbing brush. Barragry slumped, elbows on bench, head between hands and thought about nothing. That was the easiest way out. The examen was a game, a feint, a shadow-boxing stunt. MacKenna, terribly tired, sat up on the seat and studied his particular fault: how many times since my last examen? His particular fault at the moment was giving way to despair. Then he surveyed his general faults, his failures in prayer, recollection, fraternal charity, spiritual reading, acceptance of humiliation. Had he accepted in the proper spirit the humiliations of that day, the feeling that people were looking at and laughing at him with his hat perched on his head like a crow on a haycock; the shame of being closed into a small cubicle and told to strip, to change into pyjamas, dressing gown and slippers provided by the hospital, to follow a young nurse over a floor of well-waxed oaken blocks? She had placed her hand on his arm to steady him. Noli me tangere. But what did nurses in a big city hospital know or care about the ne tangas rule? Stretched flat to be photographed and feeling the hands of the nurse and of the stout white-coated radiographer pulling down the pyjamas to give the camera a clear view of his back, then lying on his side in the required crouched position, he should have thought of Christ on the Cross, Christ stripped by His tormentors. What he had felt was a virginal schoolboy shame that a young woman and an old one should handle him so.

Stripped to the waist, he stood holding his breath while his lungs were photographed. They didn't, surely to God, think he had tuberculosis. What would the camera, or the neat linen-odoured young nurse, make of the blue weals left by the discipline on his right shoulder?

The nurse helped him back into jacket and dressing-gown. She walked with him to the cubicle, said: 'Goodbye, Father. You'll have the results in a few days.' She smiled and walked smartly away. Stupefied with confusion, he wasn't even able to thank her. She called me Father. I suppose to her everything and anything in black pants deserves the title of Father; and I'm not even a collared cleric:

I'm only, in fact, something to be photographed in the search for a blemish, a quantity of flesh and skin and bone possessed and tormented by a demon in the shape of a knitting needle. Two minutes later he couldn't even remember what the nurse had looked like. He was so confused he started dressing without properly closing the cubicle door. Another nurse, passing that way, closed it for him, smiled pleasantly as if it was the most normal thing in the world for her to find in holes in hospital walls young men in and half out of clerical clothes. He remembered her face for a long time afterwards.

On the way back to the station he confessed his confusion to O'Brien and Barragry. Their taxi jammed in a mass of vehicles held up by a red light. 'I knew an old Christian Brother,' O'Brien said, 'a man from the mountains. He went to hospital for the first time when he was eighty.'

'Poor old man.' The lights changed, traffic flowed smoothly east and west along the wide quays. Two lawyers in wigs and gowns perched like vultures on the steps of the Four Courts. 'He had chronic constipation, the poor old sod. They gave him one physic after another.' Puffing Guinness barges waited for cargoes of black beer. Two shabby soiled swans were bellyflat on sleek riverside mud. The holy lake was far away, secluded by deep bogs, curtained by tall trees; clean swans there nested on piles of straw and sticks hoarded in the long linen-like reeds. 'They finally fell back on an enema.'

'Back's the word,' said Barragry.

MacKenna quoted: 'And those behind cried "Forward." And those in front cried "Back".'

'With your usual aptness, Frater MacKenna.' But today there seemed to be no gratification in being apt with a quotation.

'Oh, the poor old man,' O'Brien said, 'he nearly suffocated for shame.'

'An enema hath done this.'

'He said to me afterwards' – O'Brien opened the taxi door – 'he said to me: "Doctor, they came at me from behind."' They were laughing as Barragry paid the taximan. 'Keep enough for coffees,' O'Brien said, 'the concupiscence of the belly is at me.' In the station restaurant they had coffee and sandwiches. In the bar next door noisy

worldly men eyed them dreamily. 'I'll ring the brother,' he said. But
when he had squeezed his way back through the crowds at the barrier
to the telephone booth, he didn't ring the brother. Instead, he dialled
another number, heard the bell ring and ring and ring, but nobody
answered. There was nobody at home. He replaced the receiver and
didn't even bother to reclaim his three pennies. He didn't know
whether or not he would have spoken if she had answered. It would
have been strange to hear her voice.

The train rattled away from grey walls and then from straggling
suburban houses. But he did know that the Magnov had trusted him
all the way to Dublin as a sort of a test and that Dublin and the
woman it held in its heart, with all those irrelevant thousands
revolving around her, had beaten the Magnov and the pale Galilean,
and the bronzed martyred father founder, and the dear old Madam
Caelia who ran the House of Holinesse and all her numerous brood
and retainers: Fidelia, Speranza, Charissa, Humiltá, Zele, the gentle
Squyre hight Reverence, the groom called meek Obedience, the leach
called Patience, bitter Penaunce with his yron whip, and sharp
Remorse, and the seven Beads Men who were the Corporal Works of
Mercy, and the aged holy man Contemplation – the living image of
Brother Hazlitt – in his hilltop hermitage, and the twelve apostles and
the Connaught Rangers and likewise the Inniskilling Dragoons. He
wanted her. He wanted her. She'd be at home the next time he rang
and Petit could sleep with Dame Caelia and her three daughters, in
turn or all together in the altogether, and with the gentle Squyre and
the seven Beads Men if he felt so inclined.

The Magnov was with Brother Molloy to meet them at the station.
The sun was red behind the comical conical watertower. The white
cooling tower released from the sun's rays looked as cold as frost.
The grey Huguenot houses stood back in the shadows to stare with no
enthusiasm at the carload of dark-clothed idolaters. The shadows
were long in the woods.

The Magnov didn't talk about it, but both Barragry and O'Brien
knew that the hospital had given him MacKenna's fate by telephone.

MacKenna felt his fate even if the Magnov didn't tell him for a few days. Didn't he come from Northern places where there was premonition in men's bones? He felt his fate in his bones.

He slept now at night in the infirmary, slept late in the morning, went to a late Mass in one of the side chapels, made his meditation after a late breakfast, eschewed kneeling – which would strain his back – as strictly as the literary manual had once advised O'Brien to eschew the semicolon. In the world he had always wanted to be sacrosanct, separate and apart, and now he had his wish in a way that pushed him to the verge of panic. He was drifting off into a dream world. He had a revealing life, translated from the Italian, of Saint Paul of the Cross, and was more than a little aghast at the stories of the good man flailing himself in the pulpit in order to draw sinners towards God.

'Brother MacKenna,' the Magnov had said, 'I don't think you should take the discipline any more.'

'Yes, Father.'

'If you feel like it, wear the chain.'

'Yes, Father.'

'But rest. Rest. Don't be too hard on yourself.'

'No, Father.'

In the night he awoke with the sharp sound of blows on saintly Italian shoulders sounding in his ears. He was sweating heavily. His spine was hurting him. He knew it was his spine. He prayed desperately to Saint Paul of the Cross, but on the next day, when the light had brought back sanity, he found another life of Saint to read. He prayed constantly for the one thing he had asked of the Lord: that he might dwell in the house of the Lord all the days of his life.

Quia melior est dies una in atriis tuis super milia: For one day in thy courts is better than a thousand.

Beati, qui habitant in domo tua, Domine: in saecula saeculorum laudabunt te: Blessed are they that dwell in thy house, O Lord, they shall praise thee for ever and ever.

The beati in question would be Petit, Begley, O'Brien, Barragry, Cashman, Donnelly, Molloy, Madden, and Sadleir, et alibi aliorum plurimorum sanctorum martyrum et confessorum.

From that same psalm – it went through his head with humming monotonous recurrence – Guinan with his turned up toes and his eyes staring through thick spectacles at God's birds, could rejoice for ever because the sparrow had found herself a house and the turtle a nest for herself, where she may lay her young.

Quam dilecta tabernacula tua: Oh! how lovely are thy tabernacles O Lord of Hosts; I had rather be despised in the house of my God than to dwell in the tents of sinners.

Why, according to the translation, did the Lord have tabernacles while sinners had to make do with tents?

Over and over again he repeated: O Lord of Hosts, blessed is the man that hopeth in Thee. Every time he said it, he pulled an examen bead down or up; and one day, discovering he had thus aspirated five hundred times, he felt for a moment of soaring consolation, a little like Father Willy Doyle, only to be seized the next moment by grey glaucous fears at his vainglory.

There was great writing in the psalms. There was, too, some creature consolation of a literary nature in living secluded in the infirmary, for the curving polished corridor that led to it was lined with valuable pictures and profane books, securely locked in their cases, the proceeds of a bequest to the holy house by a cultured old layman, a relative of Father Robert. Once or twice MacKenna, walking alone to his room, was tempted to relax custody of the eyes, to peep sideways, to glimpse the procession of great shadowy names: Meredith, Poe, Chaucer, Flaubert, Dickens, Carlyle, Goethe, Ariosto. Once temptation completely overcame him. He stopped and stared, the devil rooting him to the spot, at a beautifully-bound, uniform edition of Fennimore Cooper. Sensuously he wanted to touch the books. With his fingertips he touched the glass, and there he was when Father Rector, noiselessly slipping along in old house-shoes, came upon him: 'Ah, Brother MacKenna, you like the books?'

In the awesome silence, away from the body of the house, away even, in that windowless corridor, from birdsong and the sound of wind-swayed branches, the whisper was a hoarse scream. Moreover, it was a breach of the rule of silence by a professed father. MacKenna was a little disedified. The novices, even at fusion, didn't see much of

Father Rector. How does he even know my name? He was a small shy red-faced man, his hair a waving silver mane. He had the deaf man's trick of cocking his head sideways. He had a notoriously inordinate attachment to pottering about the farmyard getting fussily in Brother Hazlitt's way. Waiting fearfully for the punitive lightning flash, MacKenna whispered, 'Yes, Father; they're lovely,' and to his unspeakable horror the little man fumbled a key from the pocket of his gown, opened one bookcase, handed him a volume of Longfellow with padded morocco covers yielding as featherbeds, relocked the case, hissed: 'God bless you, Brother. Read that.' Then he was gone as silently as he had come. He might have been an apparition, an evil spirit pretending to be Father Rector. But the good Longfellow was there, like a cushion, between his hands.

The book was a plush exotic worldling, alien on his table. For a whole day he looked at it lying there before he opened it. He had an uneasy feeling that he was doing something irrevocable. He read that life was real and life was earnest and that it was not written that the soul would return to dust. A day later he knew that for an invalid – he might as well accept the fact that he was an invalid – it was better to fall asleep to long cloying rhythms about murmuring pines and the hemlock, or about the numberless noisy weathercocks that rattled and sung of mutation, than to the swing and cut of edifying blows on the flesh of an Italian saint.

Who was MacKenna to be disedified at Father Rector, an old man tried and true in the ways of the spirit? Father Rector for all he knew, might, out among the crops and the cattle, have been blessed with the gift of tears. Father Rector knew he was sick. The old shy man had eyes for more things than the farm. Before God in the hierarchy of the Order, Father Rector stood higher even than the Magnov. The very thought left MacKenna breathless.

He suffered severely from constipation. The Magnov advised him: 'Drink plenty water, Brother. If people drank more water there wouldn't be so many ailments. How many cups of tea do you drink in the morning?'

'One, Father.'

'Drink three, Brother. Tea's a fine drink.'

'Is it my back, Father?' He was almost afraid to ask. He felt as if he was poking his nose into something that did not concern him, something that was a secret between God, the doctor, and the Magnov. In future the doctor would stand to him, as the Magnov now did, in the place of God.

'Some slight injury to the spine, Brother. The cure is complete rest. But' – a little sideways smile – 'it's by no means fatal.'

The Magnov paced slowly beside him on the blue gravel, his hand on MacKenna's elbow, and for the first time he noticed how frail the priest was. He had always thought of him as tough, agile and wiry, but now he saw how the thin hand trembled, how the shoulder-blades bunched out under a worn glazed habit; and the skin around his Roman nose and high receding forehead was almost transparent. Asceticism and age? He felt he was walking with a saint. The Magnov said: 'Patience, Brother, patience. You can get well again. Plenitudo temporis. In the fullness of time the Holy Child was born. Isn't it an exquisite phrase? God was the best writer, Brother.'

The oaks on the knoll beyond the blue gravel, the oaks in the clochar were tinged, but oh, so faintly, with bronze. The long-lost abandoned vista of avenue under the high cedars held motionless pools of entrapped sunlight. The other novices were away at recreation on the far side of the house. Was it because of his isolation from them or was it because the woods had heard of autumn that made him hear a far drifting loneliness in the cries of the birds?

'Father Minister and myself saw the dear old nun. She has always been a great friend of ours.'

'Yes, Father.'

'That's why she consented to take you. The hospital's really reserved for children.'

'Yes, Father.'

'It's a wonderful place, Brother. The patients are in the open air except when it rains. Fresh air and eating plenty onions keeps up their appetites. That's half the cure. The balconies are in a great arc facing south to the sun and the Dublin hills.'

He would lie looking at the Dublin hills while the men who were novices when he was a novice would – no longer novices, but on the next stage of their journey upwards to the priesthood – go tramping up those purple slopes, mountain wind cutting the cobwebs of study from their brains.

'There's a beautiful roofed-in altar in the centre of the arc. Mass is said there every Sunday and holiday.'

He couldn't ask: How long will it be, Father? He would bluntly ask the doctor as soon as he saw him; he would demand the truth.

'One wing is for girls, and one for boys. The girls' beds are dressed in blue, and the boys' in red. They look so healthy, so brown with the sun, so cheerful.'

Brother Hazlitt, bent double, leaning on his stick, his left hand genuinely tugging his coat-tail, came slowly from the farmyard, walked past them without speaking, his eyes cast down as no other religious in the house had his eyes cast down, his heart in heaven with the cattle. Their breath had warmed his Redeemer.

'You'll like this Reverend Mother. She's forcible and blunt, but kindly and very near to God. She has done great work there. She built the hospital out of nothing, begged money everywhere for her poor children, to cure their twisted limbs and diseased bones.'

'Yes, Father.'

'She said she'd welcome you because you could be such a good influence among them.'

'That was kind of her, Father.'

Oh, happy clouds of rooks homing to the clochar beside the holy house, tired and content after the day's foraging in flat warm fields, settling into nest within the sound of the novitiate bells.

'I'm sending Brother Barragry to Dublin with you.'

'Thanks, Father.'

The thin hand tightened its grip on his elbow: 'Brother Barragry won't be coming back to us.'

For one sickening moment MacKenna couldn't hear the squabbling of the homing rooks. He could see them with horribly sharpened clarity. They were motionless, wings extended, as if somebody had snipped jagged holes in the evening sky to reveal the darkness, the evil blackness of what was above and beyond. But for that one moment his ears were numb and when they came alive again he heard the Magnov: 'He has decided he has no vocation. But don't let that worry you. He has his own good reasons. He's a grown sensible man.'

'I know that, Father.'

'He has a great respect for your poetic talent. I only mention this because he'll be in Dublin and I'm sure he'll go to see you often.'

It wasn't possible to rejoice because he would have Barragry as a frequent visitor. That would be to be glad that another vocation had crashed on the rocks, that Barragry had taken his great talents back with him to use them, in however praiseworthy a fashion, in the world. Better be the rooks in the clochar trees. Better be bent among the cattle like holy humble Brother Hazlitt. And when I return after my recovery, as I must, how different it will be to know that Barragry is nowhere, not any longer in the same uniform, not in any house belonging to the Order, but an extern lost away in the world.

'Your duty now, Brother, is to get better. Concentrate on that. Don't be perturbed if you find it hard to keep up the habits you've developed here. But pray, Brother, pray and trust and do what the doctor tells you. You may be chosen among us all for something different, something special.'

The tinkling warning bell rang to say that the novices had ten minutes' recreation left. 'Go join the rest, Brother. All will be well in plenitudo temporis. Remember that.'

Two phrases he would always remember: 'Plenitudo temporis' and Barragry's 'Very tiresome.' Somewhere between them was everything a man needed to know.

He struggled to keep from running as he crossed the blue gravel towards the main door. He was hysterically anxious to reassure himself by the sight and sound of his brothers clustered like gabbling blackbirds around the Assisi door, waiting for the final sonorous bell. They would be his brothers for ever. But Barragry, Barragry deliberately turning his face to the world. Why? Why? Better be the two stone lions left behind by a noble lord to stand before Doric pillars and guard the tabernacle of God. Some day, those lions, like the symbol of Mark the Evangelist, would sprout stone wings and in the final dissolution go clad in the holy habit before the white throne.

At the Assisi door he gabbed with Donnelly and Petit about the new cow Brother Hazlitt had bought at a fair in the Huguenot town. Cashman, the humorous, recently ascended from the mine, had the whole tidings from Brother Molloy.

'Struck a bargain he did, like the veriest cattle-dealer of them all.'

'The Holy Ghost sharpened his wits.'

'A fine baste,' Donnelly said. 'A dual-purpose cow.'

'What's that?'

'Semper, Brother, semper.'

MacKenna's bones were all premonitions. His bones had betrayed him. He dreamt that night of a world half blue, half red, of steel silver-painted beds, suntrap balconies, sun-absorbing Vita-glass, happy brown children, tall blunt benevolent nuns, faceless anonymous nurses whose starched white aprons smelled like altar linen.

It was unusual for departing novices to say goodbye to the community. Frawley, Keown, and Curran had folded their mattresses and silently, without tear or handshake, slipped away from holiness. But MacKenna was leaving because he couldn't help it, because God willed it; he was carrying his cross; or he was, as Madden said, being carried, leaving honourably, more or less feet first. Nangle cheerily pointed out that if the worst came to the worst the hospital he was going to was only a mile away from a big cemetery on the fringe of the city. Consummatus in brevi, explevit tempora multa for his soul, if not his lumbar spine, pleased God.

'Brother Mac,' Nangle said, 'with my own holy hands I'll nail your memorial plaque on the wall outside the chapel door. Just beside the shrine of the shaking shepherd, where my enhaloed statue will stand – in tempore opportuno.'

Then they laughed and were merry together like brothers akin, because since death was not in question it could be laughed at and in the laughter the lesser actual evil could be momentarily forgotten.

And Barragry was no man to depart like a thief in the night. His hard lean face and firm handshake would, the Magnov knew, give courage to MacKenna and stiffen the general morale. The Magnov had meant what he said when he told Barragry he could trust him: he could trust him to make it clear that although it was his lot to go, it was the duty of others to persevere, that the one year of hidden life had done him all the good in the world and heaven too. Goodbyes were said in the conference room at night recreation. The lights were on, although ouside the house daylight still lingered around the clipped wire-corseted yew trees and beds where flowers were wilting in the first breath of frost. The long yellow blistered tables looked more yellow, more blistered, positively unhealthy under the artifical light. The old harmonium around which Donnelly and his choir practised, looked content again, solidly settled back in the spiritual life, the villa well over and its laxness forgotten, the lascivious challenging piano hidden somewhere in shame like the white naked statues in the locked room.

MacKenna shook hands with O'Brien. From O'Brien's pocket a sock that he had been darning during free time dangled incongrously. He said: 'A twitch in the back, Brother, does not of necessity prognosticate a long and lingering malady. I'm a doctor, you know. The surgeon you're going to is the best there is. You'll be on your feet again in no time.' He burped. He said: 'Malignant humours.' MacKenna and a half a dozen others laughed. The wraith of the Venerable Father Rodriguez smirked holily over O'Brien's broad shoulder.

'I'll come and preach you a sermon,' Donnelly said. 'Father Minister or somebody left a new book of sermons in the ad usum.'

Guinan was pressing his fingertips on one of the sticky yellow tables, then closely and curiously examining the clear prints. He said: 'They should have these things in Scotland Yard. Good luck, Frater Mac.'

Sadleir had a handgrip close as a vice, and no words of farewell but a crisp rattle of anecdotes about the accidents, the bone-breakings, and rending of the flesh, the abrasions, bruises, black eyes, gashes requiring stitches that had befallen his daft motor-racing brother: 'Hasn't a bone left in his body, that fellow. And it doesn't seem to worry him.'

'Boys of the Sadleir breed,' Madden said, and they looked at each other and laughed and knew that if they were still schoolboys they could gloriously wrestle and scuffle and pummel.

'Brother Hazlitt milks the new cow himself,' Cashman said. 'Angelus and Anima.'

'Has she got the gown yet?'

'Cashman, how do you know that?'

'Sign language from Brother Molloy.'

'What were the signs?'

'Semper deo gratias, Brother.'

'Sign language is a breach of silence.'

'If the Cistercians use it, why can't we? Are we more mortified than the Cistercians?'

For the millionth time Barragry said: 'Let us not aspire to be more than Christians.'

There were many silent handshakes and promises of prayers, and Brother Molloy, with special permission, slipped in for a moment and said: 'We'll be waiting for you, Brother. The pots are greasy. Don't be too long.'

Isolated in one corner, Barragry and Petit talked earnestly and shook hands firmly and parted for ever with mutual respect; and O'Brien, who was beadle, blew a whistle and said: 'Speech. Have you anything to say Barragry, before sentence is passed?' And everybody felt that it was a great thing to have two old men in the room, because when you were young it was hard to know what to say, and shameful to feel how near one still was to tears.

Matthews said: 'I'll be first to see you when I've the collar on, my vows taken. When I get back to Dublin.'

'Matthews, brothers all,' said O'Brien, 'has just given MacKenna a life sentence.'

'He thinks MacKenna will be in hospital until he's allowed to take his vows.'

'Heaven help you, MacKenna.'

'You'll break Shaky Horgan's bedridden record.'

'Yes, yes; not a word of a lie.'

'As a medical man,' O'Brien said, 'I'd say MacKenna wouldn't be more than forty years in hospital. But as a relgious who has acquired the gift of prophecy from reading Rodriguez, I'd say Matthews should have his vows about the turn of the century.'

'They couldn't allow him back to Dublin.'

'The lies he tells.'

'I'll ride back,' said Matthews, 'on one of my dad's horses.'

The bellows of laughter seemed to shake even the old Puritan of a harmonium.

'Speech,' O'Brien said. 'Brothers, we've only five minutes.'

'Speech.'

'Up on the table, Barragry.'

'His feet would stick to it,' Guinan said. He was still testing his fingerprints. 'Try a chair, Barragry.'

'Try the Magnov's rostrum.'

He tried the rostrum. He said. 'Few words and brief Laus Deo Semper. In these last moments I adjure you, dearly beloved brethren, to trust in the Lord. Diligently meditate as the rule prescribes. Make twice daily your examen of conscience. Read good books. Eschew the semicolon. Visit the sick and poor in hospitals. Instruct the young. Do with exactitude your outdoor and indoor works. Don't sweep the dust behind the door. Learn from Brother Petit when he corrects your Latin grammar, for he's the only one of you knows the differ between mensa and audio. Ask Brother MacKenna for his prayers, for he's the only one of you will ever see the face of God. And now, dearly beloved brethren, I approach the moment of my dissolution and my going hence is nigh at hand. Shortly I will ascend through the ceiling to camerata six to lie awake all night listening to Brother Madden snoring. But before the Lord summons me I want to say thanks, and to assure you that if I ever go into a church and see the name of one of you over a confessional I'll go somewhere else ad quietam conscientiam.'

They laughed. They applauded. MacKenna laughed. Flynn, the bereaved angelus, said: 'God bless you, Brother.' O'Brien blew the beadle's final whistle. Donnelly, not to be outdone, blew a blast on the harmonium. The rule of silence was a wonderful thing, because it meant you didn't have to talk any more, nor pretend any more. Longfellow was waiting in the infirmary.

With Barragry by your side, the city ceased to be tumult and confusion. He spoke, and every sound became as distinct and individual as his voice. He described, and the place took shape and order, became as familiar as your own old humpy town.

'Your people will be with you tomorrow.'

'They will.' MacKenna's voice was unsteady. 'It'll be a shock to them. Particularly to my mother. She depended so much on my becoming a priest.'

Barragry wore a new grey lounge suit. MacKenna was still dressed in black. He had nothing else to wear. He wasn't a cleric. He wasn't in the world. Tomorrow he would be an invalid in a bed in a hospital and his black uncomfortable poorhouse tails could go into mothballs. 'Look, MacKenna,' Barragry said. 'Your duty's to get better. Concentrate on that. Convince your people of that. I'd say you have a vocation. This illness business may only make it stronger and you'll be all the more use to the Order when you go back. They're good men. They need writers too.'

'A friend of mine at school had a grandmother.'

'People often have grandmothers.'

'But this one said that the boy who would become a priest could never lose his purity the whole way.' MacKenna looked away as he spoke. He was troubled. He had to ask that question. He didn't want to be seen blushing. The City was all around him and he felt sable and shabby.

'She must have been a nasty old woman,' Barragry said.

'No; honest, I often think, perhaps it was because I wasn't good enough that this thing came on, this pain, disease.'

'There have been pretty notable saints, MacKenna, who had shadier pasts than yours.'

Great God, I lived with this boy for twelve months and knew so little about him, never had a clue about the odd thoughts in his innocent head.

They entered the block of offices where Barragry's brother practised law. Two young typists filled the lift with their perfume, glanced with interest at Barragry, probably didn't see MacKenna. With Barragry's brother, a heavy florid, bald man, smelling of drink as the typists of cheap perfume, they lunched in the Red Bank. 'Talk at table,' Barragry said; but they didn't talk much. The brother grunted, slopped his food, drank brandy. He was a new experience for MacKenna. He was a great man for monosyllables.

'Could I borrow your car, Joe? I'll drop Mac at the hospital.'

'Sure.' Brother gave to brother the keys of the car.

'I suppose you'll practise now, Jim.'

'You never knew I was a barrister, Mac.'

'I never did.' One knew so little about a man MacKenna thought, when you hadn't known him in the world.

'Bastard was called, but never practised,' the brother grunted. 'Journalism instead. Writing muck.'

'I couldn't stand the law library. All the old men with the undergraduate minds.'

'There's money there.'

'I'd hate to be a frustrated writer making a fortune at the Bar.'

'You won't make a fortune.'

'Oh, Mac,' Barragry said, 'wouldn't you like to have him on his knees at a quarter of charity?'

'Did a week-end retreat recently,' the brother said with such honest solemnity that Barragry and MacKenna laughed; and then, hushed after laughter, saw the classical oblong house, the surrounding trees, the black-gowned novices now walking in the sunlight for the day's first recreation. In the law library they wear wigs as well as gowns, but bind themselves by no vows of poverty, obedience, nor yet of chastity. It was still another sort of community life.

Walking now, three by three, in the sunlight, do they talk of us? With the bog wind crisping for colder days the lightning flights of hungry starlings will fight for pulpy red berries in the yew trees' hearts. Or are we now part of the dark silence in which Frawley,

Curran and Keown were lost for ever to the intimate little roads of God?

In the brother's car they drove north out of the city. It was almost startling to discover that Barragry could drive a car, could guide their way imperturbably through crowded streets, could watch for signals, red lights and green, raised white-gloved hands, to find that he knew the no-entry streets and the exact lanes of traffic to follow. Why, only a few days back hadn't he been fingering his beads in the quiet of the clochar? It was a revelation to see the way he put his foot down when they were clear of the crowds. 'Runs well,' he said. 'When you're up and about, Mac, we must see the city and environs.'

'I'd love to. I never really was in Dublin. Only passing through.'

The road dipped, crossed a bridge over a small stream. 'Dean Swift used to come to that marsh to watch the wildfowl. It must have been a real marsh then. Not two-thirds a garden suburb.'

So Swift, in sybilline frenzy blind, had walked here, like Guinan, watching wildfowl. Dublin was a town with glorious memories, renowned ghosts, writers, rebels. There's a lot to see and learn when the back's better, and the knitting needle purged away.

They swung to the left where an old Celtic cross dominated a village diamond. They were back now among the fields. The hospital stood on a rising green slope. As the Magnov had said, it was a great arc facing south to the mountains and the sun. Vita glass glitteringly reflected the sunlight. There was sunlight too in the voices of the shouting brown children. Except for the bitter truth that they were bed-bound, some in splints and plasters, some on curved frames of iron and canvas, they didn't much resemble invalids. The place was a daze of noise and coloured light. As the Magnov had said, the tall nun was blunt and kind. She praised the Magnov. She said he was a walking saint.

In the boys' playroom they shook hands. 'See you day after tomorrow, Mac. You won't have any trouble keeping the heart up here.'

'Suffer the little children. It must be harder for them. At least I have sedentary tastes. They should all be out playing ball.'

On the glass partition of the playroom a nun had painted everything from Robinson Crusoe to Snow White and her retinue and to Gene Autry. The sunlight fell deflected and distorted through the gaudy colours. Clustered around a piano, four up-patients, one in a leg splint, one made birdlike by a prominence between his shoulder-blades, two balanced on crutches sang with enthusiasm but little melody about two blue eyes.

'They never heard of the rule of silence.'

'But then silence isn't only a matter of speaking.'

'It's a principle. A thing of the spirit.'

'Silence is in the soul.' They laughed. They shook hands again. MacKenna walked away, hat in hand, poorhouse tails creased awry from sitting in the car; led by a pretty little nurse who had a cupidish heart-shaped face and legs that seemed ever so slightly bandy. But that, Barragry thought as he shook hands with the Reverend Mother, might be just because of the way the blue-and-white uniform cloth clung to her thighs.

He drove back down the slope towards the village with the Celtic Cross.

In a year I've acquired some habits. How long now will they last? Life's below me there in the hollow beyond Dean Swift's marsh. And MacKenna back there, how long will he keep up his meditation and examen of conscience and he tied on a Whitman frame with all that glorious din around him? Being a gentle poet, he should derive some creature consolation from the poetic name of his rack of steel and canvas.

He stopped the car, stepped out, sat on an iron gate looking down the deep fields towards the city. Close to the houses the autumn came sooner. The ornamental trees on the city streets – trees that had lost their true vocation – were already retreating. Poor Mac and myself are like those exiled trees, bewildered down there between houses and buses and mobs of people. We're returned empties. Oh, balls, Barragry, your home is down there, and incidentally your two-legged female woman, by no means an item in the general issue to a true monk. What had you ever in common, apart from human nature, with the men who stayed: Sweeney, Hanlon, Foley, Guinan, Sadleir, Cashman, Donnelly, Molloy, Flynn, Sweetman, Petit, Madden, et alibi? This country's maggoty with returned empties, people who, like myself, took sudden upward notions, but failed to pass the tests. Or possibly I'm even being good to myself in giving myself a place among those failures, returned empties, spoiled priests, stickit ministers, whose original intentions, even if afterwards they fell by the way, must have been purer than mine. What was I anyway but a dilettante in the ways of God, a coward running to quietude because I had had too much of something that less fortunate, less selfish men would have rejoiced to posses? Wasn't I like a suburban husband taking his slice off the ration and making up for it, as he thinks, by intensified piety and domesticity?

He drove on towards the village and the Celtic cross. Dusk was smoky over the city.

And I poked my nose in among the best, and wonderful to relate, was for one whole year accepted by them as an equal: because of their humility, or simply because not even they, but only God, can know the heart. They'll go on and do great things: be tortured for their faith in Burma as a man who went to school with me was; walk to the scaffold with a man facing the ultimate horror of judical execution – I heard of a hardened criminal who dirtied his pants at the crucial moment. They'll console sinners with God's forgiveness and comfort the sick. Old people in the country know that a priest's prayer read over them on sickbed is better than the best medical potions. They'll teach the young, and preach, and bring God down from heaven. Or they'll do trivial things and be remembered by them: like two good clerics I know who built, in their sparse free time, a wooden hut to shelter the poor who came begging to their monastery door. Those clerics are somewhere in Rhodesia now. They've since built schools and a church, and the hut still stands. My hermaphroditic abnormality is that I can see the merit in all these men and will still live, once the effect of one year in the woods has worn away, in a world that would seem to them like a lion's den or a pit crawling with serpents or dear old Spenser's Cave of Despayre; dark, doleful, dreary, like a greedy cave, that still for carrion carcases doth crave, on top whereof ay dwelt the ghastly owl. And, if my memory doesn't betray me, all about it wandering ghosts did wayle and howle.

There was an ancient house, how are you? Dame Caelia, I kiss you my hand.

Well, anyhow. I shan't live alone in that cave.

Forty yards beyond the Celtic cross he pulled up at a pub he had known in his interrupted life. The hall where the phone was was brambly with bicycles. To reach it he had to lean forward at an awkward angle as if inviting a kick in the pants. This is absurd, he thought. He heard the bell ring. She was, of course, at home. Her voice was cold and flat. She said: 'Hello, Barr. Are you on leave?'

'Permanent leave. I've left.'

'Oh!' A long silence. 'It's been a long time.'

'It has. A year.' He moved to seek comfort, caught his knee painfully on a bicycle pedal, gasped. She said: 'What's that?'

'A bicycle.'

She laughed: 'Sounded more like an oath.'

'It was that too.' He explained about the bicycles. She laughed again. He explained about MacKenna. She said: 'Poor boy.' She said, after a while: 'Not you. I didn't expect to see you again.'

'You haven't seen nothing yet. But you will if you want to.'

'I want to.'

'Genuinely?'

'Oh, Barr,' she said. She was crying.

'Living among the saints has taught me a lot. Taught me how much of a hound I was.'

'Oh, Barr,' she said, 'you were never a hound.'

'The countryside down there was lovely. I'd like to show it to you some day.'

'I'd like to see it.'

It would be good to go down quietly through the woods and look secretively at the still lake, and, in the distance, the corner of the classical house showing above the trees.

Someday soon, she thought, she would tell him, before Beauchamp or Eddy did, that she had seen the place.

'I'm headed for town. Eat with me.'

'Eat,' she said. She was laughing again.

'Yes, eat. I haven't stopped eating.'

'Nor I. Nor drinking.'

'I haven't had a drink for some time.' He had money in his pocket now. Some day they'd go to see Kate, plump, midnight, good-hearted mockery of svelte demoniacal enchantresses. 'I'm thirsty now,' he said. Some day they could go to the poorhouse in the muddy town and buy the fiddler a pint and talk on equal terms with the old ruffian who had looked on the crucified Christ and seen something like a man expanding his chest. 'The Dolphin,' he said, 'in an hour.' He put down the phone, withdrew carefully from the tentacles of the bicycles. By the fire in the bar sat a piper, a pint-drinker, who played for the local band and had piped with the best at a festival in Dunedin. Barragry drank pints with him. He was home again. The world, no lasting city and all that, was nevertheless home.

But he knew with a certainty that somehow hurt, how the lives of some men can be cut into several separate pieces, linked as houses in a town are by pipes, electric wires, yet divided by brick, wood, plaster, solid partitions. Behind him as he drove to the city unseen hands built a wall the height of the sky. He was in another room, in another house.

The nurse with the heart-shaped face went off duty at eight o'clock. MacKenna liked her already. She was so young and so innocently pretty; and nurses had a very testing vocation. She tucked the clothes in around him, called another nurse to help her; and together they wheeled his bed from the noisy balcony – more noisy than usual, although he didn't know it, in order to give him a joyous welcome. The Reverend Mother had ordered that. They wheeled him through the spacious airy ward dedicated to Saint Jospeh and along tiled and terrazoed antiseptic corridors to a small isolation ward next door to the room where the night nurses ate their supper. Little pert heart-shaped face said: 'We'll break you in gently to fresh air and noise. You'll sleep better here for tonight.'

'When do I go on the frame?'

'Oh, do take it easy. That'll come soon enough. You won't find it so bad. Except for the first few days. Have you books and things to read?'

'Yes.' She looked at the books on the bedside table, also on wheels, being brought up in the rear by a ward-maid in field-grey skirt, white blouse, white cap and white apron. She made a moue. She seemed, he thought, such a child to be charged with the responsibility of looking after the sick. She wore an odd twisted ruby ring on a tiny little finger. 'We all have our own tastes in reading,' she said.

'Do you read much?'

'When I have time. Thrillers by the ton. All the things I'd love to do to the nuns.' She tucked in a stubborn corner of red coverlet. She said: 'Are you comfortable?'

'Yes.'

'Sister Grignon de Montfort will want you to do fretwork and to model in plasticine. She calls it occupational therapy. The boys make jugs and baskets.'

'I wouldn't be good at that.' Oh, if Petit could only see him now, here alone with two young women, and laughing fit to burst. Perhaps he should have felt much more embarrassed than he actually did.

'Sister Francis Regis,' she said, 'will want your advise on her paintings. She does the things on the glass in the playroom.'

'Sister Margaret Mary has a green parrot,' said the second nurse. She was tall, blonde and placid. 'It bit one of the ward-maids in the ankle.'

'Sister Colmcille will want you to teach Latin to all the up-patients so they can serve Mass.'

'I wouldn't mind that.'

'The up-patients would. They're all potential murderers. A girl isn't safe working around here.' Oh, Petit, Petit! But, oh, girl with the heart-shaped face, how Donnelly would enjoy your talk, and Cashman the joker, and Sadleir the tough, and Madden who sang comic songs.

With neat quick movements she tidied her cap before the mirror. 'Sleep well,' she said.

'Thanks.'

'Don't mention it. You're a change from what we usually get.'

She closed the door gently. Hard heels went away along the antiseptic corridor. He dozed wearily. He didn't bother to switch on the light although the switch was within reach of his left hand. He was too tired to read. Faintly from the balcony he heard children's voices, but he heard no birds, no squeaking great tit. This world was a multi-coloured arc. It was black and white, blue and white, grey and white, blue and red, all the colours of nursing nuns and teaching nuns, of nurses, ward-maids, shouting boys and girls. Light came blurred through the ground glass in the door. When the two night nurses opened that door he pretended to be asleep, because he didn't want to spoil the bubbling good humour that little heart-face had left behind her. He heard one nurse whisepr: 'He has a spine.' He tried unavailingly to remember what the figure of speech was that called a whole by the name of the part. Petit would know. He must ask Barragry the day after tomorrow.

The other nurse said: 'Sister Camillus will love him. A whole clerical student to look after.' They closed the door again. The lights dimmed in the corridor. One by one, like birdsong ceasing, the voices of the balcony children died away. Children were like birds in a way, and nearer to God, and free of the high skies of innocence.

The multi-coloured arc that was the world grew until it was a full circle. After all, the world was round. It spun like a roulette wheel around the golden hub, the altar to which God came every Sunday morning. God was everywhere. He had honestly intended to prepare points for his morning meditation, but the spinning rhythm of the multi-coloured wheel wouldn't allow him.

'Do what you can,' the Magnov had said; and the great Saint Teresa, from a bud of a mouth, in a pert pear of a face, below a nurse's white cap, told him –

> *Let nothing disturb thee,*
> *nothing affright thee,*
> *all things are passing;*
> *God only is changeless;*
> *Patience gains all things;*
> *Who has God wants nothing;*
> *God alone suffices.*